WHOSE

"Pain, heart... Campbell explores them all in *Whose Little Girl Are You?*, a suspense novel that builds to a shattering finale. Bethany Campbell is a mistress of suspense."
—Carolyn Hart

"A riveting, stylishly written story that features intriguing characters and a fast-paced, pulse-pounding plot that has as many twists and turns as a mountain highway. I loved this book, could not put it down, and didn't want it to end."—Margaret Chittenden

"With novels like *See How They Run, Don't Talk to Strangers,* and *Hear No Evil,* Bethany Campbell has become one of the top authors of suspense. . . . *Whose Little Girl Are You?* is a fabulous thriller that shows why this fan favorite is the recipient of several awards. . . . Ms. Campbell is heading back to all the bestseller lists with an incredibly powerful novel."
—Harriet Klausner

"Fascinating characters, a riveting fast-paced plot, a powerful love story, and terror that escalates with every page . . . this book has it all! Bethany Campbell just keeps getting better and better."—Margot Dalton

"A tension-packed story that builds to a bone-chilling climax."—Rebecca York

"From its grisly opening scene to its literally explosive climax, Bethany Campbell's latest thriller rockets along at top speed. A spunky heroine, a leading man who's both more and less than he seems, and a town with as many secrets as the House of Atreus make *Whose Little Girl Are You?* a first-class suspense novel."
—Janice Law Trecker

ALSO BY BETHANY CAMPBELL

See How They Run
Don't Talk to Strangers
Hear No Evil

WHOSE LITTLE GIRL ARE YOU?

BETHANY CAMPBELL

BANTAM BOOKS

NEW YORK TORONTO LONDON SYDNEY AUCKLAND

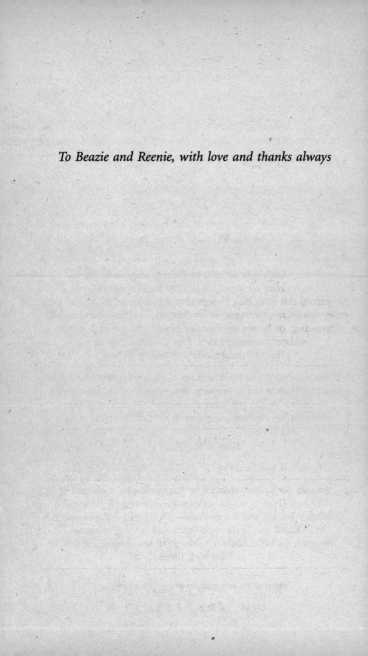

To Beazie and Reenie, with love and thanks always

In the middle of the journey of our life,
I found myself in a dark wood,
For the straight way was lost.
— DANTE ALIGHIERI

ONE

—◦◦◦—

Cawdor, Oklahoma, 1968

EVEN DEAD, SHE WAS THE PRETTIEST GIRL HOLLIS EVER saw.

The doctor's flashlight shone down on her steadily, like a spotlight. One of her eyes was open. It was blue as the bluest sky, and it stared, unblinking, off into the shadows.

The doctor leaned over and with his sure fingers pushed the blue eye shut. He straightened again, keeping the ray of light trained on her face.

Her eyelashes were long and cast still shadows across her cheeks. Her nose was small and straight. Her full lips were open enough so that Hollis could see the white rim of her upper teeth.

She lay there with her head tilted at an angle as if she were puzzled. The doctor put his foot against her face and nudged her head straight. His shoes were Hush Puppies, and the thick rubber sole left a mark on her jaw.

A sick feeling jiggled the pit of Hollis's stomach.

"A shame," the doctor said. "A damned waste. Did you boys bring what I told you?"

Hollis made himself nod.

"Yessir," said Luther. His voice did not sound scared, but it did not sound like ordinary, either.

They had been waked up in the middle of the night. They had been handed two old horse blankets sewn together with strong thread. Their orders were to get the half-blind mare and take her to the cellar door of the clinic and not to say anything to anybody. The doctor would be watching for them, they were told.

Even then, Hollis had a terrible feeling that something bad was happening and it would get worse and he could not stop it no matter what. It was like being caught in a nightmare that was stronger than you and would not let you go, no matter how hard you fought.

When they reached the clinic they'd hitched the mare in a grove of cedar trees where she couldn't be seen. The doctor had opened the door of the cellar and told Luther and Hollis to come in. The only light was his flashlight.

"I got something," he'd said. "I want you to get rid of it for me."

Somehow Hollis already knew: *It has happened at last. There is somebody dead.*

But he had not expected a girl so pretty. Or so young. She looked no more than sixteen years old.

She lay on her back, next to the basement-floor drain. Her hair was blond-like and must have hung past her shoulders, but now it was tangled and stringy and looked all dirty, like before dying she had sweat a lot.

She wore a little white gown-thing. It had blood on it. It was hitched up so high, Hollis could almost see her privates. This made him feel ashamed, so he forced himself to keep his eyes on her face instead.

Her skin was fine and smooth like a girl in a magazine picture. It was very white. Hollis wondered if she had always been that pale, or if that's what being dead had done to her.

"I want you to take this into the woods to the fire pit where the old still used to be," said the doctor. "I want you to burn it."

Hollis made himself nod again. But he thought, *Lordy God. Set fire to her. Set her on fire. Lordy God.*

"Yessir," said Luther.

"You stay with it until it's all gone," the doctor said. "I don't want anything left of it. Not one thing."

"Yessir," Luther said.

But Hollis thought, *This is a sin what we are about to do. It is a sin and a crime.* He swallowed hard. He knew right then that this girl would come back to haunt his mind and curse his soul.

They wrapped her in the horse blankets and carried her out into the darkness and slung her over the back of the mare. They each took a ten-gallon can of gasoline.

It was nine miles into the pine woods to get to the cave where the still had been. Every step of the way Hollis wanted to cry like a frightened child. He thought of God, hell, damnation, demons, spirits, and haunts. There was no moon and few stars, hardly any light. He could barely see where he was going except deeper into the tangled darkness.

But Luther, who was ten years older than Hollis, knew the way through the woods by heart. So did the half-blind mare. She plodded on, her hooves sure on a path Hollis could not see, a path he would have sworn was not there at all but that she followed as if it were inevitable.

At one point Luther said, "You ever fucked a dead girl?"

Hollis nearly burst into tears then. *I don't want to do that. I don't want him to do that. Please, God, don't let him do that.*

"No," he said. It was the first word he'd said since they'd left home.

"They're too still," Luther said with an air of knowledge. "There's no pleasure to it."

Lord God, thought Hollis. *Lord God, help me, please.* The dark woods around him seemed like the mouth of hell, swallowing him up. Although the dead girl was thrown over the horse's back, at the same time she seemed to float palely above Hollis, a spirit following him as if she were hooked to him by a thin silver wire.

They say you cannot completely burn up a human body unless you are a mortician and have the right sort of furnace in which to do it. They say that if you try to burn a body, it would take you days and days, and that the black smoke is greasy with fat, and it has a special, sickening smell that tells the world what you are doing. People are sure to notice such a long, hot, stinking fire, they say.

But this was not true. Hollis and Luther took the girl to the cave and laid her in the fire pit, still wrapped in the horse blankets.

Luther peeled back the blankets, just from the girl's upper body. He took out his knife and, to Hollis's shock, he hacked off the little finger of her right hand. Hollis nearly threw up. His knees shook, and he turned away, knowing now for certain sure he would go to hell because he had watched such a thing.

"A corpse's finger bone is powerful magic," Luther said somberly, wiping the knife clean on the blankets. "Mama Leone says so. She's been to New Orleans, she knows things like that."

Hollis shuddered, his mouth tasting sour and sick.

Luther wrapped the finger up carefully in a blue bandanna handkerchief and stuck it in his back pocket.

He covered up the girl again, unceremoniously letting the blanket fall over her face. He doused her with one can of the gasoline. Then he made a kind of a fuse-thing out of twine so that he and Hollis could run for the mouth of the cave and take cover before the gasoline ignited.

But Luther calculated wrongly about the fuse. The two of them had barely reached the cave's entrance when some force made Hollis turn back to look.

At that moment, the fire burst into life so violently, it was as if hell had erupted to capture Hollis right there. The great *whoosh* of the surging flame hit him like a blow and shook him to his bones. It knocked him backwards, singeing his hair and lashes and eyebrows.

Luther hauled him out into the night, and they threw themselves to the ground, taking cover behind a limestone ridge. Hollis's whole face ached, and he felt as if he had been hit in the forehead with a burning brand.

When the fire died down, they waited for the cave to cool, but even so, when they made their way back inside, it was hot as a chamber of brimstone.

Only bones were left of the dead girl, gray and shriveled-looking in the glowing coals. The lower jaw still grinned with a few blackened teeth, but the part that had held the eyes was gone.

"This ain't good enough," Luther said.

Hollis had feared that. They had to tend the fire and feed it, and poke the remaining bones into the hottest part of the flames. It took them thirteen hours, well past the clear sky of noon the next day. At last all that was left of the girl was a few handfuls of ash. They threw the ashes in the creek, and Hollis watched them drift away and disappear.

If anyone ever noticed the smoke that night or that morning or that afternoon, nobody ever said. People in Baird County knew better than to ask about such things. No one did ask. Not for over thirty years.

New England, 1999

A pinpoint of fire stabbed the darkness.

The temperature had dropped with such violent speed that the car door's lock had frozen shut. During winters she carried the lighter for such emergencies.

It was a cheap butane lighter of plastic, but it had an expensive gold slip-on cover. The cover was engraved:

To J.
You are the B-E-S-T
Best
Love, P.

Her heart felt more frozen than the night. She got into her car, started the reluctant motor, and set out. At first she could not think. She just drove.

That evening the blizzard had blown in with supernatural suddenness. It came shrieking down from the northern Atlantic like a thousand banshees who spun and whirled in their blinding robes of snow.

Radio announcements had been ominous with travelers' warnings; she ignored them and headed into the heart of the storm.

It was hardly how Jaye Garrett had meant to spend the night. She was supposed to stay in Boston where she belonged, to be at the advertising awards banquet. This year the banquet was supposed to be her night of nights; she was up for five major awards.

She'd made an appointment to have her hair tortured into an exquisite upsweep and crowned, quite literally, with a jeweled clip she'd bought especially from Tiffany's.

The occasion was so special that she'd indulged herself in her first honest-to-God designer gown, a strapless black number with a modestly low back and shockingly high price.

But now the black dress was hanging in the closet back in her apartment, its plastic bag unopened. The jeweled clip lay in its velvet box on the dresser, never worn. Her blond hair was disheveled, tangled by wind and dampened by snow.

This morning she had awakened with the desire to win so keen she could taste it, sparkling like champagne on her tongue. Tonight she didn't even think of the stupid awards, and all she tasted was a dark, choking dread.

Her brother, who was far away in Belgium, was sick. She feared he might be dying.

Leukemia.

When she'd heard the word, it had stunned her, stricken her like an evil spell.

Patrick couldn't be sick—he was young and strong and athletic, and because Jaye loved him so much, he was supposed to live forever.

Besides that, Patrick was a doctor, a medical researcher for a pharmaceutical company; his job was finding cures for people. He was so good that he'd been given a plum assignment in the European branch. He *couldn't* have a fatal disease himself—a just God would not allow it.

Yet a man of God had told her the news. A monk named Brother Maynard had phoned her in Boston. He was the head of the science division of the Catholic college where her mother was a secretary.

"Your mother needs you to come home," Brother Maynard had told her. "Right away."

"But my brother—" Jaye had said, shaken—"how serious is this?—I mean, he's got a wife, a child on the way—"

"It's serious," Brother Maynard had told her. "He's receiving treatment in Brussels. But I'd rather not discuss the particulars over the phone."

"Excuse me?" Jaye asked incredulously. "You'd rather not *discuss* it?"

"We need to sit down face-to-face."

"I want to talk to my mother," she'd said from between clenched teeth. "Let me talk to her right now."

"She can't. I'm sorry. That's why I'm calling."

Jaye's mind reeled, imagining still greater family disasters. She and her mother, Nona, had always had a prickly relationship, and for the past years it had bordered on estrangement.

But Jaye was seized with concern for Nona. She envisioned her mother in shock or emotional collapse.

"Why can't she talk?" Jaye had demanded. "Has something happened to her?"

"No," the monk said curtly. But again he told her to come home immediately, and he'd hung up before she could ask more.

•   •   •

She stood on her mother's porch, whipped by wind and stung by snow. She had knocked until her knuckles were skinned, but nobody answered, even though the living room lights shone brightly. She knocked harder still.

At last Brother Maynard opened the door for her. He was wearing, inexplicably, a garish Hawaiian shirt.

She entered the living room. No one was there except for her and the monk.

"Where's my mother?" she asked.

"Upstairs," Brother Maynard said. "In her room."

"Is she sick? You said she wasn't sick."

"She's not," said Brother Maynard. He was a tight-lipped little man with a gray crew cut. He made a nervous gesture to help her off with her coat.

Jaye edged away from him, keeping her coat on, as if it could somehow protect her from what was happening.

Brother Maynard said, "She wants me to talk to you."

"Why? Why you?" She hardly knew this man, and she resented how abrupt he'd been on the phone.

"This won't be easy," he said. "Sit down. Let me get you a drink." He turned to her mother's liquor cabinet. A bottle of port was set out, ready to be opened. He busied himself with drawing the cork.

She wanted to tell him that she didn't want a drink. She'd just driven fifty miles through a snowstorm and what she wanted was the truth, goddammit. Her emotions were so tumultuous she didn't trust herself to speak. She sat in the old overstuffed armchair, still bundled defensively in her coat.

Brother Maynard poured the wine and handed her the glass. "Have a few sips," he urged.

Instead, she put the glass aside. She set it on the end

table, next to the crudely painted statuette of the Virgin Mary.

Normally Jaye would have winced at the sight of this plaster Virgin. She had painted it herself when she was only nine years old, and her mother would not part with it. Nona was sentimental and loved memorabilia. The room, the entire house, was crammed with it.

Jaye tried to ignore the wine, the ill-painted Virgin, the family snapshots cluttering every wall. She stared at the monk with impatient challenge.

"A drink will help," Brother Maynard persisted. "The roads are bad. Your trip must have been—difficult."

She couldn't help herself. "Will you just the hell tell me how my brother is?"

She shouldn't swear at a man of the church, she thought in frustration, and she shouldn't snap. But she'd always had a fast temper and a faster mouth, and Brother Maynard was driving her mad.

His pinched face was somber, and his brown eyes seemed full of reluctance.

"Your brother's very sick. His hospital hopes to send him back stateside as soon as possible. But not yet. The doctors have him in isolation. They want to give him chemo treatments. As soon as possible."

Dumbstruck, Jaye stared at him. Her eyes filled with tears so that the colors of Brother Maynard's shirt blurred, jumping and dipping in a hallucinatory dance.

Isolation? Chemo treatments? How could this monk so calmly use such terrible words about her brother? And how could doctors keep Patrick in Belgium, for God's sake? None of this could be real; it was impossible.

She let her gaze drift around the room in stunned disbelief. Everywhere were reminders of Patrick—her strong, vital, and invincible brother.

There were photographs of him everywhere, far more of him than of her. She had teased him about this, but never truly resented it. He was the family favorite, hers and her mother's, too. That was how things were, and it was completely right, just, and understandable simply because he was Patrick.

In his high school graduation picture, he grinned, a classic all-American boy. Their mother said his auburn hair and freckles came from their late father's Irish forebears.

His striking dark eyes and high cheekbones were also from their father's family, throwbacks to a Sioux grandmother.

But that wide trademark grin, that was Patrick's and his alone, their mother said. Hot tears welled, blurring Jaye's vision of his smile, making it disappear.

Brother Maynard reached into his back pocket and without fumbling drew out a perfectly laundered handkerchief. He handed it to her.

He came prepared for this, Jaye thought. But gratefully, she wiped her eyes, streaking the pristine handkerchief with mascara.

"Your brother went to the hospital in Brussels with appendicitis," Brother Maynard said. "He'd been fighting a respiratory infection all winter—so they'd thought."

Jaye willed herself not to cry; Patrick would hate such a thing. She crumpled the damp handkerchief and held it tightly clenched in her lap.

"After the operation," said the monk, "he started having a fever, respiratory problems. They thought it was pneumonia or bronchitis. But the blood work showed differently. He had an extremely low count of red cells, double the normal amount of white cells, and numerous blast cells. It's acute granulocytic leukemia."

Words, words, stupid, hideous, obscene words.

Jaye wanted to rage, wail, throw the painted Virgin at the wall. But she sat unnaturally still and stared into the monk's sad brown eyes.

"Will he die?" she asked, her voice unsteady.

Brother Maynard looked away. He walked to the window, lifted the drape. Snowflakes were a white mound on the outside sill.

"He could die, yes," he said. "That's a possibility. But science does wonderful things these days. With the help of God—"

"God helps those who help themselves," Jaye said, almost combatively. "He can have a marrow transplant, can't he? That's what I thought about all the way from Boston. That's what kept me sane. A transplant could help him—couldn't it?"

Brother Maynard let the drape fall silently back into place. "Yes. If a donor can be found."

"If?" she challenged. "Can't they use mine? Isn't that what they do? Take it from a sister, a brother? My God, he can have all he needs—"

Oddly, Brother Maynard still did not turn to look at her. He only stood in that loud, inappropriate shirt of his, staring at the closed curtain.

"Is *that* what this is about?" she asked. "My mother wants to know if I'd donate marrow? Of course I will. If I have to go to Belgium, I'll go to Belgium. Do I need to book a flight? Just tell me what to do."

"It isn't that easy," Brother Maynard said. "Not anyone can be a donor. The cells have to match perfectly, if possible. It's not simply about blood type. The biology of it is complex."

Jaye rose, went to the window, put her hand on his arm, and made him turn to face her. "But family members can match exactly, right? That's how—how one brother can give another one a kidney, things like that."

Brother Maynard's thin mouth twitched uneasily. Her hand was still on his arm and he put his over hers, but she did not find the gesture comforting. It seemed strangely hopeless.

"A sibling," he said, "has a one-in-four chance of matching."

Jaye took a deep breath. The odds weren't great, but they weren't impossible. "So how do I get tested? And where? Can I do it here? Or go back to Boston?"

The man's hand tightened over hers, but his flesh was cold. "Jaye, there's no need for you to be tested. Your tissue won't match."

She looked at him in fresh confusion. "What do you mean? You just said we had a one-in-four chance."

"Jaye," he said, his eyes suddenly as cold as his hands, "he's not your brother."

"What?" She drew back, snatching her hand away. The man was obviously insane. "What are you saying? Of course, we're related—"

"No," he contradicted. "You've always been told you were, but you're not."

For the second time that day, the man's words struck her hard, so hard they stunned her.

A bit crazily she turned toward the piano, looked at Patrick's high school portrait. It stood next to her own. She stared at the pictures and remembered, dazedly, what people had said for years: *You two don't look like brother and sister.*

Patrick's hair was curly and reddish-brown. Hers was thick and blond and straight. His eyes were so dark they were nearly black. Hers were sky-blue.

She was tall, and although Patrick was not short, he

was no taller than she. She was curvaceous and uncoordinated; he was muscular and athletic.

You two don't look like brother and sister.

She and Patrick didn't look alike—yet they were alike in dozens of other ways. People who knew them well never doubted their relationship; Jaye and Patrick acted like each other, thought like each other—they talked with the same slightly clipped speech pattern. Even their senses of humor were eerily alike, although Jaye's was barbed, and Patrick's more gentle.

There were differences between them, to be sure. She was the one with the temper and stubbornness; he was the ever-amiable and sweet-tempered one, the peacemaker. But they complemented each other; in an odd and comfortable way she had always thought they made each other complete.

Jaye was filled with a giddy sickness. She took a deep breath. She felt as if she were about to take a nightmare dive off an infinitely tall cliff.

"All right," she said, "which one of us is adopted?"

I'm the one, she thought. *Mother always adored him. I was the one who got on her nerves, who disappointed her. I understand now. Now I understand.*

Brother Maynard's eyes seemed to harden. Vaguely she realized it was not from coldness but from distaste for what he had to say.

"Both of you," he said. "You and Patrick—both adopted."

Her stomach pitched. She sat down heavily in the old chair. She still wore her coat, but she felt cold to the core of her being.

Dazed, she stared up at Brother Maynard in his antic shirt. "Nona—she's lied to us all these years?"

"Yes," he said. "Your father, too, of course."

"My father," she said mechanically. It seemed a

word without meaning. He was a man she barely re-membered, a man whose obstinate nature she'd been told she'd inherited. He'd died when she was four and Patrick two. No, she couldn't attribute this lifetime of lies to him.

Tears, this time of anger, welled again. "How could she have done this?" she demanded. "How? Does Patrick know?"

Brother Maynard nodded. "I told his wife this morning. She's told him."

Jaye felt a profound and chilling wave of repellence. "My God, he's sick, he might die, and she hits him with *this*?"

Brother Maynard approached her chair. Tentatively he laid his hand on her shoulder. "He'd already had hints—from the blood work they'd done. He took the news well. He's more worried about you than himself. He hopes you won't be too upset."

Too upset? Oh, no. Not too fucking upset at all.

But she clamped her lips shut rigidly. Her troubles were nothing compared to Patrick's. She had to think of her brother.

No, not her brother, she corrected herself, her mind wheeling sickly. Then with a stubborn surge she thought, *Yes, dammit, my brother.*

She blinked back the tears. She squared her jaw, and wiped her nose briskly with Brother Maynard's ruined handkerchief. "If he's adopted, he's got blood family somewhere," she said.

"It's possible," the monk said.

"Does my mother—does Nona know who they are?"

"No. She has no idea."

"But—but—" Jaye struggled to think lucidly—"somewhere he'll have blood relations. He has to, doesn't he?"

"There's that hope. We'll pray to God there is. And that they can be found."

Jaye didn't like the feel of his stiff hand on her shoulder. But this time she didn't shake away his touch.

"If he's got family, I'll find them," she said. "There have to be records."

With a surge of hope, she thought of Shayna, her colleague at the ad agency. Shayna was adopted, and she had tried to locate her birth mother, but the records were sealed. She'd found a support organization, gone to court, got an order for the records to be opened. Such things might take struggle, but they were not impossible.

"I'll make Mother tell me everything," Jaye said with conviction. "She didn't find Patrick under a cabbage leaf. He came from *somewhere*. I'll get a detective. I'll do whatever I have to."

"Jaye," Brother Maynard said, reluctance in his voice, "there are—complications. This is partly why your mother asked me to talk to you."

He came before her. He knelt. He took her hand in his, which was cold. His voice was soft, almost a whisper.

"Listen carefully. Neither of you was legally adopted. She got you two years apart. From a doctor in Cawdor, Oklahoma. You were black-market babies. She bought you. Both of you."

TWO

HER LEFT HAND SPASMODICALLY CLUTCHED HER COAT shut as if she were protecting a chest wound.

She *had* taken a wound, Brother Maynard thought, and he had inflicted it, which filled him with distress. He was a man of science, with a retiring nature and an ascetic temperament. He had never been comfortable with emotions, his own or other people's.

He tried to pat Jaye's hand, which had gone lifeless in his. "I'm sorry," he said, and the inadequacy of the words made him feel as if a spongeful of vinegar had been squeezed into his mouth.

Jaye shook her head, dazed. She had always been lively and forthright, so much so that Brother Maynard had avoided her, embarrassed by her vitality.

But at the moment, she looked oddly vulnerable. She stared at him as if he had inexplicably hit her and might do so again.

"No," she said in a low voice. "We weren't bought in Cawdor. We were *born* there."

Brother Maynard had agreed to this ordeal to spare Nona, who had begged him tearfully, almost hysterically. But there was no way he could spare her daughter. He steeled himself.

"Yes. You were born there. But not to the people you've called your mother and father."

"No," Jaye protested. "I've got copies of our birth certificates. I keep an extra for Patrick, just in case."

He sucked in his breath and offered up a desperate prayer. *God, give me the strength to say what I must say and give her the strength to hear it.*

"The birth certificates are forged," he said. "The doctor falsified the data. It was part of the—arrangement."

He watched for her reaction, but her face looked so blank that again he was reminded of someone who had received a physical blow.

"I'm adopted?" she asked in a low, flat voice.

"Yes."

"So is Patrick?"

He nodded.

"Our mother really isn't our mother?"

"In her heart she is," he said hastily. "In her love and concern she is. But biologically—no."

Jaye cocked her head slightly, like a puzzled child. "She *bought* us?"

"She—she wanted children very much. She and your father couldn't have any. Adoption agencies were no help. They tried everything. At last they heard about the doctor in Cawdor. They contacted him. One weekend they got a call to come and get you. They drove from Austin—"

"No," Jaye said emphatically. "That's wrong. We *lived* in Cawdor. My father worked for an oil company there."

"No," Brother Maynard said. He was desperate not to waste words. "Your father *did* work for an oil company. But in Austin. No such company ever existed in Cawdor."

"But it did," Jaye insisted. "Tahlequah Oil. It failed in 1968, and my father took another job, and we moved—"

"There *was* no Tahlequah Oil," he said bluntly. "It never existed. The only times your parents went to Cawdor were to buy you and Patrick. That's how it was."

"But—" Jaye said. She clearly wanted to argue, to prove him wrong, but no words seemed to come to her.

"We never lived in Cawdor?" she asked at last. She sounded half fearful, half resentful.

"No," said Brother Maynard. "Never."

"My mother made that up? It's a story?"

"Yes."

"The same with Tahlequah Oil? She made it up?"

"Yes."

"My father," she said hesitantly, "I remember him—don't I? Barely. There are pictures of him, but—but did she make him up, too? Was he really there?"

"Yes. He was there."

"And he really died when I was four?"

"Yes. He'd had a history of heart trouble. He was older than your mother. His age, his health—these worked against them when they tried to adopt legally."

Jaye nodded. She sat for a long moment, her lips clamped together. She stared at Patrick's high school portrait on the piano, at her own photo beside it.

She swallowed. "So," she said carefully, "my brother and I have lived a lie."

"That's putting it harshly," Brother Maynard said, wanting to defend Nona, who was a good woman. "If you view it with charity, with compassion—"

Jaye pulled her hand from his grasp, and he let her, but kept kneeling before her like a penitent. He felt like one.

Color flared in Jaye's cheeks. She clutched the arms of the chair almost savagely. "Everything about our family is a lie? Everything?"

"I know that's how it seems, but—"

"No 'buts' about it," she said with sudden passion. "It's just a great, huge, damned *lie?*"

Brother Maynard winced, but he held her gaze. Obscurely he felt he owed this to her, to meet her eyes from now on, no matter what.

"How *could* she?" Jaye demanded, her voice pained and angry. "All these years? I mean, *why* would she?"

"How could she tell you the truth?" he asked, anxious to defend and protect Nona. "What she'd done was illegal. How do you tell a child such a thing?"

"She could at least have told us we were adopted. We could have coped with that—families do. But this— *this*—"

Brother Maynard felt helpless before such wounded indignation. "She and your father sincerely meant to tell you that much. When you were old enough to understand. But then he died. And she—lost courage. She couldn't bring herself to do it. She didn't know how."

She didn't know how. Jaye put her hand to her eyes and shook her head, not knowing whether to laugh or cry.

Nona, so religious and proper, had been telling the most profound of lies—for more than thirty years.

I carried you beneath my heart for nine months. I nearly died giving birth to you. And this is how you act? This is how you treat me?

She had hurled these words at Jaye in disapproval when she learned that Jaye, at twenty-three, had moved in with Adam Garrett.

She'd said the same sort of thing when Jaye eloped with Adam, and last year when Jaye had divorced him, she'd said it again: "You should have listened to your own flesh and blood. I knew he'd deceive you sooner or later. I could tell he wasn't honest. A mother knows these things."

Deception. Honesty. Flesh and blood.

In an abrupt, almost desperate movement, Jaye rose and paced to the piano. She picked up Patrick's high school portrait. She stared at it as if she were lost and he was all she had to guide her.

Brother Maynard rose, too, but slowly, as if the movement pained him.

He said, "Your mothers—your biological mothers—were unfortunate girls who couldn't keep you. But they wanted you to have good lives, better than they could give you."

She kept her eyes on her brother's picture. "Patrick and I were illegitimate. Unwanted."

His tone became pleading. "Times were different then. There was such stigma. A girl in trouble—"

Jaye held up her hand for him to stop. "Please. Spare me that. It won't sound right without violins."

She set down Patrick's photograph. She struggled for self-control. She squared her jaw.

"I'm sorry. I didn't mean to snap at you. It was

very—brave of you to break the news. But I think it's time for me to talk this over with my—with Nona."

He swallowed. "I can understand your feelings—"

"I'm glad," she said briskly. She had not broken down and cried, and she didn't intend to. Not in front of Brother Maynard or anyone else.

She turned toward the stairs that led to the bedrooms. "She's in her room?"

"I can understand your feelings," he repeated. "But you must understand hers. She—doesn't want to see you."

Jaye wheeled and stared at him. He looked almost frightened. "What?"

Brother Maynard extended his arms helplessly. "She doesn't want to see you—yet. Or talk to you. She's ashamed."

Jaye's chin jerked higher. "She should be."

Brother Maynard folded his hands over his stomach as if it hurt him. "She wants you to have time to think things over. So you won't say anything you may regret. She knows you're volatile, that you—"

Jaye's eyes flashed. "She's afraid to face me."

Brother Maynard laced his fingers more tightly over his midsection. "I know the relationship you two have had has never been smooth—and I can understand your feelings. But this is no time for anger. Right now, this isn't about you and Nona. It's about your brother. About Patrick."

She flinched. "My brother," she whispered.

"Yes," said Brother Maynard. "The rest can be worked out later."

Jaye stood taller. "I want to talk to her. Now."

"She's written you a letter," said Brother Maynard. He took it from the mantel, where it lay. "It explains

everything. She'd like you to read this before you talk."
He held the thick envelope toward her.

She didn't take it. Instead she turned and climbed
the stairs.

Beside Nona's bedroom door hung an old photograph of
Jaye and Patrick, posed with a department-store Easter
rabbit. Each time Jaye knocked at the door, the picture
quivered as if it would fall from the wall.

"Nona," Jaye demanded, "open up. I know you're in
there. You have no right to hide from this." She rapped
more relentlessly. "Nona, *Patrick* needs the truth. Open
this door or I—I'll—"

Brother Maynard put his hand on her coated arm.
"Jaye, please. She's right. This is not the time—"

Jaye shook off his imploring hand and pounded even
harder. The picture of the children and the Easter rabbit
twitched more violently on the wall. "Dammit, Nona,
open this door. I *mean* it."

"Jaye," he pleaded.

But it was too late. The lock clicked, the door eased
timidly open. Nona stood there, a thin, blondish little
woman of sixty, her face ravaged by tears. She looked up
at her daughter with pity and terror.

Jaye's heart waged war with itself. She knew Nona's
face better than any in the world except for Patrick's and
her own. It was graven on her memory, perhaps on her
soul itself. Yet she wondered sickly, had she ever really
known this woman at all?

Nona was so small and slender she always looked
delicate. Tonight she looked truly frail, standing in the
doorway of her bedroom, her chin twitching with emotion.

Jaye was half a head taller, long-legged and full-breasted. Nona had always said, *You take after my sister, Celeste. She was tall, like our daddy. I was the petite one.*

Celeste, the explanation for Jaye's height and build, had died of polio long before Jaye was born. Or had she? Had she even existed? Had she simply been another of Nona's fictions?

Nona's eyes, staring into her own, were gray-green. Jaye's were vivid blue. *Your father's family had those Irish blue eyes. You take after them in that.*

No, Jaye thought dully, meeting her mother's wary gaze. I don't take after them. I have no idea who I take after.

Before Nona's hair had turned silver, it had in truth been mouse-brown, and both Jaye and Patrick knew it. But Nona had colored it forever and always rationalized. *I used to be as blond as you, she'd tell Jaye. It turned darker after I had you children, that's all. That's the one thing you got from me. My Scandinavian blond hair.*

No, Jaye thought, looking at Nona's tinted curls. Her own blondness hadn't come from Nona. It had come from God knew where. This woman standing before her was part of herself, deeply so, yet she was also a stranger full of evasions and secrets.

Nona, who had always carried herself ramrod-straight, now stood slightly hunched, as if she expected to fend off a blow. Her face was normally a preternaturally *neat* face, not pretty, but ladylike and coolly prim.

Now it was raddled by emotion, and her eyes were red from tears. She looked so old that Jaye was startled and thrown off balance.

Nona drew herself up slightly. Somewhere out of the ruins, she managed to recover a bit of dignity, even superiority.

"I hope," she said, "that you're not going to make any more of a scene."

Jaye thought, *She's completely different. And she hasn't changed at all.*

She said, "If there's a scene, I'm not the one responsible for it."

Nona turned from the open doorway toward her room. "Come in," she said, her back to Jaye. "If you must do this, at least do it in private."

From behind Jaye came Brother Maynard's uneasy voice. "I'll wait in the living room, Nona. I'm here if you need me."

Jaye threw him a suspicious glance over her shoulder. What did he think, that Nona needed protection from her?

The monk was pale and obviously anxious to escape. Yet he held himself with an air of reluctant courtliness.

He said to Jaye, "She's cared for you your whole life. Remember that. And that right now it's your brother that's important."

Jaye resented this advice, she resented his very presence. Yet when he turned and hurried down the hall in his shirt of many colors, she was stabbed by both grief and guilt. *He's right,* she thought.

She suddenly wondered if she really wanted to be alone with Nona. But she closed the door.

Nona stood beside the bed, her back still turned to Jaye, her shoulders bent again. The chenille bedspread was rucked, and the pink pillowcase looked as if it had been clutched and dampened by tears.

Jaye had trouble breathing. The bedroom was too like the living room, overstuffed with photos and sentiment. It was like being trapped in a shrine to lost childhood.

"Turn around. Face me," she said to Nona.

Nona slowly turned. She held her hands prayerlike, clenching a tissue. The pose made her look like a fearful rabbit, but Jaye tried not to allow herself to feel pity.

"It's true?" she demanded.

"Yes," said Nona. "Of course."

"Of *course?*" Jaye repeated in disbelief. "What do you mean '*of course*'?"

Nona raised her chin. "I wouldn't have Brother Maynard tell a lie."

"You've had no trouble telling them yourself," Jaye said.

Nona shrugged with a helpless air. She clutched her tissue harder and stared at a picture of Patrick on his tricycle. "Everything I did, I did for love," said Nona.

"You bought us," Jaye said. "And you lied about it all these years."

Nona turned to her. Her eyes swam with tears, but they also flashed with righteousness. "We tried every legal way to get a child, every single one. No one would help. They said your father was too old, his health was bad—"

"How much did we cost? I'm curious. Were we expensive babies? Medium? Discount?"

"It wasn't like that. It wasn't about money. These girls wanted to keep the matter private. They couldn't keep their babies, couldn't provide for them. This doctor arranged for loving families like your father and me—"

"Tell me," Jaye interrupted coolly. "Did you get to choose us? Or were we just the luck of the draw?"

"—arranged for loving families who would treasure you and give you the best possible—"

"This was this doctor's main business? Selling babies?"

"No, no," Nona said emphatically. "Once in a while

a girl would get in trouble. He didn't believe in abortion. He knew there were good families, loving families, for such children. He had to approve of us. He wouldn't let just anyone adopt—"

"But we weren't adopted—not legally. We were sold. Like cattle. And now there's no record—"

Nona looked both defiant and desperate. "It was a private matter. It was no one else's concern."

"It was our concern," Jaye countered. "You could have at least told us that you weren't our real mother. To learn this way—"

"I *am* your real mother," Nona retorted. "In my heart and soul, you are *my* children, no one else's."

"Is that why you lied? Because you wanted to believe that so badly?"

Nona looked away, and guilty confusion seemed to settle over her like a net.

"I—I—we meant to tell you when you were older," she said. "Then John died. I had no family of my own left. It was just us. You were my children. I was your mother. I *am* your mother."

She pointed a trembling forefinger at one of the dozen framed photos on the wall beside her. In it a nine-year-old Jaye posed, not very gracefully, in a short frilly dress and ballet shoes.

"Do you remember this costume?" Nona asked, her finger trembling. "Remember when I made it for you? I stayed up nights sewing it. Because that's what mothers do."

Jaye pushed her hand through her tangled hair. "I'm not denying that. But—"

"It's not the only time I stayed up nights for you," Nona said defensively. "Remember when you broke your arm at Girl Scout camp? Remember when you had the chicken pox? Remember when you had the flu and your temperature went up to a hundred and five and a half?"

Jaye remembered all of it and far more, but Nona's protestations struck her as frantic and pitiable. She had always known that Nona's identity had been inextricably tied to being a *mother*, yet now this fact seemed warped with strangeness.

Nona stood watching her, her head thrown back as if she could recite for hours her motherly deeds. But Jaye had no heart to hear them.

Nona, with unerring instinct, sensed her moment of hesitancy. "You should take your coat off," she said. "You'll catch cold."

Jaye kept her coat on. She looked at the bedside lamp, which had a ceramic base shaped like a frog. It had been a Christmas present from Patrick when he was in college.

Patrick, she thought, and the pain struck so deep it was like having a spike driven through her chest.

"And Patrick—now he knows all this?" Jaye asked. "You picked a hell of a time to tell him."

"I had no choice. I told the truth because I love him."

"My God," Jaye said, shaking her head. "My God."

"It was because of the blood work," Nona said, raising her chin higher. "There are—peculiarities about his tissue type. He and Melinda hoped yours might match. I knew it couldn't."

Jaye's hard-beating heart missed a stroke, stumbled. "Peculiarities?"

Nona blinked back tears. She looked not at Jaye but at Jaye's reflection in the mirror. "It's rare. Very rare."

Jaye stiffened. "What do you mean?"

"It's going to be difficult to match."

"How difficult?"

Nona reached to the bureau and took up a small pink porcelain heart. Long ago Jaye and Patrick had given it to her for Valentine's Day.

"*How difficult?*" Jaye repeated.

"Very," said Nona, barely above a whisper. She turned the china heart left, then right, watching its surface catch the light.

For an instant Jaye's head swam. The room swung around her, dizzying her with images—half a hundred remembrances of things in a past that was no longer quite true.

She sat down on the edge of the bed. She put her face in her hands. "I can't believe this. I want to talk to Patrick. I need to talk to Patrick."

"It's too late to call tonight. It's after midnight in Belgium."

Jaye kept her face down. She pressed her fingertips against her forehead, which had started to ache. "Then I'll go to him. I'll get out on the first flight I can."

Nona said, "It won't do you any good to go running over there. He won't feel up to it. Besides that, he's in isolation. His visitors are strictly limited."

Jaye raised her head and eyed Nona rebelliously. "I want to see him. I'm going."

"He doesn't want us," Nona said shortly. "Melinda was clear about that. It's his express wish that we don't go to the expense and trouble of flying over there."

"Oh, I know Patrick," Jaye said impatiently. "He's just being noble. At a time like this, he needs family."

As soon as the words were out of her mouth, their irony struck her so hard, she blinked in pain. She sat and stared at Nona, as if the woman were a devious imposter who had suddenly taken her mother's place.

But Nona set down her porcelain heart and took a step toward her, something like hope on her face.

"That's it," Nona said. "That's it exactly. He needs family. He needs his blood kin. And he needs us."

Nona seized her hand so forcefully that Jaye would have had to be almost violent to shake it off.

"Don't you see?" Nona said eagerly. "We're his real family, and we need to find his biological family. His blood relations."

Nona sat down beside her, and squeezed her hand even harder. "His best chance for a tissue match is with a full sibling. But even a half-sibling would have a chance."

A kind of frantic hope gleamed in Nona's eyes. Jaye could see thirty years of deception and guilt and desperate love in that gleam.

"The best odds for him are from his blood family," Nona rushed on. "You could do that for him, Jaye. I know you could. You were always the bold one. You're the one who never lets anything stop you. That's what he needs you to do for him. Find his blood kin."

Jaye tried to speak, but could not find her voice.

Nona raised Jaye's hand to her lips beseechingly and kissed her skinned knuckles. "Please," she begged. "Not for me. For him. Please."

Jaye's hand burned where Nona's lips had brushed it. "I—I—" she stammered, "I'd do anything for Patrick. You know that. But I don't even know where to begin."

"You can start in Cawdor," Nona said. "Go there. Where you both were born. It's the logical place to start."

"Cawdor," Jaye echoed numbly.

"You have the letter? Brother Maynard gave you the letter?"

"I—I haven't read it yet," Jaye said.

"I wrote it all down," Nona said. "To make sure it was all there, all in order. Everything I know about your births is there."

She reached out with one hand and touched Jaye's

cheek. "Will you go to Cawdor?" Nona asked, her voice shaking. "Will you? For Patrick? Will you?"

What's happened is wrong, Jaye wanted to say. *And now you want me somehow to make it right?*

But she said, "Yes. I'll go."

Nona collapsed, weeping, into her arms.

Jaye, dry-eyed, stunned, held her and rocked her back and forth, as if she were the mother and Nona the child.

Nona wept herself to sleep. Jaye covered her as best she could with the pink bedspread.

Now, still dazed, she sat at the kitchen table with Brother Maynard. Before her was an untouched cup of black coffee. Beside the cup lay Nona's typed letter, all four single-spaced pages of it.

Jaye stared at the letter as if it were part of a curse. She imagined the paper crinkling into some malevolent origami beast with a beak for sipping blood.

Blood, she thought. *All of this is about blood.*

"I don't understand this marrow matching," she said to Brother Maynard. "You're a scientist. Do you?"

He cleared his throat nervously. "There are six antigens in any tissue type. They can combine in thousands of ways. Ideally the donor's combination matches perfectly." He shifted in his chair. "Even if all Patrick's antigens were common, his chance of finding a donor from the general population would be low."

"How low?"

"One in twenty thousand."

She swallowed, then squared her shoulders. "But his type's not common. So then what do his chances become?"

"Perhaps one in a million."

Oh, Christ, thought Jaye. She put her fist to her mouth to keep her lips from trembling.

Brother Maynard opened a small black notebook and showed her a series of numbers that made no sense to her.

"This is Patrick's tissue type," he said. "These are the six antigens."

He took a pen from the notebook and underlined the last group of characters in the list. "This is the culprit—DR0406. It's exceedingly rare."

Goddam you, DR0406, thought Jaye. *You little prick.* She bit the knuckle of her thumb and said nothing.

"The first five types occur among several races. But DR0406 occurs only in people of Asian ancestry."

Jaye blinked in surprise. She let her clenched fist drop back to the tabletop. "Patrick has Asian blood?"

Brother Maynard nodded. "Yes. Somewhere. It's impossible to say how far back."

"*Only* Asians have that type?"

"Yes."

"Well, then," she said with a surge of hope, "we should be looking for an Asian donor. That's a possibility for him—isn't it?"

"Yes," said Brother Maynard. "And his doctors are looking. But it's not that easy."

"Why not?"

"The overwhelming number of registered donors is Caucasian. Both here and in Europe."

Oh, hell, Jaye thought in misery.

"What about in Asia itself?" she demanded.

"There aren't that many donor centers in Asia."

"That's not fair," Jaye accused.

"I know. But it's the way it is."

She stood and paced to the kitchen counter. A simply shaped wooden parrot hung beside the stove. It had a hook screwed into its painted beak. From the hook hung a potholder.

The parrot was another present Patrick had made for Nona years ago. Jaye looked at it and wanted to weep.

Brother Maynard said, "They'll keep looking. There are new donors every day. The right one may show up."

It wasn't enough to depend on chance, and she knew it. She reached out and gently touched the parrot. "Nona's right. I need to find his blood family."

Brother Maynard was silent for a long moment. When he spoke, his voice was kind, but cautionary. "It may not be possible. I've tried to tell her that. There are no official records. The trail is thirty years old."

She kept her fingertips pressed lightly against the wooden parrot. She thought of Nona's letter, lying behind her on the table. "I know the name of the town, the name of the doctor. Roland Hunsinger. That's a start."

Again Brother Maynard hesitated before speaking. "I've phoned Cawdor information," he said. "There's no Roland Hunsinger listed. There are no Hunsingers listed at all."

She said, "I know the name of the clinic. The Sunnyside Medical—"

He said, "There's no longer any Sunnyside Medical Center listed, either. I'm sorry."

But it didn't matter what he said. He might as well not have spoken at all. She knew what she must do. There was no choice.

THREE

——◦◦◦——

SURPRISE, SURPRISE, THOUGHT JAYE: OKLAHOMA WAS NOT flat.

At least, its northeast corner was not flat. Its hills soared up into crooked ridges, then plunged into ravines and valleys, and all was thickly cloaked with woods.

Cawdor did not belong to the open plains that marked western Oklahoma. It was still of the eastern mountains with their cloistered forests.

At first sight the town seemed split into two parts, unequal in size and wealth. In truth, there were two separate towns, divided by the border between Arkansas and Oklahoma. Each town owed allegiance to its own county and its own state.

On the Arkansas side was the larger, older, and more prosperous Mount Cawdor. Here the tall churches stood triumphant, dwarfing the restaurants where liquor could not be sold by the bottle or by the drink.

But at the state line, where Mount Cawdor joined its wizened Siamese twin, just plain Cawdor, Oklahoma, the scene changed dramatically.

Cawdor served as a honky-tonk suburb for its more proper neighbor, and the few businesses strewn along the highway were mainly bars and liquor stores.

Dominating this bleak strip of commerce was a bingo parlor, run by the Cherokee Nation. The largest building by far in Cawdor, it was closed for the day.

Jaye pulled her rental car into its empty parking lot to get her bearings, to think. She had taken a hopscotch pattern of flights from Boston to the airport nearest to Cawdor. Now she stared up at the Cherokee Nation's billboard.

Bingo, she thought numbly, *here I am. Bingo.*

She looked up and down the highway. Cawdor did not feel like her birthplace. It certainly didn't feel like home. It felt like nothing at all.

I'm here. Now what?

When she'd left Boston this morning, the city was under three inches of gray, gritty snow. But here in Cawdor, the late afternoon was warm and humid, the air close. The only noises were birdsong and the rumble of an occasional passing truck.

Scattered dogwood trees blossomed in white, a stunted crepe myrtle budded pink. The gray sky hung low. It was still and vastly empty.

So what had she expected? A statue in the middle of a city park, commemorating her and Patrick's births? And on the statue's pedestal, clear, easy directions for discovering the truth about their pasts?

She could see no trace of anything that might once have been the Sunnyside Medical Center. "It was out of town," Nona had told her. "To the north. It wasn't a big building, but it was made of stone. It might still be standing."

So ask, thought Jaye.

But first she got out of her car, went to the door of the bingo parlor. From her briefcase she drew a roll of tape and one of the flyers she'd made up in Boston. She fastened the poster to the door.

At the top of the flyer bold letters asked, DO YOU KNOW ANYTHING ABOUT THE ADOPTION OF THESE TWO CHILDREN? There were pictures of herself and Patrick, their birth dates, their descriptions, the scant details of their adoptions.

She felt odd having her own face and name on the poster, yet she'd added it in hope it might jar someone's memory. In truth, she wasn't ready to think of her own parents. It was Patrick's about whom she obsessed.

Her main text was in boldface, describing Patrick's plight: THIS YOUNG MAN DESPERATELY NEEDS A MARROW TRANSPLANT! WE MUST LOCATE HIS BLOOD KIN!

She stepped back and took the measure of her handiwork.

"It pays to advertise," she whispered to herself.

The clerk behind the counter of the convenience store was a young Hispanic woman with a thick accent. Her English was limited, but far better than Jaye's crippled Spanish.

The woman let Jaye tape a flyer to the front window, but said she had never heard of Dr. Roland Hunsinger. She knew nothing of a Hunsinger family, but she did not know many—what?—*vecinos del pueblo,* people of the town.

"Is this all the town?" asked Jaye, not knowing how

to ask the question in Spanish. "Here along the high-way?"

The woman shook her head. She groped for words. "There is—there is—*una escuadra, un barrio comercial*," she said with a frustrated little gesture.

Jaye thought she understood. A square, a business district. "Where?" she asked. "*Dónde?*"

The woman said that Jaye had already passed the turnoff to the town's center. She must go back toward the border, turn right at the intersection.

Jaye was puzzled. "It wasn't marked."

"Is not marked," said the woman. "*El viento.* The sign, it blew down. Nobody put it back up."

Jaye saw why nobody put it back up.

Cawdor's commercial center was no longer either commercial or a center. It was five-thirty in the afternoon, and there was not another human being in sight.

Few buildings seemed still in use, and only one was open, a small liquor store aglow with neon signs. *How nice,* thought Jaye. *I go there. No annoying or confusing choices to make.*

She entered the store, whose interior was cramped, jammed with displays. Beer coolers took up all of the back wall except for a closed door marked EMPLOYEES ONLY. Over the door was mounted a small television. An announcer's voice droned about storm warnings.

Behind the counter stood a muscular young man, watching the television screen. His brown hair was pulled back in a ponytail and fastened with a rubber band. His eyes met Jaye's with an air of bored authority.

For a moment the brightness and closeness of the store's interior seemed to close in on her like a vise. But she forced herself to smile.

"Hi," she said. "I'm trying to find out about a clinic that used to be here. About thirty-some years ago."

"That's before my time," the man said. He looked her up and down without a flicker of emotion.

"It was called the Sunnyside Medical Center," she said.

"Never heard of it." Pointedly he turned his attention back to the television.

"It was a stone building," she persisted. "North of town. It may be called something else now."

He shrugged. His eyes stayed on the screen.

"It was run by a man named Hunsinger," she persisted. "Dr. Roland Hunsinger. Have you ever heard of him?"

Slowly, almost sensuously, he scratched at a scab on his arm. "No."

"Do you know of *anyone* around here named Hunsinger? It's important. Anything you could tell me—"

"I can't tell you nothing," he said. He turned and looked her up and down again. "I'm new here. I only been here a month."

She suppressed a sigh. This conversation was dead at birth. She opened her briefcase and took out a flyer. "Could I put up one of these?"

"I can set it out, is all."

She handed it to him, along with her card. He barely glanced at it. He set it on the counter next to a box of corkscrews and bottle openers.

"Are all the motels back on the Arkansas side?" she asked.

"Yep," he said.

Because nobody on God's green earth would want to stay here, Jaye thought, but forced another smile. "There's someplace over here to stay—surely there is?"

He pinched a scrap of something from his tongue, wiped it on his jeans. "There's one," he said.

On the counter between the Peanut Snax and Spud's Potato Chips was stacked an untidy collection of business cards. Without haste he thumbed through them, then handed her one with a gesture that was almost contemptuous.

She read:

MISS DOLL'S FAMOUS PINK HOUSE BED & BREAKFAST!
Clean Rooms! Low Rates!
Home-Cooked Country Breakfasts!
Turn South on Highway 412!
Follow the Pink Arrows!

Jaye bit at her lower lip, made her decision. "This place, it's not far?"

"No." His eyelids drooped, as if her questions had stupefied him to drowsiness.

"How far?"

He shrugged again. "Mile, mile and a half. Follow the pink arrows."

"She's open for business?"

He shrugged for the third time. He concentrated on scratching at his scab again.

"Thanks," she said with a tight smile. "You've been a big help."

He made no answer and turned his attention back to the weather report. His fingernails on the scab went pick, pick, pick.

Jaye thought Miss Doll's sounded suspiciously like the name of a whorehouse, but she didn't care. A bed and breakfast place would be small and far more intimate than a hotel.

With luck Miss Doll might have lived in Cawdor for years. She might know a great deal about it. And, best of all, she might be talkative.

But Miss Doll was not home. Her teenage granddaughter was, a sullen girl in jeans and a blue maternity smock. She looked no more than sixteen, and she wore her red hair in two braids so tight they curved up at the tips as if wired. Jaye thought she looked like a pregnant Pippi Longstocking.

"My grandma's in Tulsa playing cards at her sister's," the girl said. "She won't be back till late. But I can show you the place. It's forty-five dollars a night."

She led Jaye down a back hallway to a room with a private bath and a tiny television set on the dresser. The room was a bower of frills and flounces, calico and ruffles.

A dozen ornamental pillows, embroidered and appliquéd and tatted, were heaped at the head of the bed. In their midst sat a trio of china-headed dolls with lacy bonnets and full skirts.

"It's—very nice," said Jaye, feeling closed in again. "I'll take it."

"For how long? I got to tell my grandma."

Jaye hesitated. "Let's say two nights for starters. Maybe longer."

The girl shrugged. "There's a phone in the living room. Local calls are free. Long distance, you pay." She rubbed her stomach. Jaye saw that she wore no wedding ring.

"I have a cell phone," said Jaye.

Big deal, said the girl's cool green eyes. She turned to go.

"Wait," Jaye said. She heard the urgency in her own

voice and struggled to control it. "I came here looking for a Dr. Roland Hunsinger. Do you know him?"

The girl paused, gave her a bored glance. "No."

"Do you know anybody in town named Hunsinger?"

"I don't live here," the girl said. "I'm just visiting. I wouldn't live in a dump town like this."

"But your grandmother," Jaye said hopefully. "She's lived here a long time?"

"I don't know. She's lived a lot of places. I'll get your key. It's to the back door. And don't block the drive when you park."

She drifted down the hall, rubbing her stomach and toying with one of her stiff braids.

Jaye looked after her, wondering if her own mother—or Patrick's—had been a girl like this, caught in a small town she hated, unhappily waiting out her time.

Jaye phoned Nona to tell her she'd arrived in Cawdor, but they did not talk long. Nona was tearful because Melinda had called to say that Patrick was worse.

Jaye tried four times to call Melinda, but could not get through. The small, warm room seemed to grow smaller and warmer, smothering her. She had to get out.

She drove to a little diner on the highway. She was hungry, it was suppertime, and from the outside the diner looked like the sort of gathering place where everyone knew everyone else, where the atmosphere was friendly and gossip might flow freely.

But inside business was thin. The only patrons were Jaye, a long-distance trucker, and a pair of young Mexican men talking in quick, low Spanish.

She sat down in a booth, feeling alone and conspicuous. The worn-looking woman frying a hamburger at the grill glanced at her and sighed. She wiped her hands on her apron and came to take Jaye's order.

"No," she said when Jaye asked. "I don't know any Dr. Hunsinger."

She paused, rubbing her shoulder as if it ached. "Maybe there's Hunsingers live around here. But I don't know them. I don't work here steady. I live over in Watts."

Isn't anybody from around here? Jaye thought in frustration.

"Do you know someone who might know?" she asked. "I'm trying to find information about my brother. It's absolutely—"

The phone behind the counter rang.

"Can I post a sign?" she asked the woman, pointing at a bulletin board next to the entrance.

"Sure," said the woman. She went to answer the phone, still rubbing her shoulder. Jaye rose and tacked one of her posters to the board, which was studded with business cards and homemade flyers advertising babysitters and yard sales. At the bottom she scribbled Miss Doll's phone number next to her own.

She was no longer hungry. She left.

Jaye stopped at a service station where the only person on duty was a wiry man of sixty or so, spray-cleaning the inside of the glass front door. His eyebrows were dark, but his mustache was white and seemed perched on his upper lip like an albino caterpillar.

When Jaye showed him her flyer, she thought she saw something wary flit across his expression. The white caterpillar twitched, as if unsettled.

"Dr. Hunsinger and his family is good people," he said righteously. "They got troubles of their own. They don't need people comin' round bringing up these old stories."

Jaye's heart jolted with hope. "He's still alive?"

The man's wrinkles worked themselves into a scowl. "He ain't well. His family has got many a cross to bear." He stabbed the flyer with a black-rimmed nail. "They don't need another person comin' around stirrin' things up."

"Another person?" she asked, her pulses speeding giddily. "Other people have asked about this—"

"Doc Hunsinger is the salt of the earth," the little man scolded. "Never a person in this town needed help but he gave it. He lived by the Golden Rule, he did—"

A tall man came from the back room, rubbing his hands on a dirty cloth. He was about forty, with red hair so curly it seemed knotted. He looked Jaye up and down and smiled.

"What's the problem?"

The little man's mustache quivered indignantly. "She wants to put up a flyer about Doc Hunsinger."

"Let's see," said the redheaded man. He wore a gray uniform shirt, and over his breast pocket was embroidered the name "Dutch." He reached for Jaye's flyer.

Outside a car drove up to the bank of gas pumps, and the smaller man, grumbling to himself, hobbled out to it.

The man named Dutch read the flyer carefully. He had muscular arms thick with red hair and splotched with tattoos. He shook his curly head sadly.

"There's rumors Doc helped with a few adoptions. But that was a long time ago. Nobody remembers the details. That's for the best. The mothers that came here, they wanted privacy. To get on with their lives. Doc, he made sure their privacy was respected."

She stared at him, trying to marshal her arguments.

He offered her his hand, which was strong and smelled of disinfectant. "I'm Dutch Holbrook," he said. "I own this place. I'm also an assistant pastor out at the Wildwood Church."

A minister, she thought, her mind spinning. Surely he would help her; it was his job.

"If I could just talk to Dr. Hunsinger," she began, but he cut her off with another shake of his head.

His gray eyes, while seeming kindly, had something unnerving in their depths. "He can't talk to anyone," he said. "There was an accident a few years back. No, he can't say a word. That part of his mind's gone."

"An accident?" she asked. Her hope withered into nothingness, leaving her feeling empty and sick.

"An accident," he repeated and looked off into the middle distance. "It's purely God's mystery when bad things happen to good people. He lost his son, and his only little grandchild, too—and his health. His daughter, bless her soul, she never got over it. The son-in-law, well, he protects her as much as he can. The Lord has tested him, indeed he has."

Jaye tried to harden her heart against the troubles of the Hunsinger family; she had her own to think of. "The son-in-law," she said. "What's his name?"

"Mowbry, ma'am. Adon Mowbry. But he's not in the phone book. The family, they keep mostly to themselves these days."

"But *you* know them," Jaye persisted. "You could get me the number. I wouldn't intrude on them except for my brother. He needs—"

"Ma'am," said Dutch Holbrook, putting his hand over his heart. "I could not in conscience give you that number. Nobody in town would. We respect that family and what they're going through."

"But," she protested, "I need answers about my brother—"

"Ma'am," he said, "nobody's got such answers now but God Himself. Put yourself in His hands. Give yourself to prayer."

She sensed a strange condescension in this man, and for reasons too deep to understand she did not trust him. Instinctively she took a step backward. "My flyer," she said. "Will you put it up?"

"Certainly," he said with a benign smile. He took it to a pocked bulletin board and began to fasten it beside the notice of a farm sale. He was giving it a prominent place, but his manner seemed to say, *It won't do you any good.*

With desperate inspiration she said, "If you could find me any information, I could—I could make a donation to your church."

He finished tacking up the flyer and turned to her. "Dr. Hunsinger donated the land for our church."

He gave her a smile that showed a glint of gold. The smile said: *We're on his side, not yours.*

"Well, thanks anyway," she said. "I'll be in town for the next few days if anybody wants to get in touch."

He nodded politely, but made no reply. She went outside, got back into her car. The man with the white mustache was washing the windshield of a van pulled up to the pump. He pointedly ignored her.

As she pulled away, she glanced back inside the station. She saw the redheaded man take down the flyer he had put on the bulletin board. He crumpled it and threw it in the waste can.

Her heart drummed in resentment. But there was nothing she could do. She drove on into the night.

•   •   •

Back in her rented room, Jaye lay fully clothed on the bed, hugging one of the tatted pillows and staring, unseeing, at the pink wallpaper. She bit her lip, trying not to cry.

She had at last gotten a call through to Melinda in Belgium, but Melinda had been frightened and weepy. "What will we do?" she kept asking. "What will we do?"

Patrick's lungs had started filling with fluid, and his fever had climbed so high he was delusional. He thought he was a child again, home from school with the chicken pox, and Melinda said he kept begging for Jaye to bring him peppermint ice cream.

This image of Patrick haunted Jaye like a ghost, and she could not exorcise it. She saw him, suffering and hallucinating in an impossibly distant hospital. She shoved the pillow aside and clenched her fists so tightly that her nails bit into her palms. She clenched them harder.

A knock rattled the bedroom door. She sat up with a start.

"You got a phone call," said the granddaughter's voice.

Jaye's thoughts jumbled in anxious confusion, and she was frightened. Was Melinda calling back? Or was it Nona? Was one of them going to tell her Patrick was dead?

No, God. No. Don't let him be dead.

She swung open the door. "Yes?" The word was painful and shaky in her throat.

Miss Doll's granddaughter stood in the hall, eating a stick of red licorice. She was wearing a nightshirt with a teddy bear printed on it. Beneath the bear's picture, her round stomach bulged out like a great egg.

"Phone call," the girl repeated and kept sucking on

the licorice. She turned and started back down the hall, her fuzzy yellow slippers flapping.

"Who is it?" Jaye asked.

The girl didn't turn. "Dunno," she said around her licorice.

The living room was a thing of ruffled lampshades and figurines of angels—and dolls. There were baby dolls and rag dolls and Barbies and porcelain dolls in elaborate Victorian dresses and hats. They seemed to stare at Jaye as if she were an intruder in their exclusive territory.

The girl pointed carelessly at a pink telephone on an end table. Then she walked into the kitchen, opened the refrigerator door, and stood staring inside with a sad air.

Jaye stared at the receiver lying there, waiting for her. *It's not Melinda. It's not Nona,* she told herself, struggling to be controlled, logical. *They'd call me on my own phone. This is someone else. But who? Why?*

She thought of the flyers—she must have posted at least a dozen before coming back to Miss Doll's. Had someone decided to talk? A wild rush of hope swept her.

She picked up the receiver warily. "Hello?" she said.

"Jaye Garrett?" asked a strange voice. It was a man's voice, deep and slightly husky.

Her heart took an unexpected skip. "Yes?"

"Miss Garrett, my name is Turner Gibson. I'm an attorney."

He had no identifiable accent, and he talked with an easy, almost lazy cadence. "I'm like you," he said, "a stranger in a strange land. But I think we should talk. Do you know the Wagon Wheel Supper Club? It's right at the border, on the Oklahoma side."

"Yes," she said hesitantly. She remembered the place. It had seemed unprepossessing, but respectable.

"I know it's short notice. But would you consider meeting me there in fifteen minutes?"

She blinked in surprise. "Excuse me? Why?"

"Because you and I have something in common," he said. "We might be able to help each other. We're both looking for a certain Dr. Roland Hunsinger. And we're both looking for information about an adoption."

FOUR

—⁂—

HER HEART TOOK A HARD, JARRING SKIP, BUT SHE DIDN'T hesitate. "The Wagon Wheel Supper Club? I'll be there."

"Good. Look for a tall guy in a brown suede jacket," he said. "How will I know you?"

"I—I'm tall, too. A blonde. White shirt. Pale gray slacks."

"Fine," he said. "I'll see you there."

"Wait," she said, sensing that he was about to hang up. "My brother—can you help him?"

"It's a long shot. But maybe. I can't guarantee it."

"How did you find me? How do you know who I am?"

"You left a notice on the bulletin board at the Sooner Diner. I saw it."

She pushed her hand nervously through her hair. The explanation was logical enough; it was believable.

"These are delicate matters," he said. "Easier to talk about in person. We both want the same thing. To get in touch with Hunsinger."

"Yes," she said, but the pulse drummed so hard in her throat the word was only a whisper.

"Until then," he said.

She heard the click of his hanging up. She put the receiver of the pink phone back in its cradle. It occurred to her that it was perhaps neither wise nor cautious to go off into the darkness to meet a man she did not know.

Then she thought of Patrick, out of his head with fever and asking her for peppermint ice cream. *To hell with wisdom and caution,* she thought.

She turned toward the kitchen. "I'm going out," she called to the pregnant girl. "I don't know when I'll be back."

But the girl had disappeared, and the kitchen was empty. There was no one to hear her except the horde of posed and staring dolls.

Although the sudden appearance of the Garrett woman was a stroke of luck, it was also annoying. She was un-methodical, aggressive, and indiscreet—it was a bad combination. She would have to be handled carefully.

Turner Gibson stood at the bar, sipping his drink. Idly he watched the storm warnings on the television set mounted over the bar. A tornado watch was in effect.

Turner slouched slightly, for the most notable thing about him was his height, which was six foot three. His body was neither lean nor heavy, and like an actor's, it conveyed what he wished it to convey. Here in Cawdor he chose to make himself seem unremarkable, harmless, and safe to trust. Certain people said with bitterness that he was none of these things.

He was not a handsome man, yet he was far from ugly. His face had a misleading boyishness that he could and did use to his advantage. He wore his brown hair a bit long, with a hint of unruliness. His brow and nose and jaw were only ordinary, not classic.

He had eyes of an indeterminate color, neither green nor hazel. The eyebrows were dark and gave him an earnest look. At the moment, the line of his mouth was carefully neutral.

He watched the weather map and finished his drink. He listened to the television announcer's voice, which despite its smoothness, was foreboding: "Repeat, there are tornado warnings in effect for the following Oklahoma counties . . ."

Then the front door opened, and the blonde walked in. Her troubled gaze swept the room's interior, searching for him. *Damn,* she was good-looking; he'd seen her picture, but it hadn't done her justice.

He stood up straight, caught her eye. Mentally he was undressing her, but he gave her a smile that said, "Trust me," and "I'm not dangerous," and "I'm going to be your friend."

She did not smile back, although one corner of her mouth gave a dubious twitch as if she wanted to comply but had no heart for it.

He moved toward her. She was tall, all right, close to five ten, he'd guess. She was straight-backed and shaped the way a woman should be shaped, curved and not too thin.

Her gold hair was expensively cut and fell straight and sleek, nearly to her shoulders. The clothes were good, too, a white silk long-sleeved shirt, gray-and-white pin-striped slacks. She was pretty, but she had a distracted, almost haunted air, and she was extraordinarily pale.

The men in the room noticed her, especially those who were there without women. He could sense their sudden hunger throbbing in the air like rock music.

He reached her side, smiled down at her, and touched her arm protectively. "Jaye Grady Garrett?"

"Yes?" Her sky-blue eyes struck him as more intelligent than he had expected, and they were full of apprehension.

She looked punch-drunk, he thought with cool analysis, like a prize-fighter who'd taken too many hits, but stayed standing out of sheer willpower.

"Turner Gibson." He introduced himself in his most reassuring voice and gave her his most reassuring handshake. Her skin was icy cold against his.

"You didn't wear a jacket?" he asked with concern. "It's gotten cool out."

"I hadn't noticed," she said. She shook her head slightly, as if puzzled by her own discomfort.

He released her hand, dug into his pocket, and presented her with a business card. "I'm an attorney. The firm Truhoff, McClarty, McClarty, and Gibson."

She read the card, frowning slightly, then again raised those blue eyes to him. He felt the strong kick of a purely sexual urge. *Damn*, he thought again, but he kept his expression as innocent as the driven snow.

"You're trying to find Dr. Hunsinger, too?" she asked. "Because of an adoption?"

"Let's sit down," he said. "I'll tell you everything."

Of course, he did not intend to tell her exactly the whole truth. He could not, if he wanted to.

•   •   •

Turner Gibson seemed like such a *nice* man, thought Jaye, regarding him over the rim of her wineglass. He conveyed an air of sincerity and just plain decency.

Still, she was not quick to trust strangers. Quite the opposite. But the sympathy in his expression warmed her far more than the wine. *Be careful,* she told herself. *Right now you could be a pushover for sympathy.*

She wasn't at her most rational, she knew. Her handbag was stuffed with lucky pieces both sacred and profane. She had the gold lighter from Patrick and a rabbit's foot he had given her when they were children, a St. Jude medal and a scarf that Nona said had been dipped in a font of holy water at the Vatican.

When Turner asked her about Patrick, she let herself tell him only the barest outline of the story, keeping a tight rein on her emotions.

"My God," he said. "When did you find all this out?"

"Saturday night."

His eyes narrowed speculatively. "It's only Monday. You've had a busy two days."

He was right. The time seemed like two eons, crammed insanely tight with desperate and makeshift preparations. She didn't want to think about it, it made her head ache.

She said, "You said we might be able to help each other. How?"

Turner's gaze held hers. He wasn't a drop-dead handsome man, but she found she liked that. Since her ex-husband, she no longer trusted gorgeous men.

"We can cooperate," he said with that same level gaze. "Pool information. I have a client in Philadelphia. I'll call him Mr. D."

"Mr. D.?" she repeated warily.

He set his jaw at a thoughtful angle. "His wealth is—

well known. We're willing to pay for information, but given his circumstances, we don't want to invite extortion."

She nodded but made no other comment.

He said, "What I'm about to tell you is confidential, of course."

"Of course." Her heart knocked crazily at her ribs.

"Forty-two years ago," he said, "my client fathered a child out of wedlock. That child was born here. In Cawdor. And adopted through Dr. Hunsinger."

Another child sold, Jaye thought with a bitter jolt. *Besides Patrick and me.* Of course she had known there were others; the man at the service station had admitted as much. But until this moment their existence had seemed hazy, a mere abstraction.

Turner looked pained by what he was about to say. "My client's never seen his child. He wants to, very much. I'm sorry to say he's not well. Not well at all."

Jaye's heart twisted. "I'm sorry."

"I'm trying to find this child for him," Turner said. "We think it's a son."

"This Mr. D.—he doesn't know?"

Turner made an apologetic gesture. "It was a summer romance. In Maine. The girl's parents came between them. There were religious differences—and others. The girl was only fifteen. He was nineteen. He was told never to see her again, or he'd be charged with statutory rape."

Jaye winced.

"He went back to Philadelphia," said Turner. "She was taken home to Little Rock. Later he heard that her parents sent her here, to Cawdor. That's why I'm here. To find what I can about the son."

Jaye's brow furrowed. "This Mr. D."

"Yes?"

"He waited all this time to find out?"

"No," Turner said. "For years he wanted to find the mother. Her name was Julia. Julia Tritt. And he wanted to learn what became of the child."

She looked at him questioningly. "And?"

"She's dead," he said simply. "She's been dead over thirty years. A car accident. She was twenty years old when it happened. And engaged to someone else."

He paused, as if weighing his words. "My client never got over her. Not really. He married. Not particularly happily. They had no children. Now his wife's passed on. He wants me to find his son."

"You're in some sort of family law?"

"You could call it that."

"You've done this kind of thing before?"

"Not precisely. But he's been a longtime client."

"It's odd, don't you think?" she challenged. "You and I turning up here at the same time?"

"It's not so odd," he said. "You'll see."

She lifted a quizzical eyebrow.

He said, "What's important is that my client's case is similar to your brother's." He paused. "For both of them, there's not much time."

Her muscles tensed at the ominous weight of that phrase. *Not much time.*

He said, "We need to talk to Hunsinger. If it's possible."

"I've heard he can't talk," she said, staring unseeing at the pale wine in her glass. "That he's been injured. That he hasn't got all his—faculties."

Turner waited a beat of time, watching her. "He can talk, all right."

"What?" Shock and hope mingled too intimately to separate.

"His mind's still plenty good. I know where he lives. On a horse ranch. Just outside of town."

She looked at him as if truly seeing him for the first time. His eyes were neither green nor brown; she could not say precisely and didn't care. Because suddenly when she looked into their mysteriously colored depths, she seemed to see salvation.

He saw the change in her face, the brightness of hope touching it like light.

He hadn't lied about Mr. DelVechio exactly. But he had bent the truth, shaped and slanted it to serve him, and now she was looking at him as if he were a delivering hero. He liked that look, actually. It gave him carnal thoughts.

He hid them and gave her a brotherly smile. "Hunsinger's an old man. Past eighty. He lives with his daughter and her husband. Barbara and Adon Mowbry. I've talked to Mowbry."

Jaye Garrett's hands began to tremble. She nearly knocked over her wineglass.

He caught it with catlike quickness. Then he covered her right hand, which was cold as snow, with his own, which was steady and warm.

"Careful," he said. "Don't get your hopes up."

"But—" she stammered, "but—"

He gripped her hand more firmly. "They don't want to talk to people like you and me."

"They *have* to," she protested.

"No." He leaned nearer. "As far as they're concerned, these adoptions never happened."

"But I *know* they happened. So do you."

"The son-in-law claims nothing illegal ever took place. If it did, he knows nothing about it."

"But I have *proof*," Jaye insisted. "I have my mother's— I have Nona's letter. She tells all about it."

He wrapped both his hands around hers, but she hardly seemed to notice. "Shh," he said gently. "Keep your voice down. Listen to me. What was done here was against the law. Adon Mowbry's not going to admit to it. He *is* the law here; he's county prosecutor, has been for years."

"They'll admit it or they'll be sorry," she said hotly. "I'll see to that."

"Shh," he repeated, squeezing her hand more tightly. "Be careful. This is their turf. And people around here are very protective of Hunsinger. Haven't you seen that yet?"

She swallowed hard. "Yes," she admitted. "I've seen it."

"I've been here three days," he said. "Long enough for people to know what I'm up to—even though I've been quiet about it. You haven't been as quiet. It's possible we're being watched."

She glanced around the restaurant in disbelief. "Watched? Me? But I only got here today—"

"And how long did it take me to find you?" he asked.

Her face went pale again. She looked as if she imagined a dozen pairs of eyes secretly scrutinizing her.

But she squared her shoulders. "The important thing is my brother. What sort of doctor is this Hunsinger? Didn't he take an oath to protect life? I'll go after his license if he won't talk. I'll haul his sorry—"

"Roland Hunsinger's been retired for years. And his people will swear he's in no shape to talk."

"But you said he could—"

"I got that information from a disgruntled former servant. It cost me a lot, too. I know he was injured, badly; I don't know exactly how. He stays in the house. He hasn't been seen in public for four years."

"Oh, damn, damn, damn," she muttered. She stared

down and seemed to realize for the first time that Turner held her hand. Carefully she drew it away, settled it in her lap.

"What about his daughter?" she asked. "Maybe she knows something. There could be records—"

"The daughter doesn't talk to anybody, either. The rumor is she's got problems."

Jaye thought of Nona, sick with worry for Patrick. "Yes . . . I heard she lost her child."

"Her child and her brother. Rollie Jr. In the same accident that hurt her father. She's the only one who came through unscathed. I imagine there's a lot of grief. And some survivor's guilt as well. Her husband's got his hands full. He doesn't want to deal with people like us. And he's powerful enough that he doesn't have to."

She said, "B-but if his family's suffered, he should have some compassion—shouldn't he?"

Turner kept his eyes trained on hers. "I said he's powerful. Hunsinger owns part of that poultry operation out on the edge of town. He's got his fingers in the Cherokee gambling outpost. Most of the liquor stores and honky-tonks up and down this strip of highway? They're his."

"Even this one?" Jaye asked, with an uneasy glance around the restaurant.

"Yes," he said, with the trace of an ironic smile. "Even this one." He finished off his drink. "Now Mowbry runs it all."

She was silent a moment, staring into her wine again, her lips narrowed. "So he has family secrets to keep," she said at last.

"Yes," Turner said. "He does. And it upsets the daughter if anyone talks about Daddy's illegal activities. She wants to think he's kindly old Dr. Hunsinger, the town benefactor."

Jaye made a frustrated gesture. "So how do we find out what we need to know?"

"First," he said, "we're discreet."

"I don't have time for discreet."

"Also, we work together. We share what we know."

A wary surprise stole over her face. "You and I? Together?"

"You and I—and the others," he added.

She frowned. "What others?"

He smiled his least threatening smile. "Hunsinger didn't just sell you and your brother, you know."

She shrugged impatiently. "Well, of course. There's your client. The son he wants to find."

"What about the others?"

"I—I haven't thought much about it. I've thought mostly about Patrick."

"We know this baby selling goes back to at least 1957," he said. "The clinic was open for more than two decades. He could have been selling babies the whole time."

"Two decades?" Jaye echoed in disbelief.

"It's possible," Turner said. "So it's also possible that any number of children were sold. Not just two or three or half a dozen."

She stared at him. "How many?"

"Perhaps over a hundred."

Her mind reeled. She found what he'd said almost unthinkable. "But—how do you know this?" she demanded.

"Because a few are like you," he said softly. "And me. They've been coming here, asking questions. You're not the first. Neither am I. The truth of what happened here is starting to come out."

Dumbstruck, she blinked at him.

"And Mowbry doesn't want it coming out. A lot of

people don't. They're not going to cooperate. They don't dare. So it's important we help each other."

They're not going to cooperate.

They don't dare.

She felt numb, dizzy, slightly sick. She put her fingertips to her forehead, shut her eyes.

"Are you all right?" he asked, concern in his voice.

"I want to get out of here," she said tightly. "I feel like this place is closing in on me."

She felt him come to her side, put his hand on her shoulder. "Where do you want to go?"

She rubbed her forehead wearily. All she could think was that she wanted to see where this tangle of lies and life and death started. "The Sunnyside Medical Center," she said. "I want to see where it is. If it's not gone."

He squeezed her shoulder. "It's not gone. But it's changed. Hunsinger sold it years ago when he bought his ranch. It's a nursing home now. Pleasant Valley."

A nursing home, she thought with grim irony. The building had been turned from a gateway to birth into one of death.

"Do you really want to go there?" he asked.

She nodded, fighting the urge to bite her lip nervously.

"I'll take you."

When she rose from her seat, he put his hand on the small of her back to guide her out the door. It was not a sexual gesture, but a gentlemanly one, and she was touched by his natural air of consideration.

Without question she went with him into the gusting darkness.

Barbara Mowbry slept, her legs drawn up on the white damask couch. Beside her small, slippered feet sat the box of Godiva chocolates Adon had bought her, opened but otherwise untouched.

A video of *The Sound of Music* played on the television. It was Barbara's favorite movie, and Adon didn't switch it off for fear the change would disturb her fragile rest.

But then the phone jangled, as he knew it would. He rose swiftly to answer it.

"Hello," Adon said softly, looking at his caller I.D. WAGON WHEEL SUPPER CLUB, read the display.

"They just left, both of them," said a man.

Will LaBonny was the acting sheriff, and this was his third call to Adon tonight. LaBonny had a remarkably quiet voice, almost dulcet, but it was deceptive. He reminded Adon of a guard dog that was part wolf or jackal. He was valuable because he had savagery in him, and he was dangerous for the same reason.

LaBonny said, "The bartender says the two of them been talking up a storm."

A storm, thought Adon tiredly. Outside the wind thrashed as if in agony, and the budding bridal-wreath bushes clawed and rattled against the front window.

He carried the phone into the hallway, so that he could still see Barbara, but speak without fear of waking her.

Adon Mowbry was a tall man, once straightly built and lithe, but now, at fifty-three, his shoulders hunched prematurely, for his family troubles weighed upon him like a bag of stones. His body had thickened with the years, and his knees ached incessantly from old football injuries. On nights like this, when the air was moist and chill, they ached the most.

"Did you hear me?" asked LaBonny. "I said they left together, Gibson and the woman."

Adon sighed and massaged the bridge of his nose.

He had hoped with all his heart that Gibson was leaving town, he had fucking pined for it.

And it had seemed a done deal. Gibson had made flight reservations for tomorrow afternoon, out of Tulsa and back to Philadelphia—Adon's sources had assured him of the fact, and he was just starting to breathe easy again.

Then the frigging blonde had showed up.

And Gibson had found out about her. How could he not? She'd gone all over Cawdor posting her goddam flyers. Two people had already brought him copies, and he'd been faxed a third.

He'd shown one of the flyers to the old man, who'd nearly had a stroke when he'd seen the names and pictures.

Stop it, stop it, stop it, the old man had screamed like a spoiled child. He'd stormed, *She could ruin us all.* The woman in particular upset him.

Barbara had been in her shower, and Adon had prayed she wouldn't hear her father's rants; he didn't think she had. Adon's pale blue eyes could go as cold as death when he thought of Barbara suffering more, and although he'd quieted the old man, he'd wanted, for the thousandth time, to throttle him.

"Adon?" asked LaBonny in his soft voice.

"I don't like this," Adon said with tired distaste.

LaBonny said, "They went in his car. Took off north. Headed for the old clinic probably. I didn't try to follow. He's got to come back. She has to get her car." He paused and gave a strangely sweet laugh. "Unless they plan to shack up together."

Adon thought bleakly of this and gazed through the door at his sleeping wife. Barbara stirred, curling up more tightly, like a sick child. Adon studied her with a sadness and protectiveness that made his eyes go colder still.

LaBonny said, "Adon? What's Doc say?"

Adon turned his gaze to the room's big picture window, which looked out on the cloud-racked moonlight. The wind moaned. On television, children sweetly sang.

Adon thought again of the old man's reaction. He said, "I'd prefer not to deal with two of them."

"You want me to warn her off?" LaBonny asked. "Warn both of them off?"

Adon spoke carefully, for he always spoke carefully of such things. He feared the state police might tap his phone, and he particularly dreaded Officer Allen Twin Bears of the Organized Crime Unit. Both his father-in-law and LaBonny thought this foolish. Twin Bears would be bought eventually, they said; everyone was. But Adon remained cautious.

"I prefer not to deal with two of them," he repeated. "Barbara doesn't need this. The doctor doesn't need this." He paused for effect. "*You* don't need this."

"Do you mean—"

"It was a remark. That's all it was."

"There are things that can be done. It's a question of—"

"I've said what I had to say. I'm not telling you what to do. I don't want trouble laid at my door. Trouble is what I don't want, in any way, shape, or form. I have to fly to Dallas tomorrow. I don't want to have to worry about what's happening here."

"They can be made to feel unwelcome. It's possible—"

"I told you what I want. I told you what I don't want. Barbara should be able to have some peace. We *all* should be able to, by God."

There was a long pause. "I understand," said LaBonny.

"Good," said Adon, hoping he truly did. "Enough said."

He clicked the off button. He carried the phone into the living room and put it back in its cradle.

He was too weary to think of LaBonny; the man was the guard dog, let him guard.

Adon turned again toward Barbara. The lamplight gleamed on her golden hair. On television the children sang about farewell and *auf Wiedersehen*, about so long and good-bye.

FIVE

~~~~~

FAT BLACK CLOUDS ROLLED RAPIDLY OVER THE MOON, LIKE a pack of tumbling goblins. From time to time the moon's white light peeped down timidly over the landscape, then the goblins overran it again.

The wind racked the trees, shaking their limbs and sending flurries of young leaves into the path of the headlights. The car passed a stand of wild plum trees in bloom, and for a moment the white petals swirled in Jaye's sight like flakes of snow on the night.

Turner's profile was faintly illuminated by the dashboard lights. He had wavy hair, very thick, and the wind had disheveled it so that it hung over his forehead, reminding her of Patrick. The phantom resemblance gave her the irrational feeling that she knew him better than she did.

He said, "Feeling better?"

"Yes," she lied. Then after a moment she said, "Tell me about the other people. The ones adopted from here—please."

He flexed his fingers on the steering wheel. "Okay. Five years ago, a pair of sisters showed up asking about Hunsinger. They said their parents had always told them they were adopted, that they came from his clinic. But Hunsinger wouldn't talk to them. They didn't get much information from anybody. They went back home. To Austin."

A chill of recognition raced through her. "Austin? That's where my mother and father—where they lived when they got us."

Turner nodded. "Right. But Barbara Mowbry—Hunsinger's daughter—got upset by the incident. Her only child had been born with brain damage. Maybe the old rumors about her father triggered something psychological. Who knows? I've heard she's always been a very sheltered woman."

"And then?" prompted Jaye.

"And then, two years later somebody else showed up. A man this time. Robert Messina. Who'd grown up in Austin.

"But by that time Hunsinger had turned reclusive because of his accident. The family closed ranks against Messina. So did the town. Most people thought Hunsinger was nearly a saint. Whatever he'd done, he'd done for the common good."

"The common good?" Jaye said in disbelief. "How in God's name can selling children be good?"

"Times were different," he said. "An unmarried girl who got pregnant couldn't keep a baby. It wasn't done. She either got an abortion—which was illegal and dangerous—or she had the kid and gave it away. If she had it, she needed to keep the whole thing as quiet as possible. An illicit pregnancy could ruin her reputation, her whole life."

Jaye shifted uncomfortably. She wondered if that's how her own biological mother had felt—that Jaye's budding life was a ruinous blight on her own.

Turner said, "The people who'll talk about it say that with Hunsinger, the baby got to live. The mother's secret was guarded as closely as possible. She was safe, too."

He tossed her an unsmiling glance. "And couples like your parents, who thought they'd never be able to get a child, got one."

And they all lived happily ever after, she thought. *Almost.*

He slowed and turned west, down a two-lane highway that wound between the tree-cloaked hills. Overhead the dark clouds raced and twisted, changing their shapes.

He said, "After Robert Messina, two more adoptees came here. Separately. Last year a woman from Fredricksburg, Texas. Near Austin. Last December another man. A college professor."

"From near Austin again?" Jaye asked uneasily.

"No. Raised in Chicago. The pattern seems to break. But it doesn't. Not really."

Her heart took an apprehensive skip. "What do you mean?"

"His father worked for Lone Star Petroleum. *That's* the true common denominator. Almost all the adopting families are connected, in some way, with Lone Star."

"Lone Star? But why?"

"Hunsinger must have had somebody referring customers to him, some sort of broker."

"My God—A baby broker?"

"Exactly. And that broker lived in Austin. And had connections to Lone Star."

Jaye shook her head helplessly. "Nona says that a woman in Austin told her about Hunsinger. Mrs. Forstetter, Addy Forstetter. But that she died years ago."

"This trail's a long time cold. A lot of people who traveled it are dead."

The thought of death filled her with superstitious dread. She shivered, fighting the urge to wrap her arms around herself.

"We're almost there," Turner said. "It's just over this next rise."

She gripped her hands tightly in her lap and watched the road ahead. Old leaves blew scuttling across it, and young ones, freshly torn from their branches, danced with them.

Then the road crested the top of the hill and fell again, but on the next rise stood a building, a few windows like dim gold squares in the darkness.

Turner slowed the car and parked along the highway next to the long drive that led to the building. "This is it," he said.

Jaye thought, *This is where I was born. Where Patrick was born.* But the words seemed to have no real meaning for her, no emotional weight.

She could only think how ordinary this building looked. Ordinary and lonely, out here in these empty foothills. Before the car stood a large wooden sign announcing PLEASANT VALLEY REST HOME. It was pocked with small holes and badly in need of repainting.

The building itself sat well back from the highway. It was a square two-story structure of pale stone that seemed to flicker hazily in the unstable light from the moon. It was smaller than she had imagined, and looked old and in disrepair.

Its pillared porch had settled on one side so that the floor tilted and the roof seemed askew, like a hat put on at a drunken angle. Once the structure had been screened by a line of trees, but now only an ugly row of uneven stumps remained, erupting like tumors from the shadowy ground.

"It's not very nice," she managed to say.

"No. It's not." He cut the lights. They sat in the dark and silence.

She tried to imagine how her birth mother had felt when she first set eyes on this isolated place hidden among these desolate hills. She could not.

"Do you want to get out?" he asked. "Take a better look?"

I don't want to go any closer, she thought. *I don't even want to stand on its grounds.* But she nodded because it seemed as if anything else would be an act of cowardice.

He switched off the engine. He got out and came to her side of the car, opened the door, offered her his hand.

She took it gingerly, let him help her out. He did not hold her hand a second longer than necessary. He stood at her side, and for a moment they stared at the squat building without speaking.

"I don't feel anything," she said at last. "It seems wrong not to feel something."

"There's no right or wrong about it," Turner said. "You feel what you feel."

The wind was still high, and the air was sharp with chill. She drew in a long, shaky breath. The scent of leaves dead and rotting mingled with the first faint fragrance of spring.

He moved closer. "You're cold," he said. His breath was warm on her icy cheek.

"It's nothing," she lied.

"Take my jacket."

Before she could protest, he had stripped it off and

was bundling her into it. "Come on," he coaxed. "Put your hands in the sleeves."

The garment was still warm from his body, and the silk lining gave off the hint of his aftershave. He engaged the zipper and pulled it all the way up. His hand was near her chin and she could feel its heat.

"Better?"

"Better," she breathed. "But aren't you cold?"

He looked down into her eyes, one dark brow raised. "No. I don't feel cold at all."

He did not move away. They stood nearly motionless, their silence strangely charged. Suddenly he no longer seemed brotherly in the least, and with dismay she realized something sexual was happening between them. She thought, *Not now. And for God's sake, not here.*

She looked away from him. Beyond them, the building loomed like a mausoleum for foolish passions. She edged away from him, embarrassed by such an unfitting stirring of desire.

As if Turner realized the same thing, he dropped his hand and took a step backward. He wore a white shirt, and it shone with spectral paleness against the darkness.

He hooked one thumb in his belt and with his other hand gestured to the right of the building. "There used to be a house up there. Hunsinger lived there."

Jaye gazed at the empty spot. She could see no sign of a house, not a trace. "What happened?"

"It burned. In 1975. Just after Hunsinger retired, put the clinic up for sale. Nobody was hurt. He and his family were out of town. There was a guest house, too. For the mothers-to-be. It was torn down."

"A guest house?"

"Privacy. So they wouldn't be seen. They didn't go out. They stayed hidden."

Jaye was sickened. "It sounds like being in prison."

"It probably was. They didn't have much choice back then."

She stared at the vacant space, trying to imagine girls like Patrick's mother and her own. She visualized them as wraiths, still possessing the place, and in their bellies were insubstantial little ghost children.

No, she corrected herself, not insubstantial and not ghosts. She was real and so was Patrick; they were solid flesh and beating blood, but her blood was healthy and his was sick, and that's why she was here trying to see into the past, to save Patrick.

She turned from the bleak building, the haunted yard. "I think I'd like to go back now."

But he didn't move to go. "I wanted you to see where the house was. When Hunsinger shut down his medical practice, he moved his records into an office he'd set up in his home. They're all gone, of course."

She stopped and turned to face him again. "His records? All of them?"

"Yes."

For the first time since she'd met him, she was unable to keep tears from welling into her eyes. "If there are no records, and—and if he can't talk—and nobody else *will* talk to us, how will we ever know the truth?"

"Steady," he said, laying his hands on her shoulders. "He wouldn't have made any records that incriminated him in the first place. But the fire was convenient. It let him off the hook completely."

She blinked back the tears, waiting for him to go on.

"And," he said, "there *are* people who'll talk. I've found a few. I'll find more."

"How?"

"I have my ways," he said vaguely. "In the meantime, I'll help you as much as I can. But I want something from you in return."

The wind rose again, making her hair stream across her face. She tried to push it back, but it fluttered over her eyes and nose and mouth like a veil. "From me? What can I do?"

He bent nearer. "I'll give you my information—all of it. About the other adoptees, the clinic, Hunsinger, his family. And my client's case. Complete access to everything."

"And I give you what?"

"In return, you give me your information. Including a copy of your mother's letter."

"Of course," she said. "I'll be glad to."

"The other thing is harder to ask," he said. "But I have to."

"What is it?"

"I'd rather do this job alone," he said. "I have my own way of doing things. It would be better if you weren't—well—involved."

She was galled. "You're saying you don't want me here?"

"I can do the investigating for both of us," he said. "I can and I will."

His calm, so reassuring before, suddenly angered her. "I'm here about my brother. Not some client. My *brother*."

"I understand. And I'll ask about your brother. I'll make it a top priority."

"Excuse me," she said with feeling, "but it's not 'a top priority' to me. It's the *only* priority. And I'm not going to delegate it to some—some volunteer I hardly know. I came here to do a job, and I intend to do it."

"But you don't know how to do it," he reasoned. "You're going about it with a lot of emotion, but—"

"Maybe my emotion is my strength," she argued.

"Nobody's going to try harder than I am. *Nobody*. So who are you to tell me that—"

"See? You're getting emotional now. I have more experience in this kind of thing. And more resources. To put it frankly, it's to your advantage to—"

He stopped. He looked down the road they had come.

She followed his gaze and saw the glow of headlights beyond the rise, the brightness increasing. Then a truck cleared the hill.

Suddenly the truck cut its lights, but she heard its motor rev, gaining speed. It kept bearing down the road toward them, and she stared at it in uneasy surprise. "What—?" she started to say.

He grabbed her elbow, tried to get her back into the car, but he'd barely flung open the door when the truck was upon them. It slowed. Then a streak of flame gashed the darkness, and the roar of gunfire fractured the night. Turner seized her, hurled her to the ground, and rolled toward a drainage ditch, taking her with him. They tumbled down the shallow slope, and he flung his body atop hers, his heart thundering.

Jesus, he thought. *Jesus.* There was nowhere to run, no cover nearer than the building far across that broad, open lawn.

The truck accelerated again, then sped off. But Turner kept low, Jaye pinned beneath him, until he heard the sound of the motor fade and melt away into the moan of the wind. Then the wind was all he heard, that and the drumming of his own blood in his ears.

He pulled away from Jaye, who lay facedown. She groaned sickly. He turned her over as gently as he could. There was blood on her forehead, and her face was dirty.

"Are you all right?"

"They shot at us," she said dazedly, shaking her hair from her face. "Why?"

"I don't know," he said, "but let's get the hell out of here before they come back and try again. Can you stand?"

"I don't know."

He rose and tried to hoist her to her feet. Her knees buckled and she sagged against him. He held her to keep her upright.

"Did they hit you?" he asked, drawing back to look into her face. "Did they hurt you?"

She struggled to stand by herself. "The wind's knocked out of me, that's all," she said gamely.

But her knees wobbled again, and she started to sink to the ground. He swept her up into his arms and carried her back to the car.

He looked apprehensively down the road, but it was empty, once again deserted. She buried her face against his neck.

"I'm sorry," he said against her hair.

Then he saw that the car sat at a listing angle. The rear tire on the driver's side had been shot.

"Oh, shit," he muttered, and held her more tightly.

"What's wrong?" she asked, her voice muffled.

"They got the tire," he said. *And I'm sure as hell not going to stand out here in the open and change it,* he thought, looking down the road again. He still saw no sign of the truck, but his heart hammered as hard as before, and he knew he needed to get the woman to safety.

"I—I think I did something to my hand," she said against his throat. He could hear the pain in her voice.

"I'm going to put you in the car," he said. "I'll drive us to the building. We can get that far. I'll get you inside. There'll be somebody to help you."

Her door had swung open, and as gently as he could, he set her on the passenger seat. She groaned again and curled nearly into a fetal position. She had her right hand wrapped around her left, and she rocked back and forth with pain.

Swiftly he got in, wanting to get them both off the highway as soon as possible. "You okay?"

She nodded and bit her lip. But then she slipped sideways, leaning against the door. She had fallen into a faint.

Christ, he thought, *she could be shot and not know it, she could be dying.*

He switched on the ignition, but not the lights, and gunned the gas as hard as he dared. The ruined wheel thudded, and the car lurched and swerved, careering down the drive like a drunken dervish.

He screeched to a jolting halt, got out, flung open her door, and swept her up in his arms. He carried her up the porch, two stairs at a time. He kicked at the heavy front door as relentlessly as if he meant to knock it down.

The din of his kicking filled her ears. The sound had seemed curiously distant from her at first, an annoying intrusion from another world. But it pounded its way past her faintness and pain; it forced her mind to rise out of the blackness.

She was conscious of a door swinging open, of light, of a confusion of voices. She realized only vaguely that Turner was carrying her, because she was so much more acutely aware of the hurt stabbing like a knife at her left hand.

Then she understood that they were inside, in some sort of strange, dimly lit lobby. She had a fragmented impression of shabbiness and gloom.

She managed to raise her head and saw a pale, slender man of fifty or so. He had sleek white hair and wore a white uniform. His wire-rimmed glasses caught the feeble light so that it seemed his eyes were two flat, gleaming ovals. She blinked back at him dazedly.

"There's a room with a bed. Follow me," said the pale man.

She heard Turner's voice rumble something in reply and felt his arms tighten around her. Then she was being borne swiftly down a shadowy hall. A bright light flared on overhead. She was laid atop a bed with a bare mattress.

She rolled to her side, clutching her left hand awkwardly against her chest with her right.

"Jaye?" Turner kept saying. "Jaye?"

The pale man smoothed her hair back from her face with surprising gentleness. "What happened here?"

"Somebody shot at us," said Turner.

Jaye squeezed her eyes shut and shook her head dazedly. "I'm not shot."

"It's her hand," said the pale man. He had quick, fluttering fingers that moved over hers with a miraculously soft touch. "Oh, we've broken our finger, that's what, we've broken our pinkie. Let's see, love. Let me see."

"Jesus," Turner said, "is there a nurse in this place?"

"*I'm* the nurse," said the pale man. "The only real one, anyway. Oh, now, this hand won't look so bad when we get the blood off. But it's a *deep* cut."

Turner took his phone from his belt, unfolded it, and then swore because it was broken. "Where's the phone in here? We need an ambulance," he said.

"I don't need an ambulance," Jaye said as emphatically as she could.

"You passed out. You could have a concussion."

"I got woozy, that's all."

"Your forehead's bleeding," argued Turner.

"It's a superficial wound," the man said soothingly. "We'll have it patched up in no time."

"I don't need an ambulance," Jaye insisted. She tried to sit up, but a small, sharp pain stabbed her forehead like an ice pick. She sank back against the mattress.

"Look," Turner said impatiently to the man, "is there a phone in the lobby? I want an ambulance and the cops. We were shot at, goddammit."

Jaye closed her eyes against the glare of the overhead light. "Turner? Why'd they shoot at us?"

"I don't know," he said.

"Shhh." The man hushed her, examining her hand again. "There, there. Oh, my, we fell on the gravel very hard, didn't we?"

"Did you hear those shots?" Turner demanded of him. "You had to hear them. You're a witness."

The man shrugged calmly and felt Jaye's collarbone. "Of course I heard them. I just thought, oh, *well*."

"Oh, well?" Turner echoed with angry incredulity.

"Yes," the man said, gently touching Jaye's ribs. "I thought, Oh, again? People are always driving by shooting at that sign. Kids. That's why it's such a wreck. It doesn't pay to repaint it."

"Are you trying to say they were shooting at the sign?" Turner challenged. "Not us?"

"Well," the man said with a prim shrug, "they do it all the time. It passes for wit among them."

Turner swore again. "I'm going to find a phone." Jaye heard him stamp off.

"He'll see," said the man with an air of prissy confidentiality. "The sheriff's department couldn't care less about shooting that sign. I don't say it's right, but that's the way it is."

His words made no sense to her, and the bright overhead light made her head hurt. Even though her eyes were closed, she shielded them with her good hand.

"I'm sure they weren't shooting at you, love," the man crooned. "Just probably trying to scare you, that's all. Don't take it personally, don't be upset."

Somebody opens fire on us, and I get knocked into a ditch, she wanted to say. *But I shouldn't take it personally? Don't be upset? Jesus, Mary, and Joseph.* But she could not summon the energy to say it.

"You're shaking," said the nurse. "I'll get a sheet from the drawer."

She heard him moving, heard the slide of a metal drawer, the brisk shaking out of a sheet. Gently he lifted her hand, spread the sheet over her, then laid her hand atop it.

He smoothed her hair again. "I'm going to get some bandages and antiseptic, love. And find you a blanket. I'm going to leave you for just a little bit. Will you be all right?"

"Ummm," she managed to say. She bit her lip and covered her eyes more tightly.

"Does that light bother you?" he asked. "Should I shut it off?"

"Ummm," she said. "Please."

"I'll just turn on the night-light," he said. "And I'll be back in two shakes of a fat lamb's tail."

He switched on a bedside light, turned off the glaring overhead. "You just rest a minute, hear?" he said. Then he slipped away on noiseless shoes.

Jaye lay, feeling the thudding of her pulse. Pain shot through her finger and the cut at the edge of her palm. She slowly took her hand from her eyes, then opened them.

The room's high ceiling was shrouded in shadows.

She raised herself stiffly on her elbow, still disoriented, still shaken. The room was a glum, bare thing with dull walls and a window with a blind but no drapes. The metal dresser was empty, there were no pictures on the walls, and the metal bedside table held only an old and institutional-looking gooseneck lamp.

Where am I? she thought uneasily. *The Bates Motel?*

She realized that Turner had brought her into the building and that the building was—what?—a nursing home, which explained why the fussy white-haired man was a nurse.

This is the Pleasant Valley Rest Home, she told herself, trying to regain her bearings. And they had stopped to look at it because it had once been the Sunnyside Medical Center and—

"My God," she breathed, and fell back to the mattress again. Her heartbeat racheted to a sick, giddy speed.

I was born here, she thought. *In this very building. Maybe in this very room. I was sold here. So was Patrick.*

She closed her eyes again. She tried to comprehend that her life had begun here and so had Patrick's. Her imagination plunged down one dizzying path, then another, until she could follow none.

She thought she heard footsteps coming down the hall. She wanted it to be Turner. She wanted it to be the police. She would even welcome the strange, effeminate nurse back.

But the footsteps were shuffling, hesitant. They paused at the door. She sensed someone looking in at her. The person did not move on. She heard breathing, shallow and fast.

She was swept by a sense of being exposed and altogether too vulnerable. She forced herself up on her elbow again and opened her eyes.

For a moment, she saw a man standing in the shadowy doorway. He had long hair that hung nearly to his shoulders, and he was tall, but stooped. He seemed to be wearing ordinary clothes, jeans with a baggy shirt tucked into the waistband. She could not see his face, but she heard him inhale, a broken, short-breathed gasp.

Then he vanished. His steps were quicker going than they had been coming, but the gait was unsteady, as if he limped.

Unsettled, she fell back to the mattress, closing her eyes. She wanted out of this place. It felt evil to her. It felt haunted.

Then she heard the nurse's voice, suddenly stern. "What's wrong with you? *Excuse* me? I'm *talking* to you. Now, stop—just *stop*. Did you hear me?"

But there was no answer.

A moment later, the nurse came into the room. "I don't know what got into *him*," he grumbled. Then his voice lightened, sweetened almost into a chirp. "Are we feeling better, love? Or do we still feel we want our mama?"

His words struck her so unexpectedly that she had no defense prepared against them, none. Tears welled up and spilled between her closed lids.

Mama, she thought, and silently cried, hiding her eyes.

Back in his cubicle next to the furnace room, he shut the door and locked it, shooting the bolt into place with shaking hands. His blood banged in his ears, and his heart heaved in his chest as if it wanted to explode.

He made his way to his narrow cot and sat down. He put his elbows on his knees and his face in his hands.

She had come back for him, just as he had always feared she would.

She had lain there beneath the white sheet, her face the same dead white as the sheet, the prettiest girl he'd ever seen, her blond hair in disarray about her face. She still had the smudge on her face from where the doctor's shoe had nudged her.

Worst, atop the sheet, her right hand rested motionless, its outer edge bloody where Luther had cut off her finger.

Her hand hadn't bled then, but it was bleeding now, because her blood was flowing again, because she was coming back to life, and she was coming for him, to drag him to hell.

He knew, because she had raised up and looked at him. Her eyes were sky-blue, and they looked straight into his lost soul. He stifled a dry sob of terror.

Then his control broke altogether, and Hollis bent even lower, more abjectly, and wept into his hands like a child.

SIX

FOR JAYE, THE NIGHT KEPT CHANGING ITS SHAPE, THE WAY patterns suddenly shift in a kaleidoscope that is roughly shaken.

The nurse, Davy, had cooed over her until she was embarrassed, but he'd stopped her bleeding, splinted her broken finger, and given her a pill for the pain. She was profoundly ashamed that she'd been faint, even weepy, and she wanted no more fuss.

She was sitting up arguing that she didn't need an ambulance, when the ambulance came, siren yowling so loudly, she cringed. A paramedic and his partner made their entrance, as full of zeal and self-importance as if this were grand opera and they were the swaggering heroes come to deliver the damsel from certain death.

They wanted to strap her to a gurney, wheel her to

the ambulance, and speed her to the emergency room in Mount Cawdor. The thought made Jaye wince. Already the uproar had disturbed the residents of the nursing home—the halls echoed with their buzzers summoning help and their cries of alarm, and Davy had to bustle off to tend to them.

The more the paramedics blustered, the more Jaye insisted that she didn't want an ambulance, didn't need one, and, by God, wasn't going to get into one.

The senior paramedic fumed, his eyes flashing. He told her to hurry, that he didn't have all night to argue.

"Then leave," Jaye said stubbornly. "Because I'm *not* going with you. I'll go to a doctor on my own."

He finally stormed away like an angry tragedian, followed by his muttering partner, leaving her still a bit shaky, but triumphant for the moment.

The moment quickly faded.

As the ambulance left, a deputy arrived. If the paramedics had treated the situation as high drama, he viewed it with a boredom that verged on contempt.

The deputy's name was Elton Delray. He was a stoop-shouldered, soft-faced man with bifocals and the beginnings of a potbelly. The dim, greenish light from the bedside lamp gave his skin a strange, undersea cast.

Delray listened to Turner recount the story, then shrugged dismissively. "They always shoot at that sign."

Fresh emotion surged through Jaye, indignant disbelief. "But we were *standing* by the sign. They could have hit us."

Delray was clearly unmoved. "Kids," he said with a shrug. "From Arkansas. Get likkered up, cross the state line, find an empty car, and use it for target practice."

"This wasn't an empty car," Jaye snapped. "We were getting into it."

"They probably didn't see you."

"They had to have seen us. The interior lights went on as soon as the door opened."

"Probably didn't see you till too late."

"Too late? They could have *killed* us, for God's sake."

"You're not seriously hurt," Delray said without emotion. "You wouldn't even go to the emergency room. Mount Cawdor dispatched an ambulance all the way out here for nothing. You wouldn't go."

He might be slumped and his narrow body going slack, but his small eyes were peculiarly blinkless. They suddenly struck her as familiar, and she realized she was reminded of the flat, predatory stare of the moray eel at the Boston aquarium.

"So," she said carefully, "you think this shooting was just—mischief?"

Behind the glasses, the eel eyes stared at her as if she were so much unappealing bait. "You got reason to think otherwise?"

No, of course not, she thought. *Yes. Maybe. No. Not really.*

She could make no answer.,

Turner raised his dark brows as if he didn't understand the man. "Your meaning, officer?" he asked.

Delray turned to him, his expression unreadable. "You give anybody cause to shoot at you?"

Turner smiled disarmingly. "Absolutely not. I'm a peaceable guy."

"We've asked a few questions, that's all," Jaye said, angling her chin defiantly. "Why would that bother anybody?"

The deputy tipped his head so that his hat brim cast a shadow over his upper face. "Depends. What you been asking questions about?"

Turner crossed his arms. His shirtsleeves were dirty and one was torn out at the elbow, but his expression was so cool, he looked almost nonchalant. He gave Delray a gaze of such bland friendliness that Jaye was puzzled. "Family matters," he said.

"Dr. Hunsinger," Jaye said impulsively. "We've both been asking about Roland Hunsinger. Would somebody resent that?"

The deputy gave her a long, disdainful stare. "I doubt it. Doc Hunsinger's got no secrets. His life's an open book."

This was such a blatant lie, Jaye was about to flash a sharp retort, but Turner put his hand on her shoulder. "You're tired," he said with a gentleness that completely belied the squeeze he gave her. *Shut up,* said the squeeze with painful eloquence. *Shut the hell up. Now.*

Nettled, she looked up at him, and he gave her a smile of surpassing benevolence as he squeezed even harder. She struggled not to grimace, and she kept her eyes fastened on his. On the surface his gaze was one of concern, but in its depths she read a warning that was clear and fierce. She clamped her mouth shut.

"I guess we're lucky it didn't turn out any worse than it did," Turner said. His voice was mild, but his hand on her shoulder kept its steely hold. She nodded reluctantly.

"That's the truth," said Delray, in a tone of wise assent. "You were fortunate."

This is total bullshit, Jaye thought in fury. But she willed her face to remain rigidly blank.

"Fortunate," Turner echoed without irony. "Yes. That's how we ought to look at it."

The deputy hooked his thumbs in his belt. The stance made him look like an out-of-shape gunslinger. "It's only a rental car, and nobody got hurt bad. You're fortunate. Yes, indeed." He smiled for the first time. It made his mouth look like a slot.

"I'll remember that," said Turner.

"Me, too," Jaye said as demurely as she could, although the words tasted like ash in her mouth.

The deputy nodded to her as if to say, *Yeah, city girl. You remember. You remember it good.*

The rental car limped back toward town, its spare tire thumping. Each jolt in the curving road made pain shoot through Jaye's hand. Obstinately she ignored it.

Instead she studied Turner's profile. Back in the room she had seen the hardness in his eyes and realized there were layers of himself he had kept hidden, and until that moment he had hidden them well. Her shoulder still stung where he'd gripped her.

"Why'd you apply the Vulcan nerve pinch back there?" she demanded. "Couldn't you have been more subtle?"

"You weren't in the mood for subtle," he said easily and kept his eyes on the road.

"He made me mad."

"Mad doesn't work with guys like him."

"Well, you weren't saying anything at all," she accused. "You practically grinned and shuffled."

"Grinning and shuffling is sometimes an excellent strategy."

"It's not my style."

"Obviously," he said, an ironic twist in his voice. In the distance before them, the sparse lights of Cawdor made a poor showing. But beyond them the lights of Mount Cawdor, in contrast, were a bright, thick cluster, shinning like prosperity itself.

"He was—minimizing what happened. He tried to make it sound trivial," she complained.

"Yes. He did."

"It wasn't trivial. It was dangerous, dammit."

"Yes. It was."

"Somebody shot at us, and he acted like it was only—kids at play. High jinks. A *prank*."

"You're exactly right. Exactly."

"Then why didn't you object?"

"It would have done no good," he said with that same maddening calm.

"Do you mind telling me *why*?" she challenged. "Isn't he—derelict in his duty or something? Shouldn't you have filed a complaint? Shouldn't he put out an all-points bulletin? A dragnet? Issue a warrant? Something? Anything?"

He smiled wryly, as if to himself. "No."

"You mean that's it?" she asked. "He writes up his report and says some vandals got their jollies and it made us nervous?"

"You've got it."

"And the police do nothing?"

"In all likelihood."

"And this doesn't make you furious?"

"Fury's worthless in a case like this."

"Then what counts?" she asked in exasperation.

"Decoding the message," Turner said.

"Oh, great. Let me get out my Captain Danger decoder ring. Would you mind explaining that remark?"

"Not at all," he said with an accommodating nod. "What you were about to say to our friend Deputy Delray—"

"He was disgusting," she said bitterly. "He's got eyes like an eel."

For the first time he looked at her. His mouth curved in amusement. "You're right. I *thought* he looked familiar, like I'd seen him somewhere before. The aquarium. Damn. You're very observant."

"About what I nearly said to him—?" she prompted.

"What you nearly said to our friend Officer Eel was this: We'd been asking questions about Hunsinger. We were standing in front of what used to be his clinic when somebody drove up and fired in our direction. You were about to say, 'Is that not passing strange? Does that not seem a very odd coincidence?' That's what you were going to say to Officer Eel."

Apprehension, like a live thing, uncurled in her stomach, flexing and tingling. "Yes. Well, it crossed my mind. And it's—scary."

"It was meant to be scary. That was the first message: Somebody doesn't like these questions. They didn't want to kill us, just warn us. And they want us to get the hell out of Dodge."

"Well, I'm not. I'm staying the hell here." She said it with bravado, but her stomach gave another nervous twist.

"We'll discuss that part shortly," he said. "The first message was 'We don't like these questions.' The second was 'We can hurt you.' And the third was 'And the law doesn't give a damn. The law will not protect you.'"

"But that's—police corruption," Jaye said with dismay.

He gave her a brief sideways look. "*Really?*" he said. "Police corruption? I'm just a simple boy from Philadelphia. I never heard of such a thing."

She sighed and sank more deeply in her seat. She shook her head. "This can't be right. I haven't even been here twenty-four hours and somebody starts shooting? And the police don't care? No, this is too . . . dramatic, too extreme."

"Yes," he agreed. "And an interesting point, that. I was here for three days, and the worst treatment I got was a cold shoulder. Then you show up and suddenly all hell breaks loose."

She looked at him sharply, but he kept his eyes straight ahead and his face imperturbable.

"Me?" she said in disbelief. "You're not saying this has to do with me *personally?*"

He shrugged. "It's a possibility. And another reason you should go home and let me do the dirty work."

She raised her chin rebelliously. "What if Officer Eel's right? What if it was just teenagers behaving badly? I mean, Davy said so, too—that it happened all the time. He said it before Delray ever got there."

He held up a hand to silence her. "A minute ago you were saying that the shooting couldn't be coincidental and that Delray was corrupt."

"Well, the opposite is possible, too. That the shooting was a fluke, it's happened before, and Delray refused to get excited about it."

"You can't have it both ways," Turner said, irritation creeping into his voice.

"You're a lawyer," she countered. "You're supposed to be able to argue either side. Maybe you're even playing up all this—this sinister stuff so I'll go home. You're— fomenting melodrama."

"Fomenting melodrama?" he echoed incredulously.

"Yes. You want me out of the picture—God knows why—so you're pretending everything's more ominous than it is."

He gave her a mocking look. "Personally, I always find it ominous to be shot at. Oh, call me a fussbudget if you like, but—"

"Look," she argued, "whoever did it cut their lights

as soon as they came over the hill. Maybe they really didn't see us standing there. Or didn't see us until too late."

He rolled his eyes. "Spare me."

"Only the car was hit," she said. "I got hurt, but it was only because you knocked me down and fell on top of me."

He swore. "I don't believe you. Where'd you get this gift for logic? Wonderland? Mars?"

"I am trying to be purely objective," she retorted.

"Don't. You're no good at it."

"Well, my version makes more sense," she said with finality. She tried to cross her arms to show she wasn't going to back off from her argument. But she accidentally jarred her finger and drew in her breath with a gasp of pain.

"Are you all right?" His tone had changed to one of concern that seemed disconcertingly genuine.

"I'm fine," she lied. She held her injured hand in her lap, gripping it by the wrist.

"You should have gone to the emergency room," Turner said, studying her.

"It's not all that serious," she insisted and clenched her wrist more tightly. "Basically, I hurt my pinkie. I'd feel like an idiot in an ambulance."

They were in Cawdor now. The main thoroughfare was deserted, with most of the stores and gas stations along the highway closed for the night. Only the bars were open, their neon signs flashing like signals of quiet despair.

A few cars and pickup trucks still sat in the parking lot of the Wagon Wheel. Turner pulled in beside Jaye's rental car and parked. He turned to her. The flashing emerald lights from the lounge sign made his eyes look more green than hazel.

"I want you to see a doctor tomorrow. You have a broken finger, maybe even a cracked rib."

His demeanor had changed back to that of Mr. Nice Guy. And he was good at being Mr. Nice Guy, she thought, he was excellent. It was, paradoxically, a disturbing quality.

She said, "Davy said I seemed to be all right."

"Davy's not a doctor."

"He's had lots of experience," Jaye said earnestly. "He was a trauma nurse in Vietnam for two tours. He *knows* injuries."

"I don't want you hurting, that's all." He reached out and smoothed back her hair from her cheek. He touched her bandaged forehead so gently that she shivered. He said, "I'm sorry I spoke sharply to you."

There was something seductive in this quiet concern. She drew away from it, turning her face from his. "I'll be fine. I'm not a child."

"No," he said in a low voice. "You're certainly not. I mean it. I'm sorry I got edgy. I'm worried about your safety. That's all."

"That's very touching," she said, setting her jaw, "but I'm not going back to Boston."

She started to unzip his jacket with her good hand. He put his hand over hers. "It's cold," he said. "And you're shaky. Keep it for now."

His hand was warm on her chilled one, and it was steady while she needed all her control to keep hers from trembling. She knew she should pull away from his touch but somehow couldn't bring herself to do it.

He brushed her fingers aside and zipped the jacket back up to her chin. Then, slowly, he let his hand fall away. The otherworldly emerald light blinked and flashed, blinked and flashed.

"I'm *not* going home," she repeated obstinately, but

her voice seemed small to her. She put her good hand on the door handle to get out, but the automatic lock was on; she could not budge it.

"We'll talk about it tomorrow," he said. He got out of the car, opened her door with the electronic key. He helped her out of the passenger seat, stayed close beside her while she unlocked her car.

Why does he have to be so damned protective? she wondered uneasily. His height made her feel safeguarded and vulnerable at the same time, another paradox.

"How about we meet for breakfast tomorrow?" he asked, before he closed her door. "There's a little café in Mount Cawdor on the square. I have information to give you—remember?"

She clamped her lips together and nodded.

"And you have information to give me."

She took a deep breath. "Yes."

"And then we'll talk about—the other."

"The other" meant her leaving, going back to Boston. Again she kept her silence.

"I'll follow you to your place, walk you to the door," he said.

"You don't have to—" she protested, but he had already closed the door. He moved quickly back to his car, a tall figure in a torn white shirt, his movements smooth and economical.

True to his word, he followed her to Miss Doll's, walked her to the back door. Again he refused to let her give back his jacket. "No," he said. "Wait till you're inside. You'll have to take it off carefully, so you don't jar your hand."

He fished in the pocket of his slacks, pulled out something, and held it toward her. "Here," he said. "I found these beside the car when I changed the tire. They must have fallen out of your purse."

In his palm were her lighter, a lipstick, and a medal of St. Jude that Nona had given her to carry.

"Oh," she said. She was conscious of her hand brushing his as she took them from him. She dropped them back into her purse and drew out her key.

He stood beside her, waiting to see that she got safely inside. Again she was conscious of his height, but she pretended to ignore him as she fumbled with the lock. She damned herself; she was having another shaky spell. Without a word he took the key from her and opened the door. "Get a good rest," he said. "I'll see you in the morning. Ten o'clock?"

"Fine," she said.

"Good night," he said, and held the door for her.

"Good night," she said. She slipped inside. He shut the door behind her. The kitchen was dimly illuminated by a small light above the stove. She checked the lock and fastened the chain-bolt. She was haunted by an odd feeling of incompletion.

Ye gods, she thought in weariness and disgust, *the man was trying with all his might to get rid of her—had she wanted him to kiss her? She must have hit her head harder than she thought.*

Yet she remembered how he had shielded her from the shots with his own body, how he had carried her into the nursing home, climbing the stairs two at a time, like Rhett Butler. Something fluttered deep in her stomach.

Forget it, she told herself. *There's no time for that kind of thing.* She thought of Patrick and a kind of desperate fatigue took possession of her. She made her way to the room and threw herself onto the bed without even turning down the coverlet.

She fell into exhausted sleep among the frilly pillows and staring dolls, still wearing Turner's jacket zipped to her chin.

•   •   •

Turner locked himself in his car and drove to the nearest pay phone. He'd been an asshole, he told himself, losing his temper with Jaye Garrett. She was a scrapper, she didn't back down.

And he'd let his mask drop when he'd given her the Vulcan nerve pinch; this he also regretted. He hoped the night had been chaotic enough that she would not remember that moment. But she was smart. Smarter than he'd expected and smarter than he needed her to be.

She had to go.

Although she was bright, she was leading with her heart, and she didn't know what the hell she was doing, especially plastering her goddamn posters all over Cawdor. She'd been talking too much ever since she hit town, and she'd been too combative with Delray. She was trouble.

He pulled up to the pay phone, parked. He looked around, wondering if he was being followed, supposing that he was. But the highway seemed empty with the lonely emptiness of lands where towns are small and the spaces between them large.

He rolled down the window, slid his card into the phone slot. Since he'd been in Cawdor, he'd used pay phones because he didn't want anyone to pick up the signal from his cell phone and he didn't trust the one in his hotel room. If this was paranoia, so be it. He worked with men whose paranoia kept them alive.

He punched in Mr. DelVechio's private number and glanced at his watch. It was nearly eleven Philadelphia time, too late, probably, for the old man to be up. But on the third ring DelVechio himself answered. Pain must be keeping him awake.

"Hello," DelVelchio said. He was a big man, but he had a surprisingly high voice, and a quaver had weakened it this last year. "Who is this? It's late."

"It's Gibson. I've run into a couple of problems."

There was a pause. Turner thought he could hear the wheeze of the older man's breath.

"You still in whazzitsname? Oklahoma?"

"Yeah," Turner said, looking out at the deserted landscape. "I'm still here."

"You come home when? Tomorrow? A couple days? What?"

"Not yet. There may be new developments."

"A woman, you said," DelVechio said in his trembling voice. "You said to Anna that you stayed there because a woman. Because a woman what?"

Anna was DelVechio's nurse, and at DelVechio's request Turner confided very little to her. The old man thought she was a tyrant and suspected her of being a spy for his brother.

Turner explained about Jaye Garrett and her brother. Then he waited, listening to the distant rasp of breath in Philadelphia.

"These people," the old man said, "you find out about them. Yes?"

"Yes," said Turner. "I've already put a check on her. Tomorrow I'll ask for a profile on the brother, the mother."

"This woman," DelVechio said slowly. "To you, she is—"

"An impediment. A problem. A complication."

"Ahhh." DelVechio drew the sound out in a long, unsteady sigh.

"She doesn't know how things are done. She talks too much. She has no discretion."

"No discretion is a bad thing."

"Right. Yet she's concerned about her brother. You understand?"

"Yes. Family. I can understand that. You can understand that."

I certainly the hell can, thought Turner, but he did not say this. Instead he explained how he wished to gain Jaye Garrett's information, but get rid of the woman herself.

For a moment DelVechio said nothing. He wheezed softly. When he spoke, his voice creaked like an ancient thing. "*Fare che cosa e voi deve.* Do the thing that's got to be done. I'm an old man in need of favors. Who am I to deny them?"

"There's something else," Turner said. He glanced in his rearview mirror, but all he saw was the desolate highway leading back to Cawdor. It seemed as empty as the road to a lost civilization. "I took the woman to Hunsinger's old clinic tonight."

Almost laconically he told DelVechio about the shooting, about the warning he sensed in Delray's words and actions. "I don't know why it happened now, tonight," he finished. "I don't know if it has to do with her."

The long susurrant sound again. "Ahhh. So to find out about this woman is very necessary. In the meantime, you got some way to take care of yourself?"

"I'm okay," said Turner.

"I could provide some assistance in this matter, perhaps," DelVelchio said with diplomacy.

"Perhaps I may want some assistance. I'll let you know. And I told you before I don't trust the local law. You said you'd get me the names of people I could trust if I needed them."

"State police," DelVechio wheezed. "Allen Twin Bears. Wayne Ramirez."

Turner scribbled the names in his notebook. "Good."

"But of my son," the old man said, "you've still found nothing?"

"When I learn what the woman knows, I may make progress."

"God willing."

In his old age DelVechio had found religion, and it was more addictive to him than his painkillers. He said, "I pray to Saint Anthony. He's the patron saint that finds what's lost. Every day I pray to him."

Good, thought Turner. *We're going to need all the help we can get.*

"I also pray to Saint Joseph, Saint Jude, and the Virgin."

"That's good, too," said Turner. From experience he knew that sinners existed in abundance, but he did not give one whit of credence to saints, nor much even to goodness in mortals.

"I pray also for you," croaked DelVechio. "For your safety and success."

You're all heart, DelVechio, thought Turner. He said, "Thank you. Take care of yourself. Mind Anna. I'll keep you posted."

"Anna." The old man put an infinity of distaste into the name. "Call me tomorrow. Call me anytime. You'll have something for me, if heaven is kind."

"I'll call," Turner promised. He hung up. He did not believe in heaven or hell. He did not believe in anything his senses could not validate.

He rubbed his elbow, which was raw, scraped by the gravel. He put the car in gear and headed back toward the Arkansas border. He thought idly of Jaye Garrett and wondered if she was blond all over. In his mind he stripped her naked and imagined her both ways, blond and not.

He remembered touching her toward the end of the night, her face, her hand. He'd meant to disarm and manipulate her, but an unwanted thrill of desire had rippled through him. He hadn't expected it to happen, or for it to happen with the force it did.

The lady had better get the hell out of town, he thought.

In the years Hollis had lived in this room, no one had ever been allowed inside except himself. And no one else ever *must* come inside.

All of Hollis's magical and sacred things were here in a secret altar in his closet. All but one thing, the most important of all, and that was in the Safe Place.

But now Hollis knew the Safe Place was no longer safe. This night had been terrible, like all the plagues of Egypt rolled into one, and he thought he heard Luther's voice breathing in his ear: *Go.* He must take his things— all of them—and escape.

Every sign and portent had appeared tonight, and their meaning was as clear as if a fiery sword had rent the night sky, its blade pointing straight down at the building in condemnation.

The dead girl had come back. She knew where he was. She had looked him in the eyes, and hell had tried to close around him like a net of fire.

If he wished to save his immortal soul, he must flee. None of the thousand things he had done in this room were enough. He must make greater atonement and he would go into the wilderness, like a pilgrim, like poor Jesus Himself. He must build a church.

Hollis waited until the small hours of the morning when the building was silent except for a loose shutter that rattled feebly in the wind. Then he mopped the floor and cleaned the room and himself and put on his other set of clothes. He gathered all his things and put them in the suitcase that Luther had given him so many years ago.

Again he thought he heard Luther's voice: *Go. Build a church.*

His heart knocking at his ribs, he slipped out of his room. He avoided Davy, who would be reading in the lobby. Silently he made his way out the back door. In the backyard, he went to what used to be Mrs. Hunsinger's rose garden.

Hollis still tended the old bushes faithfully, though Davy clucked his tongue and told him it was a foolish waste of work; he should plant tomatoes instead, for tomatoes had many healing properties. The roses were worthless to everyone but Hollis. They hadn't flowered for years; they had gone back to root stock and were sterile.

By the light of a moon growing dim, Hollis knelt and began to dig with his fingers while the dead leaves blew around him, and the wind sighed in his ears like a ghost.

Go, said the wind. *And build a church.*

SEVEN

J AYE AWOKE TO THE JARRING RING OF HER PHONE. SHE DID
not know where she was and she hurt all over, as if
she'd been rolled down a hillside inside a barrel full of
rocks.

She opened one eye and stared directly into the
unblinking blue-glass gaze of a doll with a china face and
a calico bonnet. The phone rang again, and she forced
herself to open both eyes. The bed was busy with ornate
pillows.

The phone shrilled a third time. *Miss Doll's*, she
thought groggily. *I'm in Oklahoma and I'm at Miss Doll's.
Because I have to help Patrick.*

The thought of Patrick galvanized her. Her arm shot
out to snatch the cell phone. The action made her finger
throb and the aches in her body flare maliciously.

Why was she in pain? Why was her finger splinted? And why was she wearing a brown suede jacket, zipped to the neck?

Memory came, first in a trickle, then in a stream, and then in a flood. She'd met Turner Gibson, they'd gone to the old clinic, and he'd said he wanted her to go back to Boston. Then someone had shot at them and—

The phone gave another strident blare. Jaye grabbed it up.

"Hello?" she said and thought, *Somebody shot at us, but it was a sort of accident, that's all, really. A fluke, that's all.*

"Hello?" The voice was Nona's, and it sounded wobbly from tears.

"What's wrong?" Jaye asked in alarm. "Is Patrick worse?"

"No," Nona said with a sniffle. "He's better. His temperature spiked. It's down to a hundred and two."

Jaye's aches vanished, as if she'd been freed from her body and fluttered above it, free and dizzily hopeful. "He's not delusional?"

"No. But he's very, very weak. He's exhausted. He has terribly sore joints and nausea. They're pumping him full of drugs. Oh, poor Patrick."

"But he *is* better?" Jaye said, determined to strengthen her hope.

"Yes, b-but he can hardly talk. They've still got him in isolation. He can't even have flowers. He can only have a few visitors, and then if they scrub and wear sterile clothes. He's like that b-boy in the b-bubble, that story on television. And that boy *died*." She began to sob softly.

"Nona, calm down," Jaye pleaded. "We're going to do everything we can for Patrick. I've already found someone who might be able to help us."

"Really?" Nona said, like a child desperate for reassurance. "Really?"

"Yes," Jaye said firmly, and began to describe Turner Gibson as a combination of Saint Francis of Assisi, Sir Lancelot, and Jesus Christ. To comfort Nona, she shamelessly gilded her description of the man.

"And he'll help us?" Nona asked, in the same tearful, childlike tone.

"Yes, he will," Jaye soothed. "I'm going to meet him this morning. He wants to read your letter, if that's all right."

"Of course, of course." Nona paused. "He's really willing to work with us?"

"Yes," Jaye said, boldly lying. She did not tell Nona that Turner didn't like having her in Cawdor and wanted her to go back to Boston. She didn't mention the shooting or that she'd been hurt. She did what she had been doing all her life. She told Nona only the good news.

Jaye took a bath in the pink tub in the guest bathroom. There was no shower, and the pipes creaked and groaned when she turned on the water. She would have liked to soak her aching body, but she was too restless.

She saw that the left side of her rib cage was shadowed lavender with bruises and her hands looked like hell. Both palms were scraped and raw from hitting the gravel.

Wrapped in a pink towel, she stood before the fogged bathroom mirror and wiped it clear again with a pink washcloth. "Hide the children," she told her image. "There's a witch in town."

Her hair was a tangled mess, her face was white as bone, and the Band-Aid on her forehead didn't completely hide the bruise. Her splinted finger stayed thrust out, as if she were being exaggeratedly polite while drinking tea.

She plugged in her curling iron and opened her makeup case. She offered up a prayer to the spirit of Max Factor. Twenty minutes later, she opened the door of her bedroom and smelled air redolent of coffee.

The pregnant granddaughter was padding up the hall with an empty laundry basket. She still wore her fuzzy yellow slippers and the nightgown with the teddy bear on the belly. She stared at Jaye's splinted finger with obvious interest. But all she said was "Grandma's making breakfast."

Jaye held her head at a jaunty angle. "Thanks," she said, and set off for the kitchen. She didn't want breakfast—the rich aromas sent nausea skipping through her stomach. But she did want to meet Miss Doll.

Miss Doll was a large white-haired woman in a pink housecoat. The housecoat was printed all over with small dancing white poodles.

She was bent over the stove, her back to Jaye. But she must have heard Jaye's footfalls, for she turned immediately and her face broke into a smile of delighted surprise.

Her thick hair was carefully styled and gleamed as silvery as new snow. It framed a face that was aged, yet lively and still beautiful. Her eyes were guileless and blue as cornflowers. She set down her spatula and seized Jaye's right hand in a warm grasp.

"Hello, honey," she said, "you must be Miss Garrett. I'm Miss Doll. Bright told me about you."

"Bright?" Jaye echoed without comprehension.

"Bright-Ann. My little granddaughter," said Miss Doll, pulling out a chrome kitchen chair. "She told me all about you. Sit, honey, sit, sit, sit."

Obediently Jaye sat, and Miss Doll snatched up a

coffeepot and filled a pastel-blue coffee mug. With a flourish she set the mug before Jaye. "Sugar? Cream? Sweetener? Low-fat creamer? Or do you take it black?"

Jaye was taken aback by the woman's aggressive hospitality. "Black," she said.

Miss Doll opened the oven and drew out a pan of biscuits that were baked to golden perfection. She arranged them on a glass plate and set them down next to the crystal butter dish, a collection of jam jars, and a honey pot shaped like a yellow hive.

She put her hands on her hips and said, "Now I got my western quiche in the oven, it's almost ready. You want some juice while you wait? Oatmeal? A nice grapefruit?"

"A biscuit's fine," said Jaye. "I'm not very hungry."

Miss Doll snorted good-naturedly. "Honey, you come a long way. You got to keep up your strength. My quiche'll put color back in your cheeks. It'll be ready in two shakes of a lamb's tail."

"You don't have to bother, honestly—"

"It's no bother," Miss Doll said, rummaging in the refrigerator. She drew out a pitcher of orange juice and a carton of milk.

"No, really—" Jaye tried again.

Miss Doll waved away any protest. "I *love* to take care of people. That's what life's all about. Ain't it? People takin' care of each other?"

Jaye smiled in answer. She took a sip of coffee, hoping it would clear her mind. The coffee was excellent. She reached for a biscuit, and when she broke it open, it was impossibly light and flaky. The butter melted on it in a golden pool. For the first time since she'd come to Cawdor, she realized she was ravenous.

Miss Doll tried to force orange juice and cereal on

her, but Jaye begged off. The woman filled her a glass of juice anyway, then leaned against the counter. Her lips had been carefully colored the same pink as her housecoat and she pursed them in sympathy.

"I heard you had a run-in last night," the woman said with confidentiality. "With them Mexicans."

Jaye looked into the woman's wide blue eyes. They seemed ingenuous and full of concern. "Mexicans?" she asked.

Miss Doll nodded her silver head energetically. "This town's full of Mexicans. They come to work here when the chicken-processing plant opened."

Jaye's coffee cup froze halfway to her mouth. Davy had not mentioned any Mexicans, and neither had the deputy. She threw Miss Doll a questioning look.

Miss Doll's carefully penciled brows rose even higher. "There's another bunch of 'em over the border, in Arkansas," she said, sotto voce. "Mexicans, Guatemalans, Salvadorans. Lord, I can't keep 'em straight. They get to fightin' amongst themselves, the young ones."

She laid her pink-nailed fingers across her heart. "There's a bunch comes over here, shootin' up things. But this is the first I heard of 'em shootin' at people. Lord, honey, I'm sorry. What you must think of us."

Jaye set down her coffee cup. "How?" she asked coolly. "How did you hear what happened to me?"

"It's a small town," Miss Doll said with a deprecating smile. She turned to the oven, opened the door, and peered critically inside.

"No," Jaye said. "I mean *exactly* how did you hear what happened to me? Who told you? And just how did they know?"

The woman rose and faced her, the pink mouth becoming a round and innocent O. "Why, honey, I heard it at the Stop 'n' Shop store this morning. I was afraid I didn't have enough eggs for your breakfast. Folks was just talkin' up a storm about it. I'm sorry—ain't it true?"

"Somebody in a truck shot at the car," Jaye said tightly. "I don't know who it was."

"And that's how you hurt your poor hand?"

"Yes, but I certainly wasn't shot. It was an accident—"

"Well, you can bet it was them Hispanics," the woman said. She pronounced the word "Hiss-panics." "Yes, ma'am. You can bet on it. Here, let me fill up your coffee again."

Jaye tried to say no, but the steaming brew was already flowing into her cup.

"I hear you come to town to ask about your brother. He's sick?" Miss Doll asked and clucked her tongue in commiseration. "Clear from Boston, trying to help your brother?"

Jaye stiffened, then relaxed. She'd spread her posters all over Cawdor, and she *had* told the red-haired girl why she was there.

She decided to feel out Miss Doll. "My brother's adopted, and he's sick. We need to find his birth family. He was adopted through Dr. Hunsinger, when he had his clinic."

Miss Doll looked even more sympathetic. "Oh, honey," she sighed with a sad shake of her head. "That was all so long ago. And Dr. Hunsinger, he's got that Alzheimer's disease." She tapped her forehead significantly. "He can't tell nobody *nothin'*."

Jaye pretended to concentrate on turning her coffee cup back and forth on the place mat. "I heard he'd had an accident."

Miss Doll pursed her mouth unhappily. "Oh, no. It's

the Alzheimer's. Why, his mind's blank as a newborn baby's."

Jaye said, "But other people worked at that clinic. Somebody has to still be around who remembers—"

The woman held up her hands and spread her fingers, a dramatic gesture of helplessness. "Scattered to the four winds. This town's fallen on hard times. We used to have canneries here. Tomatoes. Spinach. Grape juice and jelly. But it all closed down. And the people—they left."

Jaye said, "Not everybody."

"Honey, have you seen the downtown? Or what used to be downtown? This town used to have twelve hundred people. Now we're four hundred, and half them can't speak English. We'd turn up our toes and die if they hadn't put that chicken plant here."

"When did it open?"

"Four-five years ago," Miss Doll said. "It brought jobs back, all right, but not jobs folks wants. Which is why they've brought in all these *Mexicans*. But I guess you already know more than enough about *them*."

Jaye had no stomach for listening to Miss Doll's prejudices. She tried to force the conversation back on track. "What about you? Did you live here when Dr. Hunsinger had his clinic?"

Miss Doll rolled her eyes comically and waved off the suggestion. "Me? Lord love a duck, no. I came here fifteen years ago. My husband inherited this house. He spent all our savings fixing it up. Then he fell sick and died, and it was all just as expensive as could be, and what did I have but this house? But what good does it do to dwell on it? Make the best of things, that's my motto."

"I'm sorry," Jaye said. "But do you know anybody who *did* live here when Dr. Hunsinger ran the clinic? Anybody that would talk to me?"

"Oh, honey," cooed Miss Doll, putting another biscuit on her plate, "people don't like to talk about that adoption business."

Jaye picked the biscuit up and set it back on the glass serving dish. "Why?" she asked.

Miss Doll sighed philosophically. "It's ancient history."

"Not to my brother, it isn't. I need to find his birth mother—and as much of his family as I can."

Miss Doll put her hand on Jaye's arm. It was a big hand, hot and strong. Gently she said, "Honey, did you ever think that the mamas of those babies might not *want* to be found? That's why they came here in the first place. To keep things secret."

The granddaughter, Bright, strolled into the kitchen. Her Pippi Longstocking pigtails had been unbraided, and her hair was pulled back severely into a ponytail fastened with a Minnie Mouse clip. She had changed her nightgown for jeans and a maternity top with a sailor collar.

"Is breakfast ready?" she asked sullenly.

"Almost, honey. Sit down and drink some milk. It'll be good for your baby's little bones."

"I don't care about its little bones," Bright said. But she sat down and gave Jaye a measuring look.

"Bright here, she's pregnant," Miss Doll said helpfully.

Bright shot her grandmother a look of sheer resentment, but Miss Doll ignored it. Blithely she opened the oven and took out the steaming quiche. It was high, quivering, and perfect.

Bright looked at Jaye again. "Yeah," she said, slapping her belly. "Bright here is pregnant. Like nobody could guess. Whoopty-doo."

"When's the baby due?" Jaye asked warily.

"Not soon enough," said Bright.

Miss Doll set the quiche on the stovetop to cool. She came to Bright's side. She put her big hands on the girl's shoulders and began to massage them. She said, "Bright, Miss Garrett here doesn't understand about unwed mothers. That sometimes they just want to have their babies and get on with their lives. But that's true, isn't it, honey?"

"This is the worst thing that's ever happened to me," Bright said with passion. "I hate it. It sucks."

"But you don't hate the baby," Miss Doll prompted. "You love it. You want it to have the very best life possible. And that's why you're giving it up."

"I don't love it," said Bright, her chin quivering. "It's a monster. It's in there, feeding on me, like that thing in *Alien*. Yuck."

"There, there," said Miss Doll, still massaging her shoulders. But she looked over the girl's head at Jaye with an air of satisfaction and her wide blue gaze said *See? Do you see now what I mean?*

Jaye heard her phone ringing from the guest room. She was grateful for a chance to escape and pushed herself away from the table. "I don't think I want anything more to eat," she said. "Thank you, anyway."

Hastily she moved down the hall toward the ringing. Bright's unhappy words echoed in her mind. *It's a monster. It's in there, feeding on me, like that thing in* Alien.

Had Patrick's mother felt that way about him? Had her own? She closed the guest-room door tightly behind her, as if she could shut out the troubling thought. She picked up the telephone.

"Miss Garrett," said a woman's voice. It was whispery, hesitant.

"Yes?"

"I—I heard you been asking around town. About that stuff that happened with Hunsinger. Well, maybe I can tell you something."

"Yes?" Jaye said, and it took all her willpower to keep her voice from shaking. "Tell me. Tell me, please."

The Yoo Hoo Café sat in downtown Mount Cawdor, Arkansas, beside the railroad track where no trains traveled these days. The café was a small brick structure, square as a child's building block.

Inside, its walls were ornamented with a strange mixture of sports memorabilia and cross-stitched samplers. "Warning: Killer Hogs" announced a plaque with the picture of a snarling razorback pig. "East or West, Home Is Best," gently countered its neighboring sampler.

The café had no booths, but was instead furnished with sturdy redwood tables and benches. Turner Gibson sat facing the door, drinking bad coffee out of a plain white mug.

He wore a blue blazer, a pale blue shirt open at the neck, no tie. His clothing was deceptively simple, and if one did not notice its expert cut, he might have been taken for an ordinary young businessman on a mid-morning break.

He planned to meet Jaye, make sure she was all right, and get what he needed from her. Then he would wish her luck and hustle her out of town. He had to be about Mr. DelVechio's business. The work had always been sensitive, and now it was beginning to seem dangerous, as well. He didn't need Jaye Garrett complicating it.

He had anticipated that she'd be early again, and she was. At precisely five minutes to ten she strode in the door, bringing with her a chill rush of morning air and the fragrance of good perfume.

Her face was pale, but her head was held high, and her bearing was almost cocky. She did not act or look like someone who, only hours before, had been shot at and knocked into a ditch. She carried herself as if the most strenuous thing she'd done the night before was take a bubble bath and buff her nails.

She was good at putting on a mask, he realized with grudging appreciation. That was all right. He was better.

"Hi," she said breezily, and sat down across from him. She wore simple slacks, a pale blue turtleneck, and a tweed jacket. There was nothing provocative about the outfit, but she looked so good in it, he wondered idly what she looked like without it.

Someday I'll look her up in Boston, he told himself. *Until then I play her like a piano.*

"Hi," he said, making his voice innocuously warm and friendly. "How are you?"

"Couldn't be better," she said cheerfully. "A little sore, that's all. And you?"

"No worse for wear," he lied, although in truth his elbow ached like a son of a bitch, and he'd screwed up his knee.

"Good," she said with a too-perky smile. This was annoying because he was certain that she must hurt far more than he did. "Great."

She'd done some Veronica Lake thing to her hair so that a golden wing of it fell across her forehead, hiding where she'd been hit. Around her splinted little finger she'd tied a narrow blue ribbon.

"Coffee?" he asked. "Something to eat?"

"No, thanks. Miss Doll fixed me breakfast."

He nodded at her splinted finger. "Why the ribbon? A fashion statement?"

Her smiled faded. The sky-blue eyes gave him a dead-level stare. "It's so I remember my brother. First and foremost. Did you bring the information?" she asked. "That you said could help him?"

He reached to the bench beside him, picked up a leather folder. He held it up, as if to demonstrate its substantiality, its heft. "This is it. Everything. The names and backgrounds of the other people who've been here, trying to unravel their adoptions. Plus a list of groups that try to unite adoptees with birth parents. Have you registered your brother with any?"

For the first time her briskness faltered. "Yes," she said with a swallow. "Before I left Boston. I called a lawyer in Boston that specializes in adoption law. He's supposed to register Patrick's name with all of the groups and keep me posted."

"You must have been busy before you left."

"I was."

You're a regular whirlwind when you get going, aren't you, Boston? A tall, blond, unstoppable whirlwind.

He said, "If his birth mother's registered anywhere, there's a good chance she'll be matched to him—eventually."

She pressed her lips together. She nodded.

"On the other hand," he said, "she may not be registered. She may not want to be found."

"I'm aware of that," she said, an edge to her voice. "In fact, Miss Doll made a point of that at breakfast."

"It's something you have to keep in mind," he said as gently as he could.

She stared up at the sampler about home. Then she looked away from it and said, "I brought the letter from my mother." She opened her handbag. Then she shot him a wary look. "It's just a copy. I made it at the bank."

"That's fine," he said. He laid the leather folder on the table and took the papers from her. Her hand grazed his, and his fingertips tingled enticingly. *Yes*, he thought. *I'll definitely be calling in Boston. And I'll touch more than your hand.*

She took the folder, opened it, began to read almost greedily. Her brows drew together in concentration.

"You should take your time with that," he said. "Read it very carefully. Do it on the plane. On your way home."

Her head snapped up, and her face was alight with something he couldn't name. "I'm not going home," she said. She said it with perfect confidence.

"Yes," he said. "You need to. It's for the best."

She still had that same firm calmness shining out of her. "I can't. I won't."

He fought the impulse to grit his teeth. He smiled his most trustworthy smile instead. "We have a proposition for you—Mr. D. and I. It's a good one. You won't be able to resist it."

One corner of her mouth quirked up dubiously. "You're making me an offer I can't refuse?"

The phrase rankled unpleasantly, but he kept his smile in place. He said, "You could put it that way."

She stared at him and said nothing. She looked anything but convinced.

He said, "Mr. D., in spite of his own considerable troubles, is a compassionate man. He understands your situation. And he sympathizes with you."

Her chin rose a fraction of an inch, and she stayed silent.

"He's also a generous man," he said. "And a rich one. You, on the other hand, probably aren't rich. Are you?"

She paused, as if choosing her words carefully. He knew she wasn't rich. In another folder, locked in the trunk of his car, he had her full credit report. He knew what her debts and assets were to the penny.

"I'm not rich," she said. "But this isn't about money."

"No," he said smoothly. "It's about information. And money buys information. It buys almost an infinity of sources. And resources."

She arched an eyebrow. "And you're one of those resources?"

"One of the many," he said modestly. "And I'm at your disposal. Completely. And absolutely."

Her expression changed to puzzlement. "What are you talking about?"

"About the conversation I had last night with Mr. D. He's willing to underwrite the search for your brother's parents. To pay for it."

Her body straightened like a marionette's whose strings have been jerked tight. "What?"

"My client is willing to expand the search for his son. To include information about your brother. After all, both cases are part of the same problem."

She shook her head and gave him a slight smile that told him everything he was saying was unacceptable.

"Whatever we learn about your brother," Turner explained, "might cast light on what happened to my client's son. And vice versa."

"Might," she agreed. "And might not."

"I'll do everything in my power to find out the truth for you."

"And in return?"

He lifted his coffee mug, took a meditative sip. "In return," he said quietly, "you go home."

Her cool expression didn't change. "Why is it so important that I leave?"

"I can work faster, more efficiently, by myself. And in the long run, you win."

"No. No matter what you say, your first loyalty will always be to your precious client. My brother's the charity case. Tacked on, a secondary consideration. I won't settle for that."

He took a deep breath and marshaled his next battalion of arguments. She didn't give him time to utter them.

"My leaving is not an option," she said with greater aplomb than he could have imagined. "You can work with me or not. But I'm not going."

Time to use the knife, he thought. *But slide it between her ribs gently, so she doesn't know how deeply it cuts.*

"This is hard to say," he began, trying to sound both reluctant and gentlemanly.

She didn't blink. "Spit it out," she said.

Spit it out. It wasn't the ladylike way to put it. He liked that, dammit.

But he lifted a shoulder as if in regret. "All right. You have no training for a search like this. You don't know how to question people. You're too—headlong."

Her air of slight amusement faded. "You think I'll screw up *your* search."

"I'm afraid you'll screw them both up."

"So you want to buy me off."

"No. I'm asking you to back off. And offering you a sweetheart deal in exchange."

She gripped the edge of the table. Her splinted finger with its pale blue ribbon stuck out from the others. "Take your sweetheart deal," she said quietly, "and shove it."

"You're also volatile. Too volatile."

"I'm not being volatile. I'm being more polite than I feel."

"Yes," he said. "Because you're seething. You're full of—volcanic emotion."

"You think I'm a screwup, right?"

Exactly, he thought, but it was not a politic answer. He said, "There's also the matter of your safety."

"Don't be ridiculous," she said.

Her tone bordered on contempt, and it irritated the hell out of him. "Somebody *did* shoot at us last night," he reminded her.

"That was a random act of violence," she countered. "It's happened before. The deputy said so. Davy said so. Miss Doll said so."

Turner was losing patience. "You're in denial."

"I am not."

"You just denied you're in denial."

"And you're just trying to use scare tactics."

He set down his mug, steepled his hands. "You're the one in the splint."

She leaned across the table. "You're not going to buy me off. And you're not going to scare me off. Deal with it."

"You don't understand," he said slowly and with precision, as if he were talking to a particularly obstinate child. "You're hampering your brother's cause. You want to be a player. But you bring nothing to the table. If you did, I'd be glad to cooperate with you. I'd be delighted."

She cocked her head at a sardonic angle. "Really?" she said. "Is that a fact?"

"Yes," he said. "It is."

"It's odd you should say that," she mused. "Because I got an interesting phone call this morning."

His nerves went on instant alert. But he kept his face resolutely blank. "Oh?" he said. "From whom?"

"Umm," she said, looking up at the sampler again. "You said 'whom.' I like a man who knows how to use 'whom.' "

Son of a bitch. She's toying with me, he thought with amazement. "From whom did this call come?" he asked. "Is it a person in whom I'd be interested? What—or whom—did it concern?"

She clasped her hands on the table before her. If it weren't for the bandaged finger with its ribbon, the pose would have seemed wholly businesslike. "It was from a woman. She wouldn't give her name. She says she's got information about Hunsinger. She wants to meet me."

The words woke all his hunting instincts, aroused him. "Where? When?"

"I'll tell you all about it," she said. "After I meet her. In the meantime you can sit around and count your sources and resources."

"What the hell—" he said in displeasure.

But she cut him off. "Unless, of course," she said, "you'd rather I go home and forget the whole thing."

She stood up, tucking the folder under her arm. She threw him a challenging look. "I came to the table, all right. But I'm not exactly empty-handed. And I came to play. Believe it."

She smiled in triumph, turned and left.

I'll be damned, he thought.

EIGHT

———❦———

I DON'T WANT TO MEET YOU IN TOWN," JAYE'S ANONYMOUS caller had said. "Go to Kender, Arkansas. It's about forty minutes away. Wait for me in the lobby of the Smithly Medical Annex."

"How will I know you?" Jaye had asked uneasily.

"Don't worry. I'll know you," the woman had said. There was an almost grim certainty in her voice.

"But—how?" Jaye had persisted.

"I'll know. That's all. Be there if you want to know more about Hunsinger."

Now Jaye sat on a bench in the lobby, restlessly waiting. It was forty-nine minutes after one. She had been waiting since noon.

The city of Kender, she had discovered, was small

and surprisingly busy, its hospital surprisingly large. Next to the hospital stood the annex, Kender's tallest building. It soared nine stories high, towering like a sentinel over the rest of the town.

From the start, it had seemed to her a strange place to meet. But the woman on the phone had been firm: the Smithly Medical Annex. At noon exactly.

Now the chrome minute hand on the black clock above the elevators jerked forward again. Jaye had waited an hour and fifty minutes. No one had approached her. A sickening instinct told her no one would.

She could have wept with frustration.

Perhaps, she told herself, the woman had changed her mind. Or something, anything—a crisis, an accident, even a slight mishap—had prevented her from coming. There could have been a dozen legitimate reasons. Or perhaps she had never intended to come at all. The phone call had been nothing but a particularly heartless joke.

She left the lobby with its sterile spaciousness and symmetrical benches and potted plants with shiny leaves. She crossed the street to the multilevel parking garage and took the elevator to its second tier. She had been told specifically to use the parking garage at the second level, not to park in the outside lot. That, she supposed bitterly, was only another part of a sadistic charade.

But when she approached her rented car, she saw that a folded white paper had been thrust under her windshield wiper. Her first thought was that it was a piece of advertising.

But then she saw her name neatly written on it in block letters: JAYE GRADY GARRETT.

Her heart veered in her chest and her blood began to

drum. She tore the paper from the windshield and unfolded it. The hand-printed message read:

> *I know what went on at Hunsingers clinnic. I have*
> *a list of woman who came to him, berth mothers. I*
> *will sell you this list for $25,000. I want it in cash*
> *& in small bills. Be at the pay fone outside the*
> *Stop 'n Shop store in Cawdor tonight at seven pm.*
> *I will call you and tell you wear to meet me.*
>   *Be carefull. They can eavedrop & spie on*
> *you.*

Jaye was waiting for him at a picnic table in the little park
in the heart of the town square in the heart of Mount
Cawdor, Arkansas. It was, he'd decided, the safer side of
the border, outside Hunsinger's domain.

She sat with her back straight, her hands folded in
front of her almost primly, but her expression was one of
tightly controlled excitement. She had refused to tell him
on the phone what she had found out in Kender.

He eased his long body onto the picnic bench. He
looked into her eyes, trying not to be distracted by how
beautiful she seemed to him and how full of contradic-
tions. "So?" he said.

She spoke in a low, tensely eager voice. "I can get a
list of the mothers who came to Hunsinger. I need
twenty-five thousand dollars in cash. Can you get it for
me?"

She said this with a perfectly straight face.

Turner paused. He said, "You're kidding, right?"

"No," she said and handed him the creased note.
"Read it for yourself."

Turner unfolded the paper and read it. He read it a

second time, then looked at Jaye again, his eyes narrowed.

"How do you know there's really a list?" he asked. "You can't just hand over twenty-five grand."

She leaned forward, all earnestness, grasping the edge of the table. Her ribboned finger thrust out straight and alone. "You said Mr. D. was rich."

"He is."

"Wouldn't he pay any price to find his son?"

"To find his son, yes. To invest in a rumor, no."

Her eyes held his. "But if it was good information—you could get the money?"

"Yes. If the information was good."

She sighed, pushed her good hand through her hair. The spring breeze had tousled it, and she smoothed it back in place. "You think I'm being scammed. That this is just some scheme to shake me down."

"It's possible," he said. "You've got to consider it."

She shook her head. "I wouldn't just hand over all that money, you know. I'd see what I was paying for."

"And how would you know?" he countered. "You could get a list of names that turned out to mean nothing."

"I'll make sure it's good."

"How?"

"I'll ask her questions when she calls."

He thought about it. He himself had found out nothing today. People who had been willing to tell him a bit before, if the money was right, had suddenly gone silent on him. He had the sensation of being shut out, stonewalled.

"Okay," he said without enthusiasm. "We can at least see what she's got to say. I hope she talks better than she spells."

"Right," Jaye said, but her expression had turned

troubled. Behind her was a stone statue on a pedestal, a grim Confederate officer staring off inscrutably into the April air. On either side of the granite officer small dogwood trees were burgeoning into pink and delicate bloom.

The afternoon sky was a pure blue, exactly the same blue as her eyes. *Those eyes could cause a man trouble,* he thought, *an infinity of trouble.*

"This warning," he said, "about being watched. Is this why you wanted to meet in the park?"

She pressed her lips together more tightly and nodded.

He said, "I told you that I was worried about your safety. Does this do anything to convince you I'm right?" He rattled the paper for emphasis.

She only shrugged again and stared at the pale blue ribbon on her finger.

He said, "This person, this woman who contacted you. She may be frightened. It would explain the cat-and-mouse games."

She said, "I think that's why she picked the annex. Because of the parking garage. She could slip in and out of there unnoticed. Drive in, walk in. Go in from the street or upstairs from the annex itself."

"Right," he said. "And places like that can be dangerous."

She made her expression unconcerned. "I was careful."

They sat for a moment in silence, and he watched the breeze stir her golden hair. A few petals drifted from the dogwood trees. One rolled across the table, came to rest against her sleeve. He resisted the desire to brush it away.

He said, "If you arrange to meet her, I don't want

you to do it alone. I'm not sure I want you doing it at all. Let me go instead."

She tossed her head as if she had nothing left to lose, and the motion did something odd to his heart. "She contacted me, not you."

"We'll see," he said vaguely. He put his hand over her good one. Her eyes showed that she was startled by the action, but she did not resist.

"I've wondered," she said slowly, "why she called me instead of you."

"So have I," he said. This thought troubled him more than he cared to show. He had been in town longer than Jaye, he'd made more inquiries, he'd spread around more money, and he'd made it clear he'd pay for information. So why, when information finally came, was it offered to her? He didn't like it.

She said, "Do you think they've listened in on our calls?"

Slowly he stroked his thumb over the silky skin on the back of her hand. "I've always been concerned about that possibility."

An alertness came into her eyes. "That's why you called me at Miss Doll's on her phone, isn't it? You didn't want to take a chance on the cell phone."

He gave her a small, ironic smile. She was too damned bright, and he liked that in her too damn much. He kept trailing his thumb across her hand, back and forth.

He said, "When you called me, it was from a pay phone, wasn't it?"

"Yes. Whoever left that note—I think you're right. She's afraid."

"But you're not?"

She looked into his eyes. It gave him a strange sensation, like plunging downward rapidly in an elevator. She said, "What difference does it make?"

"That's not answering the question."

"I'm afraid for my brother."

His hand went still on hers. "It's always your brother. What about you?"

"What about me?" she said, as if she didn't matter.

There was another matter that had nagged at the back of his mind. "*If* this woman has a list of the mothers—" he said.

"Yes?"

"*Your* mother might be on it," he said. "What then?"

He saw her stiffen; he could feel the sudden tension coursing through her.

"I don't know. It's not what I came for."

"You have to have thought about it," he said. His hand tightened over hers.

She bit her lip and looked away. She gazed at a puny bed of jonquils tossing their heads in the afternoon breeze.

"I've had other things to think about," she said.

"How do you feel about it?" he persisted. "Do you want to know who she is?—your mother? Or would you rather not know?"

She cocked her head, trying to look unconcerned. "Nona's my mother, for all intents and purposes."

"You don't sound completely happy about it."

"She hasn't always been completely happy with me. I wasn't the daughter she'd hoped for."

"Let me guess. Too outspoken? Too independent?"

She gave him the slightest of smiles. It was rueful.

He said, "I bet you were a handful as a kid, weren't you?"

She made no reply, and her smile died away.

He said, "And I bet you beat the holy hell out of anybody who picked on your little brother. Didn't you?"

"Yeah," she said. "I did."

She drew her hand away from his. She stood and pulled her tweed jacket more tightly around her. The sun was sinking, and the afternoon was growing chilly. She said, "If I need the twenty-five thousand dollars, will you get it for me?"

He looked at her, her pale gold hair lifting and glinting in the breeze, and he wanted her. "We'll work something out," he said.

At five minutes to seven, Jaye held her breath as Turner pulled into the lot of the Stop 'n' Shop and parked. Together they walked to the pay phone. Jaye made a pretense of looking through the telephone book that was chained to the metal post.

She glanced at her watch. It was two minutes to seven o'clock.

"I feel conspicuous with you standing there," she muttered. "I keep thinking someone's watching."

"They may well be," he said with an air of casualness that set her on edge.

She herself felt anything but casual. She glanced around the lot. Two cars had been parked in front of the store when they drove up, and a Hispanic man in a ball cap was putting gas into a battered Chevrolet.

The traffic on the highway was steady and seemed unremarkable. She did not think they had been followed, but she had the uneasy feeling that she could be wrong. What did she truly know of such things?

Across the highway was a bar, and its lot was filled with cars and pickup trucks. The bar had windows across its front, and neon beer signs glowed in them. She imagined someone sitting in that bar, watching through one of those windows.

The sky was rapidly growing dark, and the Stop 'n' Shop lot seemed like a small and precarious island of light in the lengthening shadows. When the phone rang, the sound stabbed through her like a blade.

She picked up the receiver, willing both her hand and her voice to be steady. "Hello?" she said. "Yes?"

Turner leaned close to her, so that he could listen.

"Jaye Garrett?" asked a woman's voice. It was the same voice that had told her to go to the Smithly Medical Annex in Kender.

"I waited for you in the annex," Jaye said, her throat tight. "But you didn't come."

"You got the note." It was a statement, not a question.

"Yes."

"You can get the money? The twenty-five thousand?"

Jaye exchanged a tense glance with Turner. He put his hand on her shoulder, gripped it as if to say, *Steady*.

She took a deep breath and said, "I might be able to get it. But I have to know what I'm buying. How do I know you've got what you say?"

"You've got to keep this secret," the woman said. "You can't tell people about this. Nobody."

"Who are you?" Jaye asked, praying the woman would cooperate—at least a little. "How do you know about Hunsinger?"

"My mother—she worked at the clinic. She was a nurse's aide."

"When?"

"From 1961 to 1968."

Jaye's stomach clenched and her legs suddenly felt

weak. Those dates included the years that she and Patrick had been born, but not the son of Mr. D.

Turner's hand tightened on her shoulder.

Jaye said, "Your mother—she'll talk to me?"

"She's dead," said the woman. "But she knew names. She had a list. I have it now."

"How many names?" Jaye asked, her pulse drumming in her throat.

"Five," said the woman.

"Only five?" Jaye asked. "There had to be more than that."

"There were. But five names is what I got," the woman said, stubbornness edging her tone. "That's what I know. That's what I've got for sale."

Turner squeezed her shoulder. Jaye said, "Tell me something to prove it is genuine."

The woman hesitated. "Two of these girls came from Little Rock, one from Fort Smith. Two from Oklahoma. They came from good families, all of them. Classy families, society. When a girl like that got in trouble, she came here, to Dr. Hunsinger. Their families paid him."

"More," Turner mouthed, his face close to hers.

"You have to tell me more. Twenty-five thousand dollars is a lot of money."

The woman hesitated, and her silence made Jaye's hopes stumble drunkenly. *She's going to hang up. Please, God, don't let her hang up. Please.*

The woman said, "The babies went to Texas mostly. Dr. Hunsinger didn't want to sell them in Oklahoma. It was something about jurisdiction, my mother said. Different jurisdictions would make it harder to—to prosecute and stuff."

Turner nodded, as if he understood what she meant. But again he mouthed, "More."

"That's a start," Jaye said. "Keep talking."

"The parents that bought them, they paid top money for these babies. Because, see, these were classy babies. You knew if you bought a baby from Dr. Hunsinger, you were getting quality."

God, like we were shoes or show dogs or bottles of wine, Jaye thought, gritting her teeth. She said, "I'm trying to find my brother's birth parents. Did one of those girls have a boy in 1968?"

"In 1968? Yeah, one of them had a boy. That's what's wrote down here."

Jaye's knees almost buckled, and Turner put his arm around her firmly, kept her steady.

"This girl," she managed to ask, "was she—oriental? Did she have any oriental blood, do you know?"

"No," the woman said firmly. "Dr. Hunsinger wouldn't handle something like that. He only dealt with white babies."

It's all right, she told herself. *Maybe she's wrong. Or maybe Hunsinger himself hadn't known. The girl might have had only a trace of Asian blood. That's all it would take. Brother Maynard had said so.*

"Dates," Turner murmured in her ear. "Get dates."

"Give me some dates," she said. "Tell me the date in 1968."

"No. You've got to buy that. You give me the money, I give you the whole list."

"Will you talk if I give you the money?"

"The list does the talking. I'll tell you where to meet me. Come alone. Don't bring that lawyer. I know you're running around with that lawyer. Leave him out of it."

Turner shook his head.

Jaye was fearful of pushing her luck, but she said, "I can't get the money without him."

"I don't trust lawyers."

"He's—discreet. He's not in this to get anyone in trouble."

"I want you to go to Arkansas tomorrow. Fayetteville. Meet me at the big mall. A quarter after eleven. The ladies' room. It's by the credit department in Sears. Have a big purse. Put the money in it. When you give me the money, I give you the list."

"Will you at least talk to me?" Jaye pleaded. "You must know more than you're saying. For twenty-five thousand you can at least—"

"Twenty-five thousand is cheap," the woman said with feeling. "I could have asked for four times that much, ten times. You know I could."

"Yes, I know, but—"

"Tomorrow at a quarter past eleven. In the ladies' room, like I told you. Be there."

Turner softly whispered, "Go for it."

Jaye's vision danced and she was dizzy with anxiety. "Would you meet us both—talk to us—for *thirty* thousand dollars?" She felt like a gambler recklessly upping the ante. But this had been Turner's idea, and she thought, *Hell, it's only money.*

"What?" demanded the woman, clearly startled.

"You said you could ask for more money. I'm—authorized to offer you more. If you meet us and talk to both of us, face-to-face."

For a long moment the woman said nothing. Jaye took a long, shivery breath. Turner held her more tightly.

At last the woman said, "You don't know what you're messing with."

"What?" Jaye said, startled. It was not the answer she had expected.

"You don't know what you're messing with. These people can be dangerous."

"What people?" Jaye prodded. "Who are you talking about?"

"Hunsinger's people. They run everything. There are things they want kept quiet."

"What things?"

"Things," the woman said with maddening vagueness. "I don't want to be seen with you. I don't want to take a chance."

Turner's eyes met hers. "Thirty-five," he mouthed.

"I can make you one last offer," Jaye said desperately. "Meet us, talk to us, I'll pay you thirty-five thousand dollars. It's as high as I can go."

Again there was a long silence.

"Thirty-five thousand dollars," Jaye repeated. "It's a lot of money. Just meet us and talk to us face-to-face."

"Forty," said the woman. She said it with an air of bravado, as if she didn't trust her own luck.

Jaye shook her head in frustration. "I can't go that high. But thirty-five thousand in cash—"

"Forty," the woman said, this time with more conviction.

"I'm not authorized to offer more than thirty-five—"

"Forty," the woman said firmly.

Jaye looked at Turner. He nodded.

"All right," she said, light-headed with exhausted tension. "Forty thousand. Where do we meet?"

"I—I don't want to meet around here. There's another place over in Arkansas. In the mountains. Eureka Springs. It's a tourist town. There's always people there, it's always crowded."

Turner nodded but raised an eyebrow.

Jaye understood. "How far from here?"

"An hour and a half maybe. There's these trolleys, these little green trolleys. You park your car downtown. Take the trolley. There's this big hotel there. On top of the mountain. It's called the Crescent. I'll meet you on the roof."

"The roof?"

"There's tables up there, telescopes, and stuff. A bar. Be there at eleven-twenty tomorrow morning. Bring the money. All of it. No tricky stuff."

"No tricky stuff," Jaye promised.

A sharp click sounded, then all Jaye heard was the indifferent buzz of the dial tone.

She hung up. She wanted to turn and lean her forehead against Turner's chest, just to be held for a moment. Instead she drew back from him.

But he didn't let her go completely. He gripped her shoulders and studied her face, a frown line between his eyes. "Are you all right?"

She shook her head. "I've never done anything like that before."

"You did fine. You did great."

She gazed up at him, hoping her face didn't show how naked her need was. "My God, what if that boy— the one born in 1968—is Patrick? What if his mother's name is on the list? What if it is?"

"Maybe it will be," he said, but his green-brown eyes held a worried look she hadn't seen before. *And maybe it won't*, they said.

"I need to call Nona," she said, fumbling in her purse for her phone card.

"Wait," he said. "First calm down. You don't want to sound too excited. Don't get her hopes built up too high."

Her mouth twitched, trying to smile, but all it gave

was a traitorous quiver. "Or my hopes, either. That's what you're telling me, isn't it?"

He stared at her for a long moment. "Yeah," he finally said. "That's what I'm telling you. For your own sake."

Slowly he reached out and smoothed her wind-blown hair. He brushed it gently from her forehead, stroked her bruise with his forefinger. "I don't like the idea of you getting hurt," he said.

She had to look away, draw back from his touch. Her emotions were in such turmoil, she was afraid that his kindness might undo her completely.

She turned toward the car, then looked back at him over her shoulder. "Come on," she said gruffly, "I'll buy you a drink."

"For forty thousand dollars it better be a hell of a drink," he said.

God love you, Turner Gibson, she thought. And this time, because of him, she managed to smile.

Adon did not return from Dallas until after dark. When he reached the house, he found a note from Barbara on the kitchen table. She'd written that she had taken a sleeping pill and gone to bed early.

This troubled Adon, for it meant something had upset her, but he did not know what. Felix, who ran the household, was not there to tell him, and Adon didn't know where the man was.

From the kitchen window, Adon could see that Felix's little apartment over the garage was dark, and when Adon called him, he did not answer his phone. But Felix's truck was parked in its usual place; he must be somewhere on the ranch.

Almost aimlessly Adon strolled outside and to the edge of the pasture. He leaned against the top of the fence, crossing his arms on the split rail.

The pasture was empty. The few horses that Adon had kept for his father-in-law were in the stable and would not be turned out until morning. The old man could no longer ride, of course, but seeing the horses, useless to him as they were, pleased him. And whatever pleased him soothed Barbara's soul.

Christ, Christ, Christ, Adon thought. He was angry that this fucking adoption business was rising up to haunt them again. It was like a vampire, some stinking corpse that wouldn't stay dead. He would have to depend on LaBonny to drive the stake through its heart.

Yet he was deeply disturbed by LaBonny, too. These days LaBonny watched Adon the way a scheming courtier might watch a king he thinks is growing weak and losing his grasp.

Uneasy lies the head that wears the crown, Adon thought bitterly, rubbing his eyes with the heel of his hand. LaBonny lusted after Adon's power, and he was starting to think he had a right to it, that he could seize it.

LaBonny was ruthless, but he was smart only the way a clever thug is smart. He had no idea of the energy, the cunning, and the endless dealing with detail it took to run this kingdom.

Yet, Adon thought, what a sorry little kingdom it was, no wider than this one poor Oklahoma county, its glory days past and his own domination nibbled at on every side by forces both lawful and unlawful.

Adon had power, such as it was, because the old man had empowered him; he had riches because the old man had enriched him. There were the horses, the cars, the plane, the ranch itself. There was the house on Eleuthera in the Caribbean, the bank accounts in the Bahamas and the Caymans and Lausanne.

Sometimes he wished he could leave the county behind—if LaBonny wanted to rule the sorry, fucking place, let him. He would go to Eleuthera, to the house on the beach, and live out his days on the edge of that impossibly blue sea.

Except Barbara would never go. She would never leave Cawdor. Her dead were here. For years her mother, beautiful and dead too young, had rested in the family burying ground. Now Barbara's only brother lay there, too. And the child. Her only child.

Adon saw a man's shape walking through the darkness toward him. It was Felix, the moonlight tinting his pale shirt a luminescent blue. He carried a rifle over his shoulder.

Adon waited for Felix to approach. Felix was short but powerfully built, and his Cherokee blood showed in his coppery skin, his jet-black hair. He was only a servant, and he had next to no education, but he was the one man in the county in whom Adon felt complete trust. He was rawhide tough, yet he had a streak of gentleness in his character that was as genuine as it was surprising.

Felix said, "I saw the plane come in."

Adon nodded. He had flown in his private plane to Dallas to talk to the representatives of the men who ran the drug trade through the county, using the poultry trucks. They wanted more traffic through the county, even though it was already dangerous. More. They always wanted more.

"What's the rifle for?" Adon asked Felix.

"Conchita thought there was a wild dog under the stable. She was gathering eggs and saw it crawl under, dragging a dead chicken. Skinny but with a big belly, like it was gonna pup."

"Was there?" Adon asked.

"Yeah," said Felix. "Big ugly bitch. White. Ready to pup, all right."

"You shoot her?" Adon asked.

"Yeah. I waited till the Miss was in bed. I didn't want her to know."

"The Miss" was what Felix always called Barbara, and he was fiercely protective of her. He knew she could not bear cruelty to animals.

"Good," said Adon.

"I took the carcass into the woods," Felix said. "So it wouldn't rot under the stable and stink it up. That's where I been."

The woods. That's always where the dead things are taken, Adon thought. But he nodded his approval.

Felix patted the rifle barrel. "I used the silencer. I didn't want to chance waking the Miss. She don't like it even when I shoot an ol' rat."

Adon thought of Barbara, even her chemically in-duced sleep fragile as spun glass. He said very carefully, "The Miss didn't wait up for me. Why?"

"Huh!" Felix made a sound of disgust. "That damn ol' Hollis run away and nobody can find him. Get her all upset. You know she always got a soft spot for him."

"Hollis?" Adon said, unpleasantly surprised.

Hollis Raven was yet another of old man Hun-singer's legacies, another piece of his everlasting baggage from the past. Hollis lived at the nursing home, where he was a janitor. But early on Saturday mornings, Felix fetched him to the ranch to work all day in Barbara's flower gardens, just as he had once worked in her mother's.

Hollis was not quite right in the head, and he had

no more book learning than a cat, but his very touch seemed to nurture seeds and inspire plants to flourish.

"He ran away?" Adon asked, frowning. "Why?"

Felix told him about the shooting the night before, how Hollis had looked in on the woman and then fled as if terrified.

"He locked himself up in his room," said Felix. "And Davy thought that was an end to it. Davy had his hands full, bunch of patients scared by the sirens and carryin' on. But later, he say, after everything got quiet again, he just got this *feelin'*—you know?"

Adon didn't know. His heart beat faster, and his chest felt tight.

Felix said, "Davy went to the back, looked out. Said he seen Hollis out there in the moonlight, on his hands and knees, diggin' in the dirt like a dog."

Felix paused. "So Davy yelled at him. He said, 'Hollis, what you doin'?' But Hollis had got something now, something that kind of shined in the moonlight."

"It shined? What was it?"

"Davy couldn't see. He said it was like a fruit jar maybe. He stood up and put it under his shirt, lookin' guilty, Davy said. So Davy yelled again. And Hollis run into the woods. He had a suitcase."

"A suitcase," Adon said. "Christ."

"At first Davy thinks he'll come back. But he don't. So when Hollis hasn't showed up by breakfast, Davy gets the master key and opens Hollis's room. And it's clean as a whistle. Everything's gone."

Adon snatched off his glasses in a gesture of frustration. "A shooting? Then Hollis runs away? He took *everything*?"

"Most everything," Felix said. "He don't have much. Davy found one thing, stuck back in the closet, in the corner of a shelf. A picture. A crayon picture. He called LaBonny, give it to him. LaBonny wants you to call him."

"A picture?" Adon asked with something akin to dread. Hollis was barely literate, but he could draw surprisingly well, and his pictures, though crude, had a primitive power. "A picture of what?"

"LaBonny wouldn't tell me," said Felix. "But Davy, he did. He said it was a blond woman. But that she looked dead. Laid out all wrapped up in white. Candles and crosses and angels around her."

"The doctor doesn't know this? He hasn't seen it?"

"No. I didn't tell him Hollis is gone neither. You know what they say about him and Hollis."

Adon knew, and the rumors made him sick. He raised his pale eyes to the house's second story. The old man had a suite of rooms, and he lurked solitary up in this lair all the time, like he was the Phantom of the Opera or something. Except for trips out of the state to private clinics, he allowed no one to see him except Barbara and Felix, and sometimes Adon.

Felix's gaze followed Adon's to the dark balcony, its glass reflecting the moonlight. "He was upset because the Miss went to bed early, didn't come see him. He lock his door and say he don't want to see nobody anyway. He'll go to bed early himself, and not to wake him up."

How nice, Adon thought, *if he never woke up.* Yet he needed the old man's cunning and experience; without it he would sink beneath the machinations of his rivals and enemies. And Barbara loved her father. To lose him might undo her completely.

Felix cocked his head sympathetically. "Your trip to Dallas—it went good?"

"It went all right," Adon said without enthusiasm.

"You got too much on your mind these days," Felix

said kindly. "You got a sick wife. A sick daddy-in-law. You been gone since sunup. Come in the house. I make you a nice drink."

Adon nodded, sighed again. He looked up at the stars. "I don't want Hollis to upset Barbara. Or her father."

"I understand your meaning," Felix said.

The two men looked at each other in the moonlight. Neither smiled.

The old man had been wrong, Adon thought. *We should have killed Hollis back when we killed Luther.*

He knew Felix understood this. And he knew what the other man was thinking. *It's not too late yet.*

They would, of course, have to find a way to keep it from Barbara, their beautiful, delicate, caring Miss.

NINE

—◦◦◦—

IT WAS DARK. TURNER INSISTED ON WALKING JAYE TO MISS Doll's back door. Part of Jaye wanted to believe he was being overcautious. But another part, deeper and primally wary, remembered the words of the note:

> Be carefull. They can eavedrop & spie on you.

Jaye didn't utter this thought to Turner, did not even like saying it to herself. Yet she knew he felt it, too, that sense of formless threat that filled the air like the finest of mists, pervasive and cold.

He opened Miss Doll's back gate, and when he slipped his arm around Jaye's waist, she did not resist. It was a strong arm; she liked the feel of it.

The setting hardly lent itself to fear. Miss Doll's neighborhood seemed a haven of small-town peace. A plump half-moon hung over the flowering dogwood tree. Somewhere a tree frog peeped its soft love song to spring.

The back porch was painted white and ornamented with wooden gingerbread and curlicues. Each stair was flanked by fat clay flowerpots spilling out a thick hoard of pansies.

On the back door hung an elaborate wreath of artificial flowers studded with plastic bluebirds and robins. Before the door was a welcome mat that showed a girl in a sunbonnet watering flowers.

Jaye forced herself to draw away from Turner's loose embrace so that she could dig in her purse for her key. "I'm certainly okay from here," she said as briskly as she could. "Thanks a lot."

It was his cue to leave. But he stayed by her side, so close she was swept simultaneously by comfort and unease.

Above them two sets of wind chimes tinkled in the night breeze, pastoral and melodious. He glanced at them, then gave her a wry smile. "Miss Doll's taste runs to cuteness. Is it this bad inside?"

"Worse," she said. "I'm sleeping with dolls."

"Umm," he said. "And aren't they lucky, say I?"

She found her key, slipped it into the keyhole. He put his hand over hers and drew it back from the door, leaving the key in the lock. He turned her to face him. "This place doesn't look any more secure than a candy box. Do you feel safe here?"

Her heart started to race in a way she found far too pleasant, too exciting. *This is the wrong time for this,* she thought, and willed the excitement to go away. It would not.

She tried to make her tone airy and flip. "No self-respecting burglar would chance it. He'd be killed by falling kitsch."

He put his hands on the lapels of her tweed jacket, gripped them gently. "I'd feel better if you were in a place with real security."

She thought, *Like yours?*

"Like mine," he said, his voice low.

"I'm fine here," she said, but she had become a bit breathless.

"I think you'd be safer near me."

I'd be safer here. Much safer.

"This is where I picked," she murmured. "It's where I'll stay."

But from deep within yearning whispered up through her, its message too seductive to resist. When he bent nearer, she raised her face to his.

The wind chimes jangled delicately. The tree frog piped. The breeze stirred the young leaves like a sigh. Jaye heard the almost inaudible rustle of her own clothing and Turner's.

She felt his lips take hers, gently at first, then with greater urgency and growing hunger. Her own need spiraled dizzyingly, as if rushing to meet his. A hot recklessness sparked within her, and she wound her arms around his neck. He groaned against her mouth, his hands sliding under her jacket.

Then suddenly light poured out from the kitchen windows, and the yellow bulbs of the back porch flashed on with shocking brightness. Jaye pulled back from Turner guiltily.

The back door swung open, and Bright, Miss Doll's granddaughter, stood staring at them. Her hair was back in its tight braids, and once again she was wearing the nightgown with the teddy bear on it. She shifted her weight to one foot so that her belly bulged out even more. She put one hand over it possessively.

"I thought I heard you out here," she said.

Jaye looked in embarrassed confusion from Bright to Turner. His mouth was generously smeared with her lipstick.

"Oh," Jaye said to him, her heart knocking. "Well—yes—good night. I—have calls to make. You know—my mother."

"Certainly," he said with aplomb. "Give her my best."

"I thought maybe your key didn't work," Bright said to Jaye, her tone righteous. "I came to see so Grandma wouldn't have to get up."

Jaye was nonplussed, but Turner was not. He bent and gave Jaye a matter-of-fact kiss that was quick, but not too quick. "I'll see you in the morning."

"Right," said Jaye, and tried to smooth her hair. She pulled her key from the lock and quickly stepped inside.

"Gee, sorry to interrupt," Bright said as she closed and bolted the door. But on her face was an expression of spiteful satisfaction.

Jaye ignored it. "Have there been any calls for me?"

"Nope," said Bright, looking Jaye up and down. She put her hand back on her swollen stomach and rubbed it, as if it were the reproachful symbol of the powers of sex.

"He's cute," Bright said pertly, nodding toward the closed door. "Are you going to fuck him?"

Jaye was offended. "You shouldn't talk like that."

Bright laughed. "Like how are *words* gonna hurt me now?"

For a moment they stared at each other, the woman with the damaged lipstick, the girl with the damaged life.

"You know," Jaye said quietly, "you're not as tough as you think."

Bright's chin jerked up rebelliously, and her mouth became a hard line. But then, to Jaye's astonishment, the girl's eyes filled with tears. She turned and ran down the hall as lightly as the child she was.

Adon Mowbry was angry, and this was supposed to intimidate LaBonny. It did not. These days he could practically smell the other man's weakness. The weakness had always been there, and now it was growing like a cancer.

Adon had never earned power, he had married it. Let him bluster—he could not act, had never acted, could only depend on LaBonny to do it for him. The old man, the doctor, had been a different matter. But the old man could not live forever; he was inching graveward and everyone knew it.

LaBonny tried not to let his contempt for Adon show. He stared down at his boot as he drew an even line in the gravel with his heel.

"I just get back to town," Adon said from between set teeth. "I come home expecting this problem to be over, done. I heard what happened. It was sloppy, reckless. It was *flamboyant*."

LaBonny slowly traced another line in the gravel, parallel to the first. The shooting had been necessary. Taking Adon's blame was not. "The one who shot at 'em was Bobby Midus. He was alone. The doing was his."

"What the fuck was he *thinking*?"

LaBonny gave a minimal shrug. "I reckon he thought it was a way of makin' a statement." He could not keep a sarcastic twist out of his voice.

Adon made a sound of repugnance. "The statement is that he's a fool."

LaBonny raised his head to meet Adon's pale eyes. He had the same pale eyes himself, for their families were connected, although LaBonny's people had always been the poor relations.

But the resemblance was only in their eyes. Adon was thick and going to fat, but LaBonny was tall and preternaturally lean, with a long, supple neck like a snake's. His face, too, was snakelike, a wide, thin mouth, high cheekbones, and brows so pale they seemed hairless.

He said, "Bobby's young."

"Phah," said Adon.

"He's learning," LaBonny said without emotion.

"Phah," said Adon again, with more disdain than before.

The two men stood beside LaBonny's pickup, which was parked in the curve of the long lane that led to Adon's ranch house. On either side, tall pines loomed up in black suddenness from the adjoining pastures. The pines guarded the whole length of the lane and kept this spot hidden from the views of both highway and house.

Adon's black Jeep was parked at the roadside, facing LaBonny's truck. The only light came from the half-moon just rising over the pines. It shone down on Adon's thinning fair hair, making it look as if age had already silvered it and deepening the disapproving shadows that framed his mouth.

"So they're still here," he said, shaking his head. "Gibson and the Garrett woman."

LaBonny shrugged.

"And they're still asking questions."

"Seems so."

"Christ," Adon said and put his hand to his forehead as if trying to ease an ache.

"Something's going on," LaBonny said. He delivered the news quietly, neatly, like the expert slide of a knife between ribs.

Adon's hand fell back to his side, clenched into a fist. "What do you mean?"

LaBonny's graceful neck stretched slightly, and he tilted his head. "The Garrett woman got a call this morning. Somebody—a woman—offering information."

Adon's heavy body stiffened. "Who? What kind of information?"

"About Doc. She wouldn't identify herself. She wanted the Garrett woman to meet her someplace."

"Well, where, goddammit?" Adon demanded. His jaws shook, pallid and blue in the moonlight. Their color made him look like an angry dead man.

"Couldn't hear that part," LaBonny said evenly.

Adon swore. He drew back his hand and slammed the flat of his fist against the door of LaBonny's truck so hard that the door rattled. This truck, nearly brand new, a flawless metallic blue with a customized white stripe, was LaBonny's favorite of his collection of vehicles. He despised anybody touching it, and Adon, the maggot, knew it.

But LaBonny showed no emotion. "I told you a long time ago we needed a better scanner."

Adon glared at him viciously. "I've spent a fortune on your James Bond toys."

LaBonny ignored the gibe and gazed up at the moon. Adon was rich and a college boy; of the real world he knew hardly anything. For all his fancy education, his head was full of nonsense, as an egg is full of its own meat. He demanded his spying be done, yet he knew nothing of the true cost of it or the skill involved.

"Got to keep up with the times," LaBonny said mildly.

"This conversation," Adon demanded, "who heard it?"

"I did," LaBonny said in the same tone. "Then a couple of assholes come down the highway, talking to each other on car phones, the voices got all jumbled together. Too bad. Should have a better scanner."

"Well?" Adon said pointedly. "You still have eyes, dammit."

LaBonny crossed his arms. "Well. She went to the Yoo Hoo Café. Talked to the lawyer. Then she left town—alone. Went clear up to Kender."

"You followed her, for Christ's sake?"

"Not me. Bobby Midus."

"Well, who the fuck did she meet?"

"He don't know. He lost her."

"He *lost* her?" Adon roared. "Sweet sobbing Christ on a crutch—how the fuck did he *lose* her?"

"He couldn't follow too close. They got to the city, and he got caught at a stoplight. He's not used to the city."

Adon struck the truck's door with his fat fist again, not once but twice. LaBonny watched and did not wince, but his thin mouth grew thinner still.

"I ought to cut off his balls and feed them to the hogs," raged Adon. "Shit, shit, shit."

LaBonny lifted a shoulder as if it didn't matter. He himself was deeply angered by Bobby Midus, yet he felt protective, even possessive, of the boy. It was a strange feeling, pleasantly powerful yet sometimes touched with a fierce resentment. "I tended to him when he got home. Don't worry."

Adon glared.

"Then the Garrett woman comes back," said LaBonny. "Her and the lawyer meet in Mount Cawdor, the town square. She's starting to act like she thinks she's being watched."

Adon's breath came hard and shallow. He said nothing.

"Later they go to the Stop 'n' Shop parking lot. Wait at the pay phone together. They get a call. Again she acts nervous. They talk maybe four-five minutes. I think they're arranging another meeting."

"You *think*," Adon said sarcastically.

"I noticed somebody who wasn't in town today," LaBonny said laconically. "Somebody who might have reason to go away."

Adon's nostrils were pinched and his stare was challenging.

LaBonny picked a piece of lint from his immaculate western-cut white shirt. "Judy Sevenstar," he said with satisfaction. "I saw her drive out of town this morning, about ten-fifteen. That's too late for her to go to work. And it was right before the Garrett woman left. Later I found out Judy didn't go to work. She phoned in sick. I put two and two together."

LaBonny leaned nonchalantly against the hood of his truck and let Adon digest this. Judy Sevenstar was an overweight, middle-aged Cherokee woman who lived in a trailer in Cawdor but worked in the cafeteria of the high school in Mount Cawdor.

Her mother had been a nurse at Hunsinger's clinic; she'd seen a lot in her time. And Judy Sevenstar was Hollis Raven's cousin.

"Judy Sevenstar," Adon said with anger. "That's another thing—Hollis is gone—"

"I know that," LaBonny said before the other man could finish his sentence.

"Don't be insolent. And what's Judy got to do with the lawyer and the Garrett woman?"

"Davy called her this morning, looking for Hollis," LaBonny said. "About seven o'clock. He said she got all upset, swore she didn't know where he'd got to. Later she leaves herself. She ain't back yet."

Adon's stare was intense, glittering.

LaBonny tilted his hat to a knowing angle, crossed his arms again. "You know what? I don't think Judy's coming back. One of her neighbors said when she got in her van, she had two suitcases. And she did something strange."

"What?" Adon said with a sneer.

"Judy used to have a little bird she kept in a cage. In nice weather she'd hang it on the porch. Neighbor said Judy came outside with the cage, opened it up, and watched that bird fly away. Threw the cage in the trash can. Yessir, she acted like somebody who's going to be gone a long time."

LaBonny stayed draped against the car as he watched Adon think. He said, "I reckon she thinks something might have happened to Hollis."

Adon glared at him. "Well? What in hell *is* this about him running off?"

LaBonny gave his thin smile. "Sounds like he got scared. Seeing that woman scared him. Imagine that. Scared of a woman."

Adon suddenly looked shrunken, apprehensive. "Why? He took all his things? He left only a drawing? What's it look like?"

LaBonny reached into his shirt pocket and drew out

a photocopy folded into quarters. He handed it to Adon and watched as he smoothed it. "It looks like her," LaBonny said smugly. "It looks like that Garrett woman."

Adon stared down at the crude drawing as if transfixed. A pretty, fair-haired woman lay in a coffin. Candles and crucifixes surrounded her. Over her fluttered a pair of angels, their hands pressed to their hearts as if in grief.

"Show it to Doc," said LaBonny. "Ask him if it reminds him of anybody *he* knows."

Adon said nothing. He looked dumbstruck, which both amused and gratified LaBonny. He couldn't quite keep the smirk out of his voice. "I always figured Hollis knew too much. Judy, too. I told you that four years ago. You wouldn't listen. Now they both run off who knows where?"

"You think they're together?" Adon asked, his expression sickly. He could not take his eyes from the picture.

LaBonny shook his head. "No. I reckon Judy thinks we killed him or something. So she's run. But she needs money. And that lawyer, he's got lots. That's what's up, I figure."

That's what I figure, college boy. They didn't teach you how to think like that in school, did they?

"Jesus," Adon said in a little hiss, like air leaking away.

"I got somebody watching the lawyer and the woman. So if they should happen to go somewhere and meet up with anybody—like, say, Judy—"

Adon took a deep breath. He said, "It might be prudent if they were followed. Not by that fool Midus. By you. Yourself."

"Consider it done," said LaBonny.

He smiled and put his hand to his hat brim, as if in a salute of respect. But LaBonny felt no respect whatsoever. Adon's power was falling away.

Like an overripe fruit it was ready to drop into LaBonny's hard, strong, and far more deserving hands.

The April morning spilled tender light on the forests, the unfolding leaves, the snowy blossoms of the dogwood and wild plum.

"It's pretty country," Jaye said pensively. "It's beautiful country."

The foothills had given way to true mountains, which veered up and swooped down into wooded valleys.

"You can keep it," Turner said, glancing in the rearview mirror. "I'm a city man myself."

The nearer they drove to Eureka Springs, the more steeply the mountains thrust, the more tortuously the road curved. It was as if some giant on LSD had taken a ribbon of concrete, knotting and tangling it with insane abandon.

Often the highway ran dizzyingly along the edge of a precipice, and just as often there was no room to pass or be passed. Frail-looking guardrails offered the pretense that they could protect a car from pitching over the brink and plummeting into a ravine.

It was a dangerous road. Turner was used to handling a Porsche with its racer's body and nimble steering. The rental car seemed lumbering to him, as if he were trying to guide a draft horse along the narrowest of goat paths.

Yet the road was surprisingly crowded. Most drivers seemed to be retired tourists from the flatlands, elderly men who wore ball caps and whose spouses sat sturdily beside them in the passenger seats. These men were determined to take their time, and they negotiated the twists and hairpin turns at a pace so sluggish and timid it maddened Turner.

But then in the rearview mirror, he noticed the white pickup truck again, three cars behind him. A Chevrolet, it had a darkly tinted windshield and no license plate in front.

It was, Turner thought, like fifty thousand other white Chevy pickups in Oklahoma and Arkansas. That was the problem. Back in the foothills, where the spaces were more open, he had twice wondered if he was being followed by such a pickup.

Both times it had disappeared, and he'd tried to convince himself that it had been nothing to worry about. Now he wasn't sure. But he didn't mention it to Jaye. She was already keyed up too tightly.

She had talked to her mother this morning, and her brother's condition hadn't changed. Turner knew she was deeply worried about the meeting in Eureka Springs, although she said little and kept her expression stoically blank.

He decided to try to distract her. He nodded toward the car in front of them, trundling at its cautious pace.

"If I drive like that when I get old," he said wryly, "I hope somebody takes me out, stands me up against a wall, and shoots me."

She smiled wanly. He realized he'd love to see her face unshadowed by worry. He imagined when she was really happy her pretty face could light up and be practically incandescent. *Someday*, he thought, *when this is over, I'll come to Boston. I'll make you smile, laugh. I'll make you do a lot of pleasant things.*

He glanced up at the rearview mirror. The white Chevy was still behind them, its tinted windshield glinting brightly as the flash of a knife.

He gestured at the car before them. "Look at 'em," he said. "At every curve this dude slows to fifteen miles per hour. Two miles ago a box turtle passed us. A box turtle on crutches."

She said nothing, but her smile showed the hint of a dimple. It disappeared too quickly.

He curled his lip at the driver in front of him. "When a sign says to watch for falling rocks, he slows down even more. Is that how he thinks you beat an avalanche of rock? You outcreep it?"

"You might as well enjoy the scenery," she said with a philosophic shrug. "We've still got plenty of time."

He glanced in the mirror. The white truck with the darkened windshield held its place. It was making him feel distinctly uneasy.

But he said, "The only scenery I'm likely to enjoy is you. A tree is just a tree. But a blonde in a pink sweater? That's a thing of beauty and a joy forever."

"Oh, really," she said, but the dimple flickered in her cheek again.

"No, really," he said. "You look—nice this morning."

"Nice" didn't do her justice. She wore a burgundy pantsuit with a pale pink sweater beneath the jacket. He knew clothes, and he knew hers weren't expensive, but somehow she made them look that way.

Again she wore her hair brushed to fall over one side of her face, and he supposed she was still concealing the bruise on her forehead. Her only jewelry were a pair of gold studs in her ears and her watch. On her injured finger she still wore the blue ribbon tied in a bow.

"Thanks," she said.

"No," he said, "I mean it. You look good in that color. It sets off your eyes."

"No," she said. "I mean for trying to cheer me up. That's what you're doing, isn't it?"

"No," he protested with such genuineness, he almost convinced himself. "Not at all."

"Yes, you are," she said. "And it's true I'm worried about Patrick. What if he's not on that list? What then?"

"Maybe someone who is on it can give us a lead. That's how it happens sometimes."

She swallowed, ran her hand over her smooth hair. "There's more."

"I understand," he said, and he was certain he did. "Your own mother might be on that list. That's got to give you pause."

"It's not that," she said. "I don't think about that."

"Look," he said, "I know it's got to be hard to deal with. But—"

"No," she insisted, shaking her head. "It's not that. I don't want to alarm you. But I think someone might be following us."

Jesus Christ, he thought with a start, *doesn't she miss anything?*

"What do you mean?" he asked, keeping his tone neutral, steady.

"Before we got to the mountains," she said, "the real mountains, I mean, twice I noticed a white pickup behind us. There's one back there again. It may be the same one."

"Oh," he said with false nonchalance. "That."

Her eyebrow arched. "Yes. *That*. You've noticed it, too?"

Christ, he thought, she must have been watching the

rearview on the passenger's side. And he thought she'd just been quietly staring out the window the whole way, lost in her own thoughts.

She said, "If he is following us, if it's not just a coincidence, would he be that open about it?"

Turner shrugged. "He wouldn't have much choice."

Back in the open country, where traffic was lighter, the truck couldn't keep them in sight without being visible itself. Here on this two-lane road with its hairpin curves, it was as trapped as they were by the crawling traffic.

She nodded as if she understood. "When we get to Eureka Springs and leave the car behind, do you suppose he'll follow us on foot?"

"He could try."

A line of worry appeared between her brows. "Maybe we shouldn't have convinced this woman to talk to us," she said. "Maybe we're putting her in danger."

"She's the one who set up a meeting," he said. "If he follows us, he follows us to her."

In truth, Turner wasn't wasting his sympathy on a nameless snitch willing to trade information for money. He had to take care of Jaye—and himself.

"Maybe we should have driven separate cars," she said, glancing in her own mirror again.

"No," he said. "It's better this way."

"Maybe it's a setup," she said, giving him an anxious glance. "Did you think of that?"

He'd thought of it. They were carrying a lot of cash. He said, "If this is about money, we let them take it. It's Mr. D.'s. He can afford it."

Billboards had begun to mar the roadside, touting Eureka Springs and its delights. A motel appeared, then another and another. More billboards. The traffic slowed to an even more torturous pace.

They had reached an intersection of highways, one leading to downtown Eureka Springs, another going eastward to more staid and distant cities. Turner made a right and joined the parade of cars wending into the heart of the town. Again he stole a look in the mirror. The truck was still there.

She, too, noticed, he could tell. But she said, "It's probably just a coincidence."

He nodded with a certainty he didn't feel. "Probably."

She gave a slight shudder, crossed her arms as if to fend off a chill. "But all of a sudden I'm having these melodramatic thoughts," she said. "Like I wish you had a gun."

He kept his eyes on the highway, his expression neutral. "Who said I didn't?" he asked.

She stared at him in astonishment. "A gun?"

It was unloaded and beneath the seat. But under his suede jacket, he felt the comforting solidity of his holster, waiting for the loaded gun's weight. "Yeah."

"Can you use it?" she asked.

"If I have to."

She was silent a moment.

At last she said, "This is a skill I didn't know you had."

He smiled at her. "I've got lots of skills you don't know about yet."

TEN

〜∾〜

YOU KNOW HOW TO USE A GUN?" JAYE DEMANDED. SHE was appalled yet strangely impressed.

He lifted one shoulder in a shrug. "My father was kind of a marksman. He taught me. Later I was on the pistol team in college."

This sounded plausible and benign, perhaps almost too much so. She studied him suspiciously, but he only looked at the crush of traffic in front of them and shook his head. "This is amazing. Look at it."

"So you were on the pistol team," she said. "What college?"

"Cornell," he said.

"That was in your madcap university days. Why do you have a gun with you *now*?"

"It seemed politic when one is toting forty thousand bucks."

"And you just happened to bring one with you from Philadelphia?"

"Mr. D. sent one with the money," he said. "It was his suggestion, actually. It seemed like a prudent idea. I took it."

She clamped her lips shut and glanced in the rearview mirror. The truck with its darkened windshield was still behind them. *Coincidence,* she tried to tell herself, but her heart wouldn't listen and tapped a more anxious cadence.

She hadn't questioned Turner about the cash before. Now she did. "He *sent* the money?"

"Yes."

"How could he get it here so fast? I mean you could have only asked him last night. Even with FedEx—"

"When Mr. D. wants something sent, it gets sent. He doesn't wait on FedEx. That's what being rich is about."

"You mean like—like a messenger *brought* it to you?"

"Yes. Like that."

"Along with a gun."

"Yes."

She frowned. "But he must have taken it on a—on a plane. Isn't that illegal?"

"Help me watch for a parking place," he said.

"I asked you," she said between her teeth, "if your getting that gun was legal?"

"Yes," he answered. "I'm a lawyer. I should know."

"You have a license to carry a gun?"

"Yes. Mr. D. can arrange such things. My God, the streets in this place. We're going to have to park in a lot. When we do, keep your eye on the truck."

She was nervous, disoriented, and the town itself made her feel more so. It seemed to be built on the most precipitous slope of the highest mountain, and the buildings clung to it as if defying gravity, the streets twisting tortuously.

The place was quaint, but it was also teeming and jumbled. She struggled to stay focused on Turner's revelation about the money and the gun.

"This messenger," she said uncomfortably, "did he just appear in the night, like the tooth fairy? Where is he?"

"I resent that," Turner said. "I do not have fairies come to my hotel room. The messenger's gone, returned to civilization. Good God, these lots are filling up already. Ha!"

He spotted a parking lot with an empty space and wheeled into it without signaling, his turn so swift it was almost violent. .

She caught her breath and watched for the white pickup truck. It slowed momentarily. Then it sped up and disappeared around one of the town's oddly quirking corners.

"It went on," she said with relief. But her relief swiftly died as she saw Turner thrust a clip into his automatic and jam it into his holster.

"Come on," he said. He was out of the car before she could catch her breath. He threw open her door and offered her his hand.

She stood close to him as he stuffed dollar bills into some sort of antique parking meter. The money was in an envelope in her big handbag, and it made her paranoid. She clutched the bag tightly against her chest and looked about warily, her heart still beating too fast.

Then Turner had her by the arm and was steering her toward the crowded sidewalk. "Where—" she began.

"The trolley stop," he said. "We passed one right before the parking lot. Come on. There's one coming."

She hurried to keep pace with him. No one seemed to be following them, but the streets and sidewalks were so alive with people, how could she be sure?

She felt naked in her vulnerability as they stood by the little brick trolley station. Turner asked a young African American couple if they were at the right spot to catch the trolley for the Crescent Hotel.

"Yes," said the woman. "That's the last stop. Here it comes."

Jaye saw the green trolley approaching and heard the clang of its bell. It seemed to take an interminable time to reach them. She thought she would feel safer once they were aboard, but she did not.

The trolley was crowded, and she stood as close as she could to Turner, trying to keep the purse safely between them. He put his arm around her.

She looked their fellow passengers over. They seemed a harmless lot: couples in their sixties, middle-aged women with the glitter of shopping lust in their eyes, a group of younger women who were laughing and wore matching T-shirts that said "If You Can Read This, Thank a Teacher."

The trolley spent a long time at the stop, for there was an elderly man with a walker who needed help boarding, then a flurry of resettling as someone rose to offer him a seat. *Let's go, let's go,* Jaye prayed.

No one aboard seemed even vaguely threatening. But she could sense the tension in Turner's long body, so closely wedged against hers. As the trolley jolted to a start, he drew her closer still, and she did not resist. Pressed against his chest, she felt the hard bulge of his concealed gun. It both comforted and alarmed her.

.   .   .   .

Eureka Springs was a town that, by logic, should not have existed. It would never have been built in such an unlikely place had it not been for the thermal springs that gave it its name. Long ago it had flourished as a health spa, but now the waters were polluted, the bathhouses converted to hotels and galleries, and its business was tourism, the more frenetic the better.

But above this frantic activity, as if holding itself aloof, reigned the massive and gloomily majestic Crescent Hotel. Other buildings had no yards or those only the size of postage stamps. The Crescent, palacelike, had no mere lawn; it had grounds. It claimed most of the acres at the very summit of the mountain.

These grounds, wooded and adorned with gardens, swept out around the hotel, isolating it from every other structure. The Crescent was an immense building of brick and stone, with pillars and turrets and vast stairs leading to its front doors.

The African American woman who was standing next to Jaye in the crowded trolley smiled at her and nodded at the hotel. She leaned closer and whispered confidentially, "They say it's haunted, you know."

Jaye could believe it.

The trolley shuddered to a stop and began the slow business of unloading. The man with the walker was helped out onto the pavement. The retired couples, who had plenty of time, took it. The shoppers struggled with bags that were fat with purchases.

When Jaye and Turner at last stood on the sidewalk, looking up at the Crescent's stony face, she clutched the purse with its money more tightly. The hotel was regal; it was quite august. But it was also forbidding.

The trolley's other passengers were dispersing, some heading into the hotel, some venturing toward the garden paths, still others heading downhill toward the hotel's nearest neighbor, a gothic-looking little church.

"Didn't Stephen King set a book here?" Turner asked dryly.

"If he didn't, he should," said Jaye.

The lobby was cavernous and rich, with elaborate wood trim and antique furniture upholstered in silk and velvet. A fireplace of white stone was ornate with arches and pillars and carved inlays.

A few people sat in chairs, quietly reading newspapers. Most were elderly. None looked like a spy, a mugger, or a hit man.

A young male desk clerk, who was standing with his back to them, looked prim in a meticulously starched white shirt and black vest. When he turned around, Jaye saw that he had an electric-blue streak in his blond hair and gold studs in both nostrils.

"May I help you?" he asked with arch politeness. He put his hands together, palm to palm, as if he prayed to be of assistance.

"The roof," Turner said. "There's an observation deck there—how do we get to it?"

"The elevators," said the clerk, "are that way." He pointed an immaculately manicured finger toward a wide hallway.

Jaye smiled weakly in thanks and hugged her handbag harder against her chest. She stayed close to Turner as they crossed the lobby. There were two elevators, and he pressed the up button.

At last one door groaned open, and a pair of elegantly dressed women exited, chattering in Spanish.

Jaye and Turner got into the elevator, which was ancient and had a slight air of decay. No one else approached. Slowly, massively, the door closed. Turner pushed the button for the roof terrace. The boxy little space shuddered, rumbled, and began to rise.

The elevator was as slow as it was old, and its cables creaked and groaned. But it stopped at no other floor and made its quaking progress, uninterrupted, to the roof.

The door opened as ponderously as it had closed, and Jaye looked at Turner questioningly. He smiled his nerveless smile. It did nothing to reassure her.

The view from the roof terrace was of wild and forested mountains stretching to the horizon's blue edge. The vista was marred only by a gigantic cement-colored statue on one of the nearer peaks.

The statue was clearly made to represent Christ with His arms outspread on either side in benediction. But the head was too large, the body too small, and the arms gave the whole figure an unfortunate T-like shape, like a crudely built toy airplane.

"Jesus," Turner said between his teeth. It was not said in reverence.

"Yes," said a round-faced woman next to him. "That's the Christ of the Ozarks. There's a whole Holy Land theme park over there. There's a passion play, too. Every night they crucify Jesus and He rises right back up."

"Imagine that," said Turner, but he didn't want to.

The woman turned to her two children, who were fighting over who got to look through the pay telescope. "Stop that," she ordered. "We've got to meet Daddy and go to the Wildlife Safari."

The children, who also had round faces, whined, and when the mother turned her back, the little boy kicked his sister in the shins. She howled in protest and hit him over the head with her plastic Winnie the Pooh purse.

Their mother wheeled on them and seized each child by the arm. "Robbie! Gwyneth! Right in front of Christ of the Ozarks! He can see everything you do—you ought to be ashamed."

She gave them each a shake and led them away. Jaye and Turner were left alone on the roof. She looked after the children with a troubled air, but he knew it wasn't of them she was thinking.

"We're early," he said as kindly as he could. It was true. It was five minutes before the appointed time.

She pressed her lips together and nodded. She kept looking at the closed door that led back into the hotel. It stayed closed.

The terrace stretched around them, large and empty. It had a scattering of small white patio tables with matching chairs. On one table sat an abandoned glass, half full of orange juice, and a partly eaten sugar doughnut on a paper napkin. A sparrow pecked at the doughnut. The napkin fluttered lazily in the breeze.

Turner put his arm around Jaye's shoulders. He told himself that it was to give her moral support, but he realized he liked having his arm around her. A man could get used to it.

"My brother and I were never like that," she said, still staring at the closed door. "We didn't squabble and fight like that."

"You were lucky," he said and watched the way the soft wind played with her hair. He resisted the urge to smooth it back in place.

"What about you?" she asked, not looking at him. "Any brothers? Sisters?"

"One brother," he said. Then, so she wouldn't ask more, he said, "He's dead."

She turned her face to him, her eyes as blue as the sky behind her. "Oh," she said, sounding dismayed. "I'm *sorry*."

"It was a long time ago," Turner said. It seemed like a long time ago, yet it had only been five years. His brother, Sonny, had been found in a rented room in South Philly, dead of a heroin overdose, the needle still dangling from his arm. The body was swelling, going bad. Sonny had been dead for at least two days before anybody found him, the medical examiner had said.

"Is that why you're helping me?" she asked, searching his face. "Because you had a brother, you know how it feels?"

"Yes," he said, and it was at the same time the truth and a lie. "No," he amended, and that, too, was both truth and lie.

He shrugged. He didn't want to talk about Sonny. He'd spent the last five years not talking about him. He mentioned his family as little as possible, and when he did, he seldom told the truth.

"I'm sorry," she said. She reached up with her injured hand and touched his face lightly.

They heard the sound of the door opening. Her hand froze, and she turned to look, the expression on her face both stricken and hopeful.

But it was only a wizened man in boxy black slacks and an oversize white coat with a name tag on it that said FRED. He carried an empty plastic tray. He scurried to the one dirty table and scooped up the juice glass, napkin, and doughnut. He scraped away the crumbs.

He looked up and peered at them through thick glasses that made his dark eyes appear unnaturally large. A smile crossed his shrunken face. "The bar just opened," he said invitingly. "Can I bring you something?"

"Do you want a drink?" Turner asked. He could use one himself.

But Jaye shook her head.

"No thanks," Turner told the little man.

The waiter beamed again and scuttled away, closing the door behind him. Jaye stared after him, her face stiff with control. Turner clenched his teeth and kept his arm around her. For once in his life he could think of nothing to say.

The sparrow, deprived of its crumbs, sat on the terrace wall. From the distance, the Jesus made of stone seemed to watch with expressionless eyes.

At thirty-five minutes after eleven, the door opened again. A dark woman hesitated there. She looked at Jaye, and with a dizzyingly bolt of certainty, Jaye *knew*. She drew in her breath so sharply that it hurt.

The woman walked toward them. She wore jeans and a dark sweatshirt under a navy-blue windbreaker. She carried a large red and blue plastic tote bag with a zipper. Over one shoulder was slung a worn purse of brown leather.

She looked around the deserted terrace, then at Jaye again. She ignored Turner. "Come on," she said. "There's a ladies' room down the hall. We'll go there. You give me what's in your bag. I give you what's in mine."

"You said we'd talk," Jaye said.

"We talk after," the woman said. Her tone was firm, almost bullying, but her expression was far less certain. She was a plain woman, middle-aged and going stout. She wore no makeup, and her high cheekbones and dark hair made her look as if she had Native American blood.

"We talk now," Turner said, and there was an authority in his voice, an ungiving hardness, that Jaye had not heard before.

Turner stared at the woman; she stared back. It was a clear contest of wills, and it was not an even one. Turner did not speak, but whatever the woman read in his face made her the first to look away. She dropped her gaze to the cement floor.

"You want to talk here?" he asked her with the same hardness. "Or do you know a better place?"

She shrugged sullenly. She said, "Nobody much comes up here this time of year."

She nodded toward the corner farthest from the door. She put her hands into the pockets of her windbreaker and walked away from them, head down, shoulders hunched. Then she stood at the low wall that ran around the terrace and stared out over the mountains.

Turner followed, Jaye at his side. "You came alone?" he asked.

The woman gave a short, bitter laugh. "Of course, I come alone."

He said, "You brought the list?"

"The sooner you pay me," she said, "the sooner you get it. Talk fast. Let's get this over with."

She raised her gaze to meet Jaye's eyes, again ignoring Turner. With a start Jaye realized that this woman was not merely nervous, she was terrified.

Turner must have understood, too. His voice grew gentler. "What's your name?"

"My name don't matter," she said. "It's the ones on the list you want."

"What was your mother's name?" Turner prodded. "How do I know she worked at the clinic?"

The woman still didn't look at him. She reached into her handbag and drew out a black wallet. She opened it and took out an aging snapshot, its colors going dull.

Jaye stared at the picture. It showed three women in nurses' uniforms standing beside a smiling man with fair hair. One of the women had her hands on the shoulders of a stocky, little dark-haired girl.

The group stood on the porch of the building that was now the nursing home. Over their heads hung a wooden sign suspended from chains. In dark letters it said SUNNYSIDE MEDICAL CENTER.

"That's my mother," the woman said, pointing at a dark-haired woman. She pointed at the child. "That's me."

Jaye believed her. Mother and child bore a marked resemblance, the same sturdy build, square face, solemn expression. The living woman now mirrored the woman in the photo even more eerily, as if the years had clearly proven they were of one blood.

The woman pointed at the fair-haired man. "And that's him," she said, resentment in her voice. "Hunsinger."

Jaye blinked in displeased surprise. She had not imagined Hunsinger as smiling or sociable or even quite human. But he was tall and blandly handsome.

The snapshot itself was the sort Jaye didn't think was printed any longer. It had a white border stamped with the date it had been developed: June 5, 1968.

Jaye swallowed. Patrick had been born in March of 1968. He had been in that building, among those people. This blond man had brought him into the world. These very women, perhaps, had tended him, held him.

She reached for the picture, but the woman kept a tight hold. "No," she said, and drew it back.

"Wait," Jaye pleaded. "You say your mother's dead?"

"Yes," the woman said without emotion.

"How long?" asked Turner.

The woman gave him a resentful look. "A year."

He said, "The other women in the picture, where are they?"

Jaye held her breath.

The woman glanced at the picture, her mouth tight. "The one with gray hair? She's dead, too. The other one, she moved away, got married—a long time ago. Twenty-five, thirty years."

"What was her name?" Turner probed.

"I don't remember."

"Where'd she move?"

"I don't remember."

"Who'd she marry?"

"I got no idea."

"Who else worked there?"

"I don't know. They came, they went. I was only a kid. I didn't pay no attention."

"Did you know about the babies?"

The woman's eyes grew more furtive, but she tossed her dark head rebelliously. "I heard things. Everybody heard things."

"Your mother, did she ever talk about it, about the baby selling?"

"She said the babies were better off. Everybody was better off."

"What else did she say?"

"Not to ask questions."

"Why?"

The woman put the photo back in the wallet, tucked it into her handbag. She stared off into the distance again.

Jaye said, "You told me there was a boy born at the clinic in 1968. Was it in March? On Saint Patrick's Day? Do you have the date?"

"The date is on the list," the woman said obstinately. "You'll see it when you pay."

Jaye gave Turner a beseeching gaze. *Please,* she wanted to say, *for God's sake, let's just pay her. We're getting nowhere.*

But he did not seem to notice, and the glint in his eyes was relentless. "There are five mothers on that list, five birthdays. *Only* five in eight years? That's not the impression I got of how things worked around here."

The woman's chin jerked up to a threatening angle. "The list is five people. Take it or leave it."

"Your mother—why'd she have it?"

"Ask her."

"Why do *you* have it?"

The dark eyes flashed. "She give it to me. Before she died."

"Why?"

"What else did she have to give me?"

Turner leaned closer to her, his voice dangerously smooth and low. "Do you know it's illegal to conceal evidence of a crime? It makes you an accessory. And that's what baby selling is—a crime."

The woman wheeled to face Jaye. "See?" She was angry, and tears sparkled in her eyes. "I told you I didn't want no fucking lawyer. I come to you with an honest proposition. I'm trying to help you, dammit. But *he's* trying to make me into a criminal. I knew it."

"No," Jaye protested. "I never meant—"

But Turner stepped between the two of them, pinning the woman in the corner. "What you're doing is a shakedown," he said from between his teeth. "In fancy terms, it's a form of extortion. You want me to define extortion for you?"

The woman looked wildly about her. Behind her was nothing but the width of the low stone wall and beyond that a fall of five stories. She struck out at Turner's chest and tried to force her way past him.

He caught both her wrists and blocked her way. "Answer our questions, and you get the money. Don't, and we call the law."

Jaye's stomach pitched in fear. Turner hadn't warned her he would do this. The woman seemed even more frightened. She burst into tears.

"No," she begged, trying to free her hands. "Not the law. They own the law. They'll kill me."

"Who owns the law?" Turner demanded.

"Hunsinger and his family—Adon Mowbry. They own the whole county. Let go. You're hurting me."

Jaye tugged at his arm, appalled. "Turner, don't—"

He ignored her. He leaned closer to the dark woman. "Why would they kill you?"

She shook her head so that her hair whipped about her face. "I know too much."

"About the list?"

"No—no," she almost wailed.

Jaye tried in vain to pull his arm back. "Turner, what if somebody comes? For God's sake—"

"What do you know?" His grip tightened. "Tell me, goddammit."

"Turner—" Jaye begged. "Please—"

But the woman stopped fighting. She bent her head, tears running down her face. She said, "Somebody died."

Jaye's mouth turned dry; her hand went still on his arm.

"Who died?" Turner demanded.

"A girl. One of them that came," she said. "He covered it up."

"Who covered it up?"

"Hunsinger," she said. "I don't know if he killed her accidentally or on purpose, what happened. But he covered it up."

"How?"

"I don't know, I don't know," she wept. "My cousins had something to do with it; Luther knew all about it. Jesus, I don't know. I was a *child*."

He bent so that his face was closer to hers. "Where's Luther? How do I find him?"

"He's dead!" she cried. "He knew too much, he threatened to tell, and they killed him. My other cousin's disappeared—they could kill me, too. Give me my money, dammit. All I want to do is get *away* from here. Away from *them*."

Turner bent closer to her still. "Why doesn't anybody ever see Hunsinger? What happened to him?"

"Nobody knows for sure," she sobbed. "He got hurt. There's something wrong with him. I don't know what."

"You said he owns the county. How?"

"He owns it, is all. He made a lot of money. There wasn't only baby selling. There was abortions, too. A lot of them."

Jaye stiffened in surprise. Until now people who'd defended Hunsinger had said that he'd helped illegitimate children. No one had ever hinted that he'd aborted them.

"Abortion was another sideline?" Turner demanded.

"Yes—yes. He made white girls pay high. But he did it cheap for those that weren't white. He thought it was a goddam public service, killing babies that weren't white."

She started to cry harder. "Please—please. I'll give you the list. Just let me have the money. So I can get away."

Jaye could stand it no longer. She seized Turner by his arm and shook it hard. "Let go of her."

A masklike calm came over his face. He dropped his

hands and took a step back. He reached into his pocket, offered the woman a clean handkerchief. "Wipe your eyes," he said, almost kindly.

She took the handkerchief, scrubbed at her streaked face. "Motherfucking lawyer," she muttered, but she said it without spirit and her voice choked by tears.

"Maybe you should go to the ladies' room," Turner said. "Wash your face. Jaye, you could take her."

Jaye stared at him uncomprehendingly. He was suddenly as cool and gentlemanly as the first night she'd met him. But she understood what he meant. The exchange was to be made: the money for the list.

Jaye reached out her hand to the woman, but she ignored it. "Which way to the rest room?" Jaye asked softly.

The woman said nothing. She sniffled and clutched her red and blue tote bag in one hand and Turner's crumpled handkerchief in the other. She gave Turner a look filled with hate, then lifted her chin and moved toward the door.

Jaye followed her. Without speaking, they walked down a long, dim hallway. They passed the bar, where a pair of women sat drinking colored drinks with paper umbrellas in them.

The woman pushed open the door to the women's rest room. It was tiled in small black and white hexagons, and the fixtures were ancient. No one else was inside. The doors to both toilet stalls were open. Each had a hook on the back of the door.

The woman unzipped the red and blue tote and hung it on a hook. "Go in, lock the door. Put the money in the bag, then the bag behind the toilet; leave it there. When you come out, I'll go in, check it, count it. If it's all there, I give you the list."

"You can trust me," Jaye said.

"And you can trust me," the woman said trucu-
lently. Her dark eyes flashed in anger again. "But you
can't trust *him*. That lawyer. Watch out for that one. He's
bad medicine."

Jaye stepped inside the stall, bolted the scarred door.
Her heart was thundering insanely. The money in her
purse was wrapped in separate plain packets and stowed
inside a large manila envelope.

She took out the envelope, placed it in the tote, and
put the bag behind the toilet. Then she opened the door
and stepped outside. The woman moved past her, took
her place, closed the door.

Jaye's head pounded as hard as her heart. She leaned
both hands on the sink, closed her eyes, tried to take
deep breaths. But her lungs seemed to seize up on her, to
resist taking in air. She felt a terrifying, smothering sensation, as if the room were closing in on her.

The woman stepped out of the stall. Over her shoulder was the worn leather purse. In her hand was the red
and blue tote bag.

"Is it all there?" Jaye asked. It had not occurred to
her until this moment that the money might not be the
full amount.

"It's all there," said the woman. "Here."

She reached into the pocket of her windbreaker. She
handed Jaye a small, square envelope.

Jaye seized it and tore it open.

The names and dates swam before her eyes.

Mother	From	Baby	Date
Shirley Markleson	Little Rock	Boy	Oct. 10, 1961
Cyndy Lou Holtz	Tulsa	Girl	Nov. 23, 1963
Janet Ann Banner	Little Rock	Girl	Aug. 30, 1966
Diane Englùnd	Fort Smith	Boy	Jan. 12, 1967
Donna Jean Zweitec	Oklahoma City	Boy	Dec. 18, 1968

Jaye's knees sagged, and she caught at the rim of the sink to hold herself up. She looked up wildly at the woman, whose face was impassive. "My brother's birthdate," Jaye said in a tight voice. "It's not here."

The woman's expression didn't change. "Tough," she said. She shouldered her purse and walked out the door.

ELEVEN

—◦◦◦—

TURNER WAS WAITING FOR HER, OF COURSE.

He caught her by the arm. "Not so fast," he said pleasantly. "I want to make sure my friend's all right."

The woman glared up at him. "You're gonna touch me once too often, fucker."

She was probably thinking how much she would love to rip out his heart and eat it. But he only gave her a small smile.

She started to yank her arm away, then went tautly still. The two ladies had come out of the bar. They stood in the hall, studying their bill and quibbling about whether they had divided it fairly.

Through the open doorway Turner could see the wrinkled sprite of a waiter rubbing a table clean. Beyond him a fat bartender shook a martini for a bored-looking businessman.

Turner didn't think his nameless friend would make a disturbance, not with so many witnesses around and forty thousand dollars weighing with delicious heaviness in her tote bag.

The rest room door opened and Jaye came out, paler than usual. Her eyes met his. He tightened his grip on the woman's arm.

Jaye shook her head, the dazed movement of a person who's just heard of the death of a loved one.

Turner said, "Your brother. His birth date? Is it there?"

"No," Jaye said dully. "Not even close."

The woman tried to twist discreetly away from Turner, but he held her fast, never taking his gaze from Jaye's face. Was *her* birth date on the list? Was that why she looked so shaken?

He nodded at the list. She clutched it so tightly, her knuckles were bluish white. "What about you?" he asked. "Are you on it?"

"No. Neither of us."

He turned to the woman and spoke through clenched teeth. "There have to be more names. Where are they?"

"I gave you all I had," she glared. "I can't tell you what I don't know."

"Then who would know?"

"Hunsinger," she hissed. "Him and God. Me, if I knew I'd have told you. What's it to me?"

"Money," Turner said, looking her coldly in the eye. "Money is what it is to you."

"Yeah," she said, and it was her turn to smile. "It is."

But in the end, he had no choice but to let her go.

She said she wanted a half-hour start. She got on the elevator at the same time as did the two ladies in hats. Pointedly she did not look at Turner or Jaye. She stared up at the ceiling of the elevator and held her red and blue tote bag possessively.

Then the big door heaved shut, and they could see her no more.

Jaye sat disconsolately on the roof terrace, rereading the list. On the table before her sat a gin and tonic, half-finished. She shook her head in frustration.

Turner, watching her, sipped at his scotch. "Look," he said, "the list doesn't seem like much. But it's a start. We'll track down these women. One may know something that leads to what we need. About your brother. Or maybe my client's son."

"None of the dates are right for his son," she said. "You said so before."

"I also said when one door shuts, another opens. One answer leads to another."

She shook her head. "This opens no doors. It gives no answers."

He lifted one eyebrow. "Not yet."

"I mean," she said, "altogether we knew about eight children born here. There's Patrick and me and Mr. D.'s son, and the other people who've come to Cawdor looking. We know all of their birthdays—except Mr. D.'s son, but he must have been born in March 1957."

"We know the *approximate* birthdays," Turner corrected. "Hunsinger may have fudged the exact dates."

"All right." Jaye rattled the list in her hand. "And here we have the names of five mothers and the *approximate* dates they gave birth. But nothing matches. None of the children we were looking for have birth dates that begin to match. Not even close. None."

"No," he said. "They don't."

"So this list may not even be *real*. It doesn't match a single fact we know."

He shrugged. "Maybe it matches facts we don't know—yet."

"And maybe it doesn't," she countered. "If there really are that many more names, why would that woman's mother keep just these? It makes no sense."

He leaned back in his chair, crossed his arms. "You're too honest. Think about it in criminal terms."

She frowned in puzzlement. "I don't see it."

He said, "Maybe she had blackmail on her mind."

Jaye recoiled from the thought. "Blackmail?"

"That's not to say she did it," Turner said mildly. "She might have thought these were the most likely candidates and put their names aside for a rainy day."

He lifted one shoulder negligently, like a man simply tossing out idle thoughts. "On the other hand, maybe she didn't *know* the names of all the girls. Everything was kept secret, remember? But she could have found out *these* names. For reasons of her own she kept a record."

The breeze came up, chilling the terrace. Jaye shivered and pushed her hair from her eyes, unconvinced. "But why?"

He shook his head. "Maybe to use against Hunsinger. But she was afraid to. Then when the Hunsinger babies grew up and started snooping around Cawdor, she realized the list could be worth money in another way."

"Then why didn't she offer it to somebody?" Jaye challenged.

"She was still afraid," Turner said. "But she knew the names were valuable, and she couldn't let go of them.

Finally she passed them on to the daughter. The daughter's scared, too. But she wants out."

Jaye pushed her glass away restlessly. "That's all ingenious. And the daughter goes through this whole cloak-and-dagger charade to elude Darth Hunsinger and the Evil Empire. No. There's got to be a simpler answer."

"Oh?" he said, cocking his head.

"Yes," she said with disgust. "That this list is a crock. And we just paid that—that con artist forty thousand dollars for it. I could kill her."

"First," he said, "it's not our money. It's Mr. D.'s."

"Details," she muttered.

"Second," Turner said, "you shouldn't smirch your immortal soul with thoughts of killing her. She's already worried that the Hunsinger bunch will do exactly that."

Jaye gave a cynical sigh. "That was probably theatrics. For our benefit."

"She seemed genuinely frightened."

"You frightened her," she accused. "You were rather rough on her, you know."

"Well," he said with a shrug, "there *was* my client's forty thousand at stake, as you yourself pointed out. Did you want me to just be a pussycat and hand it over?"

"Of course not," she retorted. "I'm just questioning your techniques, that's all."

"My techniques are time-honored staples of the courtroom. She hedges. I bear down. It's how it's done. But my question is, if she's genuinely afraid of Hunsinger's organization. I say yes."

"Maybe she's just paranoid," Jaye said, wanting to dismiss the whole idea.

"You were pretty paranoid yourself this morning," he reminded her. "We both were. Remember how you clung to me on that trolley?"

"I did not *cling* to you," she objected. "And it

doesn't seem like anybody followed us, because we're sitting here, perfectly in the open, and nobody's bothered us at all."

"So far," he said smugly.

"Don't muddy the water with imaginary problems," she told him. "The actual one's this—is this list for real? And if so, what good is it?"

"It's got one date that's interesting," he contradicted.

She was doubtful, almost scornfully so. "Which one?"

He unfolded his arms and pointed, with a kind of lazy authority, to the fourth item on the list. "That one."

Diane Englund   Fort Smith   Boy   Jan. 12, 1967

He said, "That date's a close one."

"No, it's not," Jaye objected. "None of the children was born in 1967. Who are you thinking of?"

His eyes met hers and held them. "You."

"No," she said impatiently. "She had a boy. And I was born in '66."

Think about it, his face told her.

Jaye shook her head. She knew the facts. She'd been born right before Christmas, December 22, 1966.

She remembered the photos in the album of her homecoming—her father must have snapped dozens. The Christmas tree had still been up. Nona was beaming, radiant, a shining triumph of maternalism. Jaye, bundled in white and capped with lace, had been a mere morsel of a person, red-faced and wrinkled—

December 22, 1966.

January 12, 1967.

Realization dazzled her like a flash of sheet lightning. The two dates were less than a month apart.

The girls went to stay with Hunsinger before they gave birth, so that people would not see signs of their pregnancy.

For how long did they hide? Two months? Three? Sometimes their confinements could have overlapped.

And if so, they would know each other.

Hope, a quick, desperate flutter of it, stirred.

"My God," she breathed to Turner. "You mean my—my mother and Diane Englund could have known each other?"

"There's a chance."

"So then," she said, her excitement rising, "any woman on this list could know others who were at Hunsinger's."

"That's what we need to find out," said Turner.

The possibilities bloomed in her mind like bright flowers. "And one name could lead to another. And another."

"If we're lucky," he said.

Her optimism was a frail and faulty craft. It had risen, but now it veered and dipped. She touched the list almost fearfully. "But all this happened more than thirty years ago. How do we begin to track these women down?"

Turner put his hand over hers. "I can do it," he said.

She looked at him, somehow believing him. Her pulses quickened crazily.

"But I've got to do it alone," he said.

No, said every beat of her heart. *No. No. No.*

"You've done your part," he said. "And Hunsinger's people are dangerous. I want you to go home. From here on, you'll only get in my way."

She turned her eyes back to the list. She stared at it hard, every name, every place, every date, every detail. "Let me think about it," she said at last.

"No," he said gently. He stroked his thumb over her

knuckles. "You owe me. I got the money. What I want in return is for you to go back to Boston. As soon as possible. Tonight."

She swallowed. She kept staring at the list. She bit her lower lip.

In the same quiet voice he said, "I'll take it from here. I bought the list. It's mine."

She stood and squared her shoulders. Without a word she picked up the list and tore it into scraps as she stepped to the low wall of the terrace.

Turner sprang to his feet. "Are you crazy?" he cried, but she had already released the pieces. They fell into space, eddied in the cool breeze, separating and drifting away like fat snowflakes.

He was at her side, and he gripped her shoulders so hard that his fingers dug into her flesh. "Are you fucking crazy?" he demanded, and his voice had turned almost savage.

She didn't care. He was hurting her, and she didn't care about that, either. Calmly she turned her face to his. She raised her left hand with its splint and its ribbon. With her index finger she tapped her forehead.

"The list you bought," she said, "is in here."

He stared at her as if she was indeed insane, and she thought, *Maybe I am.*

But she stared back at him coolly, knowing she had won. At least for the time being.

Judy Sevenstar had gone to the basement of the hotel and hidden in the women's rest room of the health bar to recount the money, not once but four times. The papery feel of the bills dizzied her with a combination of fear and power, and her mind spun with plans.

She knew the Crescent, knew its ins and outs; she

had worked there briefly as a maid when she was a teenager. She would slip out the back service entrance, and no one would see her.

Her van was parked in the farthest corner of the farthest lot of the Crescent. It was a chance, leaving it there, but she took it because she did not want to walk far carrying the money and she wanted to be safely in the open when she got in. Eureka was full of alleys and corners and niches where trouble could lurk.

She would get in the van in broad daylight, and she would take the fastest route out of town and drive on to Harrison.

In Harrison she would buy a plane ticket to Dallas. Dallas was a huge airport, a major hub, the spokes of its service radiating to every conceivable destination. When she reached Dallas, she was free, *free*, and she had the money to go anywhere she chose.

Where she would choose to go was El Paso. From El Paso she could slip over the border into Mexico, and in fucking Mexico with forty fucking thousand dollars she could live like a fucking queen.

She zipped the tote bag shut again and left the rest room, her head ducked down, her heart tripping madly in her chest. She walked down the dim hallway to the service door. There was no one in sight.

She slipped out the door, crossed the small service lot, and walked the path toward the parking lots. The money was surprisingly heavy, and her hand was sweaty on the handles of the bag.

She looked behind her to make certain nobody was following. She saw no one. Her footsteps quickened, and she thought, *Harrison, Dallas, El Paso, Juarez;* it thrummed through her mind like a mantra. *Harrison, Dallas, El Paso, Juarez.*

The van stood by itself; no other cars were parked

near. Once in it, she would be safe. She would lock the doors, so she was sealed inside it, like being inside a steel womb. And from it she would emerge reborn, Cawdor a thing of the past, behind her forever.

Harrison, Dallas, El Paso, Juarez.

The van was remarkable only for its neglect. She would sell it in Harrison, add a few hundred dollars more to her stash. In its back were her suitcases and that was all. Every other sorry thing she owned she'd left behind in the trailer.

She opened the door of the van, threw the tote bag and her purse onto the passenger seat, and climbed in. She snapped the lock shut again with a comforting *click*. Relief flooded through her, and euphoria danced in her veins.

Then something metallic and cold pressed into the back of her neck, just beneath the base of her skull. From the rear seat a familiar voice drawled, "Hello, Judy."

Her heart almost jolted out of her chest, and a bone-deep chill seized her.

"This is a gun, Judy," Will LaBonny's voice said softly, almost seductively. "And you're going to do everything I say."

The teachers with the matching T-shirts had come to the terrace, laughing and chattering, carrying drinks and bags of chips. There were five of them, and three sat at one of the tables. The other two went to the wall and gazed out at the view, exclaiming and pointing.

One of the women at the table cast a curious look at Turner and Jaye. Turner's nostrils flared, but he tried to make his hold on Jaye's shoulders appear more romantic than angry. He leaned close to her, as if whispering an endearment in her ear.

"That," he said between his teeth, "was a very stupid thing to do."

She smiled up at him, a smile of sweet docility. "I'm not going back to Boston. You need me."

Like a great gaping hole in the head, he thought. "No," he said, just as sweetly. "All I need is the information on the list. Write it down. Now."

"No way," she said. "Now let go of me or I'll start screaming and alarm all these nice ladies."

"You are goddam impossible," he whispered. He let her go, but for the benefit of all the nice ladies, he gave her a light kiss on the cheek. Her skin was cold and silky smooth as marble. He let her go.

He looked her up and down. Christ, he thought, she *was* impossible, maddeningly so, but she was also smart and gutsy. Standing there, so deceptively demure yet so defiant, she made something twist in his heart.

She was paler than usual, but her eyes were blue and smoldering as flame. The wind whipped her hair into a thick, floating skein of gold. The strange blade turned in his chest again.

"So everything I want and need is standing in front of me," he said dryly.

"You could think of it that way," she said.

"You're just a little treasure trove. You contain all the vital facts."

"That's me. Your friendly neighborhood trove."

He crossed his arms, gave her another measuring look. "Everything is hidden in your pretty head. But what if somebody blew that very pretty head off?"

She smiled again. "I'm not scared."

"And that solves everything," he said sarcastically. "But what if something does happen to you? How can anybody help your brother then? You'd better write that list down *now*, blondie."

Her smile died. "I'll make sure the information is safe. I won't take any chances with it."

"And how do you intend to do that?"

"I just will," she said.

He set his jaw impatiently because he knew she meant it.

"I've got to try to trace the Englund woman," he said. "All of them. That takes money. It takes connections."

"I'll get it done," she said.

"You don't know how," he challenged.

"I know more than you think," she said. "You talked about information brokers. I'll find one."

"You don't know *how*," he repeated.

"My lawyer will," she answered.

"You can't afford it."

"I'll max out my credit cards," she said. "I'll do it any way I can. And if I by God have to, I'll get it from you."

"*Me?*" he echoed in disbelief.

"If I don't have it, you'll have to give it to me," she said airily. "Or you won't get it either—will you?"

Christ, he thought, narrowing his eyes, *you're really something, aren't you?* He was appalled by her nerve, yet it intrigued him as well.

He put his hands in his pockets, shrugged. He sighed, then gave her a smile of reluctant acceptance. "All right. You hold all the cards."

"Yes I do," she said, her head held high. But under her bold words he heard the barest tremor of uncertainty.

Whenever Turner saw weakness in others, he studied it, scheming how he might turn such weakness to his advantage. She didn't really know what she was doing, she was improvising. She was good—but she was also an amateur.

Let's see how far you can go before you stumble, baby. Then you'll hand the power back to me.

He frowned slightly as if trying to read her mind. "You hold all the cards. So which one do you want to play?"

Her gaze met his, cool and level. "I call my lawyer. Give him these names, these facts. Tell him to hire an information broker and find out all he can about them."

He gave her a nod of restrained approval. So far the answer was right. But it should be. She'd stolen it from him.

"Where will you call from?" he asked.

Her expression grew wary. "A pay phone. Here. Now. To start this as soon as possible."

"Good." He eyed her critically, as if he were a demanding professor, she an unproven student. "Then what?" he asked.

"Then I don't wait for the information broker," she said. "I start trying to track down these people myself."

"In what order?" he asked.

She swallowed nervously. "The Englund woman. Maybe she's still in Fort Smith. If she is, she might be willing to talk."

"And if she is?"

She turned away from him. "We go see her."

He moved closer to her. He could feel the warmth of her body and wondered if she could sense his. "We should work together on this," he said. "I'm used to questioning people on sensitive issues. And some of this could get—well—emotional for you."

She kept her back to him. "I can control my emotions."

Could she? He wondered. He put his hands on her upper arms. She didn't flinch or try to resist.

"We may be traveling together," he said.

"That doesn't bother me," she said.

It's going to bother me, he thought and tried not to wince at the sensation in his groin.

"I hope we go to Fort Smith," he said in her ear. "Or Little Rock. Or Oklahoma City. I don't like the idea of taking you back to Cawdor."

She turned, looked up at him. The breeze lifted her hair to show the bruise and the cut on her forehead. He wished she'd look up at him with yearning or with affection, even if the emotion was reluctant.

Instead her attention seemed grimly focused on something far distant, not him. His hands were still on her; he stood so close that the breeze-tossed silk of her hair touched his chin, his cheek. She was close enough to kiss, but she wasn't thinking of him.

She was thinking of her brother, he could tell.

She drew away from him abstractedly, as if she'd hardly noticed how near he'd been.

"I have to find a phone," she said, and it was almost as if she were talking to herself.

LaBonny drove Judy's van. It jolted down the side road that led to the Kings River, pitching and rattling.

He smiled in contempt at its disrepair. "This is a piece of shit. How do you stand it?" Then he looked at her with his pale eyes and did the Cary Grant imitation he'd used since high school to persecute her. "Oh, Judy, Judy, Judy."

She was so scared that when they'd turned down this dirt road, she'd peed her pants, which LaBonny found repulsive. But in the backseat, Cody J. Farragutt thought it funny as hell. He was an amiable-looking freckled man in his late thirties, the same age as LaBonny. He sat with his ball cap pushed back boyishly on his head and his gun barrel pressed against the base of Judy's skull.

Cody J. smelled of sweat and spearmint gum, just as he had when they were teen-aged kids. He was fatter now, and his sideburns were turning gray, but he still wore the same expression of giddy nervousness he always got when there was going to be violence.

Behind Judy's van a third man, Bobby Midus, drove LaBonny's white truck, following them down the winding road. Bobby was the only man LaBonny would let touch his truck, although he knew the privilege hurt Cody J.'s feelings, for Cody J. had been with LaBonny the longest, from the time they were swaggering boys. They had taken Judy for a ride once back then, too.

Cody J. must be remembering the same thing. "Hey, Judy," he said, "this is like old times." He gave a thready giggle. "Like a class reunion, huh? Maybe we should sing the school song."

LaBonny smiled.

Although Judy's shoulders hunched and despair haunted her face, she somehow found the courage to shoot LaBonny a black look. She said, "Fuck yourself, both of you."

But her eyes brimmed, and streaks of tears ran in crooked tracks down her face.

LaBonny shook his head and pretended to look sad. "Oh, Judy, Judy, Judy," he said again in his Cary Grant voice.

Cody J. leaned back against his seat more comfortably. "You shouldn't say 'fuck,' Judy," he told her. "It could put ideas in a guy's mind. Remember?"

"I remember," she said bitterly.

"Who'd want her?" LaBonny asked. "She's pissed her pants."

"Wet pussy's wet pussy," said Cody J. and laughed his nervous laugh. "Hell, yes."

Judy's wrists were cuffed with Cody J.'s own Baird County Sheriff's Department cuffs. LaBonny shot her a glance that raked her up and down. "You look like a mongrel dog that's been beat and chained to sit in its own piss," he said. "But you still got meanness in your eyes. Maybe I'll have to beat it out of you."

Cody J. tickled the back of her neck with his gun. "There's more fun things than beatin'. Hey, Judy, you had a good time that night with us back in high school, didn't you?" he teased. "Didn't you? Tell me."

"Yeah," she said with dull hatred in her voice. "I had a great time."

Cody J. shifted and leaned closer to her so that his lips almost touched her ear. "Which one of us was the daddy, do you think? Huh? Don't women got an instinct about that kind of thing? Whose was it? LaBonny's? Delray's?" He gave her ear a sensual nip. "*Mine?*"

"I hope to God not yours," Judy said from between her teeth. She threw a glance of loathing at LaBonny. "*Or yours.*"

Cody J. said, "I woulda liked a little half-breed bastard runnin' around town. Long as he looked like me and not you."

Judy turned to him and lifted her lip in a sneer. "You shut up."

Cody J. patted her shoulder. "No hard feelin's, Judy. Didn't nothing come of it. Ol' Doc took care of you."

"Yeah," she said, her tone dark with disgust. "He took care of me, all right."

Cody J. laughed. "County'd be knee-deep in Indian

bastards if it wasn't for Doc. He kept a lot of good ol' boys like me and LaBonny here out of trouble. Eh, stud?" He clapped LaBonny on the shoulder.

Stud. The word made LaBonny's heart go icy. He was repelled that Cody J. would desire this broken, stinking woman; it might incite Bobby to want her, too, and the thought angered him and turned his stomach. Once LaBonny's tastes had included such things as simple, forced sex with a girl like Judy. No longer. He thinned his lips and said nothing.

The road was dwindling to a rutted path and the river was close. He heard the splash of its rushing before he saw it. Then the van bounced down one last curve, the scrub pine opened, and there was the river, wide and swollen and brown with the recent rains.

"Shitfire," Cody J. said. "It's damn near flood stage."

"More rain up this way," LaBonny said without emotion. He parked on a verge of red mud and rock. This road was hardly taken except by canoers who used it as access to the river. The spring air was still too cool for canoeing, the water too cold and wild. LaBonny didn't expect to meet any company this time of year.

He turned to face Judy. He took out his folding police knife, opened and closed the blade thoughtfully. "Why'd you meet those people, Judy? Why'd they give you forty thousand dollars? What'd you tell them?"

"Lies," she said, but he could see the fear in her dark eyes. "I told them a pack of lies, they believed me, gave me the money."

LaBonny took off his white hat and carefully set it on the backseat beside Cody J. Then he turned back to the woman. Again he began the meditative opening and closing of the knife.

"Judy," he said softly. "Please. Don't lie. Not to me. Please." He backhanded her across the face so hard that he felt her nose break beneath the stone of his big class ring. She fell back against the van's door, making sounds like a wounded animal, blood streaming from both nostrils.

"Jesus," Cody J. said, "you're gonna get blood all over the van."

"Ain't my van," LaBonny said. He glanced back at his hat to make sure no spatters of blood had struck it. He pulled down the van's visor and studied his face in its mirror. Only a single speck of crimson had hit his smooth cheekbone. He wet the tip of his middle finger and rubbed it away. He examined his hand. "Scraped my knuckle," he mused, and sucked at it tenderly.

Judy lay hunched against the door, making little sobbing noises. She held the crumpled hem of her windbreaker to her nose to staunch the flow of blood.

LaBonny gave her a sad look. "You brought that on yourself. And it hurt. I *know* it hurt. Hell, it even hurt me."

He examined his knuckle regretfully, then turned his attention back to Judy. "Now, honey, tell me why those folks gave you forty thousand dollars. Exactly what'd you give them in return?"

Bobby Midus had pulled the white truck up behind them now, parking it so that it blocked the road, just in case some fool did chance to come this way. Judy kept sobbing.

Bobby got out of the truck. Cody J. lowered his window. "Hey," Bobby said cheerfully. "We gonna rape her?"

Christ, LaBonny thought, *they both think with their dicks.* He ignored the younger man. "Cody J.," he said wearily, "give me your knife. It's bigger."

"No!" Judy screamed, her voice thick with blood and mucous. "No!"

But LaBonny held his hand out, and Cody J. laid the knife across the palm. It was a navy SEAL knife, with a blade over seven inches long. LaBonny took it and studied it with an approving frown as he ran his finger down its edge.

"Judy," he said in his most gentlemanly tone, "I asked you a question. You answer me if you want to keep your ears, your nose. I'm going to start whittling you down bit by bit, girl, if you don't cooperate."

She bowed her head. The only sound she made was a broken sob.

He sighed. "Cody J.," he said, "hold her down."

Cody J. sighed, but his fat, freckled hands closed on her shoulders and LaBonny seized her hair in his left hand and yanked it hard, so that she had to raise her face to him.

He brought the knife to the side of her head, let the blade's edge press with surgical precision where the ear joined the skull. "I got to warn you, Judy," he said in his low voice. "This is just going to hurt like a sonuvabitch."

"I had—I had a list," Judy stammered, trying to shrink back from him.

"What kind of list?" LaBonny ran the knife's blade to the underside of her ear, bore down until a drop of blood welled and trickled down her neck.

"Don't!" she begged. "My mother had a list of girls who came to the clinic. It wasn't long. Just five names."

"Now why'd your mama do that? She knew the doc didn't want no records."

"I don't know why, I swear," Judy almost babbled. "Maybe she thought it'd be worth money someday."

"But she never used it?" LaBonny asked.

"No," pleaded Judy. "Honest to God."

"Why not? She afraid what happened to Luther'd happen to her?"

"Yes," Judy said—"move the knife, please. You can have the money. Just don't cut me anymore. Please."

LaBonny gave a soft laugh. "Shhh. Now you'd be a foolish woman, wouldn't you, if you didn't have another copy of that list. Where is it?"

He moved the knife up to the edge of her eye. "You got such black eyes, just black as night. You see good out of them? Indians are supposed to see good."

She was afraid to move now; the knife hovered within a fraction of an inch from her iris. She whispered, "There's a copy of the list in the glove compartment."

"Thank you," he said. He drew back and opened the glove box. A cheap pink envelope lay inside. "This it?" he asked her.

"Yes," she said breathlessly.

He opened the envelope, unfolded the paper, read it. "Five names," he said with a slight frown. "That's all?"

"That's all, I swear to God, I swear on my mother's grave."

He bent nearer. "Swear by your eyes?"

"Yes," she cried. "Please—"

He shook the paper so that it rattled. "What do you know about these women?"

"Nothing." Judy wept. "I don't know if they're dead or alive."

"That's all the information you gave these folks? They gave you forty thousand dollars for it? For just this little list with hardly nothing on it?"

"That's right," she said. "They're rich. You can tell they're rich."

"Hell, Judy," LaBonny said with the ghost of a smile, "you should have asked them for more. Now what were you gonna do with that money? Run away?"

"Yes. That's all. I didn't want to hurt anybody. I just wanted to get away."

"Why? You don't like our town? It don't have nice memories for you?"

Cody J. snickered. "Surely you got pleasant memories of me, Judy. A hard man is good to find."

LaBonny said, "Why'd you want to leave us, Judy? Did you remember Luther and get scared?"

She said nothing. Her breath came in ragged gasps.

"Now you haven't done nothing at all like Luther did," LaBonny said soothingly. "Do you know what Luther did?"

Her eyes said she did. She did not try to nod with the knife so near.

"He tried to blackmail the doc," LaBonny said in a sorrowful voice. "But you'd never do anything like that, would you?"

"N-No," she whispered.

"He saw too much, Luther did." LaBonny began to wipe the edge of the blade back and forth across her cheek, a slow, almost loving movement. "Now you would never tell folks—strange folks from out of town—what Luther saw, would you? Not even for money."

"No," she panted. "Never."

"What Luther and Hollis saw is our secret, isn't it?"

"Yes," Judy said. She swallowed, gagged slightly. "Yes."

"What about Hollis?" he asked. "Were you gonna help Hollis with this money? Where is Hollis? Do you know?"

"You—you've done something with him," she said, tears rising in her eyes. "I know. But I won't tell. I swear."

"Good," said LaBonny. "That's real good."

"Look," she said. "You can have all the sex you want. Anything you want. You, Cody J., Bobby, too—"

He looked deep into her eyes. Something that wasn't quite a smile touched his mouth. He cut her throat from ear to ear.

"Jesus," Cody J. said in shock. "I didn't think you were going to kill her right in the van. I thought you were getting ready to *fuck* her."

"She knew too much," LaBonny said, his upper lip curling as he wiped the blood from his hand on a clean bandanna handkerchief. "I'll warrant she talked too much, too. I could see it in her eyes."

"Jesus," Cody J. said, "that's a *lot* of blood. It's like sticking a pig."

"Get rid of her," LaBonny said. "Have Bobby help you. The van, too. You know how. I got to wash up."

LaBonny got out of the van, walked to the river's edge, and began to wash his hands and arms. His long-sleeve shirt was ruined, so he stripped down to his T-shirt. He tore the shirt into bloodied ribbons and watched, without emotion, as the water carried them away.

Then he rose and went back to the men.

Cody J. and Bobby had pulled Judy out of the van and were dragging her by her feet to the brink of the river. Cody J. looked slightly sick, and Bobby was subdued, almost sullen. The kid always claimed he was born with a hard-on. It was an interesting image, but he needed to learn to be more discriminating.

"What we gonna do about that lawyer and the woman?" Cody J. asked in an uneasy voice. "Go back after 'em? What?"

"One thing at a time," said LaBonny. He handed

Cody J. the combat knife and nodded at Judy's body. "Open her up," he said. "So she'll sink."

LaBonny stood and watched Cody J. do it, slitting her open as if she were a deer being butchered. "Fill her with rocks," LaBonny said. "That'll keep her down."

"Jesus," Cody J. said. "I ain't never done this to no woman. It seems like such a waste."

Bobby shot LaBonny a glance that said he agreed. Then the boy turned his blue eyes resolutely away from the body and seemed to watch something far in the distance across the river. His handsome face was unnaturally pale.

Let them be surprised by his actions, LaBonny thought; let them be afraid of him, it would be to his advantage, keep them off guard and in line.

He gazed down at the woman with satisfaction and shook his head as if to say, *It had to be.* She had no power now, either through knowledge or sex, to expose anyone.

He looked again into her eyes, which were blind and staring and still. He had to say it one more time in his mocking Cary Grant accent. "Judy, Judy, Judy."

TWELVE

---⚜---

ORT SMITH WAS FULL OF PEOPLE NAMED ENGLUND. IT
burst with them. They must have been the founders
and the main settlers and the most prolific SOBs who
had ever lived, and they had all fallen in love with the
place and none of them had ever left. They had addi-
tional peculiarities: hardly any of them ever answered
their phones, and those who did didn't know one thing
worth knowing.

Turner had called Fort Smith information to find all
these goddam Englunds while Jaye had called her lawyer
about the list. Then they'd divided up the Englund
phone numbers like two soldiers of fortune dividing
booty and begun this unholy marathon.

The Crescent Hotel had a row of antique phone
booths along the west wall of its lobby. There were three

of them, elaborate cages of glass and gleaming oak. Jaye and Turner had each been sequestered in one of these booths for more than an hour, making phone call after phone call.

Now Jaye suddenly hung up her receiver with an air of crisp finality and knocked on the pane of glass separating them. Turner's nerves leaped to attention. *She's got something.*

She tucked her gold pen behind her ear, thrust open the door of her booth, and came to his. She nodded, her expression tense but excited.

"Thanks, anyway," he said into his own receiver, and hung up. He had pretended to ignore her while they worked, but in truth he had watched her closely. She'd used the phone like a pro, talking with concentrated zeal, taking notes with a swift, no-nonsense air.

He opened the door of his own booth. "Well?" he asked.

Her breath was coming fast, which made the breast of her jacket rise and fall in a fascinating way. She said, "I found a relative who knows Diane Englund. A cousin. She'll talk to us."

He raised his eyebrow, surprised, impressed, and more than a little irritated. *Blondie, you must have got awfully damn lucky.*

"She's in Fort Smith?" he asked. He couldn't believe it.

"In a little town called Oxford, in Mississippi," she said. "About six hours from here."

"Oxford," he said without enthusiasm.

"I talked to her brother in Fort Smith. He said he didn't remember Diane very well, but his sister did. He gave me her number in Oxford. Her name is Rita Walsh."

He studied the excitement on her face, wondering if

her hope was going to be undermined again. "And Diane's alive? This Walsh woman knows where she is?"

Jaye nodded and swallowed. "Yes. But she says this is something we should talk about in person. Not over the phone."

He frowned slightly. "You told her what this was about?"

"I told her about Patrick—I had to. She didn't want to talk to me. Why should she?"

He shook his head in resignation. It was best to lead up to these things slowly, subtly, but of course she had led with her heart. She probably always did. There was no helping it, and what the fuck, a lead was a lead.

"When did she say she'd see us?"

"First thing in the morning. Before school. She's a teacher."

"First thing in the morning," he repeated. "So when do you want to start for—Oxford?"

Her answer was exactly what he expected. "Now," she said without hesitation.

He looked her up and down. "We won't get there until after dark."

"I don't care," she said.

"We'll have to stay overnight."

She tossed her hair rebelliously. "I don't care about that, either."

"Your things are back at Miss Doll's. Do you want to go back and get them?"

"No. It'll slow us up. I don't need much to spend the night."

He met her eyes. "I don't either."

A vibration jolted between them, and the air around them seemed to thicken and crackle. A primal awareness skimmed like a drug through his blood. It sang a simple song: *I want you.* He could feel his eyes telling her that at last.

For a moment he thought she felt the same. But then her face seemed to become deliberately blank, and she looked away from him to the big stone fireplace. "All I care about is Patrick," she said. "I want to get there before this woman changes her mind."

He nodded and struggled to slow his libido to the prescribed gait. "We can stop and buy whatever we need," he said.

"Sure," she said, keeping her eyes on the ornate curves and angles of the fireplace. "I suppose I should call Miss Doll so she doesn't throw out my suitcase."

He looked her up and down again with yearning he fought to dull. "I suppose. But don't tell her where you're going."

A grim little smile curved the corner of her mouth. "I'll tell her I'll be back in a day or two."

"Right," he said, and set his jaw.

She glanced at her watch self-consciously. Still she did not meet his gaze. "Then I've got to call Belgium— God, it's already seven o'clock there."

He nodded again.

"Maybe he'll be better today," she said, her voice growing a little unsteady. "Maybe he'll be able to talk."

"I hope so," he said. He was surprised to realize how deeply he meant it. He was shocked, in fact.

She tossed him a strange, apologetic glance. "And I need to talk to my mother. She'll be wondering about me."

How prim, he thought. How anachronistic. Yet how somehow blackly appropriate to this whole mess: *I need to talk to my mother.*

"Yeah," he said.

"Don't worry," she said, "I won't let her get her hopes up." She cocked her head as if trying to convince herself that she wouldn't, either.

"That's a good idea," he said.

She murmured, "Maybe we can stop at the Wal-Mart on the way out of town. I saw one. I'll need a toothbrush, a change of underwear, things like that."

"No problem," he said.

She turned back to the phones, entered the booth again.

He put his hands in his pockets, looked off into the far, dim corner of the lobby's ceiling.

He thought of her words "a change of underwear." He thought of her in her underwear, and he thought of her out of it.

He thought, *This is turning into a real ballbreaker.*

LaBonny drove the white Chevrolet back toward Cawdor. The truck had always been a sweet and easy rider, and the highway flowed beneath its wheels as smoothly as silk unspooling.

Bobby Midus had been on duty the night before, and now he slept, his blond head leaning against the window on the passenger side.

Cody J. sat slumped in the middle, chewing on his thumbnail and staring out at the mountains with an air of moodiness. His nerve, thought LaBonny, was weaker these days, but he still had some good use in him.

"Is Adon gonna be fucking mad?" Cody J. asked uneasily. "That we let them other people get away?"

LaBonny shrugged. "We couldn't be in two places at once."

Cody J. considered this. He kept staring and chewing. Then he said, "Well, I *know* that. But will he be fucking mad, man? That we let 'em meet and all?"

"What'd you want?" LaBonny asked sarcastically. "We walk into the Crescent in the middle of the day and break it up? Besides, Judy's the one that's real trouble, not them."

Cody J. shifted uneasily and pulled the bill of his ball cap down farther. "Well," he said, his voice almost petulant, "if she gave 'em that list, now they're gonna be trouble, too, ain't they?"

LaBonny smiled and shook his head at the foolishness of the question. "That depends on how dangerous it is for them to *know* those names, Cody J. You can't know that and neither can I. They *might* be trouble. It's up to Adon to decide. And then we work from there."

Cody J. refused to be comforted. "Well, he's probably gonna be fucking mad, man. What if they don't go back to Cawdor? What if they go chasin' off to someplace on that list?"

"The blonde, she left all her stuff," LaBonny said. He knew this to be true because Miss Doll had phoned the news to Adon early that morning. "Her car, too. They'll be back. Sooner or later."

"I woulda had Judy one last time," the other man said, almost sadly. "Just for old times' sake. Knew her from way back when. Shitfire. Sometimes this job ain't no pleasure."

"Neither is the gas chamber," LaBonny said in his mellow voice.

"So I hear," Cody J. said with resignation. He reached into the back pocket of his jeans and drew out a stick of gum. He began to unwrap it.

"Don't chew gum in my truck," LaBonny commanded, his tone suddenly sharp.

"Hey," Cody J. said, affronted and righteous, "it's only *gum*, man."

"You don't chew gum in my truck, you don't smoke, you don't eat or drink."

"How can gum fuck up your truck, man?"

"I don't want your wrappers and shit in my ashtray."

"I'll throw 'em out the window, man."

"You don't chew gum in my truck."

Cody J. sighed as if his dignity had been deeply offended. He stuffed the stick of gum back into his pocket and crossed his fat arms. He stared out the window with a sullen expression.

After a few miles he sighed again. When he spoke, his tone was conciliatory. "Christ. Eureka fucking Springs. She had to go and pick Eureka. I didn't think Judy was that smart. She gave me a couple bad minutes there."

LaBonny only smiled to himself. He didn't think it had been so smart of Judy. He'd simply driven by the Buick when it pulled into the parking lot, then let Cody J. out as soon as the truck went around the corner. Cody J. had strolled back, seen the woman and the lawyer board the trolley. It didn't take a brain surgeon to figure they were going to the Crescent. It was the trolley's ultimate destination, Judy had worked there once, it was home turf to her.

And Judy, like the fool she was, had parked that rust bucket of a van right in one of the Crescent's lots. Better, as if she were cooperating with them, she'd parked it in the most isolated corner. It was child's play to pick the lock of the van's door, and they had done it so boldly and quickly, nothing furtive about it, nothing that looked suspicious in the least.

Cody J. scratched at his elbow and shook his head. "You don't think nobody'll find her body?"

LaBonny gave him one of his nearly imperceptible smiles. He didn't think so. They'd weighted her good, and the river was high.

"Not for a long time," he said.

"Well," Cody J. persisted, "what about when they do?"

"The fish're probably eating her face off right now," LaBonny said.

"What about the van?" Cody J. argued. "What if they find it, identify it?"

"Cody J.," LaBonny said. "You worry too much. It's not good for you."

Cody J. understood and shut up. He wasn't usually such a babbler, and LaBonny thought it was because he'd never before killed a woman. Neither had he himself, but it had given him a peculiar satisfaction. There was no sexual thrill in it—almost the opposite. Killing her negated the myth of the simple power women held over men. There was no longer anything simple about LaBonny's appetites, and Judy was an insult to them.

Besides, she'd needed killing. She'd always known too much, and she'd been too fucking close to Luther for his death not to eat at her. They should have killed her back when they killed Luther.

It had taken the lawyer and the bitch from Boston to flush out Judy, to force Adon's hand. Adon was cockbent over his skinny wife, he acted like a pussy himself most of the time, he'd always let his feeling for the woman run him. Now even Adon could see that there were things that had to be done. He was, of course, not strong enough to do them himself. But LaBonny was.

There was one more person they needed quit of, and

Adon was close to ready to do it, at long last. That was that fucking idiot Hollis. Then they'd all be in hell where they belonged, Luther, Judy, Hollis.

Yes, LaBonny thought, it was time.

Barbara Mowbry sat on the sunporch of the ranch house, staring outward. It had rained a short time ago, a driving spring rain that had lasted only minutes.

Now a rainbow, faint and delicate, shimmered in the western sky. The sky itself was blue again, with only a few scarves of cloud, their edges silvered by the sun.

Adon paused in the doorway, marveling unhappily at how Barbara could be so frail yet still so beautiful. In the afternoon light, her skin seemed almost luminous, as if her soul was starting to glow through it and dissolve the flesh.

When she realized Adon was in the room, she spoke, her voice soft. "Look at the sky. It looks like a picture out of a fairy-tale book, doesn't it?"

She sat on the white wicker love seat with her legs curled beneath her like a little girl, her face raised skyward. Adon moved to the table beside her and on it placed the drink he'd made for her, a very weak one. The one in his own hand was much stronger, a double.

He looked again at the sky. It did not seem truly beautiful to him. The rainbow was only a trick of physics, something to do with light and moisture and prisms. The sky's blueness was only an effect of distance. The clouds were nothing but particles of water. But Barbara seemed rapt.

"You should paint a picture of that," he said. "You used to enjoy that, painting pictures."

Her expression had been one of fragile delight, but

suddenly it altered into blankness. "Oh, no," she said. "I couldn't do that anymore. I've lost the urge."

Adon tried to cajole her. "But you were so good. Everybody said so."

"I was nothing, really," she said. "I could copy, that's all. I couldn't really create. I'm not—creative." Her expression grew ineffably sad.

Adon's mouth suddenly tasted as if it were filled with ashes. He had done it again, he thought with helpless shame. He had been trying to make her happy and done the opposite.

"Hollis could always draw better than I could," she said. "Where is he, do you think? Will he be all right?"

Hollis had lived near her, tended her, played with her when she was a child. Barbara cared for him, as she cared for all weak or wounded things, and Adon could have killed the cook for letting her know that Hollis had run away.

"He'll be fine," lied Adon. "But we'll have to send him someplace where he's supervised. For his own good. I hate to do it, but he can't run off like this. It's too dangerous for him."

"Poor Hollis," she said. "He was always so good to me. He'd talk to me—then. If only he'd talk again—that would help."

Adon nodded, but he knew that Hollis's mutism was all that had saved his life so far. It was not that Hollis could not talk; he had simply stopped speaking to anyone other than close family when he was little more than a boy. Now that Luther was dead, he spoke to no one, and that, until this foolish flight of his, had been his salvation.

Barbara reached for her drink, toyed with the glass, but did not lift it to her lips. Her hand fluttered back to her lap, empty.

"Have a sip or two," Adon pleaded. "It'll help your appetite."

"Umm," she said, and looked at the fading rainbow.

He sat down beside her on the love seat. He put his hand on her thigh affectionately. He could feel the bone. *Christ, Christ, Barbara. What are you doing to yourself?*

But she did not need recriminations, her doctor said, she needed understanding. Adon loved his wife, loved her far too much, but try as he might, he could not understand the depth of her sorrow or how to cure it.

"So how's my girl?" he asked with false heartiness, rubbing her thigh. "I came out here to see what you were thinking about so hard."

"I came out to plan the garden," she said. "But then I saw the sky and stopped just to look."

"Ah, the garden," he said with the same enthusiasm. In truth, he wondered if the conversation was wandering back into dangerous territory. The garden, in her mind, was connected with Hollis.

"The tulips aren't coming up well," she said gravely. "I'm afraid for them. The winter was so hard. Sometimes things just can't—be saved. They're too weak."

"We'll get you new tulips, stronger ones," he promised. "We'll replace 'em."

"Things," she said, "can't always be replaced."

He took her hand, disturbed at how spare it seemed in his large, thick one. "Whatever money can buy that makes you happy, you can have. You know that."

"I know," she said, not looking at him. "That's what Daddy always said, too."

Then, to his dismay, tears welled in her eyes.

"Barbara," he said in alarm.

"But what I want is—" she said—"what I want is for everything to be the way it was. I want Daddy well again.

I want my brother. I want us all to be together and happy. And, oh, Adon, I want my baby back again."

She put her face in her hands and began, soundlessly, to cry.

She let Adon take her into his arms, and he tried, desperately, to comfort her. "Oh, sweetheart," he said in anguish, "is it Hollis that brought this on?"

"I suppose," she said weakly.

"It'll be fine," he promised. "And I won't let anything hurt you again. Not ever again. I swear it."

I will do anything to protect you, he thought fiercely. *I will kill whoever hurts or threatens you in any way. I swear it. It will be done.*

As Turner drove, he watched the land and its character change. He and Jaye left the mountains behind, and as the sun lowered, they crossed the flatness of the Arkansas delta with its miles of still-barren cotton fields.

Night fell, and they bypassed the sprawl of lights that was the Elvis-haunted city of Memphis. They crossed the border, and the state of Mississippi seemed to close around them like a dark, velvet fist.

The sky was black. The land was flat, but not empty like the delta; it was clothed with the thick secrecy of pine woods. The air was warm and heavy with humidity.

The little city of Oxford was more comforting. It was the home of the state's greatest university, Old Miss. Although the town's outskirts were ringed by the usual motels and fast-food joints, they quickly gave way to its true heart, which was of the old south.

In the town square, history seemed to have penetrated every brick, every stone. It was dominated by a looming courthouse that looked both solid and spectral, ghost-ridden, perhaps, by its complex Confederate past.

But the shops and restaurants were brightly lit and busy, the streets lively with students both black and white. A bookstore whose window was impossibly jammed with displays stood with its door invitingly open to passersby.

"Are you hungry?" Turner asked Jaye. "Want something to eat?"

"No, thanks," she said with an abstracted air.

They had eaten on the move, snagging coffee and bad sandwiches and candy bars at gas stations and rest stops. She had actually eaten some goddam regional confection called a Goo-Goo Cluster, which looked to him like something that might be found in the bottom of a cage at the zoo.

As long as the daylight held, she'd immersed herself in one of her books. She might have set off this morning without her toothbrush, but she'd brought her goddam required reading. All through the long afternoon, she'd pored over *Bone Marrow Transplants: A Guide for Patients, Family, and Donors.*

When the light had started to fail, she'd whipped a penlight out of her purse and read by that. He didn't see how she kept from getting the worst headache that hell could hammer out.

For a short time this afternoon, Jaye had been happy. She'd called her sister-in-law in Belgium, and Patrick was better. His fever had dropped two degrees, and he was rational, though weak. Jaye's face had been glowing when she'd hung up the phone.

Tomorrow, she said, she "might even be able to talk to him!" At that moment she made the possibility seem more exciting than an interview with both God and the pope.

But then she'd withdrawn into herself and stayed

there. All the way to Mississippi she'd read, and her reading had been like a wall between them.

Turner knew she was concerned about Patrick. He knew she hungered to learn all she could about her brother's illness. But the wall also seemed designed to shut out Turner and to isolate Jaye from the rest of the world, to keep her alone with only her love for Patrick.

For a few tense and naked seconds in the lobby of the Crescent, he and Jaye had looked at each other with the heightened sexual awareness that shakes the body like electricity. Without words he had asked the most primal erotic question, and she had answered: *Maybe—yes, I want it, too—Maybe.*

Clearly she regretted that moment and thought it a mistake, so she had canceled and nullified it. But he was a persuasive man; it was his stock-in-trade. Should not he, of all people, be able to change her mind?

"I suppose we ought to get a place for the night," he said casually.

"Yes," she said. "And we'll pay separate bills. I don't want Mr. D. picking up the tab for a second room."

The rejection was as clear, sharp, and unpleasant as a needle thrust under the fingernail.

But was it final? Turner was not only persuasive, he was tenacious. Unspeakably so, said his enemies.

"Did you see anyplace that appealed to you?" he asked, hoping for an encouraging hint.

"There was a Budget Inn back on the highway," she said. "It's plenty good for me. If you want someplace fancier, just drop me off. We can meet in the morning."

"The Budget Inn is fine," Turner lied. "I've always liked the Budget Inn. Good buy for the money." He hated Budget Inns. They had lumpy mattresses and thin walls and plastic drinking glasses. The furniture was ugly, the housekeeping slipshod, and when you turned on the water, the plumbing shuddered and groaned.

So he drove to the Budget Inn. It was, of course, located at the highway's busiest intersection so that the building would tremble all night to the roar of passing trucks.

They parked and Jaye went with him to the office to check in. She asked for her own separate room, paid for it with her own card. The clerk looked at Turner strangely, as if to say, *Separate rooms? Are you fucking nuts, buddy?* Turner ignored him. The night was far from over.

He walked her to her room, stopped before her door. She had her purse over her shoulder, her book bag in her right hand, and the plastic Wal-Mart sack in her left. In the Wal-Mart sack were toiletry items, a new pink sweater, and a change of underwear: pink bikini panties and matching bra. She'd not bought anything to sleep in. He'd made note of that.

She put her key in the door, twisted it until the lock clicked open. She turned to him and smiled up politely. "We have to get up tomorrow bright and early. I need to call my mother, let her know we made it."

He braced his hand against the door frame, leaned nearer. "We should talk. Lay out what we're going to say to this woman tomorrow. We can't just waltz in there and blurt out anything. It's a delicate situation."

She pushed her hair back from her face, shrugged. "I'll count on you. You're the expert."

"But you're the crucial one," he said. "We're asking if she can lead us to *your* mother."

"I've told you," she said, "that's not an issue for me. If we find the woman that's my—mother, she's a means to an end, that's all. I want information from her. Nothing more."

He touched an errant lock of her blond hair. "She may want more from you. Have you thought of that?"

"I don't have any more to give," Jaye said with a coolness that was almost convincing.

"And she may not want to see you at all," he persisted, his voice soft. "The memories may be too painful. What then?"

"Good night, Turner," she said, her tone businesslike and final. She opened the door. His groin throbbed with disappointment.

"Wait," he said. "It's been a long day. I've got a bottle of wine. Maybe we could have a few drinks, discuss this a little further."

"Good night, Turner," she said again. She raised up and kissed him lightly on the cheek.

He fought the urge to haul her into his arms and kiss her until her head spun and her knees wobbled and her hormones screamed, *Take me, take me. I've got to have you.*

"One glass," he said. "There're so many things I don't know about you. I want to hear about you and your brother. I envy your closeness, I envy him. He must be quite a guy—"

"He is. Night. Have to call my mother."

She slipped inside, closed the door. He heard the depressing and excluding click of the lock. Fool, he cursed himself. Mook. Loser.

She had to call her mother. Had he fallen through some hideous loop in time and gone back to junior high school? Why was he in some godforsaken town in Mississippi lusting after a distracted blonde when back home in Philadelphia he could have satisfied himself, at a whim, with any of twenty women? Some were beautiful and bright, and some were beautiful and stupid, but nature had given them compensating talents.

Why was he getting his balls in a twist over this woman? It was insane, he was insane. He'd been in the boonies too long.

He went back to the car, got his own goddam Wal-Mart bag and the now superfluous bottle of wine. He'd go up to his own room, take an extremely cold shower, the more unpleasant the better. He'd open the wine and drink the whole bottle. What the hell.

He went to his room. He made a short, tight-lipped call to Mr. DelVechio. He checked his computer, both e-mail and fax messages, printed out the information from the brokers about Jaye's brother and mother. They seemed decent, clean-living, ordinary people. But they held her in thrall, a spell he could not penetrate.

He went to the shower like a man who is going to his own execution but no longer gives a damn. The shower pipes thundered and shrieked and spat out rust along with the cold water. *Excellent,* he thought grimly.

He was drying himself with one of the Budget Inn's Amazing Napless Towels when the phone rang. *Christ,* he thought, *who knows I'm here?* Nobody did, except for Mr. DelVechio's people. Could something have happened to the old man? Could the Angel of Death have suddenly decided it had toyed with him too long and swooped down to bear off his decaying body?

Not yet, Turner thought in sudden anxiety. *Don't let him die—not yet.*

"Hello," he said, fearing he would hear the voice of Anna, the old man's nurse, croaking out the bad news.

But it was not Anna. It was Jaye.

Her voice was hesitant, almost apologetic. "Turner," she said. "I've been thinking. If it's not too late to take you up on your offer, I'd like to have that drink after all. What do you think?"

"I think I can be there in three minutes," said Turner.

He scrambled into his clothes and thrust his key and his jackknife with the corkscrew into his pocket. He snatched up the bottle of wine and left the room. He walked the few steps to her door and knocked.

"Jaye?" he called softly.

The door immediately opened. She stood there barefoot, in her panties and sweater. She didn't say a word. She took him by the hand and drew him inside the room. She wound her arms around his neck and kissed him.

"I changed my mind," she whispered.

THIRTEEN

———❦———

S HE WAS VAGUELY AWARE THAT HE DROPPED THE WINE
bottle. It struck the carpet, rolling away with a soft,
crystal gurgle.

He hauled her close, his mouth locking on hers. His
skin was still cool from the shower, and somehow the
scent of hotel soap seemed maddeningly erotic to her.
The clean taste of him pulsated on her lips, and he
opened her mouth with his kisses so that they could taste
more deeply and greedily of each other still.

For a moment she felt paralyzed with unexpected
need; she had known she wanted his touch, but not how
much. She felt fettered by her yearning for him, impris-
oned by it.

An amazing recklessness rose in her, burning, and

his every movement fanned it higher. She arched her body against his, and her fingers laced themselves in the damp thickness of his hair.

He gasped and pulled her closer with such force that she gasped, too. *My God, he's strong,* she thought. And then, *My God, he's good.*

Desire thickened her blood, richly weighting her body with it. Her heart slammed crazily. His hands were on her, gliding over her, moving beneath her sweater, closing over her breasts with sure possessiveness.

She ached for more of his touch. But suddenly his hands went still, he drew back. He looked at her, his mouth curving and his eyes smoky with lust. He lifted her sweater her head, skimmed it off, so she stood before him in only her panties. He stripped them away.

He stared at her as he unbuttoned his own shirt, cast it off. His chest was broad and hard, with a thick haze of curly dark hair. The muscles of his shoulders glistened in the lamplight.

He lifted her and carried her to the bed.

When they finished making love, he turned off the bedside lamp and held her, both their hearts beating fast.

For a long time she lay with her face against his chest, the hair of it tickling her cheek. *Well,* she thought fatalistically, *that was shameless enough. And then some.*

Her muscles had been taut with sheer desire, then limp with satisfaction. But now her old unrest began to haunt her again. This blind plunge into sexual oblivion had solved nothing and in all likelihood had only made things more complicated.

His arm was around her, his chin resting on her head. Perhaps he could feel the tension stealing back into her body. He said, "I thought you invited me over for a glass of wine."

"It was a ruse," she said unhappily.

He laughed, kissed her forehead. "I feel so—used."

"You should," she said, and turned away from him. For she had used him, she knew. Just as he had used her. She did not wholly regret it, but neither was she happy about it.

They lay in silence. He toyed with a lock of her hair. "Worried?" he asked with the kindness that puzzled her so deeply.

"Yes," she said.

He wound her hair around his finger. "About your brother?"

"Yes."

He let the lock of hair go. His hand moved to her ear, traced its curve. "And about tomorrow?"

"That, too," she admitted.

They were silent a long moment. The tip of his forefinger trailed across her cheek, touched the corner of her mouth, stroked her lower lip lightly.

He said, "Have you let yourself think about your own birth mother? What you'll do if you find her?"

She gazed into the darkness. "No."

"Are you going to let yourself think about it?"

"No."

"Do you want me to stop asking about it?"

"Yes," she said, troubled by her own cowardice about the subject.

They fell silent again. He said, "Are you going to have trouble getting to sleep?"

She considered lying to him, but it seemed stupid after such intimacy. "Yes," she said.

"Sit up," he said. "I'll pour you a glass of wine."

She blinked as the lamp flooded the room with what seemed an unbearable brightness.

She felt the bed move, the sheets rustle as he sat up. "I wonder if I can find my pants," he mused. "I probably threw them into the next county. Ah—there."

The bed jiggled as he got up. She heard the soft sound of fabric sliding over flesh, the purr of his zipper. She didn't turn or look. She kept staring, unseeing, into the corner. She heard the soft squeak and thump of the wine cork being pulled, the crackle of paper as he unwrapped the room's plastic glasses, the babble of the wine being poured.

Then his legs were in her field of vision, his hand holding a glass of dark red wine toward her. She sat up, holding the sheet across her breasts, and took the glass. She glanced up at him almost shyly.

Concern was etched on his face. Still bare-chested, he sat beside her, his own glass in his hand. His dark hair was tousled. He clicked his glass against hers. "Thank you for changing your mind," he said.

"I don't think my mind had much to do with it," she said ruefully.

"Your mind's been working overtime," he said. "Maybe it was time to let the body take over."

She held her wine, untasted. She tried to choose her words carefully. "What happened here," she said, "doesn't have to mean anything. I don't intend to make any claims on you or anything like that."

He shrugged. "Don't worry," he said with a cynical smile. "I know your emotions are spoken for."

She looked at him questioningly, not sure she understood.

He took a sip of wine. "Patrick's a lucky man. To be loved as much as he is."

"Lucky," she said with bitter irony.

"Lucky," he repeated. "I told you I wanted to hear about you and him. Why don't you tell me?"

There he went again, she thought, being too kind. *What the hell,* she thought. *Why not?*

She leaned back against the pillow. "Nona said from the start I considered him *my* baby," she said. "From the moment she brought him home. I don't remember that, of course. I can't remember life without him."

"You weren't jealous of him?"

"No," she said honestly. "He wasn't the kind of person you could be jealous of. He was so sweet-natured, so much fun—so *good.*"

"What about you?" Turner asked. "Were you good, too?"

She tilted her glass back and forth, watching the light play on the dark wine. "No. Not me."

The corner of his mouth quirked up. "Why not?"

"I was stubborn. Horribly stubborn, Nona says. And hyperactive. And a tomboy. And she says I never had a grain of tact."

"I'm glad you outgrew it all," he said. "Especially the stubborn part."

It was a gibe, she knew, but a gentle one. She said, "Our father died when I was four and Patrick was two. Nona was devastated. For a long time it seemed there was no joy in her, only worry. So Patrick and I turned to each other."

"He liked your high spirits," Turner said.

"And I liked his good humor. And I was very, very protective of him."

"Because he was little?"

She shook her head and smiled sadly at the memory. "He talked funny. He had a speech impediment until he was, oh, six or seven. Then therapists got him over it. But it was bad. Most of the time nobody knew what he was trying to say—except me."

"I see."

"In a way, it was like having a private language. Only he could speak it. Only I could understand it. So we became sort of a nation of two."

She leaned back against the pillow, remembering. "He had this special song he'd sing me. It ended.

"And I'll L-O-V-E love you
All the T-I-M-E time—
Rack 'em up, stack 'em up, any old time—
Match in the gas tank—boom boom!

But the way he pronounced things, *nobody* else knew what it meant."

She smiled again. "He was small for his age. Sometimes other kids picked on him because of his size and the way he talked."

"So you defended him," Turner said. It was a statement, as if he had no doubt.

She nodded. "Yes. But the older he got, the more he could charm his way out of trouble. He was always the charmer."

But now, she thought, *he's in the kind of trouble that charm can't help.*

Turner raised a dark eyebrow. "And you were the scrapper?"

"Exactly." She raised the glass and took a drink.

He watched her. "Patrick was your mother's favorite?"

"Yes. But it didn't matter. He was my favorite, too. Nona and I never really saw eye-to-eye—except about him."

"You always call her Nona. Why?"

"After I got out of college, I lived with a man. She sort of disowned me for a while. It started then."

"But you patched it up—more or less."

"Less rather than more. I suppose I married him partly in some weird attempt to appease her. I shouldn't have. He wasn't—a very honest man. He lied. I hate that. I hate liars. Maybe that's why I got so upset with Nona over this."

Turner held his glass up to the light. "He lied about what sort of things?"

She shrugged. "Women. There were always other women. I couldn't take it anymore. So I divorced him. That didn't sit well with Nona, either."

"How long have you been divorced?"

"A year," she said. She was becoming uncomfortable; she had talked too much about herself. "What about you? Have you been married?"

He shook his head negatively. "No. Not even close."

"Altar shy?" she asked.

"Terminally so," he said.

Good, she thought. *I like that in a man.* It seemed the safest way to feel.

He studied her, frowning slightly. "Tell me. Why did you change your mind tonight?"

It was a question she'd hoped he wouldn't ask. The truth was embarrassing, not flattering to either of them.

She looked away. "You probably don't want to know."

He put his fingertips under her chin, turned her face to his again. "Tell me."

She sighed. "I told Nona that we'd arrived and that we were going to talk to the Walsh woman tomorrow."

His touch lingered on her face, fingers and thumb framing her jaw. "And?" he said.

She made herself keep her eyes on his. "And she

started asking questions about our sleeping arrangements. I had to tell her three times we had separate rooms. She thought we should be in separate *buildings*. She said it didn't look right, us checking into the same place."

The corners of his mouth twitched.

Her temper flared defensively. "It's not funny," she said. "Then she told me she hoped I had the decency not to 'go fooling around in some motel' with you. And after I hung up the phone, I realized she'd really made me angry. I mean I'm almost thirty-three years old, for God's sake."

"You went to bed with me because your mother told you not to," he said, his expression unreadable.

"Partly," she admitted miserably. "How neurotic is that?"

He set his glass on the night table. "Just neurotic enough," he said. He took her glass and set it beside his.

"That was one part of the reason," she said, her blood starting to speed dizzily. "The other part was that I *wanted* to call you."

He said nothing. He moved his hand to cradle the back of her neck. Her heart pirouetted.

He leaned forward and kissed her. He kissed her again and again. She put her hands on his bare shoulders, and the sheet between them fell away.

Adon pretended to read a folder of depositions about a spousal-abuse case that was coming up for trial. His mind was not on the case. It was on Judy Sevenstar.

Her death filled him with equal parts anxiety and pleasure. Anxiety because it was yet another complex secret to hide. Pleasure because Judy was no longer a menace to the order of power in the county. Most importantly, she was no threat to Barbara's fragile peace of mind.

We need no scandal, he thought. *She can't bear a scandal; she isn't strong enough.*

For years she had heard rumors of what her father had done, the baby sellings, the abortions, the crimes since. Always her father and brother had denied it; such things were not women's business, especially a woman like Barbara, as ornamental and protected as a hothouse flower.

But the whispers persisted, and Barbara was sensitive. Her brother had died. Her only child had died. Her father had become a recluse and an invalid. Why had these things happened, if not for some sort of terrible punishment?

Now, like her father, she did not go outside. She feared the staring, the gossip, the unctuous pity. She had never been at ease in the large world, and now she could not face it at all. She stayed at home in the rooms she loved. And as if in some personal, illogical atonement for the souls of her hurt and lost loved ones, she barely ate.

Tonight she was curled up on the couch, crocheting another afghan for her father. It was usually a bad sign when she began crocheting. How many afghans had she made for the old man in the past four years? Adon wondered. A dozen? Twenty? Forty?

Her little white dog lay curled at her feet, wheezing its asthmatic snores. Barbara's silvery crochet hook flashed, drawing the yarn.

Felix came into the room in his silent way. Adon looked up questioningly, but Barbara stayed bent over her needlework. The afghan looked as if it would be snow-white this time. Like a ghost, Adon thought bleakly.

"Your daddy's awake, Miss," Felix said. "And he's

eaten. He wants to know if you'll come up and watch *Wheel of Fortune* with him in a little while."

Barbara looked up and smiled self-consciously. "Of course," she said, and started to put her yarn aside.

"In a little while," Felix repeated, his voice kind. "First he wants to talk to you, Adon."

"Ah," said Adon, as if he were slightly surprised. He laid aside the deposition and rose from his chair. "I won't be long, sweetheart."

She nodded absently and bent over her yarn again, the hook flashing in and out, in and out.

Adon left the living room and climbed the long, curving staircase that led to the house's second story. He had insisted that Felix make it clear to Roland Hunsinger that he must talk to Adon whether or not he was in the mood.

The old man could watch *Wheel of Fortune* later. He had Felix tape it so he could watch it by night as he pleased. He usually summoned Barbara to be at his side, but the old man would say little to her. He tried to speak as little as possible to anyone except Felix.

Adon walked down the long hall to the south wing and knocked on the door. He knew that his father-in-law heard him, but would make no answer, so he entered.

The only light was that from the television. The sound was turned down low and strange images flickered across the screen. The old man sometimes watched rock videos because he liked the sexy, strutting, wet-lipped women. He was particularly fond of Madonna.

He would use the remote to change the channel if it was Barbara who entered the room. For Felix and Adon he made no pretense.

Roland Hunsinger sat in his recliner in the far and most shadowy corner of the room. Adon could see his feet in their expensive leather slippers resting on a stuffed stool shaped like an elephant. He could see the pale legs in their paisley silk pajamas. He could not, of course, see his face.

"Hello, Daddy," said Adon. He always called Hunsinger "Daddy" to his face. The old man had ordered him to do so long ago—"I'm Barbara's daddy and now I'm yours," he'd said after the wedding. Adon loathed using the name, it made him feel somehow diminished, and he was sure the old man enjoyed it for that very reason.

Now Roland gave a resigned wave of his hand. In the dimness and shadows the gesture was only a pale blur, but Adon understood. He pulled up the chair from the desk and sat down at a respectful distance from Roland.

Adon chose his words carefully. He had not told the old man about Hollis's disappearance, nor did he intend to. Nor would he show him the crude drawing of the dead woman; he did not need Roland to tell him what it meant. He knew.

"Daddy," Adon said, "I told you we had a problem. That lawyer and that woman from Boston that came sniffing around about the babies. We tried to dissuade them from asking questions. It didn't work."

Roland Hunsinger stiffened slightly in his chair. Adon could see the big, pallid hands gripping the armrests. The posture radiated impatience, displeasure. It said, *Get on with it.*

Adon sighed and dipped his fingers into the breast pocket of his shirt. "Then Judy Sevenstar got into the picture. She sold them a list. She said it was of birth mothers. There are five of them. I need you to look at it."

The fingers tightened harder on the armrests. Then slowly Roland held out his right hand, palm-up. Adon leaned forward, gave the old man the list. He said, "I need to know if it's genuine. And if these names can hurt us."

There was a rustle of silk as Roland Hunsinger fumbled in the pocket of his dressing gown. He drew out the penlight that Adon so hated. Barbara had ordered it for almost a thousand dollars from the Neiman Marcus catalog. It was made of platinum, decorated with diamond chips, and it had a beam like a laser.

Roland switched it on, making Adon wince. The old man trained it on the paper like a tiny beacon. Then he did what Adon had angrily dreaded he would do; he turned the light on Adon himself, shining it directly in his eyes.

Adon put up his hand to shield himself. Christ, he hated the old bastard's power games. "The names," he said, trying to keep the irritation out of his voice, "are they genuine?"

There was a long moment of silence. Then the old man spoke. His voice always sent a nearly superstitious shudder through Adon, for it was no longer human. It was mechanical and alien, like that of a particularly unpleasant robot.

"They're genuine," said Roland Hunsinger. The words came out in a sort of low wheeze with a metallic ring.

Four years ago the old man's larynx had been removed, and he could speak only with the aid of an electronic vibrating device that he held against his throat. Sometimes Adon thought this manufactured voice sounded like a particularly ominous electric guitar, and at other times it reminded him of something out of a sinister science-fiction film.

The accident that destroyed Roland's larynx had also torn away part of his jaw, and the operation to replace it had not been aesthetically pleasing. This was why the old man kept himself in darkness.

He had been handsome in his day, dashing even, envied by men, admired by women. His vanity had been almost infinite, and now he was its prisoner. He did not even wish people to know what had happened to his voice, his looks. Let the rumors abound, he said, so long as they kept the world away.

Roland Hunsinger's body was still surprisingly strong. In the room was an array of exercise machines. Sometimes he would put on the videos that he particularly enjoyed and climb onto his treadmill, walking nowhere until the small hours of the morning.

His body was still robust, and if his mind was not as agile as it once was, it was still good. He understood what went on in the county and, through Adon, he still controlled much of it. But both of them knew there were secrets to be kept at all costs.

The old man had resolutely kept details of some secrets from even Adon, and now Adon pushed to learn what was most necessary. "This list," he said for the third time, "is anyone on it dangerous to us?"

Roland turned his penlight back to the paper. He studied it for such a long time that Adon became twitchy with nerves. "Well?" he prodded.

"Dangerous?" the old man said in his cyborg's voice. "Perhaps."

Adon felt hot prickles running beneath his skin, like poisonous little stings. "Which ones?" he demanded.

The old man gave a laugh of metal and wires and circuits. "Why—any one of them," he said. "Why—all of them."

"The lawyer and the woman, they haven't come back to town," Adon said. "They may already be trying to track down those names. What should we do?"

Roland shifted in his chair, recrossed his legs. "Let me think on it," he said. He refolded the paper. "Let me meditate on it." He put the paper into the pocket of his silk gown.

"Judy Sevenstar," said Roland, "has never been an asset. Now she's become a detriment."

"I realize that," Adon replied. "It's been taken care of."

"Has it? And by whom? I'll hazard I know. LaBonny?"

Adon's heart tightened in fearful jealousy. "Yes. I hope he didn't botch it."

"I like that boy," intoned Roland. "I like him in spite of himself. He gets things done. Ha. Ha. You'd better watch him. Ha-a-a-a."

"I intend to," Adon said from between his teeth.

"He's vicious, you know. Sometimes such a quality is useful. Such as now. The future—is another matter. We'll talk of that. But first things first." Roland turned the light and shined it into Adon's eyes again. "How's my daughter?" he demanded.

"She's better," Adon lied.

"She loves me," Roland said, and the electronic voice came as close as it could to vibrating with satisfaction.

"Yes," Adon said. "She does."

"She's always worshiped the ground I walk on."

"Yes. She has."

"She's too thin," said Roland, accusation edging his words.

"I know," said Adon. Then he lied again. "But she's eating better."

"You take care of my little girl," ordered Roland, keeping the light dancing from Adon's left eye to his right.

"You know that I will."

"Give her another baby," ordered Roland. "She's been carrying on too long about that one that's gone."

"I know," said Adon. But he could not tell the old man that there could not be any more babies for Barbara. And Barbara herself could not speak of it.

"I want my little girl to be happy," said Roland.

"So do I," said Adon.

"Send her to me," Roland ordered. "I'm ready to watch my program now. God, I love that blonde that turns the letters."

"Yessir," said Adon.

He went downstairs and told Barbara that her father was waiting for her. She immediately put aside her yarn, rose, and went obediently up the stairs. Adon looked at the afghan, white as a shroud and growing row by row.

He went to the bar and mixed himself a drink, a triple.

The street was shady, but the morning sun still dazzled down through the leafy branches, throwing coins of brightness on the ground.

"Here we are," Turner said, pulling up to the curb.

Jaye's heart quickened to a strange, scurrying speed.

She did not wait for Turner to open her door. She got out of the car quickly and stood staring at the house, her throat constricting.

Rita Walsh lived on an oak-lined street that led to the campus of the University of Mississippi. A magnolia tree in the front yard was flamboyant with blossoms, and around the porch bloomed azaleas of a rich, deep pink.

The house itself gave off an air of well-kept age. It was neither a mansion nor stately, but it had been built to resemble, modestly, houses that were.

Although it rose two stories, it was not large. Instead of a full veranda, it had a small, square porch with two pillars thrusting up to support a toylike balcony. All in all, it reminded Jaye, in some odd way, of the dollhouse she had loved as a child—a perfect house for a picture-book family.

The air was warm and weighted with the exotic scents of a foreign spring. She wondered if the snow was still on the ground in Boston, if Nona had gone to work wearing the silly earmuffs she always affected in winter and at which Jaye and Patrick had always giggled. *Nona. Patrick. Me.*

Turner came to her side and gave her a questioning look. She let her gaze fall to the ground and said nothing. Together they walked to the porch, and her heart skittered more anxiously in her chest.

The two of them had spoken little this morning. He had slept in her room, wakened early, and when he saw that she was stirring, too, he'd kissed her on the forehead. He'd left and come back, bringing her coffee and a muffin.

The kindness of the gesture touched her, but she could not drink the coffee, could not eat the muffin. She was tense with worry about what Rita Walsh would tell them or not tell them. Turner seemed to understand. He did not push her to talk.

Now they stood on the porch, looking at the oak door with its brass knocker. *I don't know what this door leads to,* she thought. She exchanged glances with Turner, and she knew somehow he understood. She had to be the one to knock on the door. She raised her hand.

Rita Walsh could have been a beautiful woman if she'd wanted, thought Turner.

She was in her early fifties, tall and tanned and leanly built, with killer cheekbones and eyes of a startling violet-blue. But she cultivated that purposeful dowdiness that certain women intellectuals do. Her long hair was bushy and innocent of dye. She did not enhance herself with makeup; she wore nothing on her face except her character.

Her loose dress and leather sandals reminded Turner of the sixties. She was like a savvy, tough-minded flower child who had aged and knew times had changed, but didn't give a damn.

The interior of her house was comfortably jumbled, the furniture neither in nor out of fashion. There were books everywhere. The pictures on the wall were a mixed lot, obviously not chosen to match anything.

She served them herbal tea in mugs that didn't match, either. She sat on a tweedy couch whose upholstery was wearing thin. An enormous grayish cat with long hair sprang to the couch to lie in her lap. She stroked it and it purred, its eyes closing to slits in its fat face.

"I have a class in an hour," she said. Her blue eyes were sharp and observant on Jaye. "Then I have to get ready to go to a conference in Orlando."

"Oh," Jaye said politely. "What do you teach?"

Turner could tell Jaye was unnerved, not certain how to begin.

"Literature," said Rita Walsh crisply.

Turner said, "Ms. Walsh—or is it Professor Walsh?"

"Ms. Walsh will do," she said. Her look told him she was most certainly by God a professor and he'd do well to remember it.

He nodded and told her they were both looking for information on adoptions arranged through the clinic in Oklahoma. "We have reason to believe your cousin Diane was a birth mother. In January 1967. We need to get in touch with her if we can."

"It's a matter of life and death," Jaye said, then looked unsure about whether she should have been so impulsive with this woman.

Rita Walsh fixed Turner with her blue laser of a stare. "Tell me exactly why you want to know."

He explained, tersely, clearly. He showed her the dates and told her that there was a possibility that Diane Englund might have met Jaye's birth mother at Hunsinger's clinic.

"She might know *your* mother," the Walsh woman said to Jaye. "But how does that help your brother?" She turned her gaze back to Turner. "Or your client?"

It was a logical question, almost coldly so, but it was fair. He said, "Ms. Walsh, we have to make connections wherever we can. And hope they lead to a breakthrough."

"Ah," she said. "It doesn't sound very methodical."

Jaye leaned forward, her face pale and earnest. "Ms. Walsh, I'm coming to you in desperation. I tried to phone my sister-in-law in Belgium this morning. I couldn't get through. I don't know if my brother's better or worse."

Rita Walsh set her mug on the coffee table, which was strewn with books and magazines. She pushed the cat from her lap and stood. She went to the window and stared out at the street. She put her hands on her waist almost as if she had a backache.

"It's a terrible disease," she said quietly. "It killed my husband's brother."

Jaye looked stricken with fear and sympathy, but Turner felt a pleasant certainty flash through his system. *Oh, yes,* he thought, grateful for that doomed brother-in-law.

"Then you know," he said.

"Yes," she said, still staring out onto the quiet street. "I know."

She turned to face them again. "My cousin and I were very close when we were girls. We're still close. But what happened to her—in Oklahoma—changed her. She doesn't like to talk about it."

Turner said, "In no way do we wish to hurt or embarrass your cousin."

One corner of the woman's mouth curved to a bitter little angle. "For years she's lived in dread that someday a phone call would come or there'd be a knock at the door. And it would be an adult, a stranger, saying, 'I know you're my mother.'"

"We are not here to deliver that phone call," Turner said. "Or pay that visit."

Jaye sat stiffly in her chair, as if she were afraid to speak, to influence the fine balance of decision taking place in Rita Walsh's mind.

The woman ran her hand through her unruly hair. "Do you know Diane never told her first husband about that child? Never told him. That's how traumatized she was."

She sighed again, paced to a bookcase. "She's told her second husband. They've even told the children. But no one outside the family. Never anyone outside the family."

"We can appreciate the delicacy of the situation," Turner said. "We understand that discretion is essential."

"Discretion," said the woman, almost contemptuously. She fingered the spine of a book. "That was the name of the game, wasn't it? If you were unmarried and pregnant, it was a disaster. But, with luck, it could be a *discreet* disaster. What hypocrisy. And what a price we made young women pay."

"*O tempora, o mores,*" Turner said carefully, hoping it sounded professorial.

She cocked her head with disdainful amusement. "Exactly. Oh, the time, oh, the morals. Why is anyone ever nostalgic for those days? The way girls like Diane were treated—it was medieval. Barbaric."

"Yes," said Turner. "It was."

"When I was a girl in Fort Smith," she said, "the ministers told us that sex outside of marriage was a terrible sin. A girl who did it was a slut, and if she died without repenting she'd go to hell and burn forever. Sex was bad enough—but to have a baby? I don't think young people nowadays can imagine the stigma. Not just the shame—the sheer terror of it. And then the years of lying and guilt. But what mattered more than anything was to be *discreet.*"

"It was unfair to the girls," Turner said. "And the children."

The woman continued to stroke the spine of the book. "Yes," she said. "The children. I never heard until now that the children were sold. My God. *Sold.*"

"Yes, ma'am," said Turner.

"I remember before Diane got pregnant—or 'got in trouble' as the quaint phrase had it—there were whispers about places that 'bad girls' went to have their babies. But I never heard a word about children being sold."

Jaye had set aside her mug, and her fists were clamped in her lap. Her voice shook. "I was sold. So was my brother."

Rita Walsh looked at Jaye again. She looked at her for a long moment. She said, "I'll tell you about my cousin. And then I'll tell you where to find her."

FOURTEEN

———◦⟡◦———

RITA WALSH WALKED TO THE MANTEL. SHE TOOK DOWN a picture in a plain gilt frame and showed it to Jaye. "This is our last family reunion," she said. "It was at a farm, just outside a little town called High Mountain, Arkansas. That's where our great-great-grandparents settled when they came to America."

Jaye studied the group of people. They were lined up as if for a school group photograph, four rows deep. Their faces seemed tiny, like those of diminutive paper dolls.

Rita Walsh said, "My cousin Brian had to stand on the roof of the farmhouse to take this picture, to get us all in one shot. And that's still not all of us. There were twenty, thirty more who didn't make the reunion."

Jaye looked from woman to woman in the picture. *Which one?* she thought. *Which one has the secret? Who might have known my mother? Who might lead us to Patrick's?*

"She's here," said Rita Walsh, pointing. "That's Diane."

Jaye was jolted by how ordinary the woman looked, how completely unremarkable. Diane Englund was neither tall nor short, fat nor thin, beautiful nor ugly. No visible feature made her stand out from her crowd of relatives.

Walsh pointed to the figure beside Diane, a short, stocky man whose grin seemed good-natured. "This is her husband, Rick"—her finger moved to a squarely built young woman with an identical grin—"and this is their daughter Karen. Their other daughter, Dell, couldn't make it. She'd just started grad school in Chicago. Diane loves her husband. She's very proud of her daughters. They're a nice family. Look at them."

She almost forced the picture into Jaye's hands, then she crossed her own arms. "Diane's never seen her son. She knows the child was a boy, that's all. They said that in the delivery room. Diane only got a glimpse of him. She heard him cry. She never held him. She never saw him again."

"I'm—sorry," Jaye said, knowing the words were inadequate.

"He'd be your age now," said Rita Walsh. "He's probably very handsome. His father was—extraordinarily so. And Diane was a pretty girl. She was only fifteen. She was mad for him, absolutely mad.

"He didn't really care for her," she continued. "He wanted sex, that was all. Diane gave it to him. She would have given him anything. Then she got pregnant. He wouldn't marry her, of course. And his parents wouldn't have allowed it, anyway. *They* said Diane only did it to trap him. They said she was a tramp. That she wasn't good enough. They said a lot of things."

Jaye could think of no reply.

The woman shook her head. "She told me once that she's wondered about her son every day of her life. She's never tried to find him. She doesn't know if he's ever been told that his birth mother gave him away. Perhaps he doesn't know she exists. Perhaps it's better that he doesn't. Certainly it's easier—isn't it?"

Turner spoke. "Is it? Do you believe that?"

She turned the unwavering blueness of her gaze on him. "I don't believe in lies," she said. "But my cousin's been forced to live one. If her son sought her out, she would gladly accept him. But he hasn't."

"He might be trying," said Turner.

"He hasn't tried as hard as the two of you," she said.

"Maybe," said Turner, "we're just luckier."

She smiled, but the effect was one of sadness. "Luck *is* the wild card of the gods, isn't it? As luck would have it, my cousin is a kind woman. I phoned her yesterday, told her about you. She said to see what sort of people you were. That if you were sincere, she'd help you—if she could."

Jaye's breath caught in her chest with a small, stabbing pain. "She'll see us?"

Rita Walsh turned to face Jaye again. "Yes," she said. "There was another girl there at Hunsinger's when she was sent there. That girl might have been your mother."

Jaye felt as if the top of her skull had been stripped away, leaving her mind numb and nakedly exposed. At the same time, gravity seemed to have canceled itself, and she felt oddly as if she were floating in space.

"Thank you," she managed to mumble, but the words did not seem to come from her. Her lips had no feeling in them. Nowhere in her body was there feeling.

"It was a terrible thing that was done to women and children," said Rita Walsh. She reached into the pocket of her baggy dress and withdrew a white index card. "This is Diane's married name, her address, and phone number. She lives in New Orleans now. It would probably be best if you talk to her face-to-face."

Jaye nodded but could not find her voice.

The woman gave her a long, clinical look, like a doctor who is trying to assess the seriousness of an injury. "I'll call her, tell her to expect to hear from you. When do you think you'll go?" she asked.

Jaye shrugged helplessly.

"Immediately," said Turner. "We'll leave immediately."

Turner had watched Jaye closely. For a few moments she had seemed truly stunned, like someone who has sustained a paralyzing blow. Yet she recovered herself with amazing swiftness.

When they told Rita Walsh good-bye, Jaye had a smile in place, albeit a somewhat stiff one. Her air was perfectly self-contained, her back was straight, her hand was steady as she clasped Rita Walsh's.

Turner was tempted to take her arm as they walked down the steps toward the Buick, but something in her bearing told him she wanted to gather her own forces her own way, and she didn't want any sign of sympathy, no matter how sincere.

Once in the car he saw that she had her organizational powers up and running full-speed. "I suppose the fastest way to get to New Orleans is just to keep driving," she said. "Not to fool around trying to get a flight out of here."

"Right," he said, turning the key in the ignition.

"But we should certainly call her ourselves," said Jaye. "Find when it's most convenient for her to see us."

"Absolutely," he said, guiding the car back into the street.

"I need to make some calls," she said. "My lawyer for starters. To see if that information broker's found out anything about the other women."

That she was using her own Mickey Mouse information broker was still a sore point with Turner. He slipped her a rueful look, but she didn't notice.

She said, "I've got to try to get Melinda again in Belgium. And call Nona. But I'm not going to tell her this might lead to finding *my* birth mother. She'll go all insecure on me."

My God, thought Turner, glancing at her again. Had she already buried her own feelings so deeply that she could concern herself about the niceties of Nona's reaction?

She said, "I suppose I should call Miss Doll, too. Tell her to hold my room and see if there've been any calls. And we'll need to go shopping again. I'm going to need more underwear. And maybe another outfit." She plucked at her sleeve absently. "I'm getting really tired of this suit."

He said, "I should call Mr. D., too. I'll look for a quiet place."

"Maybe Patrick's well enough to talk today," she said. "God, I hope so."

"Yeah," he said. "I hope so, too."

"It's really good of this woman to see us," Jaye said, her chin held high. "Obviously we're going to bring back some painful memories."

"Yes. We will."

She frowned and gazed off into the shady distance. "One thing really bothers me, though."

There's more than one thing bothering you, baby, he thought, *a lot more—if you could admit it.* But he said, "Yeah, I think I know."

She gave him a questioning look.

He said, "It sounds like Diane Englund—what's her name now?"

"Kline. Diane Kline."

"It sounds as if she never knew about the baby selling. That somehow she thought she was putting the child up for legal adoption. That's going to be even more upsetting."

Jaye settled back against the seat, her face no longer wearing its mask of confidence. She looked troubled. "I suppose we'll have to tell her. I mean, if there were real records, we wouldn't be in this mess."

"I imagine the cousin's going to break the news. She seemed like a straight-shooting lady."

"And an angry one," said Jaye.

"She has a right to be angry. But who knows—it may be good for Diane Kline to see you."

She shot him a disbelieving glance. "Good? Why?"

He gave her a quick look, up and down. "You're one of Hunsinger's babies. And look how you turned out. Most excellent."

She smiled the smile that always made him a little crazy because it was haunted by a sadness that he wished he could fix. "Now you've descended to vile flattery," she said.

"I never flatter," Turner said. "I always tell the truth. I'm a lawyer. It's the lawyer's code."

For a few seconds her smile was real, amused and full of mischief. Turner's heart spun strangely, and he had a terrifying thought: *A man could love this woman. A man might not be able to stop himself.*

Jaye's courage faltered slightly when she thought of phoning Diane Englund Kline. She was secretly grateful when Turner offered to do it.

They parked close to the university, on the grounds of a historical site, the Faulkner mansion. She stayed inside the car and Turner got out to make his calls. He leaned against a decaying stable in the shade of a sweet gum tree.

She phoned her lawyer. The information broker hadn't yet sent him anything, he said, and told her to check again this afternoon. The broker expected some results, at least, by the end of the day. Was there a way he could fax her?

She thought of Turner's laptop computer, which was small, sleek, and futuristic as a space station. But she didn't want the information going through Turner. Her knowledge of the list was her power, her way of remaining a player.

"I'll find a way," she said.

She called Nona at work and told her they had found one birth mother in New Orleans and hoped she could lead them to others.

At first the news didn't seem to register. "I tried to call Brussels this morning," Nona said worriedly. "I couldn't get through. I don't know what it means."

"I couldn't get through, either. I'll try again as soon as I hang up."

"Is that *lawyer* going to New Orleans with you?" Nona asked, disapproval in her voice.

"Yes," Jaye said. "I found out this morning that he's better at talking to people about this than I am."

"Lawyers are always fast talkers," Nona said darkly.

"It's all right," said Jaye. "I'm a fast listener."

"Ho ho, miss, very funny. Are you behaving yourself with this man?"

"Yes," Jaye lied, with just the right tone of indignation.

"Don't you let him get you into bed," Nona warned. "This adoption business should show you what I've always said. There's no place for sex outside of marriage. No good can come of it."

"*I* came from it," Jaye retorted. "So did Patrick."

"Is this man rich?" Nona asked unexpectedly. "I've always heard the saying 'Rich as a Philadelphia lawyer.' Is he?"

"He seems comfortably off," Jaye said vaguely.

"Well, who knows," Nona said. "If you behave yourself, something may come of it."

I don't believe this, Jaye thought. One minute she's warning me about sex, the next she's matchmaking. "I've got to go now," she said. "Give Brother Maynard my love."

She hung up and dialed the number in Brussels. Melinda answered, giddy and tearful with excitement. Patrick had rallied. He was having a much better day. He wanted to talk to Jaye, but he wasn't supposed to speak for long; it would wear him out. There was a pause, as across the ocean a phone was being passed from one speaker to another.

Then she heard Patrick's voice say, "Hello, Jaye-Jaye."

Jaye's pulse galloped in her wrists, her throat

cramped with tears. He sounded so weak it terrified her, but he still sounded like Patrick, and it was heaven to hear him.

"Hello, Pat-guy," she said, trying to keep her own voice from shaking. She could not.

"I love you all the T-I-M-E, time," he sang, the melody wavering. "Rack 'em up, stack 'em up, any old time."

"Match in the gas tank," she recited. "Boom boom." The foolish, nostalgic words made tears sting her eyes. She blinked them back.

"Mom says you're doing—genealogical research on my behalf," he said. He said it with a breathless little gasp that made her shaky.

"Yes," she said. "I'm on my way to New Orleans. There's a woman there—she's not your birth mother—but she may be able to tell us something."

"God," he said, "that seems so weird—birth mother."

"I know," she said. "I know."

"And I'm—part Chinese or something," he said. He gave a laugh that sounded alarmingly frail. "I bet Mom's secretly really pissed about that. She paid good money and she was supposed to get a hundred percent Caucasian baby."

"You always did have a thing for egg rolls," Jaye said.

He started to cough.

Oh, God, she thought, tears burning her eyes. *Oh, God, oh, God.*

Melinda came back on the line. "I'm sorry. He's having a coughing spell. I better hang up. We love you, Jaye." Jaye could hear him, still coughing feebly in the background.

"I love you, too," she said, her voice choked, but the line had already gone dead.

She swallowed hard, then phoned Miss Doll to tell her she wouldn't be back in Cawdor for at least another night.

LaBonny wore only black briefs and an Aussie hat, one side of the wide brim bent up stylishly. He sat on the edge of his bed, cleaning his guns. On the bed slept his Doberman bitch, Sweety.

He frowned as he polished. How the fuck had Hollis vanished so completely? It was like the bastard had disappeared in a magic puff of smoke that drifted away to nothing.

The sheriff's office hadn't waited the usual forty-eight hours to put out an all-points bulletin on him; the rationale was that somebody like Hollis, who could barely talk and was close to simpleminded, was ripe to be a victim.

Sometimes young troublemakers got their kicks by abducting Hollis, driving him into the country and abandoning him to walk the long miles back to the nursing home. More than once he'd been beaten and sexually molested.

LaBonny didn't think this had happened to Hollis; in fact, he wished it had. Nothing would give him greater pleasure than for Hollis to be found dead and battered in an abandoned barn somewhere, a broken beer bottle shoved up his ass.

No, Hollis had run away. He'd taken his clothes and his blanket and his drawings and whatever little else he had. But did he have money? If so, how far could it take him? And where could someone like Hollis go?

He'd last been seen running toward the woods, one hand clutching whatever he'd unburied, his suitcase banging against his leg.

Hollis had never had a car; he couldn't drive. He hadn't gone to the bus depot in Mount Cawdor; LaBonny had checked. Nobody thought Hollis would try to hitchhike; he'd been taken on too many painful joy-rides in his time.

LaBonny rubbed the long barrel of his hunting rifle. Hollis had to be holed up somewhere, that was the answer. The county was half covered with forest, and the woods still hid tumbledown buildings, the falling remains of deserted shacks and abandoned farms.

LaBonny had expected Hollis would blunder and stumble so obviously that he would be found within a day or so. He hadn't. So it was time to go after him.

There was a knock at the kitchen door. Sweety raised her head and gave a sleepy growl. She rose and sprang from the bed, sprinting into the kitchen, still growling.

LaBonny knew who it was. He set the rifle aside and thought of answering the door in his briefs, but instead he pulled on a pair of olive-drab jeans. Tight, they hung low on his narrow hips. His naked torso was as lean and hairless as a snake's.

Barefoot, he padded into the kitchen, where Sweety was tensed before the door, her upper lip curled back to show her teeth. "Stay," he told her.

He opened the door and Bobby Midus stood there in the afternoon sun, the light gleaming on his yellow hair. Bobby had on his hunting clothes, camouflage pants and a T-shirt that hugged his chest.

He was a baby-faced young man with long-lashed blue eyes and pouting lips. But he was a bodybuilder and his neck was thick, his chest wide, and his arms bulged with muscle.

Bobby was also one of the best hunters in the county. He could bring down a deer with a shot through the eye at a hundred yards. And he knew the fucking woods as intimately as he knew the muscles of his own beautiful body.

"Christ," Bobby said, looking nervously at Sweety, who growled, her neck hair raised. "Can't you lock that thing up or something?"

LaBonny smiled at him lazily. "She won't hurt you unless I tell her to. Lay down, Sweety."

Instantly the dog lay down and went silent. But she kept her eyes fixed on Bobby's Adam's apple. "Jesus," Bobby said, but he stepped inside.

"Come on. I got to put on a shirt," said LaBonny. He headed back to the bedroom.

Bobby followed. "Is Cody J. going with us?"

"We'll pick him up," said LaBonny. He sat again on the bed's edge and pulled on a pair of socks, then his hunting boots. He rose and went to his closet. He kept it immaculately neat. He took out an olive-drab fatigue shirt with short sleeves.

He stood before the mirror, buttoning the shirt. He let his eyes drift to the reflection of Bobby, who stood in the doorway, one perfect hip cocked. He was scratching his armpit.

Bobby had watched the blonde from Boston and said he liked the looks of her, said he'd admire a piece of that. She left LaBonny cold, but he had mentioned, almost idly, that if they had to grab her, he and Bobby could go off and both have her at the same time, make it a threesome. Bobby had looked startled, but he hadn't said no. Neither of them had mentioned it since. It was as if they'd both been careful not to mention it.

LaBonny said, "You been thinking about where Hollis might hide?"

"Not much," Bobby said. "I mean how good can he hide? He's purt near an idiot."

The answer irritated LaBonny. He had a sudden fantasy of taking off his belt, pulling down Bobby's pants, and whipping his ass until it bled. It jolted LaBonny with its unexpected vividness, but he willed it to pass.

LaBonny said, "He grew up in those woods, him and Luther both. And he's part Indian."

Bobby said, "Well, he's just an old dummy. He can't even talk."

LaBonny adjusted the brim of his hat and turned his long, slender neck so that he could stare into Bobby's pretty eyes. "He *can* talk. He *doesn't* talk. There's a difference."

Bobby shrugged one big shoulder. "Well, if he *can* talk, why don't he?"

"Because he doesn't, that's all. He hasn't since he was ten-twelve years old. Nobody except family."

"How come?" Bobby asked, frowning in puzzlement.

LaBonny put his hunting rifle into its cover, zipped it up. "The doc said it's a defense mechanism."

"What the hell's that?" Bobby asked.

"It's like psychology," LaBonny said. "You ready?"

Bobby nodded, but he said, "If it's psychology that's wrong with him, then he's just an ol' retard like I said."

LaBonny stopped, his face close to Bobby's. "Well," he said with a thin smile, "if you were a retard, where in those woods would you hide?" He could smell the boy's aftershave lotion.

Bobby thrust up his dimpled chin. "I'd hide close to where I grew up, that's where. Out there by the doc's old house. The woods go on a long way past the nursin' home."

LaBonny gave Bobby's arm a condescending pat. The flesh was warm, hard, and surprisingly silky to the touch. "You can think like a retard really good," he said.

Bobby drew away sulkily, pushing out his lower lip so that his mouth looked even poutier than usual.

LaBonny walked past him. He whistled for Sweety. She leaped to her feet, eager to follow him.

"You're not taking that damn dog," Bobby complained.

"If we find Hollis," said LaBonny, opening the kitchen door, "I'll show you what this dog can do."

Bobby smiled, his good humor restored. "I bet that dog could make the ol' fool talk."

"She could make him scream," said LaBonny.

Hollis had not gone back to the home place. The home place was long gone.

The cabin had stood on a few acres near the old clinic building, and for years the family had rented it. But one Sunday, just after Dr. Hunsinger moved away, a tornado had touched down and reduced the cabin to a heap of wreckage.

Luther had been saved because he was off fishing for bream in the creek. He had lain facedown in a ditch, and the storm had passed over him, as if he had prostrated himself before the Angel of Death, and it had spared him.

That's what Luther's mother, Aunt Winona, had said. She and Hollis had been to town at Sunday school when it happened, and Miss Ellen McCoy had been singing, "Prayer of Thanksgiving":

> Sing praises to His name,
> He forgets not his own. . . .

No sooner were these words out of her mouth than a noise came like the world's greatest freight train, rumbling and shrieking. The whole church shook so hard that Hollis felt the jolting to the center of his bones. All the stained-glass windows blasted inward, spewing the congregation with jewel-like shards.

Nobody was killed, which the preacher said was God's grace, and no one was even badly hurt except for Mavis Sevenstar, Judy's mother, who was hit in the arm by a large, flying piece of glass and had a tendon severed.

Hollis himself was struck by a small sliver of blue-white glass that buried itself in his cheek. Later someone said it was a piece of the Holy Ghost descending as a dove, because that was the only picture in any of the windows that had been that blue-white color. He had bled and bled.

But the worst was to come. When Hollis and Aunt Winona went home, they discovered there was no home. The tornado had eaten up the cabin and spit it out as a jumble of rubble. Even the trees were broken off, as if they'd been no stronger than sticks.

What few possessions the family had left were scattered about the ruined woods. Of his own things, Hollis found the small picture of his dead mother, the frame's glass still miraculously unbroken. He found his mouth harp and his work jeans. That was all.

Aunt Winona said that they should not grieve for material goods and that they should thank God for sparing their lives. Luther said coldly that he wished God had spared them the goddam tornado altogether, but then, even though he was a grown man, he had sat down and cried. It was the only time in Hollis's life that he ever saw Luther cry, and it frightened him worse than the tornado.

Dr. Hunsinger had taken them in because Luther and Hollis still worked for him over at his new ranch. He let them move into the trailer house that his horse trainer had once lived in. It was a nice enough house, and people from the church gave them clothes and dishes and food.

But a week later, Aunt Winona had a heart attack and died. It always seemed to Hollis that the tornado had killed her; it had simply done it a little slower than all the other things it did. And when she was dead, that was the end of the family.

Luther started drinking and went off to live with a widow woman who had a government pension. Hollis had a sort of a breakdown and wanted nothing more than to go back to the old cabin, even though it was gone forever.

When Hollis got well, Dr. Hunsinger gave him a job and a room at the nursing home, because Dr. Hunsinger was a powerful man and he could do such things. Hollis was deeply grateful to be back in the familiar territory of his childhood. But he was changed.

The piece of the Holy Ghost had left a white scar on Hollis's cheek. He knew that God had marked him for life, and he knew why. It was because of the dead girl.

Before the tornado he sometimes had nightmares about her coming back to rebuke him for his sins. After the tornado, he had them all the time. She wanted to be whole again. She wanted a Christian burial. The fire had been a pit opening to hell, and they had thrown her in it. If she couldn't get out, she would find Hollis and drag him down with her into the flames.

Sometimes when he went to town, he would think he saw her, and such glimpses paralyzed him with terror. It could be a girl with her back to him, her hair shoulder-length and bright, pale gold. Nauseated by fear, he would think, *She's come.*

But then the girl would turn and her face would be freckled or plain, or she wore glasses, or her nose turned up, and he would realize she was just an ordinary live girl. Still, such incidents gave his life an odd, hallucinatory quality that would linger for days.

After Luther died, this quality came to dwell fulltime with Hollis. He had been shocked and grieved by Luther's death. He couldn't even think about it.

With Luther gone, Hollis had no close blood kin. He was left to keep company with sick, old people and his own spectral thoughts. The Sevenstars were kin, but they had never been close to Aunt Winona's branch of the family.

Once, after Luther died, Hollis had walked to town, and Judy Sevenstar had confronted him. She'd almost dragged him into an alleyway.

"I know that you know that something bad happened at Hunsinger's," she'd hissed. "I know somebody died there, and you knew it, and Luther knew it, too."

Hollis had been stricken with fear. He shook his head, *No, no, no.*

But Judy narrowed her eyes. She grasped the front of his shirt. "Luther knew, he said he had proof. What was it? Do you know? Do you?"

The question made his world go black at the edges; it swam and wavered in his gaze, and terror knocked his heart against his ribs. He could not speak, only keep shaking his head: *No, no, no.*

"That old doctor had him *killed,* Hollis. He'll kill you, too, if you don't be careful. You think he's so good to you, but you better watch out."

Hollis had always been frightened of Dr. Hunsinger, even though the old man had been astonishingly charitable to him. But people said things about Dr. Hunsinger and Hollis.

Hollis had no father, which was shameful. He did not remember what had happened to his mother, and

Luther and Aunt Winona wouldn't talk about it. They would just say they didn't know, nobody knew.

Other people said that because of Hollis, she had gone off and died of shame because he had no father. All he knew of her was that she had been pretty, a tiny woman with bright eyes, a pointed chin, and long, shining hair.

Yet these same people sometimes whispered that Hollis *did* have a father and that it was Dr. Hunsinger. Luther and Aunt Winona wouldn't talk about this either. And they said he must never, ever ask anyone else because something bad might happen.

The doctor had become both a good and terrible figure to Hollis. He was like God, who allowed evil things to happen, yet at the same time could be kind and the only one powerful enough to save you. He was to be obeyed, respected—and feared.

Then something strange had happened to the doctor—an accident—although Hollis didn't understand how an accident could happen to someone so powerful. The old man was still alive, but he never left his house anymore. But Hollis got the feeling that he knew everything that happened and that, to a degree, he controlled it. He had become even more like God, because now he stayed completely unseen.

Dr. Hunsinger and the dead girl and death and hell had become all mixed together in Hollis's mind, and when the dead girl *did* come back that night, he could think of nothing to do except run to where none of them could find him.

So he had not gone to the home place. That, he realized, was the first place people would look.

So he had found another place, deep and secret and safe.

He did not think that anyone had ever known about

this place except for him and Luther. And Luther was dead—but then so was the blond girl, and she had come back.

Hollis went out only at night, but even so the dead girl had sent him a sign and a warning. He found a dead dog in the woods, white as bone, its belly big with its unborn young. It was hard work in the stony ground, but he buried it, he prayed over it, he tried to give it peace.

Now he crouched in his hiding place. Long ago the place had had two entrances, but now there was only one, almost impossible to find. Inside it was dark, but Hollis had brought his candles.

He had lit them, and against the stony walls he'd propped the pictures he had drawn of the dead girl at rest. He was building an altar of stones that was more than an altar.

It would be a coffin, too.

FIFTEEN

—⦿—

I T WAS LATE AFTERNOON AND RICHLY SULTRY IN NEW OR-
leans.

"We could check into a suite at the Windsor Court,"
Turner said, his voice full of temptation.

But Jaye opted for a hotel she could afford, an aged
inn in the Garden District that billed itself euphemisti-
cally as "no frills." She paid for her own room.

"It's not a fleabag," Turner said gallantly, and just as
gallantly he did not pressure her to share his room. He
had put temptation aside, he realized, and was letting her
choose their way.

"You're keyed up," he said, massaging the back of
her neck. The gesture filled her with emotion; it was
exactly what Patrick used to do when she was nervous.

He said, "We're not far from the park. Let's take a walk."

Now they strolled the shade of St. Charles Avenue, and Jaye savored the perfumes of a southern April. She was tired of their endless miles in the car and raised her face skyward, glad to have trees and blueness overhead.

In the Spanish moss an unnatural glitter caught her eye and she blinked in pleased surprise. "Turner, look," she said, pointing up.

Like colored tinsel, beads glittered in the branches. Strings of them hung from the live oaks, as if the trees wore jewels woven into their mossy beards. The rainbow hues gleamed crystalline in the late-afternoon light.

Turner gave a one-cornered smile. "Mardi Gras ended less than a month ago. This is a parade route. People on floats throw beads. Some go wild."

Jaye thought this delightful. All along St. Charles, beads dangled from the telephone wires, they hung on lampposts like crooked leis, they glittered from porch roofs.

"Wait," he said. "I see a good one. I'll get it for you."

They stopped beneath a tulip tree. He leaped like a basketball player and captured a necklace out of the branches. The beads were metallic green, purple, and gold.

He put them around Jaye's neck. "Those are the Mardi Gras colors," he said. "The purple's for justice, the green's for faith, the gold's for power. Maybe they'll bring you luck."

His hand lingered near the beads, then moved to stroke back an errant strand of hair. He smiled and she found herself smiling back. Justice, faith, and power: they seemed excellent forces to have on one's side. Suddenly she realized she had the urge to kiss him right there on St. Charles Avenue, in full daylight.

A streetcar went trundling heavily by. Turner took a strand of her hair between his thumb and forefinger, stroking it. "Maybe that was the famous streetcar named Desire," he said.

Maybe it was, she thought, but she felt it was wiser to say nothing. She looked away.

He dropped his hand, began to walk again. She fingered her beads and stayed by his side.

He glanced upward and said, "The beads get caught up there and then bit by bit they fall. All year long it rains beads in New Orleans. And just when they're about all rained out, there's another Mardi Gras."

"I'd love to go some year," she said wistfully. She and Patrick and Melinda had planned to go last year, but then Patrick got transferred to Belgium—he'd promised her they'd go when he came back. *And we will,* she told herself. *He'll get well and we will.*

They had reached the billowing green lawn of the park. The gardens spilled out a tropical lushness of flowers, and the air was heady with their scent. Evening was starting to fall, and a pair of black swans floated on the lake.

"Have you ever been?" she asked Turner. "To Mardi Gras, I mean?"

He gave a rueful chuckle. "Yeah. In college. Oh, *God.*"

She gave him a sidelong smile. "Oh," she said. "*That* kind of trip."

He nodded. "Humanity at its lowest ebb: the drunk college boy at Mardi Gras."

"What did you do?" she asked, amused in spite of herself.

"I'll never tell you," he said with an expression of mock misery. "You'd lose all respect for me."

"No," she said, shaking her head. "I wouldn't.

You've done too much for me. If a person respects anything, it ought to be kindness. And you've been very kind."

He stopped, drew her to the side of the path. He took her left hand between his. She still wore the splint on her finger. She had put on a fresh ribbon, thin and dark blue. He toyed with it.

She took a deep breath and said, "I took a separate room for a reason."

He nodded wryly. "You don't have to explain."

She said, "I—did it because of Nona. She's in a state. She's worried about everything. Me included."

"I understand," he said. He tightened the knot on the bow, then gently straightened the bow itself.

She swallowed. "But when Nona's upset, well . . . she can do things that make her more upset still. She's perfectly capable of calling the hotel to make *certain* we have separate rooms. I know she is."

He lifted his gaze to hers, and the look he gave her made the beat of her heart feel both sweet and painful.

She said, "I want you to be with me again tonight, Turner."

"I want it, too," he said. He bent and kissed her lips. The trees gossiped softly in the breeze. The black swans glided on the darkening lake.

Night was falling in Cawdor, cool and soft. Adon's Jeep appeared, heading toward the usual meeting place, the curve in the lane.

LaBonny leaned against his white truck, waiting. The brim of his Aussie hat was tilted low, and he clenched a toothpick at an assured angle between his teeth.

He watched as Adon parked his Jeep and got out. Adon looked angry, but also haggard. He was wearing down, LaBonny noted with cool interest. He was wearing out. The man had never had the strength to seize the county, and he didn't have the strength to hold it.

Adon could huff, he could threaten and complain, but he was growing ridiculous in LaBonny's eyes. Old Doc's bastards had started flocking home in earnest to roost, and as they did, LaBonny had realized that bit by bit he could pry Adon's power from his unsure grasp.

Adon said, "First you let that lawyer and that woman get away from you—"

"They'll be back," LaBonny said. His tone was like that of a calm adult correcting an excitable child. "Their luggage is here. Her car's still here."

"God knows what they're finding," Adon complained. "And they're *still* on the road. The Garrett woman calls Doll, but she doesn't say where they are. How'm I supposed to find them?"

LaBonny took the toothpick out of his mouth, pretended to examine it. "You're a smart man," he said. "Make them come to you."

It was more taunt than compliment. Adon's nostrils flared. "And Hollis," he said, "you were supposed to find Hollis. Why haven't you?"

"There's a lot of woods out there," LaBonny said, almost lazily.

"How can you be so damn sure he's even *there*?" Adon demanded.

"He can't be anywhere else," LaBonny answered. He cocked his head and nodded with confidence in the direction of the woods. Each day that he watched Adon unravel, he felt surer of his own strength and cunning. He said, "He's out there all right. Somewhere."

"Then keep looking, dammit," Adon said. "Sweet Christ, aren't the three of you together smarter than one idiot?"

This was the tactic LaBonny had used on Bobby Midus, and he didn't like having it turned on himself. He said, "Bobby's the best man around here in the woods."

"Wrong," Adon said, narrowing his eyes. "He's obviously only second best. You get back out there tomorrow and look again."

"I've used up my days off," LaBonny said. "I'm back on duty tomorrow."

"Take some sick days," Adon ordered.

"Fine," said LaBonny with a shrug. "You want me to take more men?"

Adon scuffed his shoe and stared at the gravel irritably, but his shoulders were slumped. "Not yet. The fewer people know your business, the better."

LaBonny watched him for a minute, gauging the other man's growing helplessness. Without the old man, without old Doc, Adon would be nothing, a puppet who had lost his puppeteer. LaBonny toyed with the strings himself.

He said very quietly, "We saw sign of him."

Adon's head snapped up. "What do you mean?"

"We went to where the old Raven place used to stand," said LaBonny. "There was no trace of him there. But we hiked around over behind your place. Yonder."

He could see Adon's flabby body tense, even in the failing light. "My place?"

LaBonny crossed his arms and hid a thin, little smile. "Anybody shoot a dog around here?"

"Felix did," Adon said, almost suspiciously.

"A bitch? Big white mongrel?"

"Yes."

"What'd he do with it?"

"What'd he do with it?" Adon echoed with displeasure. "He threw the damn thing in the woods to rot."

"Well, somebody buried it," said LaBonny. "All nice

and properlike. Piled stones on top of it. Sweety found it. She knew there was something dead down there."

"Christ," Adon said in disgust.

"Now that's not the thing a normal man would do," LaBonny said, cocking one of his snaky hips. "But Hollis, he would. There was even a flower laid on the top. And a little cross buried with her. Made out of sticks. Cute."

He reached into his breast pocket and drew out a white handkerchief. He unfolded it to reveal a small cross, no more than three inches high, cut and notched together with a penknife.

He held it toward Adon. "Want it?"

Adon swore again and ignored it. LaBonny shrugged and broke the thing in half, tossed it away. He shoved the handkerchief into his back pocket, then hooked his thumbs under his belt.

"Wasn't so very far from your house," he said.

Adon's back stiffened, and his chin shot up aggressively. "How far?"

"Half a mile, maybe less. I think he's watching you."

"Watching?" Adon snapped. "Jesus Christ almighty—why?"

"Maybe he's scared of you. Wants to keep his eye on you."

"Well, did you fucking search that area? You *should* have. Watching me—the crazy sonuvabitch."

"Couldn't. It was getting dark."

"You go back tomorrow," Adon ordered hotly. "You search every square foot. You find him, hear me?"

"Consider it done," LaBonny said mildly.

"But don't let my wife see you," Adon added. "And if there's shooting, keep it down. It upsets her to hear shooting."

LaBonny nodded agreeably. If he had Bobby with him when Hollis was found, it wouldn't take more than one shot. Bobby was pretty with that rifle, just as pretty as a picture.

"Get started first thing in the morning," Adon muttered, and stalked back to his Jeep. He got in and slammed the door.

LaBonny stayed lounging against his truck, his long legs crossed. Adon started the Jeep, backed it up. He turned it around forcefully but with the awkwardness of a man in the grip of too much emotion.

LaBonny switched his toothpick to the other side of his mouth and watched Adon go. He didn't know if Hollis was really watching the ranch house or not. It was simply an idea that had occurred to him and one he knew would prey on Adon's already raw nerves.

When the Jeep was out of sight, LaBonny unzipped his fatigues. He took a long, lingering piss on Adon's lane. The rising moon cast down its light, and his urine twinkled like jewels in the grass.

By the moonlight, Hollis reburied the dog's stiffened body. He had dragged it to another spot deeper in the forest, and gouged out another hole with a piece of sharp-edged limestone. He knew he should not do this, but he could not stop himself.

She's got to be buried decent, he thought obsessively. *Oh, bury her, bury her. Cover her, cover her up.*

He fashioned another cross to lay on the corpse. He scraped the earth back over it, patted it down. Then he began to collect stones for another cairn to protect the grave of the poor, murdered dog.

A time to cast away stones, he thought tearfully, *and a time to gather stones together . . .*

For that which befalleth the sons of men befalleth beasts; even one thing befalleth them: as the one dieth, so dieth the other; yea, they have all one breath; so that a man hath no preeminence above a beast . . .

All go unto one place; all are of the dust, and all turn to dust again.

His hands were bleeding by the time he put the last rock in place. He rose and began to walk, unsteadily at first, still crying.

Late this afternoon in the woods, he'd heard the men's voices, at first distant. He'd stayed hidden in his dark place, listening to them come nearer. He'd held his breath, as if by that act he could make himself invisible. And it had worked. They had passed him by as if he did not exist.

It was only later, when he came out, that he saw that they had found the dog's grave and what they had done to it. Their desecration had terrified him. It was as if no matter how hard he tried to serve death and please it with the correct rites, his work was undone, and death was laid bare again in all its ugliness and guilt.

And he had yet to finish his other altar—so many more stones to be hauled, to be set carefully, reverently, in place. He should begin immediately. Yet he did not.

Instead he went to the edge of the woods but not beyond. The moon was too bright tonight. He stood in the shadows, staring at the ranch house. Only one dim light was on, high up, in the old doctor's window. Hollis touched the little medicine pouch that hung from a string on his neck. *This is the key to everything,* Luther had said.

Hollis knew he should not be there, that he was tempting fate, but coming to see the house was like burying the dog. He could not stop himself from doing it. So he wiped his tears away on the dirty sleeve of his shirt and stood watch over the doctor, for reasons even he himself could not understand.

• • •

The hotel was a small Victorian one with a sagging double-tiered portico and green hurricane shutters. It radiated that air, so common in New Orleans, of aged and mildewed elegance, but evening was kind to it. Moonlight made it look romantic rather than decayed.

It was protected from the outside world by a stern, high fence of wrought iron. Here and there strings of colored beads dangled with unseemly rakishness from its sharp tips.

Jaye looked up at them with a puzzled expression. "Why don't children climb up there and get them?"

"Because any kid in New Orleans who wants beads gets about fifty pounds of 'em every Mardi Gras," Turner said. "Someday the weight of the beads is going to sink the place into the sea."

He opened the wrought-iron gate for her. She said, "Maybe someday I'll see it—Mardi Gras."

I'll take you, he wanted to blurt out. *I'll take you to every parade, I'll catch all the best beads for you. I'll rent us the most elaborate suite with the biggest, deepest bed in town. I'll get you up there and undress you until you're wearing nothing but all the necklaces I've caught for you. And one by one, I'll take them off you. . . .*

But he did not say it; it was too reckless. It hinted at long-term attachments, and it gave him an eerie feeling that he could be sexually obsessed with this woman, wanting no other. That was a dangerous attitude for a man like him, one he had avoided his whole adult life.

"It *is* pretty down here," she said dreamily. She stopped and drank in the view for a moment.

An ancient live oak in the courtyard dripped Spanish moss, and starlings quibbled sleepily in its depths. The hotel cat, a fat yellow tom with a stumpy tail, stalked possessively across the lawn and disappeared into the shadows of the banana shrubs. The front stairs were flanked by beds lavish with hibiscus and azaleas, and old-fashioned lampposts stood along the walk like soldiers.

But Turner paid no attention to the scenery. He studied Jaye's profile, its edges gilded by the soft glow from the lamps. The light glinted on her hair, making it spark a darker gold; it cast long shadows from her lashes; it glistened enticingly on her lips.

You're beautiful, he wanted to say.

Instead he said, "Do you need to call your mother again?"

She gave him a small, embarrassed smile. "She'll worry if I don't. Right now she doesn't need that."

"I'll give you some time alone then," Turner said. "I need to check in with Mr. D.'s people."

She nodded. "I have to call my lawyer again, too."

Turner nodded, said nothing. *The list,* he thought with a shriveling feeling in his stomach. *She needs to call about the damned list.*

Her attorney had still received nothing for her this afternoon. He'd told her to call him at home tonight. And Turner chided himself. He needed to stop thinking of what he wanted to do to this woman in bed and figure out how in hell to get the list from her.

But a pleasant idea occurred to him. If he was good enough in bed—and he intended to be very good indeed—and if he kept winning her trust, she just might relent and *give* him the list. Along with anything her cut-rate information brokers had found for her. It would be for her own good, he told himself. His people could do the job better than hers.

Very well, then. He would combine business with pleasure and woo the information out of her. He looked at her again, bathed in that golden light, surrounded by the perfumed air, and he thought, *Oh, my dear, you won't believe the things I'm going to do to you.*

The hotel's lobby was not impressive. The floor had once been a sleek checkerboard of tiles, but now many of its squares were chipped or snaked by cracks.

The furniture was Victorian antique, but shabby. The crystals of the chandelier were dim with age, and the silk wallpaper looked careworn. There was an elevator even older and more creaking than the one at the Crescent, an elaborate cage of tarnished brass bars.

But Jaye's room, though small, was adequate. There was no phone, no television. The bed was a bad Victorian reproduction, but it was clean and comfortable enough. The drapes and bedspread were of matching dark red satin, which gave the room a rich and rather sinful air.

She sat on the bed's edge and used her cell phone to call Nona. Nona was in an excitable mood because she'd been able to talk to Patrick for all of five minutes.

"He said he was hungry for my peanut butter pie," said Nona. "He said you can't get pie like mine in Belgium. Oh, I wish I could go and take that boy some pie. I'm baking some peanut butter brownies. I can ship *them* overseas. I'll see he gets some of Mama's cooking. I'll make him some cookies, too. Snickerdoodles. He always loved snickerdoodles."

"Maybe he can't have food from somewhere else," warned Jaye. "I mean he's still in isolation."

"But he's *rallying,*" Nona corrected. "He's going to be out soon. Didn't you think he sounded like he was rallying?"

No, Jaye thought sadly, *he'd sounded like he was going*

to cough himself to death. But she couldn't say that. "Send the brownies," she said. "Send the cookies."

"And you're going to find his birth people," Nona said with confidence. "Everyone is praying for Patrick's health and that you find these people. Brother Maynard and all of the other monks are doing novenas. I was just on my way to church to pray and light candles. You're going to succeed. I know it."

Jaye gritted her teeth. In her worst moments, she imagined the only way she could find Patrick's mother would be by a bona fide miracle. But Nona, of course, fervently believed in miracles. Jaye had given up her faith in them years ago. She said nothing.

"And Patrick *will* get well," Nona said. "Are *you* praying for him?"

"Yes," Jaye said, and it was the truth. But her prayers were desperate and makeshift.

"There are big cathedrals in New Orleans," Nona said. "You should go to one and pray for him there. And light candles."

"I will."

"Promise?"

"Yes." She didn't want to. She'd long ago left the rituals of the church behind, and religion had become a highly private matter to her. But if such an act would give Nona comfort, she would do it.

"Are you behaving yourself?" Nona asked with one of her sudden switches of tone. "With that *man*?"

"Yes, yes," Jaye said wearily. She steered the conversation elsewhere, then said her good-byes. She dialed her lawyer's number. "Murray," she said. "It's Jaye. Did the information broker find out anything yet?"

"Yes," said Murray. "He's got quite a bit on one of the girls and a good start on a second. Where are you? Do you have access to fax facilities?"

She looked around her little room with its imitation antique furniture. "This place is pretty minimalist. But the office has a fax, and you can send anything to me in care of them."

She gave him the number. She had checked the hotel's fax capabilities without telling Turner. It made her feel slightly guilty, but it also gave her the sense of independence she wanted.

"Let me get this through to them," Murray said. "Then I'll call you right back."

She hung up and waited. She rose and paced the room, pausing to look in the cloudy mirror that hung over the dresser. She still wore the slacks and short-sleeved sweater she'd bought yesterday in Eureka Springs.

In Oxford this morning, she'd bought another change of clothes and a kind of tote bag so that she wouldn't have to check into a hotel with no luggage.

I'm Nona's daughter, after all, she thought. *Worried about how I appear to a desk clerk.* She played nervously with the Mardi Gras beads at her throat.

At last her phone rang again. She snatched it up.

"Jaye, it's Murray," the lawyer said. "You're all set. It should be waiting down there for you."

He paused, then said, "But, Jaye, don't get your hopes up. This first report—I'm afraid it won't do much good."

Her skin prickled apprehensively. "Why not?"

"The fax explains it better than I can," he said kindly. "But there's sure to be something more promising tomorrow."

Jaye's mouth suddenly went dry. She wanted to ask him what he meant, but she knew the answer was waiting for her downstairs.

"Anything else I can do?" he asked.

"No, thanks, Murray. I'll talk to you tomorrow. Wait—you didn't say anything about any of the search services, the ones that unite adoptees and birth parents. No word?"

"No, sorry. I'd tell you immediately if there was. If Patrick's birth mother's registered, it could still take a while to match her name with his. We'll have to be patient."

"I know," she said. But patience seemed the most threadbare of her virtues, worn out and used up.

"And, Jaye," said Murray, a different note in his voice, "did you tell me the name of this lawyer you've teamed up with?"

"It's Gibson. Turner Gibson. From Philadelphia. He's in family law."

"Did you want me to check this guy out, Jaye? Or do you trust him?"

She hesitated. She thought of lying naked in Turner's arms last night. "I trust him," she said softly.

"Okay, kid," Murray said. "Sorry. Old Murray gets overprotective sometimes. Go get your info. Sorry there's not more, but there will be. Take care."

She said good-bye and hung up. Her heart banged in her chest even harder, she could feel the pulse in her throat jumping. She took a deep breath and went downstairs to get Murray's fax.

An hour had passed, but Jaye hadn't phoned. Turner didn't know what it meant and hoped fervently to God that she hadn't changed her mind. He called her.

She answered on the second ring. "Are you all right?" he asked.

"Yes," she said in a strange voice. Her tone was tentative, careful, one that sounded unnatural from her.

"Did you call your mother?"

"Yes," she said.

"Is everything okay?" he asked.

"Yes," she said.

"Did you get a hold of your attorney?"

"Yes," she said in the same maddening way.

Don't overwhelm me with all these details, he thought in frustration. He said, "Did he have anything for you from the information broker?"

"Yes. He—faxed it."

"*Here?*" Turner said in disbelief. The rooms didn't even have fucking phones, for God's sake; he was beginning to think he was lucky the place had electricity. The hotel had atmosphere going for it, but damn little else. "He faxed it to their office," she said hesitantly. "I picked it up there."

That's what this is about, he thought with an almost fatalistic intuition. *She's read it and it's upset her.* He chose his words carefully. "Would it help you to talk about it?"

There was a long moment of silence. "Maybe. Could you come to my room?"

"Sure," he said. "I'll be right there."

He didn't know what in hell was happening, but she certainly did not sound in the mood for seduction. He sighed and picked up the expensive bottle of Merlot he'd bought, just in case his luck changed.

He walked down the worn flowered carpeting of the hall and knocked on her door.

She swung the door open and looked up at him, her sky-blue eyes intense and unhappy. "Come in," she said.

This was, he noticed with disappointment, no replay of last night. She was fully dressed, and whatever was on her mind was clearly not erotic. She turned her back to him as soon as he entered, went and sat on the edge of her bed. She stared at a pile of faxed sheets spread on the dark red silk coverlet.

He set the wine on the bureau. "That's the information your lawyer sent?"

She nodded, her jaw set.

"Are you going to let me see it?" he asked.

"You might as well," she said and looked up at him with an expression he didn't understand.

He realized that meant either bad news or no news or a combination of both. "You look like you could use a drink," he said. He nodded toward the wine. "Should I open this?"

"Sure," she said without enthusiasm.

He fished the corkscrew out of his pocket. "You want to tell me why you're so glum?" he said.

She shook her head in frustration. "It's like Judy Sevenstar sold us the keys to five doors. Well, one of them leads exactly nowhere: Donna Jean Zweitec."

"The last name on the list," he said, drawing the cork.

"Right," Jaye said bitterly. "And the date she gave birth was closest in time to Patrick's birthday—less than five months. She might have known someone, she might have had a name that could lead somewhere—somebody's name, *anybody's*—"

He unwrapped one of the glasses on the dresser. He waited for her to go on.

"She's dead," Jaye said, a bleakness in her voice. "She died seven years ago. She was only forty-two. *God.*"

With a steady hand Turner filled a glass half full. "It doesn't have to mean we've hit a wall," he said. "There may be family, somebody who can tell us something."

He moved to her side, offered her the glass. She ignored it, shook her head so that her golden hair swung.

"She was a nurse, Turner. A missionary nurse in

Africa. She died in Kenya in 1993. In an outbreak of some sort of fever."

"Here, drink this," he said, urging the glass on her. She sighed and took it.

"She'd been in Africa for nineteen years. She considered it her home. They buried her there."

Turner was careful to show no reaction. He stepped back to the dresser, poured a second drink, his hand still steady. "Any relatives left in the States?"

"Her parents are dead. She had one older sister. And she's a nun—a Carmelite nun—in North Carolina. A discalced Carmelite nun."

Turner regarded her over the rim of his glass. She leafed through the faxed pages with an air of disappointment that was close to grief. "What's a discalced Carmelite nun?" he asked.

She threw out her injured hand in despair. "She's cloistered. She's taken like—like—a vow of silence. She can only talk to other nuns. And not even to them very much. She's certainly not going to talk to *us*."

"It's only one door closed," he said as kindly as he could. "There are four more. And one's going to open tomorrow."

"I don't even want to think about that," she said, flashing him a wild look. "And why should the one path opening be toward *my* mother? I don't want to find her. I want to find Patrick's, dammit."

"Maybe she can help get you there," Turner said.

"And maybe she can't," she said. "Here. Read it and weep."

She handed him the faxed pages. He skimmed over them. Donna Jean Zweitec, born in Oklahoma City in 1951. She'd attended St. Anthony's High School until spring 1967, then transferred the following spring to St. Boniface High in Spartanburg, South Carolina.

There was no explanation given in the fax. But Turner knew what had happened between that fall and that spring. She'd given birth to a baby, a boy. Was that why the family had moved to Spartanburg—to put the incident behind them?

In 1970 Donna Jean Zweitec had started nursing school, and in 1972 she volunteered for missionary service. The church had sent her to Kenya, where she served faithfully until her death.

Turner frowned to himself. She hardly sounded like a likely candidate for a teenage pregnancy. Had it been a love affair, a foolish experiment, a rape—what? Who could say after all these years?

Beneath the faxed sheets on Donna Jean Zweitec was another sheet with a name, a few facts, and a great deal of white space.

He muttered the name aloud. "Diane Marie Englund Perry Kline."

"What good does that do us?" Jaye asked in despair. "We've already found *her*. We're going to see her tomorrow. We're way ahead of these so-called information brokers. I don't know why I'm paying them to look up dead people and nuns and people we've already found."

He scanned the information again, thin as it was. "No. They've got the basics here on her—this is the key. Pretty soon the computers will be spitting out a lot of information—down to the brand of dish soap she uses."

Jaye sat holding her wine, still-untasted. She shook her head. "What good would that do? When she's already agreed to talk to us?"

"It'll help us to know if what she says is the truth," he said.

For a moment her face went blank. Then she said, "Oh." Her eyes met his.

He nodded. "Let me borrow these sheets, all right? I'll give them back. But let me fax this to the brokers I always use. Just to double-check. All right?"

She looked momentarily doubtful, but then she nodded. "I suppose. It seems wasted effort, though."

"No effort's wasted if it helps your brother," he said. The odd thing was that at the moment, he absolutely meant what he said.

She took a long, tremulous breath. "And Mr. D.," she said. "To help Mr. D. find his son."

Turner did not really give a damn about DelVechio at this point. But he set aside the faxed pages and raised his glass.

"Then to your brother," he said. "And Mr. D.'s son."

She gave him a small smile that quivered slightly and quickly died, but she touched her glass to his. "Yes," she said.

They drank.

Then he set his glass on the bedside table. He bent and took her face, her beautiful face, between his hands. "You cried when you read the fax, didn't you?"

She blinked in surprise. "A little," she admitted. "Not much."

She nipped at her lower lip as if she were ashamed of herself. That small movement made his heart turn over in his chest. "Scared about tomorrow?" he asked.

She lowered her head and nodded. "Terrified."

"That you won't find out anything about Patrick?"

"Yes," she whispered.

"Or that you'll find out more than you want to know about yourself?"

She didn't meet his eyes. "That, too."

He tilted her face toward his. He started to lower his

mouth to hers, then saw the pain in her expression. "Maybe this isn't the time for this," he said, and hated himself for saying it.

"Oh, Turner," she said, "hold me—please. Make me stop thinking—for just a little while."

SIXTEEN

─◦◦◦─

H ER HEART DRUMMING, SHE RAISED HER MOUTH TO HIS.
For an instant he hesitated, then pulled her
into his arms and kissed her, almost roughly yet with
strange tenderness. Need went tumbling through her,
yearning and keen.

His mouth seduced and cajoled, but it also con-
quered, and his tongue tasted like warm honey against
hers.

Then his hands were on her upper arms, and he
pulled her to her feet. He drew back slightly. In his eyes
urgency warred with control.

"Take off your sweater," he said, his voice tight.

He took a step backward. She saw the desire crackling in his gaze and wanted to fan it into flame, strong

and devouring. Slowly she pulled off her sweater, let it drop into a small, soft heap on the floor.

He gave her a small, taut smile that told her he was more than pleased. "I'm going to take the rest of it off you," he said softly. "I want to see you."

With fierce swiftness he unfastened her slacks, almost ripping them. Then he took a deep breath and shook his head. "No," he said. "Slowly. I want this to last."

Deliberately he eased her out of her remaining clothes, letting them fall one by one to the floor. She stood, tense and quivering, as he undid her bra and bared her breasts. The bra dropped, a small silky pool beside her outer clothing. "My God," he breathed. "You *are* beautiful."

He framed her breasts with his hands, his thumbs stroking the pink nipples into sensitive peaks.

"So beautiful," he said, his eyes feeding on her, his touch slow and maddeningly sure, making her ache for more.

"Now," he said, his voice thick with controlled desire. "You undress me."

She raised her hands and with trembling fingers began to unbutton his shirt.

He wore nothing beneath it except a gold chain and medal. When the shirt was half undone, she parted it and kissed his breastbone. She felt the tickle of his dark hair, the warmth of his flesh, the thunderous beat of his heart. She smelled the scent of his cologne.

His mouth swept down and covered hers with urgent hunger. His hands swept over her bare back, then her hips. His groin was hard and warm against the throbbing of her own.

She was borne away, intoxicated by the sexual power

they wielded over each other. He started to fumble with the remaining buttons of his shirt but then he literally tore it off, and she heard the rip of the sundering threads.

Her fingers awkward with eagerness, she undid his belt buckle. He fought his way out of his clothes, and at last the two of them were naked together, flesh hungering for the touch of flesh. He lowered his head and kissed her breasts, teasing them until she reached orgasm from the touching alone.

She wanted the sweet oblivion of sex, and he gave it to her again and again.

When he entered her, the last of her control shattered like the thinnest and most fragile facade of glass. She cried out against his lips and he drank her breath, his body shuddering as he carried them into a darkness so deep it was both like dying and being reborn.

He lay with her sleeping in the crook of his arm. He stared into the shadows of the now-darkened room.

They had made love with an intensity that verged on despair. It wasn't the despair or the intensity that bothered him. It was the idea, the very words *making love*. What had happened between them, for all its sexuality, seemed more to him than simply sex.

He wanted her too much; it had become a weakness, an obsession.

Emotion wasn't something he'd planned on bringing to the equation. And he was bringing more than she did. Emotion was something that she was tired of, exhausted by, didn't want. He desired her. She desired escape.

He had undressed her until she was almost naked—but not quite. He should have untied that damned blue ribbon from her finger, freed her from it if only for a fraction of an hour.

He had the eerie feeling that even now there were three of them in bed: Jaye, himself, and a haunting, stubborn presence who never went away—Patrick.

It was not that Turner thought Jaye's love for Patrick was incestuous—he knew instinctively it was not. But her overwhelming concern for her brother was like a preying beast that denned in her heart and devoured all her emotional energy.

It seemed stupid and petty to be envious of a brother whose marrow was rotting away. Yet here Turner was, jealous of the poor bastard. Because the poor bastard had one piece of abiding luck: Jaye loved him.

Turner realized that no one had ever loved him as deeply and unselfishly as Jaye loved Patrick. In all likelihood no one ever would.

He smiled bitterly to himself. Hell, it was better for her that she not care for him overly much. For if she did, it would not be him she loved, but the illusion he had created to win her trust.

He was not proud of what he had done or what he was. He had been an underprivileged boy who had become an extremely rich man whose only goal was to retire at forty with five million dollars in securities. He had gone into criminal law not out of a love for justice but out of spite.

His father had been a police officer, a violent and corrupt man who'd always gotten away with both violence and corruption. His mother drank to forget about it. His brother went to hell. And Turner had ignored it as much as possible and concentrated on getting richer. He had hated his father, resented his mother, failed his brother.

Jaye hated lies and he had lied to her outright; he had twisted and withheld the truth from her more times than he could count. He saw no choice but to keep on doing so.

What good was the truth at this point? If he told her the truth, he would lose her. If he kept on lying, he might still lose her. He had twisted the reality about himself to her so many times that it was like a Gordian knot.

"*Oh, Turner,*" she had said, "*hold me—please. Make me stop thinking—for just a little while.*"

Christ, Christ, he needed to stop thinking himself. Lying had begun as a necessity, a means to the end he wanted. He tried to believe that he had not trapped himself hopelessly in his own machinations this time.

Damn, he thought wearily, he was sick unto death of DelVechio. The old man was like a wily demon who had caught him in a blood-signed contract. Yet he needed to be about the old schemer's business. He had to hie himself out of this room and back to his own to use his phone and his computer.

Jaye had been downhearted because her information broker had discovered so little. Turner believed that there was more to be found and that he knew how to find it.

He rose on his elbow and smoothed her silken hair back from her cheek. He resisted the desire to kiss her lips and wake her so that they could tangle themselves even more deeply in the sensual web they were weaving.

Instead he gave her temple a chaste kiss. She stirred sleepily.

"I've got to go, love," he said. "I'll let myself out."

She snuggled against his shoulder. "Turner?" she said.

He did not let himself kiss her again, but once more he stroked her hair. "Yes?"

"You're a good man, a kind man. And I meant what I said last night about not making any claims on you."

Make them, he thought. *But I'm not a good man or a kind one.*

"Go to sleep," he said gruffly. "I'll see you in the morning."

He rose from her bed, feeling empty and more alone than he'd felt since his brother's death.

Roland Hunsinger had slept late this evening.

Barbara had not seen him. She had fallen asleep on the couch again, her yarn work still in her hands. Her little white dog lay curled at her feet, looking like a toy made out of ostrich feathers.

Felix came silently into the room, his harshly boned face grave. "He's up from his nap," he told Adon in a low voice. "He's eaten. He'll see you."

Adon rose stiffly from his chair. He had drunk a bit too much. On his third Bombay gin martini, he hadn't bothered to add ice or vermouth.

The old man would notice, of course. Sometimes he was like a carrion crow and saw everything. Yet, paradoxically, at other times he seemed to notice nothing of importance at all.

Adon nodded toward Barbara. "Stay with her," he said to Felix. "Watch her."

"I won't leave her," said Felix. He sank into the chair Adon had vacated and laced his big-knuckled fingers together. His face impassive, he picked up the Tulsa newspaper that Adon had dropped when the print grew too blurry to read.

Adon made his way up the stairs as steadily as he could. He knocked at Roland's door, waited a moment as he was expected to, then went inside.

The television was on, of course, but tonight it was turned to rodeo. The old man liked to watch the clever horses used in calf roping, but he was most fond of bull riding. He always enjoyed seeing a rider thrown and menaced, the more violently the better.

In his youth he had seen a man gutted by a Brahman's horns. It had impressed him mightily, and he lived in hopes of seeing such a thing again.

"Hello, Daddy," Adon said, careful to keep his voice from slurring. All he could see of his father-in-law was the old man's veined feet propped on the elephant-shaped footstool.

"Felix says Barbara's already asleep," the old man said from the shadows. His electronic voice managed to vibrate eerily with displeasure.

"Yessir," said Adon.

"She's always sleeping lately," Roland complained. "And she's too thin. What's the matter? Is she sick?"

"Well, sir," lied Adon, "the doctor says it's a touch of that chronic fatigue syndrome thing." He pulled out the desk chair and sat down in his designated place.

"Phah," Roland said with disgust. "In my day there was no such fucking thing. It's something these new doctors made up. Iron is what she needs. Give her iron. Make her eat liver, that's what."

"I'll do that," said Adon.

"Women are too skinny these days," Roland grumbled. "They look like boys. They look like sticks. This afternoon I saw *Some Like It Hot* on television. That Marilyn Monroe looked like a woman ought to look. She by god had some tits on her. An ass. A belly. Makes you want to get some."

It depressed Adon that Roland sat up there in the dark lusting over a woman more than thirty years dead. He mumbled, "Yessir."

"Barbara needs meat on her bones, if she's going to get pregnant again. She needs good, red blood. I've *told* her that."

I'm sure you have, you insensitive old dickhead. "I have, too," lied Adon.

"You've been drinking," the old man accused. A weird shrillness, some sort of feedback, rose and echoed in his voice.

"I may have had one too many," said Adon. "I guess I lost count. It was an accident. It won't happen again."

"A real man can hold his liquor," Roland said contemptuously, and there was the same high-pitched ghostly reverberation in his voice. "Is that why Barbara doesn't get pregnant? You're not a real man?"

Adon thought, *If it wouldn't break Barbara's heart, I'd see you dead. I'd gladly kill you with my own hands, you disgusting old bastard.* He said, "She's had no complaints."

"She was the most beautiful girl in this county," Roland said. "There wasn't ever a man who saw her who didn't want her. But the only one she ever by god wanted was *you*. So I by god let her have you. You were smart enough in your way. You could serve a purpose—in your way. But then my son ups and dies on me, and all I got left is one child to my name—me, who brought a thousand into the world."

"It's true irony, sir," Adon said stiffly.

"So I've depended on you," the old man said. "But I sometimes think you don't got the *cojones*, the nuts, the balls for it. Everything came to you too easy. Maybe I should hand the whole operation over to somebody else. Jesus. Can't hold your liquor. Can't make a baby that'll take. Only one you did make didn't turn out. Hell. I brought a thousand babies into this world. You can't even bring one that's a keeper."

Adon stiffened as if struck. The one child he and Barbara had had was a sweet little boy born with a brain defect. He stared at the old man in hate.

If Barbara dies before you, I will kill you, thought Adon. *In the most horrible way possible. For years after, men will talk about the way I killed you.*

From the television came the sound of rising excitement from the rodeo crowd. Adon turned to see a cowboy flung from the back of a dun-colored bull. The rider hit the dirt hard, tried to get up, and could not. The bull came, plunging and dancing toward him, hooking its horns.

But the rodeo clowns sprang forward. One lured the bull away, the other dragged the cowboy to safety. "Ha!" cried the old man. "Nearly got him! Damn!"

From between his teeth, Adon said, "Miss Doll heard from the Garrett woman today, but she couldn't find out where she's at."

"Miss Doll is not a woman of subtlety," said Roland in his twanging voice. "She gave good head in her day, but she is not a woman of subtlety."

"The list," Adon said as patiently as he could. "You said the list they have doesn't matter."

"I didn't say *that*," Roland rebuked him. "One thing can lead to a goddam other. I said I'd think on it and I have. I don't want any city lawyer mixed up in this. And I want shut of that woman entirely. I don't want her snooping anywhere *near* this business. It's a can of worms. Dangerous for me, you, everybody. She's got to be stopped. Her in particular."

Adon's stomach pitched queasily. "But what if she doesn't find out anything?"

"What if she does?" Roland retorted. The words echoed on the air with a whine. "You need to find her is what."

"I can get her back here," Adon said.

"You should never have let her get away."

"It was LaBonny's fault," Adon said. "He went after Judy Sevenstar instead."

"*You're* supposed to be in charge of LaBonny. His failure is your failure."

"I said I can get her back. But is it—necessary?"

"God damn your eyes, *yes*. You want everything we got to come crashing down?"

Adon felt the gin churning in his stomach, trying to climb, hot and sour, back up his throat. All he wanted was his wife back, well, and with no one to molest her peace. But he said, "Nossir."

"Then we got to *divest* ourselves of that woman," Roland said, as if only a simpleton would not know.

A fatalism settled over Adon, as if someone had put an unspeakably heavy cloak on his shoulders. "What about the lawyer?"

"Boy," said the old man, "let me explain the facts of life to you." Then he gave a laugh that quavered like a thick metal string, queerly plucked.

And Adon thought of Hollis, who was doomed, even though the old man didn't know it. He had hoped Hollis would be the end of it, but now he knew that it could not be the case. *The killing can never stop*, Adon thought. *Not until we're all in our graves ourselves.*

At the heart of New Orleans very little seemed new.

The streets of the Garden District were old, the houses that lined the streets were old, the tall trees that cast streets and houses in shade were old.

And although Jaye had thought that Oxford, Mississippi, was the deep south, this was deeper still. The foliage was thick and tropically green. The flowers bloomed with almost indecent fecundity, and the morning air was heavy with the scents of jasmine and sweet olive.

But the inside of Diane Englund Kline's house had no sense of the south to it. The furniture was almost defiantly modern, streamlined metal upholstered in black. The walls and ceiling were an immaculate white.

Jaye recognized the framed lithographs on the wall—Alexander Calders, black and white with startling touches of red. These red accents were repeated sparingly throughout the room. A well-shaped piece of pottery on the white mantel, a scarlet pattern running through a black and white rug, a black vase with three crimson silk flowers.

The effect might have been forbidding, but was not; Jaye found it quite beautiful in an austere way. She and Turner sat on the black couch. Before them, on the black coffee table, sat a white tray with a red coffeepot and matching cups.

Across from them sat Diane Englund Kline. In the angularity and ultra-modernity of the setting, she alone seemed softly rounded and old-fashioned. She was also clearly nervous.

She had none of her tall cousin's self-possession. She was short, with round pink cheeks and curly hair that owed its perfect blondness to a beautician. She had a snub nose and a rosebud of a mouth and wore a blue caftan.

She held her hands clenched tightly together in her lap. Her eyes darted about the room as if she did not want to meet the gaze of either Jaye or Turner. Turner had said he liked the feel of the house.

"The decorating isn't typical," she said, a nervous flutter in her voice. "I mean it's—very contemporary.

I—we—don't get into that antique thing they have down here. This"—she made an uneasy gesture that took in the room—"is my husband's doing. He's a graphic artist. He's got all the taste. Not me."

She clasped her hands together again, then pressed them between her knees as if imprisoning them. She stared down at them. "Also," she said, "I have allergies and so do my daughters. It's easier to keep down dust and mold—in a house like this. You know. Simple."

She went silent and kept on staring down at her lap. Part of Jaye's mind thought, *She hates this. I hate doing this to her. I wish we'd never come.*

"We don't have pets or plants," Diane Kline said, as if apologizing. She didn't look up.

Turner spoke. His voice was gentle without being unctuous or condescending. "Mrs. Kline, it was kind of you to see us. We appreciate it more than we can say."

The woman said nothing. Her chin trembled, and Jaye, dismayed, thought, *Oh, God, she's going to cry. We've made her cry.*

Turner said, "Would it be easier if we just asked you questions?"

The blond head nodded. "I'm sorry," she whispered. "I've never talked about this much with anyone—except family."

Turner said, "I told you how we got your name— through a woman whose mother worked at the clinic. The mother kept a list. We're not sure why. There were five names on it. Yours was one. I promise you that this knowledge doesn't have to go any further than you want it to."

"It's all right," she said in a small, shaky voice. "I've put my name on a register. So that if m-my—son—ever wants to—locate me, my name is there."

Jaye blinked in surprise. "You put yourself on a register of birth mothers?"

"More than one. It was only a few months ago. It was like something inside me finally said 'It's time.'"

"Your cousin didn't tell us that," Turner said.

The woman straightened her shoulders, raised her head. She stared at one of the lithographs on the wall. "I love my cousin. But I don't tell her everything."

"Of course," Turner said.

Jaye found that she could not take her eyes off the woman. Diane Kline was younger than Nona by a good fifteen to twenty years. *Is this the age my mother would be?* she wondered. *And Patrick's? Did this woman know my mother? Were they frightened girls together?*

Turner said, "The woman who worked at the hospital—her name was Sevenstar. Mavis Sevenstar. Does that ring a bell?"

"Yes," said Diane Kline, her pink mouth hardly moving. "I remember."

"Do you know why she'd have your name?"

She licked her lips. "We weren't supposed to use our real names. The whole time I was there, they called me Patty Jones. But sometimes—there'd be a slip."

Jaye's heart clenched into a cold, tight fist. If the girls hadn't used their real names, they'd be next to impossible to track. She shot Turner a worried look.

"Mrs. Kline—" he began.

"Call me Diane," she said. She kept her head down, but she raised one hand and began to pick at a loose thread of her caftan.

"Diane," said Turner, "how did it happen that you went to the Hunsinger clinic?"

She took a deep breath. "There were—homes—they called them. Homes for unwed mothers. But my parents didn't want to send me there. It was—a stigma. And there were too many people. My mother found out about Hunsinger."

"How?" asked Turner.

The short pink nails plucked at the blue thread. "There was a woman in Fort Smith. She could set up such a thing. Her name was Mrs. Nations. I don't know how my mother found her. She arranged for me to go."

Turner's eyes narrowed. "Do you know any more about Mrs. Nations? Her first name? What her connection was to Hunsinger? Is she still alive?"

Diane sighed. "Her first name was Dorothy. She was from Oklahoma. Later she remarried, moved away. That's all I know."

"How old a woman was she?" asked Turner.

"I don't know." Diane shook her head. "I never saw her."

"Did your parents pay her to arrange things?"

"Yes. I didn't know—my parents didn't know—nobody knew they were *selling* children." She put her face in her hands and began to weep.

Jaye felt paralyzed with pain for the woman. But Turner was on his feet, at Diane's side, putting his arm around her protectively. "You were a child yourself. It's not your fault. It wasn't your parents' fault. You're right—they couldn't have known."

"Mrs. Kline—Diane—" Jaye said earnestly. "Look at me. I was sold. So was my brother. We—we've had a good life. Our mother loved us very much. She and my father were too old to adopt legally. He died when we were little. But she did all she could for us in every way. She put us both through college. She—did everything."

"Look at her, Diane," Turner said. He squeezed her shoulder. "See? She's one of Hunsinger's babies. She turned out just fine."

Diane raised her eyes. They glistened with tears. She looked searchingly at Jaye. "You're beautiful," she said simply. "What do you—what do you do? For a living, I mean . . ."

"I'm in advertising," Jaye said, a knot in her throat. "In Boston."

"Are you married? Do *you* have children?"

Jaye tried to smile. "No."

"But you've had—a happy life?"

"Yes," said Jaye. "Except that my brother's sick. I need to find his blood relations."

Turner handed Diane his handkerchief. "Her brother turned out fine, too. He's a doctor. Many of the adoptive families were well-to-do. They came from Texas and had connections to an oil company—the same one, Lone Star. All of the children that we know of who were adopted went to families with ties to Lone Star."

Diane stared up at him, bewildered and questioning.

"No," Turner said. "None of the adoptees we know of could be your child. But the chances are that your son went to a Lone Star family, too."

Jaye longed to say something that would comfort the woman. "I can't tell you how much my mother wanted children," she said. "We were—her life."

Turner hunkered down by Diane Kline's chair and took her hands in his. "From the dates we have," he said, "we think you might have been at Hunsinger's at the same time as Jaye's birth mother. Was there any other girl there with you?"

She looked beyond Turner at Jaye, tears rising in her eyes again. For a moment she was silent. "Yes," she said at last. "There were two."

The words jarred Jaye with unexpected force. "Two?"

"Yes," she said tiredly.

Turner held her hands more tightly. "Did either of them give birth shortly before Christmas?"

Diane swallowed. "Yes. Both."

And one of those girls, Jaye thought with a sick tightening in her stomach, *was my mother.*

"Was either child a girl?" Turner asked.

Diane glanced at Jaye again, then looked away. "Both."

A muscle twitched in Turner's jaw. "Do you remember the dates?"

"No. Right before Christmas. Close together. Maybe two days apart. They stayed on a few days after. Then they went home. And there was just me."

Jaye winced at the thought of a fifteen-year-old girl, pregnant and frightened, in a strange place for Christmas.

Turner said, "These other girls, did you know their names? Their real names?"

Diane nodded. "One was Linda O'Halloran. She was from Oklahoma City. The other was Mary Jo Stewart. She was from Little Rock."

Jaye's heart began a rapid stammer. *I just heard my mother's name. But I don't know which one it is.*

Turner looked into Diane's eyes. "Can you tell us any more?"

Diane said, "I never saw Linda again. She was older than us. In her twenties. Mary Jo—I actually met again. In college. At the University of Arkansas. I recognized her immediately—and she did me. We spent three years each pretending the other didn't exist."

"And then?" prompted Turner.

"And then one night she phoned me. She wanted to meet and talk. And—we did. We became friends in a strange sort of way. We've stayed in touch. She's still in Little Rock."

Turner seemed to weigh his words carefully. He stroked Diane's hands. He said, "Do you have any idea which of those women was Jaye's mother?"

Wordlessly Diane nodded and stole another glance at Jaye.

"Which?" Turner asked.

She bit her lip, then looked Jaye in the eye. "It has to be Linda O'Halloran. Mary Jo's found her daughter. Last spring. It's what made me decide to look for my son."

Jaye could only stare mutely at the woman. She should have felt a hundred emotions, some part of her mind supposed. But she felt nothing, only numbness.

She saw that Turner, his face concerned, was watching her reaction. She wanted to smile, to shrug, to show him she was all right. She felt her mouth give an odd little twitch, that was all.

He turned back to Diane. "You said Linda O'Halloran was in her twenties. What did she do?"

"She said that she was a cocktail waitress."

"Did she say anything about the father?"

Diane bit her lip again and shook her head. "No," she whispered. "She didn't talk to us much."

"And the Hunsingers," Turner said, "you lived with them?"

"We stayed in kind of a guest house. A woman brought us our meals. Her name was Winona. Winona Raven. She was a—Native American."

"Did you know anyone else that worked for Hunsinger?"

"Only by their first names. Winona had a son and a nephew we saw sometimes, working around the place. But they weren't supposed to talk to us, and I can't remember their names. The nurses at the clinic? I remember Mavis Sevenstar. There was an Ann, a Nancy, a Jeanmarie."

"What about Hunsinger himself? Did you get to know him?"

"Barely," Diane said in a quavering tone. "I didn't want to know him."

Jaye found her voice at last. "Linda O'Halloran," she said. The name felt strange, almost ominous on her tongue. "Do I look like her?"

Diane gazed at her almost guiltily. "No. Her eyes were blue. But her hair was brown. She wasn't tall like you."

"Oh," said Jaye. She could think of nothing else to say.

Suddenly Diane sneezed, covering her lower face with Turner's handkerchief. She sneezed again and again, and when she finally stopped, she seemed physically weakened. Her shoulders sagged, and her face was mottled with red.

"I'm sorry," she said in a thick voice. "It's the allergies. Stress brings them on. I'm sorry."

Jaye nodded and tried to smile, but her mouth gave only another impotent twitch.

Diane Kline crumpled the handkerchief in her fist. "I passed them on to my daughters," she said. A vague expression came to her face. "I've always wondered if I passed them on to my son. I hope not. Oh, I hope not."

Then she bowed her head and began to weep.

SEVENTEEN

T HAT," JAYE SAID AS TURNER STARTED THE CAR, "WAS
hard. It was too *damn* hard. I hated myself for doing
it."

She said it, her voice tight. It was the first time she'd
spoken since they left the house.

"It wasn't pleasant," Turner admitted. "It had to be
done."

Jaye sighed in emotional exhaustion and raked her
hand through her hair.

"She's a nice woman," Turner said. "Emotional—
but nice. If her son tracks her down, I think he'll like
her."

"Well, he certainly *should*," Jaye said. She crossed
her arms and stared out unhappily as they passed the

houses of Prytania Street. Then she bent her head and put her hands over her eyes. "Christ, what a mess."

He pulled over to the curb, parked, unsnapped his seat belt and hers, and put his arm around her. With his other hand, he took her chin between his thumb and forefinger. "Hey," he said in concern, "are you okay?"

She shook off his hand. "Yes, dammit, and don't be nice to me or you'll make me cry. Haven't you been noble enough for one day?"

"Obviously, the answer is yes," he said, but his arm stayed around her.

"Besides," Jaye pointed out, still keeping her eyes hidden from him, "she kept your handkerchief."

"I brought two," he said.

"Oh, God, you *would*," she said with irritation. "Well, I'm not going to cry. I just need a minute, that's all."

"If it would help," he said in a low voice, "I could take you back to the hotel and try to make you stop thinking about it, like last night."

She gave a strangled little laugh that was edged with tears and swatted at him. "That's disgusting. Don't make me laugh, either. I don't *want* to laugh."

"I'm too noble. I'm too disgusting. Don't make you laugh. Don't make you cry. Make up your mind," he said.

She let her hand fall to her lap, composed her face. She still didn't want to look at him. "You were very good with that woman," she said. "I was worthless."

"I don't have much at stake," he said. "A client. Not a brother. Not a mother."

She shook her head in frustration. "I don't need another mother. I've already got one, and I can't handle her. And I don't see how finding another one is going to help Patrick."

He rubbed her shoulder. "The past is like a maze. You don't know where a path can lead until you follow it."

She stared moodily out the window. Down the sidewalk came a tall young man with dark curly hair. He pushed a little boy in a stroller, and the boy had curly dark hair, just like his. As they drew closer, she saw that they both had the same dark eyes. *Parent and child*, she thought. *So simple and clear and neat. Parent and child.*

"You can get lost in a maze," she said, watching the man and the child pass.

"Not if you keep your head," Turner said. "And you will. I know."

She turned to him in gratitude, managed a shaky smile. He leaned forward so that his forehead rested against hers.

Oh, Turner, she thought in confusion. *You're becoming indispensable. I hate to admit it, but you are.*

She drew back, looked into his green-brown eyes. "All right," she said. "What do we do next?"

He exhaled through clenched teeth. "We learned about three more women. Mary Jo Stewart. Dorothy Nations. Linda O'Halloran."

She tried to keep from wincing at the name Linda O'Halloran.

He said, "Diane says Mary Jo Stewart will talk. So first we get in touch with her. And we try like hell to find Dorothy Nations. If she's still alive, she could tell us a lot."

She nodded, but tensed at the thought of what he was going to say next.

"And," he said, tucking a strand of hair behind her ear, "we need to find Linda O'Halloran."

An unpleasant sensation swept her, like tiny cold spiders crawling beneath her skin. Her stomach tightened and she wondered, *Is this what cowardice feels like?*

"Frankly," she said, "I'm not crazy about the idea of finding her. I mean, excuse the expression, but this whole conception is new to me."

He laughed and kissed her ear. "That's my smart-ass girl. Come on. Let's drive someplace and start doing our incredible telephone-relay team shtick. I'll call Mary Jo Stewart, see if she'll meet us in Little Rock."

"Little Rock?" Nona said dubiously. "You're going on with that man to Little Rock?"

"Yes, if she'll agree to see us," Jaye said. She had told Nona about meeting Diana Kline, of hoping to meet Mary Jo Stewart. She said nothing about Linda O'Halloran.

The car was parked by the art museum, and Turner had gotten out, leaving Jaye to make her calls in private. She could see him working his own phone as he leaned, one hip cocked, against the Buick. She could not hear him, but his frown was earnest as he talked, his hair tousling in the morning breeze.

"You two are traveling together an awful lot," Nona said. "In my day, people didn't do that. People cared about the impression they made."

I don't give a damn about the impression I make, Jaye wanted to say. "We're traveling on business," she said instead. "Lots of people do it nowadays."

"Make sure you stick to business," Nona warned. "You're supposed to be helping Patrick, not playing footsie with some shylock."

"A shylock is a loan shark," Jaye said.

"You know what I mean," said Nona. "Tell me—this woman you met. Did she seem like a *nice* woman? Dr. Hunsinger promised that all his girls came from good homes, that they weren't, you know, floozies."

Except in my case, Jaye thought. The less Nona knew about that, the better.

"She seemed like a nice woman," Jaye said dutifully.

"These girls—they know they did the right thing, don't they?" Nona asked. "Giving those babies to loving families who could take care of them?"

They didn't have much choice, Jaye thought, remembering Diane Kline's tears. "They did what they had to," she said.

"I hope they learned their lesson," Nona said piously. "I've always hoped they made only one mistake and didn't go back down the primrose path. I mean, some probably did, and that's worried me."

Her tone became confiding. "That's why I was always strict with you," she said. "A girl that gets in that kind of trouble—well, you never know. I wanted to make sure you hadn't inherited a tendency toward that sort of thing."

The words hit Jaye like a dash of ice-cold water. Suddenly she realized why Nona had always been so straitlaced and Victorian about sex. *My God, you worried that I came from flawed stock. That my mother had a streak of whore in her and that I do, too. That I'll go bad the way she did.*

Jaye's jaw was tight when she spoke. "That's why you always wanted Patrick and me to be so—puritanical?"

"Well, you especially," Nona admitted. "Boys are different. Boys will always try, of course. It's their nature."

Jaye pushed her hand through her hair in frustration. *I've got to end this conversation,* she thought. *Before I start screaming.*

"I've got to call Patrick," she said in a choked voice. "It's past five in Belgium."

"He's better today, but he had tests all morning," Nona said. "They wore him out. Maybe you shouldn't bother him. Talking tires him."

"Good-bye, Nona," Jaye said without further argument. She pressed the cutoff button and dialed Brussels. Melinda put her on the phone to Patrick, who did indeed sound weak.

"What kind of tests?" Jaye asked.

"Christ," Patrick answered, his words labored, "every kind. Platelet counts. Chest X ray. CAT scan. I don't want to think about it. Tell me how you're doing, blondie."

"Blondie's doing fine," she said. "We're talking to more people, finding more names. We're trying to arrange a meeting in Little Rock."

"Going there with Mel Gibson?"

She smiled that he had the strength to joke. "*Turner* Gibson," she corrected. "Much better-looking than Mel."

"Nona's worried that you're boinking him." Then with a flash of his old impertinence, he added, "Are you?"

"Nona's been worrying about me boinking somebody ever since I turned nine," Jaye said. "Do you realize she's always been such a prig because she's afraid we might have inherited evil, lustful, sexual natures?"

"Well, I inherited one," he said. "And I can't tell you the pleasure it's given me."

Oh, Patrick, I love you, she thought with a dizzying wave of emotion.

"What? What?" he said, his voice sounding farther away than ever. "Oh, crud, Jaye, they want me off the phone. They just brought in something to eat. They *say* it's something to eat. It looks like—it looks like—"

His words trailed off. His usually nimble mind and quick words had failed him, and the lapse made her suck in her breath painfully.

"Gotta go," he said breathlessly. "Gotta go."

"Good-bye, Patrick," she said. "I love you. And we're working hard for you."

He didn't seem to hear her. He repeated himself, like a very old man. "Gotta go. Gotta go."

Someone in Belgium took the phone away from him and hung it up.

For a moment she leaned her elbows on her knees, pressed the heels of her hands against her eyes. She said a "Hail Mary." For years she had gone without reciting the rosary; now, in the past week, she had done it a hundred times.

She straightened and looked out at Turner, who was leaning against the hood and talking with such concentration into his own phone. *Back to work,* she told herself sternly. She tried to call Murray, but when she learned that he was out of the office, her spirits plunged again.

"He had a client with an emergency," said Myra, his secretary. "Call back in the afternoon. Around two o'clock."

"This is an emergency, too," Jaye said, desperation winding her voice tighter. "He said the information brokers should have more for me today. He *promised* they would."

"Maybe," said the secretary. "A fax just came in, but it's marked confidential. I'll need his approval to send it on. I'll have to wait for him to phone in."

Jaye choked back a swearword. "Call me as soon as he does. In the meantime, I have three more names for the brokers to check. Can you relay them? I need immediate action on this—immediate, Myra. I can't emphasize that too much."

"I'll get it done when I can get it done," said the secretary with a put-upon air.

"Right *now*, dammit," Jaye said angrily. She rattled off the three new names, made Myra read them back to her. "I'll call every hour on the hour to see if you've done it," she warned. Then she said a terse good-bye and hung up.

Her head throbbed, and a pain stabbed at the base of her skull like a needle trying to pierce its way into her brain. She ignored it and dialed her own answering machine at her apartment in Boston. There were no new messages of importance.

She dialed her office voice mail. Messages from frustrated clients, exasperated artists, a petulant male model wanting to know why she hadn't confirmed his casting. Nothing that mattered.

She called Miss Doll's number to tell her that she would probably be gone at least another night.

A busy signal buzzed in her ear like a large, angry insect.

While Jaye found difficulty connecting with anyone, Turner had reached a woman who was a live wire crackling with energy and information.

Mary Jo Stewart, a widow, worked in Little Rock as an assistant director of a women's family-planning service called Choices. She had a warm, low voice with a southwestern twang, and so far she had answered his questions with remarkable frankness.

"We specialize in counseling pregnant teens," she said. "I don't want to see any more kids have to go through all that garbage and back-street intrigue that we did. Hunsinger was a money-hungry quack. Worse than a quack."

Turner raised an eyebrow in interest. The woman sounded angry, but hardly irrational. "Worse?" he repeated. "How so?"

"He was a butcher," she said with disdain. "I was never able to have children again. I had all kinds of trouble after the birth. Two years later I had to have a complete hysterectomy. I was only eighteen."

"I'm sorry," said Turner, and the word *butcher* repeated like an evil echo in his mind. A girl had died, Judy Sevenstar had said.

"What happened with Hunsinger—don't think that such a thing affects only a woman's body," Mary Jo Stewart told him. "It messed with my head for a long time. For years I couldn't see a baby without thinking of what he'd done to me. That's why it became so important for me to find my daughter."

Her strong voice trembled.

Turner said, "I'm glad you found her."

"So am I. And so, I hope, is she. And guess what? Tada! I'm a grandma, too. She's got two little boys of her own now."

"Congratulations," said Turner.

Mary Jo said, "Look, I've *been* through an adoption search. I know what it's like. And Hunsinger screwed up the records and falsified them every which way, so it's even harder for us. I'll do anything I can to help."

"If we came to Little Rock would you talk to us?"

"Absolutely," she said. "I meant what I said about helping. I knew I couldn't rest until I finally saw my daughter—even if it was only to know that she was okay, that she'd had a decent life at least. She is, she did, and she's a lovely girl." She chuckled. "It's been a bumpy ride sometimes, getting to know each other. A bumpy ride for *both* of us. But it's been worth it."

Turner smiled a one-cornered smile. He had a hunch that Mary Jo Stewart was a woman well worth knowing. Bumpy ride and all.

He said, "Diane Kline said there was a third young woman with you at Hunsinger's. A Linda O'Halloran."

"Oh," she said. *"Her."*

His smile died. A chill of apprehension prickled up his spine. He said, "You didn't like her?"

"Not especially," she said with an ironic little laugh.

"Why not?"

"If you come up here, maybe we'll go into it then. It's not something I care to discuss over the phone, okay?"

"I understand," Turner said, and what he understood was that the news about Linda O'Halloran would not be good. He thought of Jaye. *I don't want her hurt, goddammit.*

To the Stewart woman he said, "Linda O'Halloran—do you have any idea where she is today?"

"None," the woman said. "I always supposed she went back to Oklahoma City. She worked in a hotel restaurant there, the Empyrean Room. I never followed up on her."

Turner thanked her and told her he'd be in touch again soon. He hung up. On impulse he dialed Oklahoma City information.

A prerecorded voice asked him the name he was searching for. "O'Halloran, Linda," he said.

There was an instant of silence, and far away he

imagined chips and circuits electronically searching in vain for such a person.

Then the mechanical voice came back. "The number is 555-8932." It made a programmed pause and repeated itself. "The number is 555-8932."

Shit, Turner thought. *It can't be the same woman. It can't be.*

But he dialed the number with something akin to superstitious dread in his heart. The phone rang nine times. Then a woman answered.

"Hello?" she said. She sounded sleepy, and she had what Turner thought of as a whiskey voice—low and husky to the point of roughness.

"I'd like to speak to Linda O'Halloran," he said.

"Yeah. This is me," she said. She made a sound like a stifled yawn.

"Ms. O'Halloran," he said, "my name is Turner Gibson. I'm an attorney from Philadelphia. I'm trying to find a Linda O'Halloran who used to work at a hotel restaurant in Oklahoma City in 1964, the Empyrean Room."

"Yeah," she answered. "That's me. I'm the one." She yawned again. "A lawyer? What's this about? Did somebody die and leave me a lot of money? Like in my dreams."

"Ms. O'Halloran," he said, "there's a Dr. Roland Hunsinger in Cawdor, Oklahoma. I was told that in 1966 you—"

She cut him off. "Omigod," she said, her voice suddenly a wail, "omigod, *no.*"

"Ms. O'Halloran—"

"No, no, no, no, *no!*" the woman cried. "You let me alone! You let me alone!"

"Ms. O'Halloran, this is a matter of great im—"

"I don't want to hear about it," she said. She began

to cry hysterically, great gulping sobs. She hung up on him so hard, his ear rang from the impact.

Christ, Turner thought, but he dialed the number again. He got a busy signal. He waited two minutes. He dialed again.

He got an answering machine. "Hi, this is Linda, but I'm not home right now. Leave your message and number at the sound of the beep."

Quickly Turner gave his number and repeated his name. "Ms. O'Halloran," he begged, "please call me. All I want is information. I'm trying to trace two people, a boy born in May of 1957 and a young woman who had a son in March of 1968. The father of the boy born in '57 wants to recognize the relationship. The boy born in '68 needs a marrow transplant. In both these cases time is cru—"

Linda O'Halloran's voice, tearful and full of resentment, came back on the line. "You leave me *alone,* God damn you!" she stormed.

"Ms. O'Halloran, just hear me out," Turner pleaded. "If it's a question of money, I can—"

"Don't *ever* call here again, you prying sonuvabitch. What's over is over. I never want to talk about that time. Never. It's over. It's done. Go fuck yourself, you fucker."

She hung up on him again. He tried three more times. He got no signal. She had disconnected the phone.

Together Turner and Jaye walked in the shade of the live oaks. He'd told her they needed to talk.

Jaye jammed her hands deep into the pockets of her slacks. The motion hurt her broken finger, but she hardly noticed. She tossed her hair rebelliously.

"So she doesn't want to talk," she said of Linda O'Halloran. "So what? I'm just a bad memory to her.

Well, she's no memory at all to me. Why stir it up? Let her be." She shrugged.

Turner took her by the elbow, stopped her, made her look at him. "I just wanted you to know I found her, that's all. I'll have to try to see her. If you want to stay out of it at this point, I'll understand—"

Jaye shook her head stubbornly. "Why do we need to see her at all? Diane Kline's talked to us about 1966. Mary Jo Stewart's agreed to. But 1966 doesn't even have anything to *do* with Patrick. He was born in 1968."

Turner leaned nearer, staring into her eyes. "She may know *something*. So I'm going after her. As soon as we talk to Mary Jo Stewart."

Jaye raised her left hand, a gesture for him to drop the subject. "Fine," she said. "Do what you have to with her. But leave me out of it."

He took her wrist firmly. The blue ribbon had come partially undone from her little finger. He began to redo it. He said, "What if I can't leave you out of it?"

She watched his fingers, so precise and steady on the ribbon. Her heart beat harder. "What do you mean?"

He said, "You may be the one person in the world who could make her talk."

A grim and reluctant resignation swept over her. *I don't want to. It's the last thing I want. I don't even know why it scares me.*

"There's more," he said, lacing his fingers through hers. "I can bring reason to the table to convince her. I can bring the issue of ethics. I hope I can bring tact. But you always bring something I can't."

"What?" she breathed.

"Passion," he said. "So much passion."

She bit her underlip, possessed by a sudden, irrational impulse to cry. "Oh, hell," she said miserably. "I'll do whatever I have to do. You know that."

"Yeah," he said. "I know that." He kissed the splinted finger.

She looked away. The museum gardens were riotous with brilliantly hued flowers, exotic foliage. For a moment the colors swam and blurred in her vision.

Turner ran a forefinger across her knuckles. "Look," he said. "I know it's got to be a shock to you—all of a sudden knowing who she is, where she is—"

He stopped, kissed her injured finger again. "And it's got to sting a little, that she doesn't want to talk about it. But it has to come as a shock to her, too, after all these years. A lot of these mothers might react the same way."

She shook her head, said nothing.

"You want me to take you someplace, buy you a drink?" he asked.

"No," she whispered. She took a deep breath and faced him again. "I have things to do."

With one hand he held her injured one. With the other he touched her face. "It wouldn't be a sin to take half an hour for yourself, you know."

"I have to get that information from Murray. Can I use your computer?"

He smiled a little ruefully. "You finally trust me enough to use my computer?"

"Yes," she said, and squeezed his hand. "I finally trust you enough."

"Let's keep it that way," he said.

She nodded, suddenly feeling shy with him. She had experienced intense emotions with this man, so many that she was beginning to feel a bit frightened.

"Promise?" he asked, his tone gently teasing.

"Promise," she agreed.

His fingers still twined through hers, he bent and kissed her.

．　　．　　．

All morning long, LaBonny and his men had slogged
through the storm but found no trace of Hollis.

The rain was so cold that LaBonny regretted bringing Sweety. Wet and shivering, she cowered close to his
legs, whimpering when the thunder rolled. LaBonny
thought Hollis deserved to die just for the discomfort
he'd caused the dog.

Bobby Midus kept bitching, complaining that the
ground was too wet for a man to make out either sign or
track. Wherever Hollis was, said Bobby, he had to be
drier and warmer than they were; he was probably holed
up somewhere laughing his crazy ass off.

In the meantime, said Bobby, here they were hump-
ing along like grunts in some goddam monsoon in some
goddam Vietnam movie. And Hollis, like the goddamn
Cong, was hiding, the goddamn invisible man.

Hiding where? LaBonny wondered, his ill temper rising. *Where?*

Then Bobby found the entrance to a cave even *he*
hadn't known existed. He said he'd heard of a cave in
these parts, but he'd never believed it. And now, son of a
bitch, here it was.

LaBonny's blood went wild with an excitement that
was almost orgasmic. *Got him!* he thought. Hollis Raven
was a dead man.

For LaBonny *knew* what this cave was. It was the
place Luther had blabbed about, the old revenuer's cave,
the place where he'd said he and Hollis had taken the
girl's body and burned it all those years ago—it had to
be.

The cave's entrance was blocked with dirt and vines
and brush, but once Bobby started heaving aside the
deadwood and stripping away the briars, LaBonny could
clearly see the opening.

"Shit, man," Cody J. said, wiping his face wearily, "a

rabbit couldn't get in there." He stood to the side, his rifle raised.

"Hollis could," Bobby said ominously.

The rain kept driving down, and Bobby kept swearing and grunting as he tore through the last of the grapevines and strangle briers. The beautiful skin of his cheek was cruelly scratched, and the water streamed from the bill of his cap as from a drain spout.

Cody J. backed up two steps. "Be careful, Bobby," he warned. "If he's in there, he could come at you."

"Let him," Bobby fairly snarled. "I'm so sick of hunting the son of a bitch, I'll kill him with my bare hands." He dragged down a mass of dead creeper vine. "You hear me, Hollis? I'm comin' in there, and I'm gonna kill you with my bare hands."

"Hush," cautioned Cody J. "Don't make him mad. He's crazy enough."

But Bobby didn't care. When his anger turned to rage, it possessed him so completely that he became wild and fearless; it was one of the most intriguing things about him, thought LaBonny.

"Hollis, you goddam motherfucker," Bobby cried with passion, "I'm gonna dance in your goddam blood!"

And you will, you pretty thing, LaBonny thought, leveling his own rifle. *You will.*

But Hollis wasn't in the cave.

Sweety entered first, low to the ground, her stub of a tail tucked under. But she didn't bark. She didn't growl. The only sound in the woods was the rain pelting through the branches and striking the soaked earth.

When the men entered, the air of the cave was cool and motionless. It was heavy with mustiness that was scented with antiquity. LaBonny shined his flashlight about the interior.

They were in a sort of small room of roughly surfaced limestone. It was not high enough for any of them to stand up straight; they had to hunch over, nearly doubled, as if the cave had turned them into bent old men.

There was a short corridor that ended abruptly after a few feet, blocked by stone debris. "It used to go farther," Bobby breathed on the moist air. "But its ceiling done fell."

"Why?" Cody J. asked nervously. He looked up into the shadows that hung over them so closely.

"Because it's a cave," Bobby said contemptuously. "Caves *cave in*."

The gray walls glistened with damp, and the floor beneath their boots was littered with rotting leaves, small bones, and animal droppings. LaBonny saw a brown spider delicately picking its way out of the light's beam. The place was thick with crudely spun webs. Another spider retreated into the dirty white silk of its trap.

Bobby looked at the moving spider and hit it with his gun butt. "Christ, a brown recluse," he said. "This whole place could be crawling with them. Let's get out of here."

LaBonny's stomach churned coldly. He hated poison spiders, and the recluse was the worst of all. Its bite could make the flesh rot off the bone. He slung his rifle over his shoulder and seized Sweety by the collar, dragging her back into the rain, leaving the other men in the dark.

"Hey!" cried Cody J. "The light!"

But LaBonny didn't care. He wanted his dog *safe*.

Bobby came stumbling after him. "Shit," he said, brushing at his face and slapping at his clothing. "Them spiders get in a place like that and eat up everything until they ain't got nothing to eat but each other."

Cody J. pushed past him, stamping his feet and

swearing. "Man, it smells like a goddam tomb in there. Hollis ain't been *there*, I guarantee you."

"When we find him, I'll by God put him there," vowed LaBonny.

"I'm gettin' too old for this," Cody J. said, casting a resentful look at the cave. "My joints ache. I didn't sleep good last night. Ached and done had nightmares. Dreamed Judy rose up and walked out of that river, lookin' for a golden needle to sew her stomach back shut."

Bobby laughed in disgust. "Sew your own mouth shut. Your granny told you too many spook stories."

"Had to get up twice last night to put linament on my knees," complained Cody J. "I'm probably coming down with the rheumatiz. It runs in my family."

"Mouths run in your family," sneered Bobby.

LaBonny ignored them both. He squatted and ran his hands over the dog's smooth, quivering body, searching for any sign that she'd been spider-bitten. Her hide felt like drenched silk stretched taut, and her nipples were hard as cold little pearls to his touch.

"You all right?" he asked her tenderly. "My baby all right?"

Adon lifted the phone in his study. It was still dead. The goddam spring storm had knocked the lines out.

He wondered darkly if it was only here, out in the country, or if the service was down for all of Cawdor and Mount Cawdor. He would get through to that spying old bitch Doll Farragutt eventually, he knew. But could Doll call out? Had she reached the Garrett woman yet?

Christ, how had it come to this? He had never planned for his fortunes to be joined with those of Roland Hunsinger. From boyhood, he had heard the rumor that Hunsinger's money and power were anchored in blood.

Adon had gone off to college wanting to study poetry and literature, but there was no future in it. So he had gone into law.

He had not meant to come home and join his father's dusty country practice. He had meant to go far away to romantic cities and sophisticated adventures. But he had not.

He became his father's partner. With that partnership, he uneasily entered into his father's alliance with Hunsinger. He had never meant to sink into it this deeply.

But somehow, while he'd slipped from youth to early middle age, little Barbara Hunsinger had grown up into a startlingly beautiful and delicate woman. And she loved him. She'd loved Adon. It was a miracle.

Now the storm wind seemed to pluck at the walls of the house as if trying to pick it apart, bit by bit. The rain swarmed down the windows, blinding them to the view beyond.

From the living room, he could hear the sound of the television. Barbara was there, curled up on the couch in her white robe and her pretty little white slippers with the open toes. Her little dog was asleep beside her. Next to her was her lunch on a tray stand. He knew the food was untouched. He ached with his need to protect her, to rescue her from her sorrow.

But it was becoming so hard. So hard. When Hollis and the Garrett woman and the lawyer were gone, Adon knew he would have to find a way to kill LaBonny, or LaBonny would destroy them all. It must be done. The old man had told him so, and had told him how to do it.

Adon leaned his elbows on his desk and put his face

in his hands. Perhaps at this moment LaBonny was murdering Hollis; he prayed that it was so.

Through the closed door came the voice of Julie Andrews, gloriously singing that the hills were alive with the sound of music. Adon wept.

EIGHTEEN

———◦◦◦———

LIKE A PACK OF HOUNDS WITH SUPERNATURAL POWERS, the investigative agency had tracked down the three remaining women on Judy Sevenstar's list.

The information from Jaye's broker flashed onto Turner's glowing computer screen. Then it hummed and clicked through the built-in printer, transforming itself from electrons to ink.

There it all was, retrieved from cyberspace: their married names, their addresses, occupations, phone numbers; their pasts and their presents.

They all shared a common background in Arkansas and Oklahoma, but little else—except for what was unrecorded, their sojourns with Hunsinger. Their levels of education varied, and they were scattered from St. Louis to Hawaii. One was married, another divorced, the third had remained single.

Turner could reach only one of them by phone. Neither Janet Banner nor Cyndy Holtz answered.

Shirley Markleson Mathias did. She had been fifteen years old when she bore a son in 1961. Now she had been married to the same man, a choral music director, for thirty-one years. She was a mother and grandmother, a Sunday-school teacher and church secretary in Lincoln, Nebraska, where she had lived for the past three decades.

Turner reached her at her home. Jaye was beside him while he talked, tensed, her eyes full of anxiety.

Shirley Mathias had a bad cold, but was cordial until he mentioned Hunsinger. "I don't know what you're talking about," she said with sudden sharpness. "You have me confused with someone else."

"I don't think there's any confusion," Turner said as amiably as he could. "We desperately need people who'll—"

"I don't know what you're talking about," she repeated.

"Anything you say will be held in the strictest confidence—"

"I don't know what you're talking about," she snapped a third time. "You've got the wrong person." She hung up on him. When he redialed, the line was dead. Like Linda O'Halloran, she'd unplugged the phone.

"She's playing hard to get," he said as he flicked shut the phone. "I'll try again later."

He and Jaye sat at a picnic bench on the museum grounds. "Sorry," he said and put his hand over her injured one.

She sighed and nodded at the flimsy computer

printout that lay on the table, weighted by a pinecone, its pages fluttering.

She no longer seemed to feel the need to conceal information from him. She hadn't asked him to shake hands, to make any sort of promise or pledge. She seemed simply to assume that they no longer kept secrets.

She pointed at the date Shirley Mathias had delivered her son in October 1961. "Look at that. It seems so long ago," she said in sad wonder.

It was a long time, thought Turner. Women like O'Halloran and Mathias probably saw it as an eon ago, a time so distant they had earned the right to disclaim it.

He said, "I'll stay after her. After all of them. Ready to hit the road for Little Rock? It's a long ride."

"I should try again to get Miss Doll," she said. "So she doesn't throw out my clothes and have my car towed away."

She reached for her own phone. "I've still got to get through to Murray, too," she said worriedly. "His secretary said he wanted to talk to me personally. I don't know what's up. I hope it's something good for a change."

Turner rose. "I need to get a cup of coffee. You want one?"

She shook her head. "No, thanks." She managed an anxious little smile.

He nodded and made his way toward the museum coffee shop. He knew Jaye was secretly disappointed at the information her broker had furnished on the three remaining women. She had wanted more than bare statistics.

But Turner knew such information usually started in a trickle, then widened to a stream and then to a river of facts. Most of these facts would be trivial and many would be useless.

The river of information could broaden into a flat, featureless sea of minutiae in which an investigator could drown of boredom. But once in a while, the flood produced a treasure of some sort, perhaps a single pearl, and a vigilant watcher would find it.

He got his coffee, headed down the museum's steps and back toward its grounds. He saw Jaye sitting in the shade, her hair rippling like silk in the breeze. She was talking intently on the phone—too intently, he thought.

He frowned. He walked toward her, waiting for her to lift her head and notice him, acknowledge him. She did not. She listened, she spoke, she listened again.

Her injured hand was pressed against her breastbone, almost as if in supplication. She hung up just as he reached the table. She looked at him, her face aglow.

"That was Miss Doll. She said she's been trying to get me, but they've been having trouble with the phone lines—thunderstorms. Oh, Turner, somebody's been calling there for me, a man, she said, and he says he knows something about Patrick. He wants to talk to me in person. I've got to go back to Cawdor."

Her words came out in a breathless tumble. She rose from the bench, eager to go, and her cheeks, usually pale, were hectic with excitement.

He held up his hand like a traffic cop. "Wait a minute," he said. "Who is this guy?"

"He won't tell her. She says he sounds at least middle-aged. But he said he knew of a girl who had a baby in Cawdor in the middle of March 1968. He said she was a girl with long, straight black hair, that she looked a 'little foreign.' She's still alive—and he knows where to find her. Turner, it *has* to be her. It *has* to."

She started for the car. "Hold on," he said, laying his hand on her arm. "Why doesn't he just phone you? Miss Doll's got your phone number. Christ, you posted it all over Cawdor."

She stopped, looking unpleasantly surprised by his suspicion. "Maybe because it's confidential. Other people have wanted to talk to us face-to-face. Maybe he wants money—other people have."

"And maybe he's a con man," Turner said. He didn't like the feel, the very texture of this. "Or just plain crazy."

"Then I'll have to find out, won't I?"

She tried to draw away from him, but he was insistent. "So where was this guy when you were in town?"

"Maybe he didn't hear about it right away," she argued. "It's actually more convincing *this* way—that he doesn't just pop out with an answer as soon as I ask the question. That he turns up when it *isn't* convenient for me."

"I'm sorry," he said, but he stayed, unmoving, in her path. "It just sounds too good to be true. How many people in Cawdor did you tell about Patrick's Asian blood?"

"Oh, God," she said in exasperation, "I don't know."

"Any?"

"Yes—I can't remember how many. Turner, I've got to check it out. If you don't want to come, just say so. I'll take a cab to the airport, catch a flight into Tulsa or northwest Arkansas."

"Then how will you get to Cawdor?" he demanded.

"I'll rent a car," she said, with a frustrated toss of her head.

"You've already got a rented car in Cawdor."

"So what?" she shot back. "I'll rent another one. You

think an extra car rental means anything at a time like this?"

For a moment they looked each other up and down almost combatively. "We should be going to see Mary Jo Stewart in Little Rock," he said.

"This man sounds like he has what I need to know," she countered. "Mary Jo Stewart wasn't even there the year Patrick was born."

He'd seen that set of her jaw, that glint in her eye before. Originally she'd wanted to tag along with him, and he'd been hot to be rid of her. Now he recoiled at letting her go off alone. Not to Cawdor. Especially not to Cawdor.

"It's all right," she said. "I'll call a cab. You go on to Little Rock. I'll stay in touch."

He sensed a peculiar inevitability, almost a fatalism, settling over him. The sunlight, dancing so restlessly among the leaf shadows, seemed to dim.

"No," he said. "We're in this together."

From somewhere in the trees a mockingbird sang its sweet taunt in praise of the beauty of the day.

LaBonny stood among the cedar trees in the pouring rain, watching as Bobby Midus and Cody J. dug into the sodden mound.

Sweety, water streaming from her sleek coat, danced and whimpered.

"Christ," said Bobby Midus, his pretty mouth pouting in disgust, "he done it. He's went and buried that same old dog again. Phew!"

LaBonny looked on in angry repugnance. All morning and most of the afternoon, and this was the only sign they'd found of Hollis—the damned dog's carcass had been dragged to another godforsaken spot and reburied.

Even the floods of rain couldn't wash away the stink rising from the grave. Cody J. took a step backward, flinging up his hands with revulsion. He almost dropped his field shovel. "Shit," he said. "Cover it back *up*."

"No," LaBonny ordered. "Uncover it all the way." Between his fingers he twiddled the little cross Hollis had made for this second grave.

"Why?" Cody J. protested. "Man, this thing'd gag a maggot."

"Because I say so," LaBonny said. The dead dog had lured Hollis out once; it might do so again. Next time LaBonny would have somebody staked out, watching.

"Hollis is crazier than a snakebit pig," Bobby grumbled, but he went back to digging.

LaBonny looked off into the pines, which were blackish-green in the stormy light. The rain streamed off the brim of his Aussie hat and made the world look struck with flickering silver.

Then he turned back to stare dispassionately at the dead dog. "Drag it to the edge of Adon's property," he ordered. "Right in front of the plum grove by the barn."

"Drag it?" Bobby said with abhorrence. "Damn thing's gonna leak and stink all over."

"Make it easier for Hollis to find," said LaBonny.

"I ain't gonna touch the damn thing," Bobby sulked. "I don't have gloves."

"Cody J.," said LaBonny. "Do it. Make sure it leaves a trail."

"Jesus H. Christ," swore Cody. "What a job. I should have been a fucking mailman."

But he reached down and grasped the dog by its hind legs. The bones made a liquid sound at the joints, as if they might tear away. Cody J. swore again, but he kept dragging the dog through the rain-bent grass.

LaBonny and Bobby stayed upwind from him,

Bobby laughing and making jokes at Cody J.'s expense. "Know what kind of dog that is, Cody J.? A rottweiler? Get it? A *rot*-weiler."

Cody J.'s face had a stiff, resentful look, his mouth turned down and his nostrils pinched. He refused to look up and he refused to answer. The dog left a trail of slime and patches of white hair. Occasionally small white worms spilled from the carcass and writhed blindly on the wet ground.

Sweety followed daintily and at a distance, sometimes stopping to sniff the liquid that had oozed from the dog. When she tried to lick up a spot, LaBonny sharply ordered her to stop. She raised her sculpted head, looking abashed, and did not do it again.

At last Cody J. had dragged the dog to the stand of wild plums—almost three-quarters of a mile. LaBonny told him to put it on the east edge of the grove, where no one from the house could see it; the barn would block the view. Cody J. gave it a last yank into place, then dropped it with a wet thump. He stepped back, his face even grimmer than before.

LaBonny stayed upwind. He nodded at the dog's corpse. "Bash its head in," he said.

Cody J. looked at him in pained disbelief. "Jesus, LaBonny, you gotta be kidding—the brains are gonna be worm puke by now."

"Smash it," LaBonny said in a tone that was colder than the rain.

With a sigh, Cody J. took his trenching tool from his belt. He raised it high, then swung it like an ax down on the dog's skull. It cracked apart like a rotten cantaloupe.

"Jee-sus," Bobby gasped and took a step backward, turning his head to avoid the stench. "What's *that* for?"

"To make it harder for Hollis," said LaBonny.

"Harder to what?" demanded Bobby.

"To drag it off and bury it again."

Bobby took another step backward, his full upper lip curled in petulance. "What makes you think he'll bury it again?"

LaBonny gave him a dead-level stare. He tapped the little wooden cross against his wet palm. "He's got a thing about it."

"Well, I'm getting a thing about it, too," Bobby retorted. "I'm getting a thing about this whole fucking day. We're *never* gonna find him in this shit, man."

He glanced at the gray sky in despair, then his blue eyes flashed angrily at LaBonny. "He's holed up someplace, I told you from the first. I want to go home. I want a shower and a bottle of whiskey, and I want Dolores to come over and love on me till I'm warm again."

Dolores was a little Mexican girl who worked at a convenience store on the highway, and Bobby claimed she could suck a golf ball through a garden hose. She was pretty and well-rounded and giggly, and Bobby was silly for her. LaBonny disliked her with the intensity of a man who senses a natural enemy. It would, he often thought, be tempting to show her exactly how much he disliked her.

Bobby eyed LaBonny, then cast a sly glance at the dog shivering next to his knee. "You oughta take that dog home, LaBonny. She's gonna get sick. Dog with a thin coat like that, she shouldn't be out all day like this."

Do you think you can play me? LaBonny thought in contempt. *Like I was a cheap tin flute?*

"That's right," he said with a tight-lipped smile. "I'm taking her home. But one of you stays, to watch that thing." He nodded at the ruined body of the dog. "I think it's gonna be you, Bobby."

"What?" cried Bobby in dismay. "*Me?*"

"You," LaBonny said, drawing the word out and

puckering his lips. "Cody J.'ll come round about midnight to spell you."

"Me?" Cody J. asked, incensed. "I'm goin' home, spend four hours in the shower washing the stink of this thing off me. I ain't coming back to smell it anymore. Christ, man—I'm *tired*."

"Goddammit," Bobby said furiously, "I want to be with Dolores tonight."

"I want Hollis," LaBonny explained with a tilt of his head that was almost flirtatious. "And if I get what I want, I'll make you happier than Dolores ever will."

Bobby's expression became wary. "What's that mean?"

"Five thousand to the man who gets him," LaBonny said, smooth as silk. They knew he had the money. He'd gotten the lion's share of Judy Sevenstar's cash.

"And," he added, "the very special regard of myself. And of Adon Mowbry. But especially me."

"Well, hell," Cody J. said, shaking his head in frustration. "Five thousand dollars is five thousand dollars. But what if Hollis figgers it's a trap and don't come?"

"He'll come," LaBonny said. "He can't help himself." He smirked and tapped his temple.

"Where'm I supposed to watch for him from?" grumbled Bobby. "The barn?"

"You watch all those sniper movies," LaBonny said, amused at the boy's bad mood. "You figure it out."

"Best place'd be up in the loft," Bobby said sullenly. "At least it's dry."

"Put the silencer on," LaBonny ordered. "Adon don't want the missus or the old man to hear."

"What's wrong with Adon's missus, anyway?" Bobby demanded. "Used to see her out all the time. Good-looking woman. Great tits. Now you never see her a'tall."

"She's got nervous troubles," said LaBonny, unwrapping a stick of gum.

"Since that accident?" asked Bobby.

"Yeah," said LaBonny, putting the gum in his mouth. "Since the accident."

"She lost her baby and her brother," said Cody J. "And her daddy got all banged up."

Bobby raised his chin as if in challenge. "I heard stories that Hollis is her big brother, but she don't know it. That old Doc knocked up a pretty little Indian gal. I heard that's how Hollis got simple, old Doc yanking him out by his head with them forceps. Is that true?"

LaBonny shrugged. "I don't give a damn about his life story. Except the end. I want it to end."

"Man, if he gets within a hundred yards of me, I'll blow off his frigging head," Cody J. vowed with weary resolution. "He's made me freeze half to death and stink like dead dog."

"No," LaBonny said. "I don't want him killed. You can wing him, take him down. But don't kill him."

Bobby pursed his sensual mouth and looked more suspicious than before.

"But *why*?" Cody J. practically wailed.

"Because I want to do that myself," said LaBonny, catching Bobby's gaze and holding it. "I'll show you how to do it right."

"We'll be there this evening," Jaye told Miss Doll. "By about eight o'clock. I'll see you then." She snapped shut her phone and met Turner's dubious eyes. He wasn't happy with her, she knew.

But all he said was "Ready?"

She nodded. He took her arm and led her out the door and onto the sun-baked airfield. They followed the pilot across the tarmac to where the Cessna glittered in the afternoon light.

"Chartering a plane," Jaye said ruefully, "it sounds so . . . decadent."

"Not as decadent as driving all the way back to Cawdor," Turner said, narrowing his eyes against the sunlight.

The pilot's name was Frank Talbeaux; he had a limp, a Cajun accent, and a large tattoo of a vampire bat on his arm.

The plane itself was mostly red and white, but it had one blue wing, and its fuselage was dented as if by hail. Its nickname, stenciled in chipped red paint, was La Pouffiasse, the slut.

Jaye had to admit that it wasn't as if they were chartering a Lear jet, but even hiring the Cessna made her feel extravagant. Turner argued Little Rock would have been a hard-enough destination by car. Cawdor would have been even more punishing.

They'd stood on the grounds of the art museum thrashing it out while squirrels gamboled across the lawn and the mockingbird sang.

"It makes more sense," Turner had maintained. "I call my secretary, have her arrange a flight. We can be in Cawdor by nightfall."

"I can't afford it," she'd said stubbornly.

"You don't *have* to," he'd countered. "*I'll* rent it. I've got an expense account, dammit."

"I don't."

"It doesn't matter. You come as my guest. It's no skin off Mr. D.'s nose."

"But," she'd pointed out, "you wouldn't even be *going* to Cawdor if it wasn't for me."

"You've shared your information," he said. "I share my transportation. It's a fair deal."

Before she could think of a reply, he put his hand on the nape of her neck. The gesture gave her shivers, in spite of the day's warmth. "On this trip, kid, it's like the Bible," he'd said. " 'Entreat me not to leave thee, or to return from following after thee: for whither thou goest, I will go. . . .' "

"The devil can quote Scripture for his own purpose," she'd breathed, but she'd known he'd won. She'd agreed to the flight.

But as they mounted the spindly stairs of La Pouffiasse, she still felt the niggling, unpleasant sense of being a parasite on the wealth of the mysterious Mr. D.

"I feel like a mooch," she said as she strapped herself into the small, hard seat.

"Then you're not a very good one," Turner said, settling beside her. "Or you'd have mooched a better ride."

She looked uneasily around the plane's cramped interior. There were beer cans and sandwich wrappers on the floor, and a fly buzzed lazily around the cabin.

"Maybe we should have waited and taken a regular flight," she said uneasily.

"This is faster," Turner said.

"*Merde!*" cried the pilot, swatting the fly. "*Je te fous une baffe!*" He flicked the dead insect from his control panel as he settled into his seat. Over his shoulder he said, "Please don't play those phones and 'lectronic things. They fuck up the signals."

"Don't want to fuck up the signals," Turner said, an eyebrow crooked. He stowed his computer under the seat.

With a clatter and a roar the Cessna's engine came to life, vibrating so hard that the cabin rattled like a shoe box being shaken by a giant.

Turner faced Jaye and smiled lazily. "If we were in Philadelphia, Mr. D. would see that we had a *much* better plane. Sorry about this."

The clamor grew louder; the cabin shivered until its very metal threw off a pained, high-pitched hum. Jaye gritted her teeth and shouted in his ear, "Who's more powerful than Mr. D.? I want to sleep with *his* lawyer."

Turner laughed.

The plane began to bobble and lurch down the runway. The motor made a sound like a continuous thunderclap, and Jaye thought she could hear rivets shrieking. She took a holy medal from her purse and the scarf Nona said was dipped in the Vatican's holy water. She clutched the medal in one hand and the scarf in the other.

She closed her eyes tightly and thought, *Patrick, Patrick, Patrick.*

LaBonny was driving home through the rain when his beeper vibrated against his thigh like an unwanted caress. He reached under his slicker and withdrew the pager. Its display window showed him the too-familiar code that signaled Adon wanted to meet him in the lane. And he wanted to meet *now.*

What did the weak, spoiled fucker want now? Why couldn't he just call and at least give a hint? It disgusted LaBonny, Adon's fear of the telephone, his cowardice about leaving any sort of a trail. It was the lawyer in him, thought LaBonny, the politician. And Adon was scared shitless of Allen Twin Bears of the state police—of an Indian, for Christ's sake—LaBonny found this shameful.

He set his teeth together and put the beeper back in its holster. Sweety was in the back of the truck in her canine carrier, protected by a tarp. He'd wanted to get her home, get into a long, warm shower with her. He had a special·dog body scrub that he used on her that made her fur glistening and soft.

He was only a mile from his own place, but he pulled into a drive, turned around, and headed back toward the Mowbry ranch.

The rain lessened, dissolving into the finest of mists, and fog was forming in the valleys between the hills. The ravines filled with it as with cloudy rivers, and it trickled thickly even in the ditches that ran beside the roads.

LaBonny saw no beauty in the fog embracing the low places of the earth, no otherworldliness; he saw only menace. Hollis could be out there slipping through the fog like a phantom, and Bobby, up in the loft with his rifle, would never see him.

A haze hovered low over the flattest of fields, which this evening were empty of horses. Adon's farm lane ran between two such fields, and the vapor danced across it like ghosts playing hide-and-seek.

Adon stood in the road looking like a ghost himself. He wore a black raincoat and he carried, absurdly, a black umbrella. Behind him his black Jeep glimmered in the mist.

LaBonny parked, sighed resentfully, got out of the truck. He adjusted the tarp over Sweety's carrier. The dog whined, eager to go home. "Steady," LaBonny consoled her.

He walked up to Adon, his slicker making a silky, brushing sound. "What is it?" he asked, looking down at the smaller man.

Adon looked mournful and lumpish in his black coat. The mist had pasted his thin hair to his skull; it speckled his glasses.

"The Garrett woman, the lawyer, they're coming

back," Adon said. He shifted his umbrella from one chilled hand to another.

"When?" LaBonny asked. He looked down at Adon's silly rubber overshoes. They were the sort of effete thing worn by a man not cut out for a real man's work.

"Soon," Adon said. "Doll phoned. She said they're coming from New Orleans by private plane. Landing at XNA."

LaBonny nodded. XNA was the region's newest airport, off in the boondocks where the noise of planes would bother only cattle and chickens. "When?" he asked.

"About eight tonight," Adon said. He shivered with the cold.

"It'll be later," LaBonny said, "if this keeps up." He glanced up at the low, impenetrable lid of clouds and knew he was right. It always pleased him to show more savvy than Adon.

"It would be best if they didn't come back at all," Adon said.

You mean it would be best if they die, LaBonny thought without emotion. He said nothing. He only lowered his eyes and stared down at Adon's round, moist face.

"You understand?" Adon asked.

LaBonny gouged a trough in the wet gravel with the heel of his hunting boot. "I understand," he said.

A small burst of rain began to rattle down, and Adon moved the umbrella to shield himself from it. "Second," he said, "it would be helpful to know exactly how much they know and with whom they've been in contact."

With whom, LaBonny thought with contempt. Only a pussy college boy talked like that. It was another sign that Adon wasn't fit to run the business of the county. *With whom,* for Chrissake.

But LaBonny said, "Find out who knows what? Consider it done."

Adon pulled the collar of his black raincoat tighter. "Third," he said, "when they leave—"

When they die, thought LaBonny.

"—it should seem natural," said Adon. "You take my meaning?"

It should look like an accident, LaBonny thought. "Yes," he said. "That can be done."

But he also thought, *It's coming down to a lot of killing, Adon. With the blood all on my hands. Not yours. I'm the piper that you have to pay.*

"You haven't found Hollis yet," Adon accused. Suddenly the expression on his soft face looked surprisingly dangerous.

"Shitty weather," said LaBonny. "He's laid low. He'll have to come out sooner or later. I got a man posted."

"Any sign he's been watching my house anymore?" Adon asked. The lenses of his glasses were misty disks in the fading light.

"Yeah," LaBonny lied. "Bobby saw some fresh tracks. It's all right. Like I say, I got him on watch."

Adon made an ineffective gesture, something like a shrug. "It should be done by now."

"Stop the rain," LaBonny said evenly, "and I'll get it done."

Adon looked at him, his mouth like a black slit. He was not amused. "Get to XNA. Wait for that plane. We'll all rest easier once this is done. And remember—it should seem natural."

LaBonny nodded and said nothing. He had his own plan forming. If they got Hollis, too, tonight, they could put all the fucking bodies in the spider cave and blast it shut, burn the car, sink it.

The less evidence strewn around the county, the better. If anybody asked, the story would be that the lawyer and the woman drove off through the rain, nobody knew where, it was as simple as that.

He watched as Adon went to his Jeep, opened the door, and climbed inside. With an almost prissy motion he closed the umbrella and shook water drops from it. Then he pulled his door shut, turned on his lights and wipers, and headed down the lane to his home. His warm, his brightly lit, his undeserved home, thought LaBonny, standing in the cold rain.

He turned back to his truck, readjusted Sweety's tarp. "I'll take you home, darlin'," he murmured. "And I'll make this all up to you, soon as I can."

They were fogged out of the XNA airport, the Fayetteville airport was just as bad, and Tulsa was under a tornado warning, with three funnels sighted so far. *Maybe,* thought Turner, *this is for the best.*

Frank Talbeaux, with much swearing, turned La Pouffiasse away from the sodden north of the state and headed back toward Little Rock. There, too, it was raining, and he landed her in a soup of mist.

Turner and Jaye sprinted across the damp tarmac, their heads down. Talbeaux scurried behind them, muttering furiously in French. "What's he saying?" Jaye whispered.

"Don't ask," replied Turner.

They made it inside the airport, and Talbeaux headed straight for the men's rest room. Turner suspected he had a flask in his battered valise.

At the commuter flight gate, stranded travelers filled the seats, looking disconsolate. At the check-in counter, a clerk with an angry air avoided making eye contact with anyone. Behind her was the status of the current sched-

ule. Nothing was flying in or out of northwest Arkansas
or northeast Oklahoma.

The atmosphere of the waiting area was heavy with
worn patience and despair. Its trash cans overflowed.
Castoff newspapers littered the few empty seats. The
floor was streaked with tracked-in rain.

Turner could use a drink, a strong one, Cutty Sark,
straight up. "Want to see if this dive has a bar?" he asked.

Jaye nodded, but in her expression worry was com-
bined with distraction. "I need to call Miss Doll. Tell her
we're delayed so that she won't wait up."

She was already taking her phone from its holder.
He put his hand on her upper arm.

"Maybe we should stay here for the night," he said.
"We could talk to Mary Jo Stewart. We're on her turf."

But Jaye had that stubborn glint in her sky-blue eyes,
that set to her jaw. "I want to get there as soon as I can."

"It's already past six o'clock," Turner said. "There's
no knowing when this weather'll let up."

"When it lets up, I'll be ready," she said, dialing. "If
you want to stay, I'll get a standby ticket on one of the
commercial flights. Or maybe I could rent a car and
drive."

Christ, he thought, she was like a terrier. Once she
got a hold of something, she never let go. He sighed
harshly in resignation. "We'll talk about it. I'll tell
Talbeaux we'll be in the bar," he said, and set out to track
him down.

Talbeaux was in the rest room with whiskey on his
breath, fairly reeking of *eau de* rotgut. Maybe he'd pass
out and they'd *have* to stay in Little Rock. No, he thought
grimly, at this point Jaye would hitchhike to Cawdor,
she'd crawl there on broken glass.

When he found her again, she was standing alone in
a corner by a machine that dispensed soft drinks, her

golden head lowered. She was on her phone, gripping it so hard that her knuckles were pale, and she was listening intently.

He gave her a one-cornered smile to tell her he'd let Tableaux know where to find them. She did not smile back. Her face was stiff with displeasure, and when her eyes met his, they flashed with something beyond anger, something akin to hatred.

That blue laser gaze held his for only an instant and then she looked away, as if she could not bear the sight of him. She turned her back on him.

Something inside Turner seemed to fall down and die. A foreign emotion swept over him, dark and consuming. He supposed it was guilt.

She knows, he thought, looking at her straight back, her implacable shoulders. *She knows*.

Jaye felt sickness, but she also felt a small, cold rage that froze the core of her heart. "You're sure?" she said to Murray.

"I'm positive. Listen, I tried to get you all afternoon. I couldn't."

"We were on a plane," she said. Her jaw felt stiff, as if it were wired. "A very small plane. I couldn't use the phone."

"With *him?*" Murray asked, apprehension in his voice.

"Yes," she said, and the rock of ice at her heart's center took on another cold layer. "With him."

"But," said Murray, "you said he's not there right now?"

She could feel Turner's eyes on her back. She sensed his presence as if he threw off some sickening and poisonous radiation.

"He just came back," she said. "Just now."

"Jaye, be careful. I don't know what it all means—" Murray said.

"But you're *sure* about this, Murray?" she pleaded. "There's no mistake?"

He paused. He said, "There's no mistake, Jaye. None. The man he's representing is Mafia. Turner Gibson is a mob lawyer."

NINETEEN

❧⟡❧

H E SAW HER SNAP THE PHONE SHUT. THERE WAS SOME-
thing ominously final in the gesture. It made a bitter taste rise at the back of his throat.

Very deliberately she put the phone back in its holster on the strap of her purse. Just as deliberately, she
turned to face him, her face as pale and hard as a frozen
pond.

The eyes that had once looked on him with gratitude, with admiration, even affection and desire, were
cold with loathing.

He raised one hand, a gesture of apology. *I can explain everything,* the gesture tried to say. But the expression in her eyes didn't change.

"That was my lawyer," she said, her voice flat.

"Yes," Turner said. "I can tell something's happened. I should have told you before this—"

She looked at him as if he were a particularly vile insect. "I know who Mr. D. is," she said.

"Yes," he said with a nod of agreement. "Mr. D. is—"

"Edward DelVechio," she finished for him. "Bloody Eddy."

"Wait," Turner said. "It's a nickname that's easy to misunderstand. It goes back to his days in the meat-packing industry. He—"

Her words came down like a blade, cutting him off. "He's a murderer."

"Let me explain this," Turner said. "It's been *alleged* that he's a murderer. It's never been proven in a court of law."

She tossed her head. "Because *you* got him off. A killer is walking the streets because *you* got him off."

"My firm represented him, yes"— Turner felt as if he were contorting himself desperately to avoid being impaled on a hook—"and the court found him not guilty."

She tilted her head, her eyes narrowed as if seeing him for the first time. "But you're his fair-haired boy, aren't you?" she asked sarcastically. "You're his bright young man, the one who really brought it off, aren't you?"

Turner hated the damnation flashing in her eyes, and he truly believed he did not deserve it. "No one lawyer in a complex trial can take full credit for anything—"

Again she cut him off. "You get them all off, don't you?" she said. "Him, all his—his henchmen—his whole dirty outfit."

"I've represented more than one person connected

to Mr. DelVechio," he admitted. "But you have to understand this about the law—"

She was having none of it. "You've got him off of big charges—and small ones. Haven't you?"

He wanted to deny it. He wanted to give her all the intricate and elegant arguments that he could spin out as silkily as a spider. But looking into her face, he knew better. He had defended DelVechio against murder, against racketeering, against income-tax fraud. Always successfully.

"You're nothing but mob yourself," she said with contempt. Her nose was wrinkled as if she smelled evil rising off him like the stink of rot. "What do you call it? A consigliere? Like in *The Godfather*."

He felt a flash of anger himself. "No," he shot back. "A consigliere is Mafia, I'm not. I'm a criminal lawyer. That's all. Whoever walks in the door, I can choose to defend—yes or no."

Her expression grew haughtier. "And Mr. DelVechio just kept walking in your door, eh? And you kept choosing yes."

"I'm good at what I do," he said. "I like a challenge." It was true.

"Good at outsmarting justice?" she asked, one eyebrow raised.

"I give my client his money's worth," he said. And that, too, was true.

She took a step closer to him. "Are you really looking for DelVechio's son?"

"Yes," he said, holding her gaze. "I am."

"But"—she made a gesture of incomprehension—"but why *you*?"

"He likes me. He trusts me." Then he decided to add the final and most important truth. "He can afford me."

"Jesus," she said in profound disgust. "And you're

supposed to find this—this poor, innocent man who has no idea who his real father is and say, 'Surprise, your daddy is a Mafioso named "Bloody Eddy." He's up to his neck in organized crime, he—he kills people, he steals and he cheats, but suddenly he wants to *know* you, be part of your *life*—' "

"DelVechio's human, too," Turner said. "He and his wife had no children. He always wanted to find the boy. His wife objected. When she died, he decided to—"

"Decided to *what*, for God's sake?" she demanded. "If he has any feeling for this son, the best thing he could do is *never* let him know the truth. *I* wouldn't want to know *my* father was a Mafia thug. Who would?"

Her voice had risen dangerously. He took her arm, even though she tried to push his hand away. "Quiet down," he said. "People are starting to stare. He doesn't want to harm his son. There's money involved. A gift he wants to give."

"Money?" she said in disbelief. "You mean blood money."

"I mean a gift," Turner retorted. "Mr. DelVechio's never been proven guilty of any—"

"And every dime you've spent since we've met is the same thing, isn't it?" She sneered. "Blood money. *Dirty* money. *Mob* money."

He put up his hand in a placating gesture. "Sometimes, Jaye, the end justifies the means—"

She amazed him by drawing back her handbag and striking at him with it. The holstered cell phone caught him across the bridge of his nose hard.

"Don't pull that Machiavellian garbage on *me*," she ordered, her eyes snapping like blue flames. "You paid for that plane with Mafia money, didn't you? And Judy Sevenstar's list, too—didn't you?"

"It was Mr. DelVechio's money," Turner reasoned.

He felt a warm, slow trickle of blood oozing down his upper lip.

The waiting travelers in the gate area, previously leaden-eyed and depressed, were now alert, watching the scene with greedy interest.

"You let me think you were in family law," she accused him. "You didn't say it was a goddam *crime* family."

He unfolded a handkerchief, dabbed at his upper lip. He could taste the blood dripping down the back of his throat. She had a hell of a right.

"And the things you *said* to me," she hissed in barely controlled rage. "Did I *trust* you? Did I *promise* to trust you?"

He supposed he had no right to defend himself. He forced himself to stay silent.

"Even quoting the Bible at me," she fumed. " 'Entreat me not to leave thee . . . Whither thou goest, I will go—' "

"I meant it," he said.

"You make me *sick*," she said, her lip curled.

He couldn't help it; he began to argue his own case, the urge in him was bone deep. "I got you the list," he said. "I got you to Oxford and New Orleans and this close to Cawdor again. I've stayed with you every step of the way."

"Under false pretenses," she shot back, her eyes bright with furious tears.

"If I'd told you the truth," he said, dabbing his lip again, "you would never have talked to me. Nobody would have. Secrecy was necessary."

"Not secrecy," she retorted. "Lies. God. I went to *bed* with you. A Mafia lawyer—all the time playing Mr. Nice Guy. A knight in shining armor on a white horse. My God. I *hate* you."

She drew back her purse to give him another hit, but his hand shot out, seizing her wrist. He heard a woman gasp. He heard a child giggle.

He stepped closer, looked down into her blazing eyes. "You want airport security here? Keep up the melodrama."

"Let go of me," she ordered from between gritted teeth, "or I'll rip your hand off."

"I'll let go, all right," he said, leaning nearer, "but first hear me out. I'm *not* a Mafia lawyer. I'm a criminal lawyer. If I take DelVechio as a client, I do my best for him, same as if I was a surgeon who took him as a patient."

"How noble," she said scornfully.

"Under the law, every accused person has the right to a defense. Even Eddy DelVechio. That's a basic American principle."

"Now you're hiding behind the Constitution," she accused. "Shakespeare was right. 'Let's kill all the lawyers.' Let me go."

He released her.

"Now get away from me," she said. "And stay away."

He said, "I don't want you going on to Cawdor alone."

"Get away from me," she repeated mechanically, not even looking at him. "And stay away."

She began to walk purposefully toward the boarding desk. He followed, staying close by her.

"Let me take you as far as Cawdor," he pleaded. "Just so I can see everything's on the up-and-up."

"I'm buying a ticket," she said. "If you come after me, I'll make a scene like you won't believe. I'll call airport security. I'll tell them you're harassing me, stalking me." She wheeled to face him. She pulled back her hair from her forehead to show the fading trace of her bruise. "I'll say you did *this*," she threatened. She held up her splinted finger. "And *this*."

"But that's a lie," he objected.

"Then you should understand perfectly how it works," she said.

She walked away and left him standing there.

She bought a standby ticket for XNA. She called Miss Doll for the third time that day—or was it the fourth?

"I'm sorry to keep bothering you," she said. "I'm still having travel problems." She said nothing about Turner, but she was vaguely aware she was still talking too much, babbling too many unnecessary details out of nervousness.

She said she hoped that she'd be on flight 442 to XNA, that she'd rent a car and drive to Miss Doll's, that Miss Doll should not wait up late or get up early for her, that she did not know what time she'd get in.

"Rent a car?" Miss Doll said, sounding shocked. "But, honey, you already got one sitting in the driveway."

"Yes, well, I'll have to hire somebody to drive one back to the airport," Jaye said. "I'll figure it out later."

"It seems a shame," Miss Doll said, "renting two cars. Why those companies, they charge you an arm and a leg."

Jaye tried to sound philosophical and said that things went that way sometimes. She asked if the man had called for her again.

"Yes, he sure did," Miss Doll said. "He called no more than half an hour ago. But I said you was having weather problems. He said he'd call back in the morning."

Jaye's already hasty heartbeat sped up erratically. "Did he leave any other message?"

"No, honey," Miss Doll said, her voice laden with sympathy, "he didn't. He makes it clear he wants to talk to you, not me."

"I'll be there as soon as I can," Jaye promised. "If he calls again, tell him that, please—*please*."

"I will, sugar. And don't you get yourself all worn out. You sound tuckered." The woman paused. "I got a nephew who could drive that rental car of yours up there and meet you," she said.

"No . . . no," Jaye protested. Although the offer was tempting, something seemed wrong with it, but she was too numb and fatigued to think it through.

"You could pay him a little something," wheedled Miss Doll. "It'd be cheaper than renting a second car."

A tiny ray of reason broke through her confused thoughts. "He couldn't drive it," she said. "I have the keys."

"Ahhhhhhhhhhh," said Miss Doll. "I didn't think of that."

Jaye told her good-bye, closed the phone, put it away. She looked around the gate area. The atmosphere of impenetrable ennui had settled over it again, as if the travelers were all prisoners in some particularly enervating anteroom of Hell.

Turner had disappeared, going off in the direction of the nearest bar with the limping, profane pilot. Outside the rain strummed and clicked at the big windows, the runway glistened wetly, and the mist made colored rings around the lights.

She put her hand to her forehead and squeezed her eyes shut. She felt foolish and betrayed. Her anger with

Turner ebbed and flowed, mixing with disgust at her own stupidity.

Why had she taken him at face value so easily? How could she have been so hideously gullible?

Because, she told herself with angry defensiveness, Turner was not merely deceitful, he was monstrously deceitful. He seemed good, kind, tender, trustworthy—a goddamn Boy Scout, she thought with impotent fury. Tom Hanks and Jimmy Stewart rolled into one tall, slightly boyish package, designed to be irresistible.

It was bad enough to have fallen into his silky web of lies—did she have to fall into bed with him, too? She was as feckless and easily misled as the girls who had been forced to go to Hunsinger.

She could never tell this to Nona, of course. *I slept with a member of the mob. I slept with a Mafia lawyer.*

And not just any mobster or any old echelon of the Mafia, she thought miserably, but Bloody Eddy DelVechio, who was probably at least a godfather, a boss of all bosses. If Turner was angry because she now spurned him, he'd probably have a horse's head put in her bed.

Giddy with shock, she began to imagine telling Patrick about this fiasco. And Patrick, of course, would be a smart-ass, making her laugh about it against her will.

He would say something irreverent like "Well, at least the Mafia is Catholic."

Or he would say, "Well, Jaye, if you're hunting for marrow, a guy named Bloody Eddy sounds like a good start."

Or Patrick would say, "Why'd you fall in the sack with him? Did he make you an offer you couldn't refuse?"

Silently she began to laugh at herself. At the same time tears seeped between her closed lids. *Oh, yes, Pat-*

rick, she thought. *He made me an offer I couldn't refuse. He said he'd help you.*

She forced her emotions down, subdued them by sheer willpower.

It's all right, Patrick, she thought. *I'll help you myself. I'll do it alone.*

She dried the trace of the tears she'd allowed herself. She squared her jaw, folded her arms, leaned back, and closed her eyes again. She needed rest, she told herself, not recriminations or self-pity.

She had to conserve her strength for whatever waited for her in Cawdor.

Turner resisted the strong desire to get blind, stinking drunk. He sat at the bar nursing a light beer and wishing it were battery acid.

"*La gonzesse?*" said Frank Talbeaux, sitting on the barstool beside him. "I saw her hit you on the nose. You and her are—*phhhhtt?*"

I don't know, Turner thought gloomily.

He shrugged. "It's a little tiff. She'll get over it."

Talbeaux gave an expressive shrug. "So are we going on to this Cawdor place? Or not?"

"Yes," Turner said and took a drink. He wasn't letting her go off to Cawdor alone. She might take another swing at him, but he'd chance it.

"If I sit around all night in this place," said Talbeaux, "I have to charge you the overtime."

"So charge me the overtime," Turner said. He didn't give a fuck. It wasn't his money. It was Bloody Eddy's bloody money.

And yeah, Turner supposed it did have the whiff of murder and fraud and a dozen other crimes about it. But no crimes that were ever proven.

Thanks, in part, to me. Thanks in very good part to me.

"I hope we're not here all night long," grumped Talbeaux. "Little Rock is *le trou de ball du monde*—asshole of the world."

Wrong, thought Turner, *the absolute asshole of the world is me. Myself. It is I.*

He looked at his watch. It was nine-forty-five.

It occurred to him, almost idly, that it was not too late to call Mary Jo Stewart.

After all, if the woman had thought of anything new, anything at all, Jaye would want to hear it. Turner had insinuated himself into Jaye's good graces once—almost despite his own volition—by being able to help her brother.

He could by God do so again.

Turner opted for the public phones. He left Frank Talbeaux in the bar. The pilot was sipping bourbon and flexing the muscles of his forearm, admiring the way it made the wings of his vampire tattoo wriggle.

Mary Jo Stewart answered on the fourth ring. "Ms. Stewart. Turner Gibson here. I hope it's not too late to call."

Her rich voice sounded alert, a bit nervous. "No, no, not at all," she said. "God, I was just thinking of you."

His intuition prickled electrically. "Really," he said. "You must be psychic. I've been thinking about you and our conversation."

"I talked to my aunt today, in Rockford, Illinois," she said.

"Yes?" he prompted, wondering what in hell the aunt in Rockford had to do with anything.

"My mother," said Mary Jo Stewart, "never wanted

to talk about my little 'incident.' The business with Hunsinger. She practically made a career out of not talking about it."

"Yes?" Turner said in the same tone.

"Well, the poor woman went to her grave without telling me a lot of things. And one of them was how she found Hunsinger in the first place. You know, how she arranged to send me there."

"Yes?" he said for the third time.

"She's been dead for—oh, ten years now. I miss her every day."

"I'm sure you do," Turner said.

"Well, she and her sister had been estranged for years. It's one of those family things, you know? About my grandmother's will. About who got a silver epergne, for God's sake. It'd be hard to make you understand."

Turner understood all too well, for the law had taught him. The human heart was so full of strange nooks and curious crannies, he could well imagine sisters driven asunder by less than a silver epergne—it could have been a hairbrush, an inkwell, a thimble.

"Unfortunately, these things happen," he said.

"My aunt's two years younger than my mother. She moved to Rockford when I was only eighteen years old. We lost touch, then there was this inheritance thing. Even though I tried not to take sides, there was a rift. But after you called, I started thinking. Maybe she knew how my mother found out about Hunsinger. So I phoned her."

Turner waited, suddenly on edge.

"She knew," Mary Jo Stewart said simply. "She remembered."

There was a beat of silence. Then she said, "It was a woman named Juanita Bragg. With two gs. My aunt said she was a nurse. That she arranged things like that. Abortions. For girls to go away. Quiet adoptions. All those things."

He held the phone clenched between his jaw and shoulder and scribbled *Juanita Bragg* in his notebook.

"I looked her up in the telephone book," the Stewart woman said. "She's still in town. She lives in a fancy sort of retirement apartment complex."

Turner's blood beat hard in his throat, as if it had suddenly become too thick to pump. He put a hand over his free ear to shut out the airport noise, to hear nothing except Mary Jo Stewart. "You talked to her?"

"Yes," she said. "Just tonight. She was coy with me. I think she wants money."

Money I've got, Turner thought, with a dizzying surge of pure adrenaline.

She said, "I don't quite know how to handle this. You said you might come to Little Rock. Would it be anytime soon?"

"I happen to be in Little Rock right now," said Turner, his mouth suddenly dry. "Grounded. The weather."

There was a pause, a long one.

"Maybe it's fate," said Mary Jo Stewart.

The Riverside Retirement Village was, Mary Jo Stewart told him, "a chichi place. *Very*." She added, with a touch of bitterness, "The baby-brokering business must have paid well."

Turner took down Juanita Bragg's phone number, promising himself to send Mary Jo Stewart a dozen roses, maybe two dozen. As soon as he hung up, he dialed the Bragg woman's number.

She answered almost immediately. "Residence of Juanita B. Bragg," she said in a rasping purr of a voice. "Juanita B. Bragg speaking."

Turner explained who he was. "Ms. Bragg, I've been told that in the past you helped some young women, as they say, 'in trouble.' That this help involved a certain Dr. Roland Hunsinger in Cawdor, Oklahoma."

"Sooo," said the woman, "who gave you my name?"

"Mary Jo Stewart," Turner said. "You talked to her very recently."

There was a long moment of silence, and his heart beat with painful force. Again he covered his other ear, so he would not miss a word she uttered. At last she said, "You're her lawyer?"

Turner hesitated. "I'm representing more than one person in this."

"Like who?" she drawled.

He said, "One's a man from Philadelphia. He thinks his son was born at Hunsinger's clinic in 1957. He wants to find him. It's important to him."

Another long silence. This time when she answered there was a heavy sweetness in her voice that reminded Turner of too-ripe fruit. "I used to know a thing or two that happened in 1957," she said. "I'd have to stir my memory. Refresh it, you might say."

And I've got a good idea how you'd like it refreshed, Turner thought cynically.

He said, "I'm more concerned about another birth. A boy, born March 17, 1968."

She gave her overripe laugh. "From 1957 to 1968? That's a long stretch. You don't want much, do you?"

"I'm willing to pay for solid information," said Turner.

"I see," said the woman. "Just how much?"

Turner said, "That would depend on just how solid the information is."

"We-ell," she drawled, "I kind of kept a little diary in my day."

"What sort of little diary?"

"Oh, names," she said, almost flirtatiously. "And dates. Situations. Who paid for what. That kind of little diary."

"Just what years might that little diary cover?" Turner asked.

"Ooh," she said, "about 1956 to 1969. About that range."

"And how many names do you have in that little book, Ms. Bragg?"

"Thirty-five or so, I'd reckon."

"Of the girls? Or their families?"

"Both," she said with obvious satisfaction.

Turner felt awestruck with revelation; he almost fell to his knees in gratitude.

"Ms. Bragg, would you be interested in talking business?"

"I'm *always* interested in talking business," she said. "It's what keeps a girl like me young at heart."

Bless your rapacious old soul, he thought with another rush of euphoria.

"I'm in Little Rock at the airport right now," he said. "How soon could you see me?"

He held his breath.

She made him wait the space of three heartbeats. Then, coquettishly, she said, "No time like the present, honey."

He glanced at his watch. It was exactly ten o'clock. He thought, *Jaye, you're going to love this.*

He said, "I'll grab a cab. I'll be right over. I may bring a young woman with me, a client."

"A woman?" she said, sounding a bit disappointed.

"A client," he repeated. "See you shortly."

He hung up and made his way back to the bar. "I've got to make a side trip," he told Talbeaux. "Wait for me." He nodded at the half-filled bourbon glass in the man's hand. "And take it easy on that shit, will you? Or I'll find myself another pilot."

Talbeaux narrowed his dark eyes. But he gave a Gallic shrug and nodded, his air bored. "Your *petite amie*, she's probably gone," he said. "Your girlfriend."

"What?" Turner asked, stunned by sudden apprehension.

"I heard them announce it while you was on the phone," said Talbeaux.

"They were boarding the flights to Tulsa, to XNA."

"What?" Turner repeated, not wanting to comprehend.

"Cleared for landing," Talbeaux said with another shrug. "As for us, I wouldn't mess around too long if I was you. This filthy weather, it might shut everything down again."

Turner hardly heard him. He had already turned away and was half striding, half running toward the gate.

With a nauseating plunging of his stomach, he saw that the waiting area was no longer crowded. It was almost half emptied. A line of passengers was trickling out the door to descend to the wet tarmac. He could see others outside scurrying toward a waiting propeller plane.

"Jaye!" he cried, but he could not see her. "Jaye!"

Desperately he tried to elbow his way to the front of the line going through the gate.

"Hey, friend," cautioned the male attendant at the door, blocking his way.

"I'm looking for a blond woman," Turner said,

wondering wildly if he should knock the man aside. "About this tall." He made a sharp gesture, chin-high.

"I remember," the man said, eyeing him harshly. "You're too late. This is the Tulsa flight. She was on the one to XNA."

Turner looked out the big windows in disbelief. The other passengers were staring at him with a mixture of hostility and nervousness. "Step back, buddy," said the attendant.

"But—" said Turner.

"That's the flight," the attendant said with a curt nod toward the windows. "Taxiing off. Step back now."

He watched, helpless, as a small plane trundled down the runway, picking up speed, its wing lights flashing. Faster it went, and faster still, growing smaller in the darkness.

TWENTY

───∼∽∼───

BOBBY MIDUS HAD LAIN IN THE HAYLOFT FOR HOURS,
cursing Will LaBonny.

The hay tickled and pricked Bobby, its dust itched
his nostrils, it made his sinuses seep and throb. Mixed
with the dust was the odor of horse dung, hanging in the
air like a too-heavy perfume.

From below he heard the occasional stamp of the
horses' hooves, the gentle nickers and blowing sounds
they made, content in their stalls. He envied them, wishing he were snug in his own place with Dolores all silky
and naked beside him.

The rain had stopped, but it still dripped monoto-
nously from the eaves. It had left behind a moist coldness
that had wormed itself into the very center of Bobby's
bones.

The loft door was open two feet and propped with a bale to keep it from creaking back and forth. Through this opening, he could see the veiled moon turning the clouds a tarnished silver. By this dull light, he could just make out the swollen white dog lying next to the plum grove.

For two and a half hours Bobby had stretched out on his stomach like a sniper, the headless dog in his rifle sight. But now he sat up miserably in the loose hay. Sometimes he heard the rustle of mice creeping among the bales. He hated mice—their hairless little hands and feet, their long, naked tails.

An owl lived in the loft, and Bobby had been disgusted to find that while he was in sniper position he had accidentally rested his elbow in fresh owl shit.

Owl shit, mouse shit, horse shit, Bobby thought bitterly. He wiped his running nose on his sleeve and wished it was LaBonny in his crosshairs and not that damned dog with its smashed head.

LaBonny was getting too big for his britches these days; he acted like he was goddam Hitler and Cawdor was his fucking Third Reich. Once Bobby had looked up to the man, almost idolized him. He'd envied his power and wanted to imitate his air of cold, remorseless control.

Lately, though, LaBonny made him uneasy. It was more than the killings, though that was part of it, God knew. Suddenly LaBonny was pulling them into depths that were dangerous and inescapable.

Having one murder on his hands—Luther's—had bothered Bobby little after it was over. Luther was such a nobody, he almost didn't count except as sort of an initiation rite.

Bobby had been only seventeen then, proud to be taken along. He and Cody J. and LaBonny had run Luther off a back road he often took. LaBonny had chosen the spot carefully, the crest of the high hill that led down under the old Sumpter County railroad trestle.

When Luther saw the three of them get out of their car, he'd known he was in mortal trouble; you could see it in his face. It was downright comical, and afterwards, though Bobby had been shaky with nerves and excitement, he'd laughed about it.

Luther had tried to lock the truck doors against them, but LaBonny, cool and efficient as a machine, simply shot the lock off. He'd been like the goddamn Terminator or something. Luther had fought when they'd hauled him out, but he was no match for the three of them.

They'd beaten him until he was on his hands and knees, barely able to support himself, drooling blood into the dirt. Even then the fool was trying to crawl away, as if escape from them were possible. It was LaBonny who struck the death blow. He took a crowbar, raised it high, then smashed in the top of Luther's skull. It caved in like a walnut shell under the blow of a hammer.

LaBonny rolled him over on his back, and Cody J. and Bobby had each taken another swipe at his head with the crowbar. LaBonny said that's how it should be. Cody J. sighed and smashed in Luther's face, and Bobby, to prove himself, stove in his forehead so hard a bit of Luther's brain flew up and landed on the hood of his truck.

"The brainmobile," Cody J. joked in his aggrieved way, and Bobby, feeling a little crazy, laughed until his stomach hurt. LaBonny only smiled thinly.

Bobby found the death thrilling, yet peculiarly exhausting. They put Luther's body in his pickup behind the wheel. They'd aimed the truck downhill, straight for the trestle's thick iron supports. They'd started the engine, put it in gear, gave it a hard push with their own car—and let gravity take its course.

Christ, what a sweet crash it made—the kind a boy dreams of making when he smashes together toy trains. The impact shook the air like steely thunder, while metal screamed and the trestle gave off a whine like a plucked string. At that instant, Bobby felt powerful and anointed, sealed into an elite fellowship.

Cody J. was his brother in blood, and LaBonny was even more, like a father or a priest. It was as if LaBonny had touched Bobby's boyish soul and turned it hard and potent.

That had been almost four years ago. Bobby had swaggered because he was in LaBonny's innermost circle, one of the warrior knights of Cawdor, and nobody messed with them, nobody *dared*. There were men to fear and obey in the country, and he was, by God, one of them.

But lately LaBonny had started getting *weird*, and rumors began to circulate. For a long time he'd lived with a blond girlfriend, Genevra. She started to complain loudly that he was getting meaner and kinkier with her, that he couldn't get it up otherwise.

This gossip had shocked Bobby, who felt like he himself was always ready for a woman. But Cody J. whispered it was true; that even in high school LaBonny took his sex rough or strange or both ways at once—or he didn't take it.

One day Genevra disappeared, simply vanished. LaBonny said she'd gone to live with a cousin in Wisconsin, but nobody had ever before heard that such a cousin existed. And nobody ever heard from Genevra again.

Then LaBonny took up with a blond girl from Tulsa

who moved in with him. She was a short girl, but squarely built, with wide shoulders and narrow hips, and she wore her hair cut like a boy's. She always wore jeans and cowboy boots, and she never used makeup, but it didn't matter. She was beautiful, with long-lashed blue eyes and full, sensual lips. Her name was Cara.

Cara had stayed until six months. Then one day she showed up, crying, at a doctor's waiting room over in Mount Cawdor. She had a black eye and a split lip, and when she walked, she hobbled like something inside hurt her terribly.

Later that day somebody else saw her waiting at the Phillips 66 station, where the Greyhound bus stopped. She had a single suitcase and stitches in her lip. When asked where she was going, she said, "I'm getting as far the hell away as I can, and I ain't never coming back."

She got on a bus headed for Dallas, and nobody ever heard from her again. LaBonny never mentioned her. Once Bobby made the mistake of asking what happened between them, but LaBonny only looked at him with such a pale, flat gaze that Bobby knew better than to ask again.

There were other rumors, including the one that LaBonny had hurt a whore in Oklahoma City so bad she nearly died. That she didn't press charges because she was scared of him.

Cody J. had been there that night. He said the girl was a little square-built blond with real short hair.

"That whore looked a lot like Cara," he'd told Bobby. "You know who else looks like Cara?" He'd paused for effect. "*You* do."

This had infuriated Bobby, primarily because it was true. He'd threatened to shoot Cody J. dead if he ever said such a thing again.

But sometimes in recent months Bobby caught LaBonny looking at him in a way that made Bobby uneasy. Bobby was a beautiful young man, and he thought he knew that look for what it was. At first it even gave him a strange thrill of power, as if *he* were the one in charge instead of LaBonny. LaBonny, after all, was a man to be courted, curried, and pleased. It was good to be in his favor—and it was dangerous not to.

But Jesus, thought Bobby, LaBonny didn't *really* think that Bobby would ever *do* anything—did he? But, God, the way LaBonny was throwing his weight around lately, like he was Lord High Mucky-Muck of everybody, what would Bobby do if—

At the edge of the plum grove there was a sudden shift in the pattern of shadows. Bobby tensed. His hands tightened on the rifle.

It had been a movement; he was sure of it. Slowly he lowered himself into the sniper's position. He looked through his night sight, located the place where he had seen the shadow move. It could be a scavenger, he knew—a coyote, a 'possum, even a wild pig.

But a man stepped from the shadows. He was lean and hunched, and he bent over the dog tenderly.

Hollis, Bobby thought, with a rush of triumphant excitement. He no longer noticed the pricking of the hay. He no longer noticed its dust stinging his nostrils. He was a hunter, and the prey he had waited for so long had come at last.

Adon desperately wanted a drink, but not now, not yet. Tonight of all nights, he must keep his mind clear.

He sat in the living room, listening to Mozart and pretending to read a law article. He did not like Mozart, but he'd read that the music had a soothing effect on a troubled mind. And his mind was troubled.

Doll Farragutt had been calling all evening with conflicting reports: the Garrett woman and the lawyer were flying back tonight by private plane. No, they were not flying back, the weather was too dangerous. No, now she said they were coming from Little Rock by commercial flight.

"She called again," Doll said breathlessly. "She didn't have time to talk. They were getting ready to board. But I've got the flight number. They'll be here within the hour."

"Both of them?" Adon asked.

"Well, I *suppose*," Doll said testily. "She didn't say any different."

He didn't like having Doll phone him this way, she lacked the subtlety that Adon usually insisted upon, but he needed the old woman's information. He was careful of what he himself said. "You and she'd discussed someone picking her up?" he'd said.

"Yes," said Doll. "But she—"

Adon cut her off. "But no names were mentioned?"

"No, but—"

"Thank you very much," he said. "I appreciate it." He hung up before she could say more.

He immediately paged LaBonny. He sent him the flight number and its time of arrival. LaBonny paged back, so Adon knew the message was received and understood. LaBonny knew what must be done, he would devise a way to do it.

Adon had a sudden, nightmarish image of his house as an isolated castle, protected by a moat. But the moat was filled not with water, but blood, and tonight the blood would freshen and grow deeper.

It has to happen, he told himself fatalistically. *There's nothing to be done about it. Nothing.*

He did not see or hear Barbara come into the living room. He looked up only when he heard the little dog bounding behind her, its paws thumping softly on the carpet.

"Darling," he said, pleased she had returned to him.

But then he saw the strain in her face and the fear in her eyes. "What's wrong?" he asked in concern.

She stood there in her white nightgown and peignoir. Her little feet were bare, and the blue veins in them stood out in a way that hurt him to see.

"I was just getting ready to take my pills," Barbara said. She opened her hand to show him the two red capsules. "I heard a sound. From out by the barn. Like something's hurt."

She looked so stricken that Adon's stomach pitched with guilt. *Christ, Christ, don't let it be Hollis. Don't let everything happen at once.*

LaBonny had said he'd set a trap for Hollis, and Bobby Midus was in the loft of the barn, waiting for him if he showed. Bobby was an excellent shot, the best in the county, Adon told himself. If he shot Hollis, it would be clean, there would be no suffering.

He rose from the couch with an air of hearty confidence that he did not feel. "Well, let's just see," he said. He switched off the recording of Mozart. He walked out onto the sun porch. He opened its outside door.

The night was silent except for the soft dripping of rain from the eaves into the garden. Barbara had moved to the doorway between the living room and the sun porch. She pulled her peignoir tighter and crossed her arms as if she were chilled.

The little dog danced across the tiles of the sun

porch's floor, its nails clicking. It stood at the open door, its head cocked curiously. But no sound troubled the night except for the gentle runoff of the rain.

"See?" Adon said kindly. "Nothing. You must have imagined it."

"I didn't imagine it," Barbara said. "It was like a cry. Of pain."

He shut the door and went to her side. She was shivering. He put his arm around her protectively. "Whatever it was isn't crying any longer. It's all right."

"What could it have been?" she asked, looking up at him with anxiety in her eyes.

"An owl," he said, kissing her forehead. "A coyote. There are wild things in the woods."

"Something got caught," she said, and shuddered harder.

"It's nature's way," he said. "It's how things survive."

He tried to draw her closer, but she resisted. "They prey on the weak ones," she said unhappily. "On the helpless ones."

"Come inside," he said, taking her thin hand and leading her back into the living room. "You'll get a chill. I'll walk you back to your bedroom. You can take your pills. Then I'll tuck you in bed."

She stopped and stared back at the darkened sun porch. "I keep thinking of Hollis," she said unexpectedly. "I'm afraid for him."

"Hollis will be fine," he lied. "Would you like a glass of warm milk? It would help you sleep."

"No," she said sadly. "I don't want milk."

She began to cry. Adon, feeling helpless and damned, put his arms around her.

"There, there," he said. *Such meaningless words.* "There, there."

.   .   .

Turner paused before the doorbell of Juanita Bragg's apartment, steeling himself to stay calm. He could have grabbed Talbeaux out of the bar and followed Jaye immediately. But he hadn't.

He'd had this meeting with the Bragg woman, and it could be of crucial importance. He didn't want to jeopardize it. If she had the information she said she did, and he got it, he could go to Jaye then, and he wouldn't be empty-handed.

He didn't trust Jaye's so-called informant to have anything more than an itch to make fast money. But she could hardly connect with this man before tomorrow. Turner could go to her with real information; he could get back to Cawdor in just a few hours. If he had to beat on Doll Farragutt's door in the middle of the night like an idiot to get Jaye to listen to him, so be it.

He raised his hand and rang Juanita Bragg's doorbell. He heard it chime inside, a complex ding-donging that went on for a full ten seconds. He heard the yap of a small dog.

The door swung open and a woman with dyed red hair peered up at him. She had a face like a ruined dumpling. She was in her seventies, perhaps, short and lumpily built. She was wrapped in a full-length robe of magenta silk trimmed with magenta ostrich feathers at the neck. Behind her stood a miniature dachshund, growling and shrilly barking.

"You must be the lawyer," she said with a smile. The smile deepened the creases and wrinkles in her face and made her small eyes almost disappear.

"Turner Gibson," said Turner, extending his hand. "And you're Ms. Bragg."

She took Turner's hand tightly between her own, which were spotted and knobby and covered with rings.

Her nails were long, pointed, and bright red. "Call me Juanita," she said. She smelled of perfume and strong wine.

"Come in, come in," she crooned, pulling at his hand. Almost in the same breath she spoke sharply to the dachshund, "Doody—shut up!"

Doody shut up. Sullenly he waddled to a rug before the artificial fireplace. With a disgruntled sigh, he lay down.

Juanita Bragg's living room was crowded with furniture and decorations that had been chosen to look lavish, but somehow failed. It had velvet drapes that were too heavy and silk upholstery that was too shiny. The carpet was the color of oxblood and dotted with too many imitation Persian rugs.

She led Turner to an imitation antique settee that looked as if it been copied from something found in a Victorian whorehouse. "Sit," she said, releasing his hand and fluttering her fingers with their long nails. "Sit, sit, sit. Would you like a little drink?"

Before the settee was a low, matching table with intricately carved legs. On it were two pressed-glass goblets, an open bottle of port, and a silver-plated dish overflowing with peanuts.

"No, thanks," said Turner.

"Well, I just may indulge myself," she said in her voluptuous voice. "If you don't mind."

She'd already indulged herself about half a bottle's worth by Turner's estimate, but he smiled tightly and nodded, even though the last thing he needed was for the woman to have one too many. He had a strong intuition that she was a mean drunk.

"Ms. Bragg," he said. "It's late, I have a long trip ahead of me tonight, so I'll get to the point. You said you had a kind of diary about your dealings with Hunsinger. With perhaps thirty-five names of girls and their families."

She poured herself a drink with surprising accuracy, not spilling a drop. She gave him an appraising glance. "Thirty-six," she said. "I recounted." She sat down in a silk-upholstered wing chair. She crossed her ankles daintily, like a lady.

Turner made his tone friendly, almost intimate, yet clearly respectful. "You said you'd be willing to sell this diary?"

She took a sip of her drink. Here manner, flirtatious only moments earlier, had gone hard as chilled glass. The little eyes looked calculating and suddenly stone-cold sober. "For a price. For a *good* price."

He leaned forward, putting his elbows on his knees. It was a casual pose, and he hoped a disarming one that said *You can feel comfortable with me. You can trust me*.

He said, "We'll talk money in a minute. First I need to know something about the validity of this list. Will you tell me about how you got involved with Hunsinger? And came to make these—arrangements."

"I was a nurse. I worked for him when he practiced in Hot Springs."

Turner hid the jolt of surprise he felt. He'd never before heard that Hunsinger had had a practice in Arkansas. "Hot Springs?" he said. "How long ago?"

Suddenly the coquette was back. She put her fingertips to her mouth, and a small laugh jiggled from deep within her. "How long ago? I hate to even say."

He smiled indulgently, but said, "Ms. Bragg, the more—shall we say 'frank?'—you are about these things, the more you'll be rewarded."

The coquette vanished and her eyes became hard

again. "It was 1956," she said. "He lost his license in this state."

"Why'd he lose his license?"

"Some irregularities with drugs," she said. "And the abortions."

"So then he moved to Oklahoma?"

"Yeah. Land was cheap there. There was an old spa for sale. There used to be springs in that part of the state. You know, hot springs, healing springs, that kind of stuff. But they got polluted. So he got a deal. He started his clinic."

"And you stayed in touch?" Turner said. "You sent him clients?"

She took a sip of her wine. "I referred *patients* to him."

"Of course. Excuse me."

She tilted her head and regarded him with a superior air. "These girls had a medical condition. They needed a doctor. Things were different back then. See, what concerned me, what touched my heart, was that these girls needed *help*. Somebody had to help them. That somebody"—she touched her breast delicately—"was *me*."

"I see. And how did people know to come to you?"

"Back then, you had a medical problem like that, you asked a medical person. I was a medical person. Word got around, I guess. That I could help."

"I see." He paused, pretending to search for words. "He was arranging illegal adoptions. Selling babies. Did you know this?"

He had expected her to lie, to act innocent or shocked or both. "I figured it out soon enough," she said.

"Eventually you stopped sending girls to him," Turner said. "Is that why?"

"No," she said. She gave a distasteful little shrug. She took another drink, a big one.

"Then why?"

"He screwed some of them up," she said, looking away.

He thought of Mary Jo Stewart. "Yes," he said, trying to sound understanding. "I've heard that."

"And the times changed," she said with a tired sigh.

"Changed how?"

"Changed every way," she muttered, shaking her head. "The pill and free love and hippies and drugs. People's attitudes changed. I mean, Woodstock and the Age of Aquarius and all that shit—excuse my French. People weren't moral anymore. This country's gone to hell in a handbasket."

Turner didn't allow himself to smile at the irony. Did she really believe the country had been more moral when she and Hunsinger flourished? Or was such a statement only the result of the staggered logic of the port?

"Today a girl gets knocked up," she said with a gesture of disgust, "more'n likely she'll keep the kid. Nobody gives a damn. People got no shame."

"The list of girls," he said gently. "Why'd you keep it?"

She met his eyes again. She gave a crooked, one-cornered smile. "Why're *you* here, honey?"

"Because you know things," he said.

"Bingo," she said with another wave. "Give the man sixty-four silver dollars. Give him a case of Mars bars. Christ, reliving all this makes me need another drink."

"I'll pour it," said Turner, wanting to control the amount. He picked up the bottle and poured the glass a third full.

"You could top that off," she said.

He acted as if he didn't hear her, and placed the bottle well out of her reach.

She gave him a challenging look. "You probably think I wanted to blackmail somebody, don't you?"

Exactly, thought Turner. *Just like Judy Sevenstar's mother thought about doing.* "The idea never crossed my mind," he lied. "Anyone can clearly see you're not that kind of woman."

"That kind of woman," she said and sipped her port. "I'll tell you what kind of woman I am. I grew up in the Depression, that's what."

"Times were hard," Turner said with a sympathetic nod.

"I *know* what it's like to go without," she said, her voice suddenly quavering. "I vowed I'd never live that way again." She looked around the room crammed with its imitation luxury. "I've done all right for myself. I've done all right."

"You've done splendidly," Turner said.

"When I got extra money, I *invested* it," she said, narrowing one eye wisely. "I invested it *smart,* too. I bought Wal-Mart stock when it was next to nothing."

"An extremely shrewd move," said Turner.

"I'm not rich," she said, waving a forefinger with its scarlet talon of a nail. "But I'm *comfortable.*"

"This is a lovely place." Then, shamelessly, he added, "Exquisite."

"I never had to use that list," she said, raising her chin haughtily. "I didn't have to. But I always kept it. Like insurance."

"Insurance is always prudent. Very prudent."

"Someday," she said, lifting her penciled brows, "some person might *want* it."

"Exactly," said Turner. "And that person has come. I am that person."

"I was ahead of my time," she said almost dreamily. "I was a sort of feminist hero."

"Indeed you were."

"I helped those poor downtrobben—downtrodden girls."

"Absolutely."

"And heroes should be rewarded."

Turner took out his checkbook. "Let's talk about this reward," he said.

LaBonny drove through the mist toward the airport.

It was near now, a few miles beyond the next rise. The airport was so new, so set off by itself that the road to it was long, dark, and lonely. It was a road from which a couple, like the lawyer and the woman, might easily take a wrong turn or an unexpected direction and disappear.

Cody J. sat morosely in the passenger seat. He was sulking because he'd spent all day in the cold, wet woods, and although it was now night, there was more work to be done.

Even his most trusted men could be like mules, thought LaBonny. Lately they had been stubborn, even childish. Cody J. acted like a man who's grown tired of the rigors of his job and Bobby was a balky young rebel, cocky, but not completely certain of what he was getting into. Yet LaBonny knew that he owned them both; he had sold their souls, and they couldn't unsell them. Each killing bound them more tightly to him.

His phone rang. *What now?* he thought with irritation. He flipped open the phone. "Yes?" he said curtly.

"It's me," said Bobby Midus. He sounded excited, almost antic.

You'd better make this worth my while, LaBonny

thought. But he had a pleasant image of Bobby, exiled alone in the cold night, far from the swarthy Dolores.

"You know that varmint that was causing trouble?" Bobby asked, almost bubbling. "Well, I by God *got* him."

LaBonny's taut nerves went more rigid. *Varmint* was the code word for Hollis. So this was to be Hollis's night, too, was it? The more the merrier. "Did you kill it?" LaBonny demanded.

"Hell, no," Bobby said, obviously offended. "You said not to—"

Shut the fuck up, LaBonny thought. He was not a jellyfish paranoid like Adon, but he knew cell phones could be monitored, and Bobby, of all people, should know it, too.

"You put it in a cage or something like that?" LaBonny asked.

"Something like that. Now what?" Bobby paused. "It's bleeding sort of hard."

"If you don't want it to die," said LaBonny—*and you don't, you pretty dumb-ass*, he thought—"you better stop it."

"Well, I ain't no veterinarian," Bobby said and laughed.

"You heard me," LaBonny said, his temper growing more evil. "Are you where I told you to be if this happened?"

"Yeah," Bobby said with a note of defiance. "Well, sure."

If Bobby captured Hollis, he was to haul him off to the hay shed in the near pasture, where there was a road of sorts. They had left the trucks there the last two days when they hunted, for of *course* they couldn't park near Adon's precious house. Sickly little Barbara or the old man might see.

Bobby's voice took on a whining note. "When you coming? I done told you there's a problem. And I'm fucking tired. It's been a long day."

"I'll get there when I get there," LaBonny countered. "I can't be every place at once."

"Well, it's goddam cold out here," Bobby complained. "My heater ain't working right. How long is this going to take? You know how long I been up today? It's been—"

"As long as I have," LaBonny bit off. He snapped the phone shut and thrust it back between the seats of the Blazer.

Christ, he thought irritably, *he had to do everybody's thinking for them. None of these sorry bastards could function without him.*

Cody J. turned to him, his expression resentful. "Bobby got Hollis?"

"Yeah," LaBonny said. "He got him."

And you're disappointed, aren't you, you little shit, because you wanted the bounty money on him for yourself, didn't you?

"Jee-sus," said Cody J. in disgust, "you mean we gotta tend to *that*, too, on top of everything else?"

"That's what it means," said LaBonny coldly.

The clouds opened again and fat, splattering drops began to hammer the windshield. LaBonny turned on the wipers.

"God," moaned Cody J. as the new downpour drummed on the hood of the car. "Not *again*. We're gonna have to build a fucking ark, man. Ain't this night ever gonna end?"

LaBonny saw the lights of the airport complex shining through the haze and the rain. "It'll end," he said.

. . .

Jaye hurried through the rain, her head down. She clutched her cheap carry-on bag, and before she could reach the double doors of the terminal, her thin clothes were drenched.

"Be careful if you have to drive tonight, miss," said a middle-aged businessman, scurrying beside her, a magazine held over his balding head. "There's a tornado watch. Two funnels sighted. I just heard."

Jaye gave him a sickly smile of thanks. *Great,* she thought. *My brother's dying, I've slept with a Mafioso, and now tornadoes. Maybe we could have a locust plague and a rain of frogs.*

She would never tell Nona about Turner Gibson. Never. Never. Never.

She would say something like, "He was a such a mild-mannered little man, and he turned out to be married. I was shocked when he made a pass. I left him in the dust." And then she'd say, "It was a terrible experience. Don't ever ask me about it again."

She reached the double doors, pushed her way inside. The airport was new and spacious, but it had an air of incompletion, a sort of sterile emptiness that was unwelcoming.

Well, she thought grimly, she hadn't come for the decor, she'd come to meet the nameless man who might know something about Patrick. She would rent another car and drive to Miss Doll's. She'd take a long, warm bath and get into a warm nightgown. But before she climbed under all those quilts, she would kneel and humbly pray that Patrick's mystery man could tell her what she needed to know. She would pray until her knees went numb and her back was sore.

Possibly she would also bang her head against the bedpost to punish herself for Turner Gibson.

How could I be so stupid? Why didn't I see he was too good to be true?

She passed the baggage carousel and headed for the booths housing the car rental agencies. She wondered how much more money she could bleed from her charge cards before they shut down her credit. Well, if she had to borrow from Nona, she would; she could always get a bank loan to pay her back.

How did I let myself end up in bed with that man? Would somebody please examine my head?

A small man with childishly round cheeks and a freckled nose approached her, his expression shy. He wore a ball cap that sat too low on his head and made his ears stick out. The cap added to his boyish air, but she saw that his sideburns were graying and his face showed the marks of early middle age.

He said, "Miss Garrett? Miss Jaye Garrett?"

She stopped and gave him a questioning look. He drew nearer. "I'm Miss Doll's nephew, Cody," he said. "She said it was a waste for you to go to the expense of renting a whole other car. She sent me to bring you home to her. She sent this here umbrella for you."

He handed her a lady's compact umbrella, tucked in a little fabric case covered with pink roses. "It's wet out there in that ol' parking lot," he said, and pulled the bill of his cap lower.

"You're Miss Doll's nephew?" she said hesitantly, not wanting to seem rude.

He shuffled his feet and gazed down, as if it embarrassed him to talk to a woman. "Cody J. Farragutt," he said. "Doll's husband was my mama's brother. I ate over there tonight. With Doll and Bright. It's my night off. She said I should come pick up you and your friend."

He looked about, as if trying to pick out her traveling companion. "My 'friend' stayed in Little Rock," she said more sharply than she'd meant to. "He won't be joining me."

The man looked slightly stunned. "He won't?"

"No," she said, not wanting to talk about it.

"Well, Miss Doll said there was two of you coming," he said. He sounded like a schoolboy who was afraid he'd gotten something wrong and would be punished for it.

"No," she repeated. "Just me."

"He won't be along at all?"

"I have no idea of his plans," she said. "My work with him is—over."

He shuffled his feet, looking uncertain.

She said, "It was kind of you to drive all the way out here, but you shouldn't have. I can rent a car."

"No, ma'am," he said. "Miss Doll would skin me alive if I let you do that. She gave me my marching orders, ma'am. And she knows how to do it."

Jaye smiled. He obviously knew Miss Doll's style.

"I got to drive back to Cawdor anyhow," he said logically. "So you might as well come along. Bright wanted to come with me, just to get out, you know, but Miss Doll wouldn't let her. It being late and the tornado watch and all."

Jaye shivered in her wet clothing. She looked at the umbrella, not remembering if she'd seen it at Miss Doll's. But the man's manner was so earnest, and he was obviously familiar with Miss Doll and Bright. Why should she be paranoid?

"You ready to come, ma'am?" he asked. "I'm parked in a five-minute loading zone." He reminded her somehow of an overage puppy, clumsy and too eager to please.

She gave him a grateful smile. She walked out the

door with him. A white Blazer was parked in the loading zone, its motor running.

He opened the passenger door and she got in, fastened her seat belt. She expected him to get in on the driver's side, but he did not. Instead another man emerged from the shadows of a nearby pillar. He was tall, wearing an army camouflage slicker and an Aussie hat. He slid swiftly into the driver's seat, and simultaneously the man with boyish face got into the backseat behind her.

"Oh," she said, startled. "There are two of you." With a quick, nervous jerk she undid her seat belt, reached for the door handle. "Really, maybe I ought to—"

But she heard the automatic locks click shut, and the car was already in motion, heading out of the lot and down the dark, lonesome road.

TWENTY-ONE

————◦◦◦————

A N HOUR LATER TURNER GOT BACK INTO THE WAITING
cab, his pulses banging like drums. "To the airport,"
he ordered.

The cabbie sighed and turned on the windshield
wipers. The mist had turned back into drizzle, steady and
cold.

Turner snapped open his briefcase and took out the
object that had lashed his heart to such a helter-skelter
pace: Juanita Bragg's diary.

It was not the original diary, of course; that was
locked in a safety deposit box. This was a photocopy that
Bragg had kept stashed in a safe at the courtesy desk in
the lobby of the Riverside apartments.

She had wanted cash for it—her asking price was
three hundred and sixty thousand dollars. "All the

names or none," she said, tapping her long nails on the edge of her chair. "At ten thousand dollars a name."

He argued passionately, because it was expected of him. He got her down to one hundred and eighty thousand, to be delivered to her by courier before five o'clock the next afternoon.

She didn't want to let go of the photocopy until the money was safely in her hands. Turner argued with even more passion, cunning, and eloquence than before. As collateral he left her his gold Rolex, his computer, and a promissory note signed in the presence of the night clerk, who notarized it and put it in the safe.

Turner took his gold penlight out of the briefcase, snapped it on, and began to read down the list. He skipped the earliest years, even though that was where Mr. DelVechio's lost ladylove might be listed.

He went directly to 1968. Juanita Bragg had kept her records neatly, the items one to a page and the details listed in a clear, bold hand.

One name and date leaped out at him:

Suzanne Elaine McCourt—fifteen years old—small, slender, brunette Sophomore, Little Rock Central High School
Due date, mid-March, 1968
Time to be spent with Hunsinger: three and a half months
Parents: Brendan and Kita McCourt, 2809 Bluebird Road, Little Rock
Arrangements made by father.
                                    Rec—$100. December 1967

Turner's stomach clenched with excitement. There were no other names of girls who had borne children in

March 1968. Suzanne McCourt could be Patrick's mother.

He read the entry for the McCourt girl again. She was small, slender, brunette. Although the father's name clearly bespoke Irish origin, the mother's did not.

What kind of name was Kita? Could the woman have been Japanese or Korean, a war bride? The dates would allow either possibility.

Don't get too excited, he warned himself, setting his jaw grimly. He looked back into the 1966 entries. There was Mary Jo Stewart's name, her parents' names, and her Little Rock address. There was no listing for Diane Englund, who had come to Hunsinger from Fort Smith. Or Linda O'Halloran, who had come from Oklahoma City.

He looked for estimated birth dates of the other adoptees he knew were seeking their biological parents. There was none that fit Dr. Roy Spain, or the Cloony sisters, or Debbie Lattimer.

But there was one entry that could be about Robert Messina, who'd been born in mid-March 1957. Turner marked it and thought, *Good luck, Messina.*

He hesitated before leafing back farther in the pages. DelVechio's son had been born to a girl from Little Rock, Julia Tritt. Would her name be here? Suddenly he didn't want it to be.

But she was.

Julia Ann Tritt—seventeen years old—beautiful brown-eyed blonde
Junior, Little Rock Christian High School
Due date, early March 1957
Parents: Rev. William Robert and Deena Davis Tritt

> Time to be spent with Hunsinger: four months
> Arrangements made by aunt, Donna Davis Snelling
> Rec.—$50.

Turner felt an odd sense of relief, of freedom even. There was information here, but nothing new that was useful to his search. Wherever the son of Julia Tritt and Eddy DelVechio was, his name was unknown, still untraceable.

He smiled cynically. There was much information in the photocopy, but none that DelVechio wanted, and he'd be outraged at the price tag. Turner was already rehearsing his fast-talking riff to justify the expense.

But he had more important business at hand. He took up his phone and dialed his secretary, Melissa Washington. "Hello, Wonder Woman," he said in his most seductive tone. "Put on the magic bracelets. I've got a job for you."

She'd been asleep, she was disgruntled at being wakened, but Turner cajoled her into cooperation.

A list of thirty-six women would be coming. But immediately he must have information on the McCourt girl; phone the brokers now, he said. He didn't care what time it was in Philadelphia.

Next, as soon as possible, he needed one hundred and eighty thousand dollars, cash, no bill larger than a hundred. A private courier was to take it to Juanita Bragg and deliver it personally.

"And tell the courier to get back my watch, computer, and my promissory note," he told her.

"Turner," wailed Melissa, "*what* are you up to? You say you're in Little Rock *now*?"

"Heading back to Oklahoma. Coming up on the airport right now. I'll call you first thing in the morning. Phone me if anything important comes up."

"Turner—"

"Got to go," he said. "Got another call to make."

He hit the cutoff button, took a deep breath, and dialed Jaye's number. She should be on the ground by now, maybe even at Miss Doll's.

I'll say exactly the right thing, he promised himself; *she won't hang up, she'll have to listen. Please, God, make her listen.*

Turner realized that this was probably the first prayer he'd said since he was nine years old and his dog was hit by a car. He'd prayed with all his heart for God to let the mutt live.

He tensed, listening to the ringing on the other end of the line. It went on for a long time. Then a recorded voice recited, "The Bell customer you are calling is unavailable or has traveled outside the Bell coverage area. Please hang up and try again at a later time."

Turner closed the phone and thought again about his dog. It had, of course, not merely died, but died horribly and before his eyes.

Why think of a stupid dog, dead nearly thirty years? he thought contemptuously.

He opened the phone again and dialed Miss Doll's number.

She answered, sounding edgily chipper, not in the least sleepy.

"This is Turner Gibson, a friend of Jaye Garrett's," he said. "Has she made it there yet?"

"Why, no, honey," said Miss Doll, suddenly sounding befuddled. "I don't know for sure if her plane's even in yet. It's a long drive from that airport. But—I thought you was with her."

"We had to separate for a little while," he said. "I had business here."

She was silent for a moment. "And you're wanting to talk with her?"

"Yes. It's urgent."

"Well, you got a message for her?"

Turner hesitated. "Yes," he said. "Tell her I have important information that may help her brother. That I'm at the Little Rock airport, and we're starting for XNA immediately. I'll be in Cawdor as soon as I can. I'll come for her."

"Come for her?" Miss Doll said in apparent surprise. "You mean here?"

"Yes," said Turner. "Tell her—this is crucial—she *has* to see me."

"I'll tell her," vowed Miss Doll.

"Emphasize that what I've found out could be vital to her brother. I have a lead to find a marrow donor. Will you be sure to deliver that message?"

"I will most certainly deliver that message," said Miss Doll sweetly. "Cross my heart and hope to die."

Neither man had said or done anything overtly threatening.

Yet Jaye knew to the core of her heart that something had gone wrong when doors locked. Their metallic clicks echoed through her mind with a resonating sense of entrapment.

"Wait!" The word burst from her without her volition and automatically she reached for the door handle, tugged, and tugged again.

But the car was already moving, picking up speed, and the handle was as immovable in her grip as the bar of a cell.

Already the illuminated airport building was retreating into the distance behind them. The Blazer slipped out of the pool of light that marked the parking lot and plunged into the blackness beyond.

"I've changed my mind," she said as calmly as she could. "I want to go back. I'd rather rent a car, after all." But even as she spoke, she knew with sickening certainty that the words were futile.

The driver turned to face her. He was a man of almost serpentine leanness. He gave her a closed-lipped smile that turned his mouth into a tight, curved line. "Go back?" he said softly. "We couldn't have that."

Don't show them you're afraid. Don't. Don't let them know what you suspect. Seem gullible. Make them let down their guard.

She licked her lips. She had a foreboding of disaster, yet her deepest instincts kept hammering the same message through her nerves: *Don't panic. Play dumb. Watch for an opening.*

She gave the man a shaky smile in return. "I'm from the north. I'm not used to such hospitality."

"It's just our way," said the lean man. He turned toward her with a fluid motion, offered his hand. "My name's LaBonny. Will LaBonny."

His skin was hard and cold to the touch, but she clasped his hand firmly. "I didn't mean to be jumpy," she said. "But it really would be nice to go back for a minute. I should have used the rest room. My kidneys are about to burst. On the plane I drank so much coffee—just to keep awake. You know."

"There's a place ahead," he said. "It won't be far."

She could see nothing ahead except darkness as far as the horizon.

"I *really* have to go," she said and gave a self-conscious laugh.

"It won't be long," he soothed.

"I hope not." She crossed her legs. She fidgeted. "Are you related to Miss Doll, too?" she asked in a perky voice, as if trying to distract herself from her discomfort.

"We're friends," he said.

"If there's a convenience store ahead, maybe we could stop there. I could use the rest room—and buy her a little present. Some chocolates or something. It was so *sweet* of her to send you."

He nodded agreeably, and she thought, *Miss Doll— she set me up. Why? What for?*

She fingered her phone in its holster attached to her purse. It was switched off, but it was a link to the outside world. If only she could keep it close to her, if only she could find a moment to dial 911 . . .

The lean man, LaBonny, reached out and switched on the radio. Guitars twanged. A singer moaned about being a thousand miles from nowhere.

LaBonny gave her a look that seemed perfunctory, almost bored.

"Where's your friend?" he asked casually. "We thought you were coming with your friend."

Turner, she thought with a stab of something like hope. *Turner, these bastards don't know where you are.*

"Our business together is done." She tossed her head as if she had nothing in the world to fear. "Things have changed. I need to get home."

His eyes flicked up and down her body. "You find anything out about your brother?"

"Oh," she said innocently. "You know about my brother? Miss Doll told you?"

"Right," he said.

She nodded enthusiastically. "Yes," she lied. "I did get news. Right before I got on the plane. I got a call from Belgium. That's where my brother is—Belgium. They've found a match for him in the international marrow bank. I don't have to look for his family anymore."

LaBonny threw her a sharp look. The dashboard lights made his bony face seem almost skull-like.

Jaye made a happy gesture. "So it's over. Poor Turner Gibson—he didn't get anything at all. But he's glad for us."

"They're expecting you back home?" LaBonny asked carefully.

She nodded with false cheer. "I still can't quite believe it. I'll spend the night at Miss Doll's, then go home. The search is over. The story has a happy ending. My mother's meeting me at the airport tomorrow. With reporters. There's going to be a story on Boston television. New Hampshire, too."

The lie about news coverage was a sudden inspiration. If these men believed the media was waiting for her, surely they wouldn't dare do anything to her—would they?

The tall man showed no reaction. He did not take his eyes from the road. When he spoke, his voice had a peculiar deadness.

"Reporters?"

"Yes," she said, rummaging through her purse, wondering what she had that could be used as a weapon. Keys, her lighter, a spray bottle of perfume, a rat-tailed comb . . .

She said, "Great human-interest story. You know— worldwide search for a marrow donor. They're going to want our reactions. My mother'll cry quarts. It'll be great. The *Boston Globe* will probably do a story, too. I know a lot of people at the *Globe*. Media's my business." She gave him a modest smile.

"Christ, LaBonny, *television*?" said the freckle-faced man. "A *newspaper*?"

The driver's neck swiveled and he shot the man a quick glare. Then he gave Jaye another of his tight smiles. "You'll be quite the star."

"I'm just happy about my brother. And that this wild-goose chase is over. We weren't getting *anywhere*." She gave a self-deprecating laugh. "I wasn't cut out to be a detective. It'll be good to get home."

LaBonny seemed to reflect on this for a moment. "You didn't tell any of this to Miss Doll?"

She shrugged carelessly. "When it happened, it happened so fast there really wasn't time. Besides, I figured I'd surprise her. She's really been *wonderfully* supportive. Is that convenience store close?"

He ignored her question. "She said you were supposed to talk to somebody here. About your brother."

She gave a sad little sigh. "Probably somebody who wanted to shake me down. It doesn't matter. I don't need to see him now. My brother's got his donor."

He nodded thoughtfully. "What about your friend? He's still searching?"

She felt the stiff form of the rat-tailed comb in the depths of her purse. Such a comb could be a weapon, she knew, it could be used to stab. She'd taken self-defense classes.

She said, "He's going back to Philadelphia. He's probably en route now. His client called him off the search. He was spending way too much money." Confidentially she added, "He really *did* abuse his expense account."

From the backseat, Cody J. spoke. His voice sounded oddly taut. "So you mean it's over for both of you?"

"Yes," she said. "Thank God. He was an awful man

to work with. So paranoid. I'm glad to be done with him."

LaBonny said, "And he's already gone back to Philadelphia?"

She nodded with an air of finality. "I watched him get on the plane. To make sure he was gone from my life for good, to tell the truth. I mean, he had this very strange conspiracy mentality." She wrinkled her nose in distaste. "Weird."

They drove on into the night. The lonely voice of a singer warbled that there was no time to kill. Far ahead she saw a light, dimmed by the mist.

"Oh," she said with pleasure, "is that a gas station or a store or something?"

"I reckon," LaBonny said in a flat voice.

"Then we can stop," she said in triumph. "Oh, God, have I got to go. Five more minutes and I'd—You don't want to hear about it." She laughed.

"I'll make you a deal," he said.

She looked at him in surprise. He kept his gaze on the wet ribbon of road.

He said, "While you're in the rest room, you let me try out that phone of yours."

Instinctively she put her hand on the phone. She'd counted on taking it with her. It was her lifeline.

"Oh," she said, disappointment in her tone, "I'm afraid the batteries are down. It's dead."

"You used it in the airport," said Cody J.

"Yes," she said brightly, "but it was going out then. I could barely hear."

"I'd just like to try it," LaBonny said. "Mine's not working. I've got to make a call."

The convenience store was in sight now, bathed in fluorescent light. It was only a cinder-block square, but to her it looked like a palace of sanctuary.

LaBonny held out his hand, and there was something implacable in the gesture.

To hell with it, she thought in despair. *I'll lock myself in the rest room. I'll write a message on the mirror. I'll beat on the wall to alarm the clerk. I'll crawl out the window and escape. I'll do by God something. They won't get me out of there without a fight.*

She handed him the phone. He slowed, put on his blinker to signal the turn into the convenience store's lot. She held her breath.

A phone rang. She jumped in spite of herself. At first she thought it was hers and that LaBonny would know she'd been lying.

But it was his, she realized in confusion. He took it from between the Blazer's seats and unfolded it. "Yeah?" he said. He listened intently for what seemed a long time. "Yeah? That's interesting. Yeah. I'll deal with it."

He shut the phone again.

"I'm *so* glad to see this store," she said. "I can't tell you how—"

He slowed, veering to the side of the road then stopped so abruptly, it jolted her. They had not yet reached the convenience store; the turnoff was still fifty feet away. The distance between her and its safety suddenly seemed an unbridgeable gap.

"What—" she began.

LaBonny unsnapped his seat belt and leaned toward her. His angular face was gilded by the lights from the lonely little store. His eyes narrowed. "Where'd you say your friend was?"

"On his way to Philadelphia," she said with blithe conviction. "Could we get on—"

"You saw him get on the plane?" he said.

"Yes," she insisted, but foreboding swept over her like a great, chilly wave.

He drew back slightly. Then coolly, with swiftness
and precision, he backhanded her across the left side of
her face. Pain knifed through her cheekbone, her head
knocked against the passenger window, and tears welled
in her eyes. She blinked them back and glared at him in
astonishment and outrage.

He brought his face so close to hers that she could
feel his breath on her lips.

"That call—it was about your boyfriend." His voice
was almost a whisper. "He's not on his way to Philadelphia. He's coming here. Right now. You lied to me, Miss
Garrett. Don't *ever* do that again."

He said this with a soft sternness that she found
more frightening than anger. He sighed. Then he drew
back from her, studied her with an air of godly detach-
ment, and hit her again.

Hollis lay in the hay shed in the darkness, weeping silently and clutching his shattered elbow. The sides of the
hay shed were open, and the cold and dampness of the
night rolled over him, chilling him to the bone.

He knew who the man with the gun was. It was
young Bobby Midus, one of the men, it was whispered,
who had murdered Luther. Bobby had shot him and
dragged him here and now stood over him with his gun
and did nothing to help him.

Hollis wept in fear and hurt. At times the pain was
so intense, it consumed him like fire, but at other times it
lifted from him in a strange and peaceful way. It was as if
his soul rose like a mist out of his body, trying to escape.
In these moments he felt only a pleasant numbness, and
his thoughts came slowly, but with a cold, foreign clarity.

Bobby hadn't killed him outright. Why?

Instead Bobby had ripped Hollis's shirt and tied a

piece of it around his upper arm, pulling it so tight that the arm felt deadened, as if it no longer belonged to him.

Then Bobby had hauled Hollis, sobbing, to his feet. He'd half carried, half pushed him for more than a mile through the woods, swearing all the way, saying all the worst words, and taking God's name in vain.

Hollis had fainted twice, and once he'd had a vision of a great angel in white robes swooping down to bear him away. But when the creature was right over him and the gold of its hair was dazzling him almost blind, it suddenly changed from an angel into the dead girl.

Her face was white as snow, and her eyes were sad and full of accusation. She held out her hands to him, and one hand was stained with blood, like Jesus's hand, and she was begging him to give back her severed finger.

He'd struggled out of that vision screaming incoherently, and Bobby had stuffed a dirty cloth in his mouth to shut him up. He'd dragged Hollis upright again and once more forced him to keep stumbling through the night.

Now the hay was slick and matted beneath him, and it smelled of moldy rot. Why hadn't Bobby killed him, he kept wondering, why? And at last in one of the strange, clear moments, he knew the answer: Bobby had kept him alive because worse things were to come.

They were going to let the dead girl come for him and drag him screaming down to hell. He sobbed harder, and the cloth stuffed in his mouth almost made him strangle. He wished he had the strength to rise and run, because maybe then Bobby would have to shoot to kill him, and that would be better than this. But he had no strength.

Then pain surged back in a sickening tide and he heard a telephone ring. A telephone couldn't ring in a hay shed, so he knew he must be having another waking dream.

He could hear Bobby talking to someone who wasn't there, and nothing he said made sense to Hollis.

Then Bobby went silent again. All Hollis heard was the dripping of the rain off the edge of the shed's roof. Then there was a wet, rustling sound, and he realized it was made by Bobby's boots in the wet hay.

He felt the toe of Bobby's boot digging into his ribs. "Hey, Hollis," Bobby said. "Guess what? You and me are gonna be here awhile. But then we're gonna have company. LaBonny's coming. You know LaBonny, don't you?"

Hollis knew. He was terrified of LaBonny. Judy Sevenstar said LaBonny was the leader when the men killed Luther, and if Hollis and Judy weren't careful, LaBonny would have them killed, too. Hollis tried to rise, but he could not. He managed to crawl a few feet, then collapsed again in the wet hay.

"You want to run away, Hollis?" laughed Bobby. "That ain't nice. LaBonny's bringing some folks to meet you—remember that woman from the nursing home, Hollis? The one that scared you? She'll be here. We're going to kill you and put you in that spider cave together and seal it up. Won't nobody ever find you till hell freezes over."

Hollis sobbed into the hay, knowing his immortal soul was at stake. He hadn't finished his altar; he hadn't done all the ceremonies he'd hoped would lay the dead girl to rest.

Yet, he thought desperately, if she came, he could give her what she wanted, and perhaps she would spare him and let him go to heaven. In panic, he clutched the little leather bag that hung on a string around his neck.

"Hollis," Bobby said, "what you always grabbing at that bag for? What you got there? Let me see."

Bobby knelt beside him and reached for the pouch. Hollis twisted sideways, holding the bag more tightly. *Luther had said, "This is the key to everything. Keep it. Hide it."*

Hollis could not let it go. He could not—if he did, he would fall into fire and everlasting damnation and pain a thousand times worse than this. He needed it to appease the dead woman who stalked him for so long.

But Bobby Midus's hand closed around the pouch and tore it from Hollis's neck. Hollis screamed against the rag in his mouth. He thrashed wildly as Bobby struggled to unknot the string that fastened the pouch shut.

Hollis felt his hand strike something hard and wet, and his fingers closed on it instinctively. He knew the thing from its feel, from working all those years on Doc Hunsinger's farm. It was a baling hook.

It was rusty, the handle warped, but Hollis didn't notice; he grabbed it as a drowning man might grasp a lifeline. He saw hellfire dancing around him, and he lunged into a sitting position and drew back the hook.

"What—" Bobby said, his voice perplexed, and Hollis saw that phantom horns grew on Bobby's head as if he were a demon and that when he spoke, a flame of darkness glimmered in his mouth. With all his strength, Hollis swung the hook toward that flame.

La Pouffiasse made a landing that rattled Turner's teeth. He paid off Talbeaux, gave him a bigger tip than he deserved, and made his way across the wet tarmac toward the terminal.

The building was nearly empty. Only one car rental

place was still open, and its desk clerk looked as if he was shutting down for the night. He was an obese young man with curly black hair and round cheeks that were so pink, they were almost scarlet.

Turner rented a compact because it was the only thing available. It was a small gray thing with a snub nose and blunt tail. It looked like a metal cocoon that contained some sort of grub that would, perhaps, hatch one day into a real car.

He headed toward the highway the clerk had said would take him to Cawdor. It was half past midnight. He took a chance on calling Jaye. He dialed and stared at the mist beading on the windshield. Once more he heard the operator's recorded voice tell him the customer he had dialed was unavailable.

He hit the cutoff button and drove for a few minutes, thinking, *Maybe she doesn't want to hear from me. Maybe Miss Doll hasn't given her the message about Patrick yet.*

He dialed Miss Doll's number. So what if he woke her up? He'd buy her a bottle of champagne or something to make up for it. But she answered with surprising swiftness.

"Oh, yes, she's here," Miss Doll said jovially. "She's looking forward to seeing you. She's in the shower right now. But she'll be waiting for you."

She'll see me, he thought. *She's waiting.*

"How far away are you?" Miss Doll asked.

"A half hour. Maybe a little more," he said. "Would you have her call me when she gets out of the shower? It's important."

"If the phones work," Miss Doll said with cheerful wryness. "It's been hit-or-miss all day. This rain. We'll have to grow webs on our feet."

"Have her try," he said. "Please."

"I will," she said.

"And if she can't reach me, tell her I'll see her soon."

"Oh, we'll be waiting," Miss Doll fairly chirped. "With bells on."

He shut the phone, thinking, *It can't be this easy. She can't forgive me just like that—can she?*

In all likelihood Jaye wanted only to hear what he had to say about Patrick. It didn't matter; it was an opening. Somehow he'd make her listen to him. Making people listen, convincing them, was his business.

The mist turned to rain, thin pelting drops of it, and he drove on, rehearsing how he would apologize to her. First he would give her the information about Patrick. And then he would explain as he had never explained before.

LaBonny had driven her to a back road and tried to slap and bully the truth out of her. His blows were calculated, executed with a sort of horrible control, as if pain were a science he had studied and that he liked very much.

"Your brother hasn't found a donor—has he?" he demanded, shaking her. He threw her against the Blazer's closed door. "If he had, your lawyer friend wouldn't be coming here. You're still looking, aren't you? The two of you?"

His coolness both terrified and infuriated her.

"No," she lied desperately. "I came to get my things—that's all. I want to go home. Let me go home and I'll never tell anybody—"

"The truth," he said without emotion, and struck her across the cheek. "Why'd the two of you split up?"

Her stomach quaked with rage and fear, but she said, "My part in it was over. I *told* you. So we went our separate ways."

LaBonny exhaled, a long sighing sound as if he was losing patience. "He's coming after you. Why?"

"I don't know. I—"

Again he hit her, and this time she felt the inside of her lip split and tasted blood pooling in her mouth.

"Who knows you're here?" he demanded, his voice dangerously soft.

"Everybody—my mother, my lawyer—"

"What you said about the media was a lie, wasn't it? Wasn't it? Do you want me to use a knife? Cody J.'s got a nice one, a big one."

She screamed and howled and pretended to be so hysterical she could tell him nothing.

Disgusted, he reached into the glove box and drew out a pair of handcuffs. The chain that joined them clinked almost merrily. Her heart shriveled at the sight of the gleaming metal, and the touch of steel on her wrists almost made her vomit. But she choked back the sensation and kept up her mad babble of pleas and protests.

He cuffed her hands behind her back with terrifying swiftness; he was a very strong man. Then he took a greasy cloth from beneath the seat and jammed it into her mouth to gag her. Even then she did not go silent. She made small, choked, whimpering sounds.

LaBonny took her leather folder out of her cheap carry-on bag. He began methodically to go through her papers. Her heart plummeted.

She had copies of the faxes and e-mails about all the women on Judy Sevenstar's list. She'd written down their names as well as those of Dorothy Nations, Mary

Jo Stewart, and Linda O'Halloran. She watched him pore over the pages.

His eyes rose to meet hers. "Quite the detective, aren't you?"

She shook her head and kept her eyes wide with fright she did not have to feign. His lips twisted in disdain. He set the folder carefully on the dashboard. Then he reached for her.

Oh, God, she thought.

He thrust one thumb into the side of her mouth and with the other hand yanked the gag out so hard it ripped on one of her incisors.

"You were on the road a long time," he said, grasping her hair and twisting her head so that it nearly touched her shoulder. "How many of these women did you talk to?" He nodded at the folder with its sheaf of printouts.

"None—they didn't want to talk to us," she said desperately. "They just wanted to forget the whole thing. I swear."

"Who did you see?" he hissed. "What did they say?" He gave her hair another wrench.

If I ever get loose, Jaye thought in profound fury, *I will kick your crotch to God's own hell.*

But she whimpered and said, "I swear—I swear. Please don't hurt me anymore—please—I'm going to pass out."

He brought his face near hers and spoke with unsettling quietness. "Your ears are pierced. You got pretty little earrings. I could tear them out of your ears with my teeth. Don't make me do it."

"Hail, Mary, full of grace," babbled Jaye, letting tears well and spill. "Blessed are thou among women, and blessed is the fruit of thy womb, Jesus—"

"She's not gonna tell you nothing," Cody J. said in disgust. "She's too scared. Shut her up and let's go to Doll's."

LaBonny drew back from Jaye, his mouth twisted. "I've got to get a message to Mowbry."

Jaye slumped in the seat, blubbering and praying and frantically thinking of a way to escape. She saw LaBonny dial a phone number. He waited, staring at her papers, his jaw taut. Someone must have answered, for he began to speak into the receiver.

"Names," he said tersely. And he read them, all of them that she had written down. "Ask Doc, then call me. All right. Signal." Then he hung up.

Who'd he call? Why? She thought desperately. *Why are those names important to him?*

"Pray for us sinners now and at the hour of our death," she said in a helpless, stumbling whisper, and immediately began the prayer again.

"Make her stop that Catholic crap," Cody J. complained. "It's spooky."

LaBonny ignored him. Jaye kept up her ragged stream of mumbled words. She kept her head bowed as if in abjection, but her eyes were on LaBonny. He seemed to be waiting for something.

Then he took a beeper from his belt. Its small light was flashing, a green dot winking off and on in the darkness. He examined its display window, his eyes narrowed.

Although Jaye strained to read it, too, she could make out nothing. But LaBonny seemed to understand perfectly.

"Well," he said with an unpleasant smile. "Well." He flicked the beeper off and put it back on his belt.

Jaye kept her lips moving, even though hardly any sound came out.

"O'Halloran," LaBonny told her. "That was the name you shouldn't have on your list. What do you know about the O'Halloran woman?"

From the backseat Cody J. said, "Let me and Bobby have her. Bobby *wants* this one. He said—"

LaBonny took a fistful of her shirtfront and jerked her toward him. For the first time his face showed anger. "Fucking stop that. Tell me what I want." He drew back his hand to slap her again.

"We never talked to her," she cried. "Don't hit me again—please. Whatever you want to know—just ask."

In the greenish glow from the dashboard, she saw LaBonny's expression change to one of cold superiority. It was as if for a few seconds he had been thrown off balance, but now he was back in full control.

Slowly he lowered his hand. "That's right. Whatever I want to know. All I'll have to do is ask."

She did not know what idea had come into his mind, but from his expression she knew it involved pain.

He stuffed the gag back into her mouth slowly, almost lovingly. "I don't have to ask you. I'll ask your boyfriend. He won't like seeing you hurt."

He leaned over, kissed her gently on the cheek. At the same time he pinched her breast so painfully that she cried out against the gag.

He turned and spoke over his shoulder. "Cody J., you and Bobby wanted to rape somebody? I just might give you your chance. I might take a piece of her myself."

He leaned close to her again. "But I'll warn you, sugar," he said in his dulcet voice, "I won't do it like the other boys."

.   .   .

Turner was on the outskirts of Cawdor when the phone rang.

Jaye, He thought with a surge of the sort of excited apprehension he thought happened only to schoolboys.

But the voice was not Jaye's. It was a woman, and she sounded more than a little drunk.

"Mr. Gibson," she said. "I'm sorry to call so late. I gotta do it while my courage is up. Is it too late? Did I wake you up? What time is it?"

A sickening disappointment stabbed him, but he kept his voice cool, professional. "I'm up. It's not too late. What can I do for you?"

"You—you called me earlier today. You—asked me about some things. You asked about some—personal things."

Christ, he thought. He knew that voice, and he wasn't happy to hear it again. *Christ, oh, Christ.*

"This is Linda O'Halloran," she said. "In Okka— Oklahoma City."

Jaye's mother.

She sounded as if she was about to go on a crying jag. He kept his own tone steady and friendly. "I remember. What can I do for you, Ms. O'Halloran?"

She sniffled. "I can't believe this. It's like fate. I left Oklahoma years ago. I just came back a couple months ago. I thought it was safe to come back. That all that stuff was forgot. I've done my best to forget."

Carefully he said, "Are we discussing what I asked you about earlier?"

There was a long pause. He thought he heard the clink of ice cubes in a glass. "Hunsinger," she said. Her voice was bitter and thick with tears.

"Yes," he said. "Dr. Hunsinger. Do you want to talk, Ms. O'Halloran."

"Yes," she said. "No."

Turner was in Mount Cawdor now, and the power lines were causing interference with the phone's transmission. It crackled and cleared, then crackled again. "It's all right, Ms. O'Halloran," he said. "You only have to tell me what you want to."

"You don't know what it's like," she said. "A man can't know."

The transmission cleared and he pulled to the side of the road, hoping the connection would hold. "I'll try to understand," he said.

She paused again. "I met Hunsinger when I worked at a place called The Empyrean. He—kind of came on to me. I knew what he did."

"What he did?" Turner said.

"That he did abortions. And girls came to him that had to have babies and keep it secret. He made a lot of money at it. He liked to flash it around. I wasn't impressed. I had a guy. But Hunsinger told me to come to him if I ever—if I ever needed a friend."

He heard the clink of ice cubes again, a pause as she drank. He said, "And it turned out that you needed a friend?"

She started to cry. "You never think it's gonna happen to you, you know. And this guy I loved, I thought he loved me. But I got pregnant, and—*pow*—he drops me like a hot potato. I mean, like the song says, he was gone, gone, *gone*."

"It's all right," Turner said, trying to comfort her. "I understand. It's still painful."

"By the time he left," she said, "it was too late for an abortion. So I had to have the kid. I had no choice."

The kid was Jaye.

She sniffled again, and it sounded as if she was using a handkerchief. "I didn't have all that much money," she said. "So Hunsinger made an 'arrangement' with me. He said if I'd sleep with him when he came to Oklahoma City, he'd let me work it off. Twenty-five dollars a visit. So I promised."

She began to cry again.

When she finally quieted again, she said, "I'm sorry. This is real hard."

Turner said, "Nobody blames you. You didn't have much choice."

"I let him have my baby," she said. "I never even saw her. The nurses told me she was pretty. Real pretty. I guess I'll never know."

She's very pretty, Ms. O'Halloran. Enough to break your heart. I know.

"I wonder about her all the time," she said. "A week doesn't go by that I don't think about that kid. God."

Turner took a deep breath. This was a path down which he didn't want to travel, but there was no turning back. "So," he said, "you've decided you'd like to find her, your daughter?"

"No," she said with surprising sharpness.

He was both relieved and puzzled. "No?"

"What's done is done. I got no business butting into her life at this point. I wish I knew for sure she went to good people. I'd rest easier, that's all."

He thought about it. "I could probably try to check that out for you, Ms. O'Halloran. If it'd put your mind at ease. I can't guarantee anything, of course."

"No," she repeated morosely. "Maybe it's better not knowing."

He frowned. "Excuse me," he said. "I don't understand. How can I help you then?"

"I just want people to know what Hunsinger's

done," she said with sudden passion. "I want it out—all of it. Every dirty thing he did."

He tried to reassure her. "The baby-selling business is going to come out. I can promise you that."

"There's more," she said. "There's a lot more."

Warning signals shot through Turner's system. "What do you mean?"

"I sent somebody else to him. That was the worst thing."

"Yes?" He waited for her to go on.

"The person I sent, it was my sister."

"Your sister?"

"Listen," said Linda O'Halloran in a rush, "she wasn't like me. She had *potential*. She was beautiful, she had brains—everything. She was like a prodigy. She had a scholarship to the University of Southern California. Me, I always hated school. She was different. She was going to get life by the tail, do everything right."

"This is a younger sister?" he asked.

"Eight years younger. When our mother died, she came to live with me in Oklahoma City. She did her senior year here. And then she got the scholarship. And she went to California."

Turner could guess what happened next. "But something happened."

"It was a big whadamacallit. Campus. Too big. She felt lost. She got involved with some guy. She'd never tell me his name. But then she called me in a panic, because she's knocked up."

"So you sent her to Hunsinger?"

"For an abortion," she said. "I didn't want her to go through what I did. I wanted her to get her education. To have her future. I called Hunsinger. I asked if I could pay for it the same way, like before. He said yes."

Turner waited.

She said, "She never came back."

His stomach pitched uneasily. "She didn't come back?"

"Hunsinger sent a car for her. He did things like that. You know, like he ran this fancy service. He was supposed to have the car bring her back. She never came. I never saw her again."

"Ms. O'Halloran—"

She said, "I think he killed her."

TWENTY-TWO

———∞∞∞———

A GIRL HAD DIED, JUDY SEVENSTAR HAD SAID.
    "You think," Turner said, "that Hunsinger killed your sister."

"Yes." Her voice was low and shaky, yet filled with enormous bitterness.

"When did this happen?" he asked.

"April tenth, 1968," she said. "He sent a car for her. A woman drove. Her name was Dorothy. That's all she'd tell us. Dorothy."

Dorothy Nations of Oklahoma City, thought Turner. *Your friendly local arranger: abortions and illegitimate births. Transportation provided.*

"I walked her to the car," said Linda O'Halloran. "I asked her again if she wanted me to go with her. She said no. I stood at the curb and watched them drive off. I—she—I never saw her again."

"You didn't take the license number?"

"I never thought to. I never thought there'd be a need. And then it was too late."

"What did Hunsinger say?"

"That she ran off. That some boy came for her. That she left with him. He said she had it all arranged, it was obvious. At first I believed him. I *wanted* to believe him."

The rain drummed on the roof. The windshield wipers did their boring dance. Turner found himself staring through the rain at the church billboard. "And then?" he asked.

"And when I didn't hear from her I *couldn't* believe it. She wouldn't do that to me. I was all the family she had."

She paused, and he had the intuition she was refilling her drink, fortifying herself. She said, "I wrote to California; I called. Nobody there ever had word of her, either. It was like she fell off the face of the earth. So I went to Hunsinger. I said I wanted the truth."

She took a long, quavering breath. "He said the truth was my sister was a slut and so was I. He said that Lisa never put a foot inside his clinic. That when this Dorothy drove up, another car was waiting there. It had a man in it. Some of the nurses saw it."

"This car—did he describe it?"

"He said it had California plates, but he knew she'd been in California. I must have told him. I don't know. I just don't know."

"Ms. O'Halloran—"

"He *said* my sister got out of Dorothy's car and into the man's. He *said* he had four witnesses. And—and he said if I went around making accusations against him, he'd sue me for slander. He said he'd take me to court and show I was nothing but a blackmailing whore."

Turner ground his teeth and stared at the church sign.

"I didn't have any money. Who was I? Nobody," she said, despair in her voice. "What could I do?"

"Nothing," Turner said quietly. "You could do nothing."

"Except blame myself," she said as if he hadn't spoken. "Because I sent her to him. Me. I was the one. I kind of started going downhill then."

Turner imagined the journey downhill had been long and hard. He heard it in her voice.

"I went to Fort Worth," she said. "I got married a couple times. I got unmarried, got 'em annulled. Nothing ever seemed to last."

"Any children?" he asked, trying to sound merely curious out of polite concern. *Maybe you've got sisters, Jaye,* he thought. *Or brothers besides Patrick.*

"No," she said. "I think maybe Hunsinger screwed up my plumbing. There were two I lost, early on. Maybe it's just as well. I wouldn't have been much of a mother."

She started to cry again, quietly. "I heard Hunsinger's still alive. But he's had a stroke or something. I hope he's suffering, the old bastard. I hope he pays for all the hurt he's caused. I want justice."

Turner was a lawyer, and he knew the odds on justice prevailing were not good. But he said, "There's an old saying: The truth will out. Let's hope it does."

"Christ," she wept. "Such a world that made such things happen to women. And the men involved, they just walked away scot-free. Christ."

She was about to slip into a crying jag, a long one,

Turner could tell. He was desperate to get a few last facts before she lost herself in incoherence and tears.

"Ms. O'Halloran," he said. "Are there any facts you can give me about your sister? Her full name. Her appearance. Any identifying marks or scars."

"Lisa Lou O'Halloran," she sobbed. "She was a beautiful girl, beautiful, beautiful. Tall, with blond hair. Very fair skin—she sunburned, sunburned so easy I teased her about going to Calforna—California. Blue eyes. Sky-blue. And smart. Smart as a goddamn whip."

Jaye, Turner thought sickly. *She'd been like Jaye.*

"Shouldn't be dead," Linda O'Halloran mumbled. "She sh-shouldn't be dead."

Turner calmed her as best he could; he promised to call her back in the morning. At last he got her to say good-bye. After he hung up, he stared out the window at the rain for a long time, wondering what he should say to Jaye.

He thought about the dead girl.

He knew now why Jaye's appearance in town had caused consternation. The Hunsinger family had more to hide than flesh peddling, probably at least a manslaughter charge.

He took his gun out of his briefcase, loaded it. He took off his jacket, strapped on the holster, put on the jacket again.

At last he put the car back into gear. He drove on, crossed the border.

Jaye lay alone on the floor of the backseat of LaBonny's Blazer, gagged, her hands cuffed behind her. LaBonny had roped her ankles together with something like clothesline, and it cut painfully into her flesh. He had thrown her handbag at her so it had hit her in the face, then tossed a filthy blanket over her that smelled like dog.

Her nose hurt, her face throbbed, but desperately she tried to think. The men were going after Turner, LaBonny had made that clear.

Now the Blazer was parked, the men were gone, and she was alone. She thought the Blazer was parked in the alley that ran behind Miss Doll's.

Dammit, I hurt, she thought, but then she thought of Patrick and Turner. She could help no one, not even herself, where she was. *To hell with hurting.*

The men had gotten out of the car quietly, only a few moments ago. She had heard the *snick* of the automatic locks snapping shut again behind them.

Now a dog hair tickled her nostril and she sneezed. *Get rid of the bloody blanket,* she thought. She began to wriggle, and once she started, she realized that she was not helpless, she was not immobilized. Her wrists were cuffed, but she could move her hands, her fingers.

Say uncle? Patrick used to taunt, when their quibbling turned to wrestling and he pinned her to the floor. *No,* she would spit back. *Never.*

Did LaBonny think tying and handcuffing her made her helpless? Well, LaBonny, fuck him, was wrong.

If she could get out from beneath the blanket, she could do more. She could squirm her way between the front seats. She could hit the door lock on the driver's side with her elbow or foot, spring it open.

She didn't need her hands in front of her to open a door. With enough maneuvering, she could get out. But once she was out, what good was that? What then?

Match in the gas tank, she thought. *Boom boom.*

She nearly wept, *My lighter. I've got my lighter.*

She knew exactly how a Blazer was made; she had driven one until last year. If she could get out the door, she could lean against the car, ease her way to its rear, and screw off the gas cap. The Blazer had a gas cap that was exceptionally easy to manipulate.

She had done it in subzero weather wearing mittens. She had done it so often she could do it blindfolded. *I could do it with my hands tied behind me,* she thought with mordant irony.

She could click on the lighter, set fire to something like a fuse, and drop it into the gas tank. *That* would put a crimp in LaBonny's goddam plans.

Rack 'em up, stack 'em up, any old time—
Match in the gas tank: boom boom.

It would be dangerous, she knew. But it was the only plan that could fasten itself down in her spinning mind. She managed to shake herself free from the blanket, squirmed until her back was against her purse. Fingers awkward, she snapped it open. She fumbled for her lighter. She felt it, her hand closed around it. Then her knuckles brushed the scarf. The scarf—she could use it as a fuse.

Thank you, God. Thank you. Thank you.

Somehow she'd have to stuff one end of the scarf into the gas tank and set the other end afire. Then she'd have to hit the dirt, roll like hell, and pray. She'd probably burn half the skin off her body.

It's better than dying.

She gritted her teeth and told herself that what mattered was not letting LaBonny win, God damn his eyes.

Say uncle.
No. Never.

But writhing her way into the front seat was harder than she'd thought. She could not do it feet first, the way she first tried; she needed her feet for leverage, to push off.

She stopped, breathing hard, her body aching, and

looked out the window. She recognized where she was and knew she'd been right. The Blazer was parked in the alley that ran behind Miss Doll's. The closest house was dark; it looked empty and neglected.

Half a block away she could see Miss Doll's back porch, its yellow light aglow. There was light from within the house as well, but faint and from only one window. And somewhere in the yard's dense shadows, LaBonny and Cody J. waited for Turner.

They'll kill him. They'll torture us for what we know and then kill us both.

Her heart beating violently, she looked again at the vacant house. Its yard was full of rank bushes and high grass. A woman could hide there—for a while.

The lighter in her hand was already slippery with sweat.

Once again she tried to insinuate herself into the front seat, this time headfirst, like a burrowing worm. But she found herself wedged between the seats, sweaty and breathless with struggling. Her hands locked behind her created a trap she hadn't expected. They made her body too wide to squeeze between the seats, and no matter how hard she struggled, she could not force herself farther.

She gritted her teeth, extricated herself, and fell onto the backseat again. *I was so close,* she thought, tears of frustration burning her eyes. *I was so close. I saw the lock. It was only a few feet from my face.*

Her heart banged against her ribs as she tried to angle herself to slip between the seats. *Christ, Christ,* she thought. *Patrick, you never had me in a fix where I had to work like this.*

She tried again, panting and sweating. This time she contorted her body until her muscles began to twitch and stab with pain. But somehow she twisted and squeezed half through and half over the seat backs until she surrendered herself to gravity and dropped.

The fall was awkward, and it hurt. She found herself flat on her back, winded, her head on the driver's seat. Her pinioned arms were trapped beneath her, and the console between the seats pressed into her spine like a stone.

She tried to fight upright to a sitting position, but she was almost exhausted and had to stop a moment and rest, her chest pounding. It was then that she saw the glow of approaching headlights strike erratic shadows in the Blazer's interior. A car was coming.

Turner. Oh, my God, Turner. Not yet, Turner. Not now.

Turner pulled to a stop behind Jaye's rental car. Miss Doll's house was nearly dark, but not quite. Maybe the old woman had gone to bed and maybe she hadn't, it didn't matter; he wanted Jaye *out* of there.

He wanted to get her someplace more private, where he could talk to her without interruption. A place where they could be alone and where he knew she was safe. He had Juanita Bragg's diary in his briefcase, and he hungered to show her Patrick's date of birth, the name of the woman who must be, please the gods, his mother.

He was counting on that date, that name, to buy her forgiveness. But what he would tell her of her own mother, about the dead girl who had been of her own blood, he did not know.

One thing at a time, he told himself. *One thing at a time.*

He uncoiled his length from behind the wheel and stepped out of the car, seizing the briefcase. He hurried through the rain, head down, to reach the back porch.

But then—unexpected and unexpectedly near—he heard a shrill jolt of noise, the blast of a car's horn. The blare of it on the quiet night was so clearly *wrong* that he turned toward it automatically.

As he did, a man's figure lunged out of the shadows. It happened with a nightmarish swiftness. Turner's hand flew to his jacket for his gun. But a second, taller man was already on him, cutting off his breath with a choke hold and jamming a gun against his cheekbone.

"Stay quiet," the man hissed. "Or die. I've got your girlfriend. You're coming with us."

The horn kept braying, its sound shattering the night.

The other, smaller man cried, "Jesus, LaBonny, it's her. What's she—"

At that moment the horn went silent.

Turner fought for air, conscious of the gun barrel drilling into his cheekbone, and the words echoed drunkenly in his mind: *I've got your girlfriend.*

Jaye, he thought, choking for breath. *Oh, God, Jaye.*

"She must have—" began the smaller man.

"Shut up. Get her," the tall man ordered in a harsh whisper. "Don't let her do it again."

The other man moved off swiftly through the rain and shadows.

"Listen to me, you son of a bitch," the tall man said in Turner's ear. "You tell me everything you know or I start cutting the girl. I'll cut her apart a piece at a time."

She hadn't meant to hit the horn. She'd struck it with her elbow in her battle to position herself. The sound had split her soul with terror; it was like the very trumpet of doom and she had sounded it.

She tried to heave her body upright, and—*oh, God,*

no—hit the horn again and was pinned against it. On and on it blared.

No, no, no.

Cursing her own folly, she wrenched herself into a sitting position in the driver's seat. She wriggled to insinuate her body between the steering wheel and the door to reach the main lock button. She found it and, gasping, contorted herself to press it. The locks snapped open with a beautiful, liberating *click.*

Thank you, Mary, Mother of God, she thought almost drunkenly. She groped for the door handle, found it with her right hand. She pulled on it. Miraculously the door opened, but the interior light flashed on.

Oh, God, she thought in horror, *oh God oh God oh God.*

She thrust her feet out the door, found the ground, slid to a standing position, and leaned against the car, her pulses banging in her temples. The door fell shut. She was in blessed darkness again.

As swiftly as she could, she eased toward the rear of the Blazer until she was next to the gas cap. It opened easily.

Thank you, Mary, thank you, Jesus. Thank you, Father, Son, and Holy Ghost.

She fumbled to unscrew the inner cap with her right hand. It, too, came undone with astonishing ease. *Oh, Patrick. Oh, Patrick.*

She still gripped the lighter, slick with sweat, in her left hand, along with the scarf. She switched the scarf to her right hand. She flicked on the lighter.

I'll L-O-V-E love you
All the T-I-M-E time—

A man was running toward her. She thought she saw the glint of a gun in his hand.

She set the scarf afire. It burned her hands. She thought of Patrick, she thought of Turner, she thought of Nona. . . .

Rack 'em up, stack 'em up, any old time—
Match in the gas tank—

"Listen, you cocksucker," hissed the tall man. "Get back in your car. I'm taking you and the bitch for a ride."

"Why? This is a mistake," Turner choked out, trying to stall. "We've got no—"

An explosion shook the air. Down the alley a fiery light bloomed in the sky, a great, billowing chrysanthemum of flame. A man screamed out in agony.

The man called LaBonny swore.

Miss Doll's back door flew open. "What's happening?" she screamed. "What's—"

LaBonny leveled his gun at her. "Get back in the house," he cried. "It's none of your business."

"There's a *fire!*" Miss Doll shrieked. She did not seem to see LaBonny's gun.

Turner brought down the side of his left hand on LaBonny's wrist in a cracking blow and with his right drew his own gun. LaBonny had somehow kept his grip on his pistol. Turner didn't hesitate. He shot the man in the stomach point-blank.

Miss Doll screamed.

LaBonny lurched closer to Turner. The gun slipped from his hand. He clutched Turner by both shoulders, as he might a long-lost comrade. Then he sagged, burying his face in Turner's neck.

For a moment he remained in this parody of an embrace, gasping and gurgling. Then the man's grip loosened, and he sank down Turner's body as if he was going to kneel before him. For a moment he swayed drunkenly on his knees. Then he fell in a heap on the ground. "Sweety," he said in a rasping voice, "get him."

Turner stared down at him in stunned astonishment. He had no idea what the man's words meant.

On the porch Miss Doll was screaming. The lights in other houses were flicking on; he heard unseen people calling out questions, but the words made no sense to him.

Jaye, he thought again. *Jaye.*

He ran blindly in the direction of the flames. The second man lay behind the burning wreckage, holding his face.

Turner hunkered down beside him, hauled him up out of the dirt by his shirt collar. "The woman?" he demanded. "Where is she?"

"I'm hit," the man wept. "Something hit me." Blood ran down his forehead, covering his face.

Turner shook him. "The woman—where is she? Tell me. Or I'll by God throw you on the fucking goddamn fire."

"She was in the car, in the car," the man babbled.

Oh, Jesus, Turner thought. He let the man drop back to the dirt. He sprang up and ran toward the burning hulk that had been a car. But he could not get close enough to open a door. He could see nothing within the interior except antic flames. Dark smoke, heavy with the smell of gasoline, boiled up into the rain.

"Jaye!" he screamed. "Jaye!"

Once again he tried to approach the wildly dancing fire, but the heat scorched his face, driving him back. Then he heard a sound from beside the alley, a woman's moan of pain.

He spun on his heel. He looked about wildly. And then he saw her.

She was lying in the tall grass with her hands behind her. She was hurt, he could tell, and his heart knocked against his ribs.

He dropped to his knees beside her and started to take her in his arms. She tried to cry out, but the sound was strangled. He realized the back of her clothing was burned, and he felt blood on his hands. He was terrified to touch her, for fear of hurting her more. He took the gag from her mouth, and she gasped rawly for air.

He flicked open his phone and dialed 911. "I want to report an injured woman," he said. "And I want the state police. Not just the local police. I want the state police. I want—I want Twin Bears and Ramirez. And the FBI. There's been a hostage situation."

Jaye stirred and turned her face toward his. Her eyelids fluttered. "Turner," she said. Her voice was weak.

"I'm here, baby," he said.

"Will you hold me?" she asked. The pain in her voice clawed at his heart.

"I'm afraid I'll hurt you," he said, stroking her forehead. In the shimmering light from the fire, he could see that it was bruised.

"I don't care," she said.

Gently, holding her by her shoulders, he raised her so that she could rest against his chest. She fainted. He did not let her go until the state police arrived. Only then did he let the medics take her.

Adon sat in the darkness, waiting. Barbara had long been asleep upstairs. Indeed, her pill might soon be wearing off. He would have to cajole her into taking another.

He could hear the old man upstairs. The rock music

channel played music with a heavy, insinuating beat, and Adon could hear the old man moving on his treadmill, each step a soft thud that took him nowhere.

The rain had eased again. For a while it had poured down as in a biblical flood, and during that time Adon had thought he'd heard distant noises: a crash, as if from an explosion, sirens. Perhaps he had really heard them, perhaps not.

When his beeper signaled a message, he felt strangely cold. It would be LaBonny, telling him it was over. The lawyer and the woman were gone now. It would look like an accident. Had that been the crash he'd heard? Had that caused the ghostly scream of sirens in the distance?

That would be good, he told himself. That would be fine. It would give them a few more months of peace. That's all Adon needed, really. Just a few more months. Just a little peace.

But when he looked at his beeper, the code message was not from LaBonny. It was from Elton Delray, to meet Delray in the lane as soon as possible. Adon sighed.

He went to the hall closet and took out his new rain jacket with the hood. He put on his rubber boots to keep his feet dry. He could not find his own black umbrella, so he took Barbara's flowered one, which hadn't been out of the house in years.

He went to the garage, got into his Jeep, and headed for the lane. The trees curved over it, their branches black and dripping, looking like trees from a wicked forest in a fairy tale. He didn't have far to go, but he turned on the heater. He had always disliked being cold.

He parked and waited in the Jeep, his lights cut. There was no sound but the dripping of rain on the roof, so he turned on the CD player.

Pavarotti was singing something about "*ah, lo paterno mano*." Adon didn't understand it, but he always found the man's voice comforting.

Then he saw the lights of a sheriff's department car coming up the lane. Adon shut off the music, put up the hood to his rain jacket. He got out of his car and opened Barbara's flowered umbrella.

The headlights of the car caught him hunched under the umbrella, and he supposed he looked foolish in his maroon hood and shiny boots, and the light reflecting off his glasses.

Delray kept the headlights on. He got out, looking slumped and tired. With his back to the light, his face seemed gaunter than usual. Adon realized that someone else was sitting in the car, another deputy, probably Cornell Henley. It was all right, Adon told himself. Cornell was a good boy. He knew how the system worked.

Adon looked at Delray's shadowy face. "Is it over?" he asked. "All of it?"

Slowly, sadly, Delray shook his head. "LaBonny's been shot," he said. "He's hurt bad. He's in the Mount Cawdor Hospital, but they're going to airlift him over to Tulsa. Maybe he's gonna die. Maybe not. The lawyer did it."

Adon felt an odd little chill run over him, as when he was a child and would get a shudder that made people joke, "A goose just ran over your grave."

He could only clutch his umbrella and stare at Delray. "The girl's hurt, too, but not so bad," Delray said, tilting down his hat brim against the rain. "So's Cody J. Cody J.'s scared and he's talking, Adon. Talking up a storm."

Adon lifted his chin. His hands were cold and wet around the umbrella handle, and his glasses were starting to mist. His knees shook slightly, but he held his ground. He tried to make his voice steady. "What's—what's he talking about?"

Delray put his hands on his gun belt. "That you had Luther Raven killed. Because he tried to blackmail Doc." Delray nodded toward the house. "Luther'd said Doc killed a girl back when he was running his clinic. That Luther'd seen the body burned and he had proof. So old Doc had him killed."

"Ahhh," said Adon. It was neither a denial nor an admission. It was the only sound that was drawn out of him, as if by a phantom hook, and the breath of it was visible in the cold air.

Delray crossed his arms, and there was a certain resignation in the gesture. "State police asked Cody J. about jumping the lawyer and the girl. He told 'em everything. He wants to cop a plea. If somebody's going to death row, he don't want it to be him."

Adon nodded, then bowed his head slightly. He felt tears of fatigue rising in his eyes.

Delray said, "They asked him if there was any more mixed up in this thing tonight. He told them about Bobby Midus. Said Bobby Midus had Hollis out in the hayfield, waitin' to kill him. It was your orders."

Adon watched the water run in little rivulets down the channels of the gravel. The channels were muddy at the bottom. There had been so much rain, the stones were washing away. It would have to be replaced when the weather was more clement.

"State police went out there. Hollis hurt Bobby somehow, Adon. He got him with a baling hook. He's in the hospital, too. And I suppose he's gonna talk, too. He'll have to, to save his own skin."

"And Hollis?" asked Adon with a vain flicker of hope. "Is he dead?"

"No. Bobby shot him, but he didn't kill him."

"Hollis," Adon said in a small voice, "he's not talking—is he?"

"No, but they say maybe a doctor can make him."

"Hmm," Adon said with an abstracted thoughtfulness.

"Adon," said Delray, "I shouldn't be here. But you and Doc, you done many a good thing for me and mine in my time. The law's out of our hands this time. The state police are in charge. They'll be sending somebody for you soon. To bring you in. To question you. And Cody J. and Bobby Midus—they're both gonna rat you out. I'm sorry."

"I thank you, Elton," Adon said. "You're a gentleman." He managed an avuncular little smile.

"I'm going now," said Delray. "You take care, Adon."

Adon kept his smile in place. He watched the deputy climb back into the car. He waved at both men as they turned to drive back down the lane. He saw Delray wave back.

Adon lowered his foolish umbrella and closed it. It hadn't really been able to keep him dry. He stood for a moment in the rain and the dark, thinking.

Cody J. was talking. Bobby Midus was talking. A doctor might be able to make Hollis talk. It would all come out. The dead girl, so many years ago. If only the old man had come clean then, but he hadn't. After that, crime had built upon crime. Now the lawyer and the woman were closing in like Greek furies, about to bring it all out in the open . . .

Adon got back into the Jeep. Before he closed the door, he shook out the little flowered umbrella as best he could, saw that it was neatly furled, and snapped its dainty strap in place. He drove back to the garage and parked his car.

He took his rain boots off at the door so that he would not track rain or mud in on the carpet. He hung up his rain jacket on the kitchen coat tree, then put a towel under it to catch the water. He set the umbrella carefully in the corner, its point on the same towel.

Felix was gone tonight. Adon had given him the night off and sent him home. There was no one in the house but family.

Adon walked in stockinged feet to his study and unlocked his safe. He took out his automatic, with the silencer attached. He put in the clip. Holding the pistol behind him, he climbed the stairs.

He could hear the old man's rock and roll music and the thump of his treadmill.

He walked into Barbara's bedroom. She slept under a white coverlet, her head on a ruffled white pillow. Her little white dog was at her feet. It opened its eyes and wagged its tail sleepily. It did not lift its head. It yawned.

Oh, my love, my love, thought Adon, *I have tried in every way I know to save you pain, and now this is all that I have left to give you. I love you, my darling.*

His hand shaking, he put the gun to her temple. The gun made a strange little noise, like a breath being exhaled. Her body jolted and was still. In the semidarkness, it was as if a dark flower had suddenly appeared in her hair, and its dark leaves flowed down the pillow onto the sheet.

The little dog leaped to its feet and whined. Adon turned and shot it. Another soft exhalation came from the gun, but it made the little dog fly across the room as if thrown from a catapult. It made a dark mark on the pale wallpaper and fell to the floor, silent.

Adon imagined the old man in his room, and he thought Barbara would want her father spared. Adon was tempted. Death, he thought, was in many ways too good for the old man.

He picked up the little dog and laid it down again at Barbara's still feet. He took up a white notebook and a white pen from her bedside table. He wrote a short note that, he hoped, explained everything.

Then he walked softly down the hall. This time he did not bother to knock. He opened the old man's door.

Roland Hunsinger had finished working on his treadmill. He had climbed on his bicycle and was pedaling as he watched MTV. He turned his head when the door opened.

"What do you want?" he asked in his metallic, vibrating voice.

"Peace," said Adon, raising the gun. "I want peace."

He fired once. The top of the old man's head flew off, spattering blood over him and the stationary bicycle. He slumped over the handlebars, and his feet slid from the pedals. The light from the television shone on his exposed brain, made the blood running to the floor glisten.

Adon closed the door and went back to his and Barbara's room. He lay down beside her. He put his arm around her. He kissed her cheek, which was still warm.

Then he put the barrel deep between his teeth. Like a lover, the gun breathed its small sound into his mouth.

TWENTY-THREE

AT THE MOUNT CAWDOR HOSPITAL HOLLIS WENT WILD with fear and pain. They struggled to ready him to operate on his elbow, but he fought against being undressed.

He fought even harder when they tried to take away the filthy little leather bag he was clutching convulsively.

Until the moment they touched the bag, his cries had been incoherent. But now he was screaming out a word, the same word over and over again: "No! No! No! No! No! No! No! No!"

"My God, knock him out," an intern snarled impatiently. "He's going to wake up the whole town."

The kindest of the nurses tried to reason with Hollis. "Please, Hollis, let me have it for just a little while. Nothing will happen to it, I swear."

She was a pretty little Native American nurse, with long dark hair held back with a clip. She kept stroking his forehead, patting his good arm. At last she calmed him slightly.

"Now," she whispered, "let us have this. So we can take you to the operating room. I promise you can have it back as soon as you're through."

But Hollis began to cry. And he began to babble something that resembled language.

"I'm giving him a shot," said the intern.

"Wait," said the little nurse, and put her ear to Hollis's jerking, muttering mouth.

"What?" she said softly. "What?"

"She'll come for me," Hollis seemed to say in a slurred voice, as if he was drunk or had had a stroke.

"She'll what?" asked the nurse. She tried to take his hand in hers. "You can trust me. What did you say?"

"If they c-cut on me, she'll c-come for me," stammered Hollis. "She'll take me to hell."

"Nobody's going to take you to hell," soothed the nurse. "We'll fix you up just fine, you'll see."

But he jerked his hand from her grasp and clutched the dirty bag to his chest. "I gotta give it *back*," he sobbed. "I gotta give it back."

An older nurse approached with a syringe. "Sorry. You're making me do this."

"Give it back to who?" persisted the small nurse. "Hollis, let me help you. Give it back to who?"

"To the d-d-dead girl," Hollis wept, but the intern held him down while the other nurse stuck the needle into him. It took only seconds for him to quiet.

"Poor man," said the little nurse. She had seen Hollis walking up and down the roads since she was a little girl and she'd always felt compassion for him.

The other nurse took the dirty leather pouch from

his limp hand. "What is this?" she asked sourly. "Some kind of Indian thing? A medicine bag or something? Ugh, it's filthy."

"Let me see," said the intern with a frown. He unknotted the bag's string and poured the contents into his hand. His face paled slightly.

"What is it?" asked the older nurse.

"Christ." The intern's expression was one of horror mingled with disbelief. "I think it's a finger. A mummified human finger."

Turner paused at the open doorway to Jaye's hospital room. The state police and the FBI had not let him come to her until now, two days after the carnage behind Miss Doll's. At the sight of her his heart vaulted in his chest.

She did not realize he was there. She sat awkwardly propped up in her bed, drinking fruit juice through a straw and staring at an old movie on television. Humphrey Bogart was telling Ingrid Bergman that in this crazy world the troubles of two people didn't amount to a hill of beans.

Jaye's chin quivered, and she looked as if she was going to cry. Turner felt an unpleasant lump in his own throat.

Flowers, many of them from him, were everywhere, dazzling the room with color. But she looked wan. She had an ugly bruise on one cheekbone and another on her forehead and a scrape on her chin. She sat at an odd angle, because of the burns on her back. Her hands were thickly swathed in bandages past the wrists.

The flowers next to her, on the bedside tray, weren't his. Instinctively he knew they were from Patrick and what she'd chosen to have closest to her.

He swallowed but struck a nonchalant pose, one hip cocked, his hand braced against the door frame. He pasted a crooked, I-don't-give-a-damn smile on his face.

He said, "So—are you speaking to me? Or not?"

She turned to face him, her eyes wide with startlement. "Oh," she said. The glass nearly slipped from her bandaged hands. Drops of apple juice spattered on her chest and on the sheet. "Oh, *damn*," she said in frustration, struggling to set the glass back down on the bedside tray.

He moved to her side and took the glass from her hands. He pulled a handful of tissues from the box, wet them from the water glass, and began to dab at the spotted sheet. "I asked if you were speaking to me," he said.

She stared at him warily. "I guess so," she said at last.

He stopped rubbing at the sheet. "Would you let a guy kiss you hello?"

She drew in her breath. She turned her eyes from him and looked at the television screen, where Humphrey Bogart was walking off into the mist with Claude Rains.

"I guess so," she said with something like resignation.

He bent and kissed her on the mouth for a long time. Then, because it felt so good, he kissed her even longer. When he drew back, she gave him a look as if to say, *I don't know what that meant. Maybe it meant nothing.*

He wet the tissues again and brought them near the stains on her breast. His eyes locked with her wary ones. "May I?" he said.

For a moment they stared at each other. Slowly, almost helplessly, she smiled.

"No, you horny bastard. You said you wanted to talk. Talk."

He touched her bruised cheekbone. "Did LaBonny do this to you?"

Her smile died. "Yes."

His forefinger traveled to her scraped chin. "This, too?"

"No," she said, collapsing back against the pillows. "I did that. I took a dive into the gravel after I dropped the scarf in the gas tank."

His hands settled on hers, above the bandages. "And this?" he asked, touching the gauze.

"I didn't dive fast enough," she said sadly.

He nodded. He'd heard. She had second-degree burns on her hands. She'd been hit on the edge of her left hand by a flying shard of metal that had cut through muscle and severed the tip of her little finger.

She was lucky, her doctor had said. She'd carry some scars, but other than the lost fingertip, there'd be no permanent damage.

"What about your back?" he asked, running his hands up her upper arms.

"The same," she said. "Some burned spots, mostly first and second degree. Some of it no worse than a bad sunburn. A few cuts. I'll live."

"Good," he said, stroking her upper arms again. "Good."

"And you—" she said—"you weren't hurt?"

He shook his head sadly. "No. You took all the punishment. You were a brave girl."

"No. Just desperate," she said.

"Sometimes it's the same thing," he said.

She glanced away, her eyes sweeping the room. "You sent so many flowers," she murmured.

"I wished I could send you all the flower fields of California," he said. "All the orchids in the tropics. All the cherry blossoms in Japan."

She didn't smile at his fancifulness. She stared at the flowers and said, "You shot LaBonny."

He sighed. "Yeah. I did."

"But you didn't kill him."

"No. I didn't."

"I wish you had." Her voice was bitter.

He brushed her hair back from her forehead. "I think the state of Oklahoma'll do that for you."

He paused. "Did anyone tell you Miss Doll's under arrest? As an accessory. She won't talk, but the kid has."

"Bright?" Jaye asked in surprise.

"She told the police everything she knew. They've put her in a foster home. The adoption Miss Doll had arranged wasn't exactly on the up-and-up. The authorities will see that it is."

"The poor kid," she said. "A foster home. She'll be better off."

He paused again. "They found Judy Sevenstar."

She swallowed hard. "When?"

"This morning."

"It's our fault," she said hopelessly. "We shouldn't have talked her into meeting us."

He gripped her shoulder. "It's Hunsinger's fault, dammit. And LaBonny's. And Adon Mowbry's. She's not the only one that was killed. You know that, don't you?"

She closed her eyes and shook her head. "Some of it. Not all of it. Sometimes when people talked to me, I was kind of—out of it. I know there was somebody named Luther. And somebody else named Hollis; they wanted to kill him. And there's something about a girl, years ago. It all gets mixed up for me. The pain pills . . ."

He told her clearly and concisely about Hollis. "Bit by bit, he's telling the story," Turner said.

Jaye frowned slightly. "I thought he couldn't talk."

"He *wouldn't* talk. He's starting to. To a psychiatrist. And a nurse he likes."

"He ran away? Because of me?"

"He hid in the woods. There was a cave. It was where the girl's body was burned. He went there. LaBonny found one entrance. He didn't know there was a second one."

She shook her head in incomprehension. "This— Hollis. He was as much a victim as the girl was. Will he ever get well?"

"He'll get better. He'll get care now. He should have had it years ago."

She nodded, almost to herself. "That's good."

"The police sent the finger to a lab for DNA testing," Turner said carefully. He added, just as carefully, that there was a woman who had come forward and said the girl might be her sister.

She shuddered. "My God. How horrible." She looked down at her left hand, the one wrapped most thickly in white. She said, "That girl. I—I feel kind of connected to her. I'm supposed to look like her. I've lost a little finger, too. Or part of one. It's weird. It's like somehow we're related."

"You are," he said simply. "She was your mother's sister."

She looked up at him sharply, disbelief in her eyes.

He told her Linda O'Halloran's story. "Her name was Lisa," he said. "She would have been your aunt."

Jaye's expression had grown strange. "Aunt? I'm sorry. It just seems—incomprehensible. I guess I should feel some sense of loss or—something. But I don't feel anything. It seems wrong not to feel anything, yet—" She faltered.

He said what he'd told her the first night they met. "There's no right or wrong about it. You feel what you feel."

She shrugged helplessly. "Is that why they—they came after us? They knew I was related to the girl who died? They were afraid it'd come out?"

"Yes. But they won't hurt you again. They won't hurt anybody."

She nodded numbly. "I heard about Adon Mowbry," she said. "It's terrible. But it—doesn't really register, either."

"Not yet," he said. "Things like this—they take time."

A starkness came into her eyes. "But Hunsinger never talked? About the children he sold?"

"No," he said. "He never admitted anything."

He saw the sudden glitter of tears rising, although she tried hard to blink them back. "Then how will I ever find out about Patrick? About who his mother is?"

Turner reached into his inside pocket. He drew out a copy of Juanita Bragg's listing of Suzanne McCourt. "I've found her," he said.

Her lips parted. She said nothing. She stared at him.

He told her about the Bragg woman and Suzanne McCourt Alison. "Her father was a GI in World War Two. Her mother was Japanese, a war bride. When Suzanne got pregnant, she was only fifteen. So was the father. Her parents told her the baby was born dead. They sent her to California to keep her away from the father. But when he was eighteen, he followed her, married her. They're still married. They have two grown daughters and a son."

"Oh, Turner," Jaye whispered. "He has full sisters? A brother, too?"

"They'll cooperate fully," he said. "I'm flying out there this afternoon. If anybody's marrow matches Patrick's, I'll get that person to Belgium. I'll fly with them, if it makes you feel better."

"No," she said in a choked voice. "I can't let you do that. It's not right—"

"No," he said. "It is right. You put your hands into the fire to save my life. I wish to God it was me that felt those flames and not you. I'd give my heart's blood for that."

"I didn't do it just for you and you know it," she protested, but she had started to cry. Her bandaged hand shook and she couldn't get a tissue out of the box. The whole box fell to the floor. He bent and retrieved it, took out a couple of sheets, wiped her eyes. He made her blow her nose as if she were a child.

"Stop crying," he said. "You're not good at it. You've never given yourself enough practice. There, that's it. Blow again."

He made her ease back into her complicated nest of pillows again. He said, "Call Patrick. Call Nona. Get a nurse to dial for you. Tell them that I've gone to California."

"I can't let you do this—" she protested.

"I owe you," he said simply. "And I wish I could guarantee this is going to save your brother. I can't. While I'm gone, I want you to think about two things."

Brusquely she wiped away a last tear with her forearm. She was paler than he'd ever seen her. She said nothing, only watched his face, waiting for him to go on.

He said, "First. I want you to think about your mother. About what she's been through and everything she gave you."

"I have," she said. "I've thought constantly. She's coming tomorrow to take me home. I'm going to have to stay with her awhile because of this—" She waved one hand with exasperation. "But I think Nona and I are going to get along better now. I never really appreciated—"

"No," he said quietly. "Not that mother. The other one. Linda O'Halloran. She read about you in the papers. She saw your picture. She wants to meet you. Promise me you'll think about it."

He saw that the idea stunned and terrified her, perhaps on a level too deep for her to understand.

He reached into his pocket and drew out a card. "This is her phone number and address. You can phone her. Or write her. Or do nothing at all. It's your choice."

He set the card beside Patrick's flowers.

"I don't know if I can do it." Her voice was almost a whisper. "I'm not ready. Maybe I'll never be."

"I understand that," he said.

She studied his face. "She—sounds like a difficult woman."

"She's had a lot of problems in her past. She'll probably have a lot in her future. That's the way it is."

Jaye stared down at her bandaged hands. He knew she didn't need any more complexity in her life, and that included Linda O'Halloran. It probably also included him.

He, to whom words always came easily, hesitated,

searching for the right ones. He threw out everything he'd rehearsed. He tried to speak from his heart.

"The other thing is that I misled you from the start. I was wrong to do it. But I swear to God I'm not a member of the Mafia."

She gave a small shrug, as if she didn't want to debate it.

He said, "I've defended mobsters, but I'm not one. I've defended murderers and embezzlers and drug traffickers, but I'm not any of those things, either. That's God's truth. I want—your forgiveness. I'm trying like hell to earn it."

She gazed at an expensive bouquet of tulips he'd sent. "You don't have to buy it, Turner. I gave it to you when you walked in the door."

"Jaye," he said, "for a little while in Mississippi, in New Orleans, it was as if—you were mine. God knows I was yours. Can it be that way again?"

She could have smiled and opened her arms to him. But she didn't. Instead she stared at the daisies Patrick had sent her and at last she said, "I don't know."

"Maybe it'll just take time," he said.

"Maybe," she said, without meeting his eyes.

And maybe not, he thought.

"I'll be in touch with you about Patrick," he said. "And you know how to get in touch with me."

"Oh, yes," she said. "I know."

"Can I kiss you good-bye?"

"Of course."

He bent and pressed his lips against hers. Her mouth beneath his was warm, but somehow, this time, the touch of it was tinged with regret. It tasted slightly salty from her tears.

He drew back slightly. "I love you," he said.

She looked away and said nothing in return.

· · ·

Suzanne McCourt Alison's middle child was a daughter named Tara. Her bone marrow matched Patrick's. She flew to Brussels with both Jaye and Nona.

Jaye did not invite Turner. She made it clear that it was not his place to be with them. What was at stake was a family matter, and the family was not his.

The transplant was, said the doctors, a seeming success. Everything, Jaye thought, should be fine now. It was not.

Jaye had told Turner she had forgiven him. She realized this was not true. He had lied to her, and because of it she feared him. She was grateful to him, but some part of her held back fiercely from letting herself feel anything more.

She could not answer his letters. The one time he phoned her, she found herself unable to talk to him.

"I'm sorry," she said. "I'm thankful for everything you've done. I mean that with all my heart."

"Will you see me?" he asked.

She looked at the scars on her hands. She thought, *The burned child fears fire.*

"I don't think so," she said.

"It would be best if you didn't call again," she told him.

There were too many things for her to sort out. Patrick was back in the United States now, and Melinda had had her baby, a boy named Patrick Jr. He looked exactly like Patrick—and Patrick's newly discovered sisters and brother, the Alisons.

With the Alisons Patrick had a second family. Being Patrick, he fit in with them from the start, and they loved him. Nona, unwilling to be left out, had nothing but praise for them and began to act as if they were her relatives, as well.

Jaye knew only Patrick could pull off such a thing so flawlessly. She herself felt restless and at loose ends. Patrick could handle a complex family with ease. She could not and felt a small, painful sting of jealousy that made her despise herself.

She had received a letter from Linda O'Halloran asking her to come and visit, but the words seemed stiff and melodramatic, and perhaps not quite sober. The letter said little of Linda O'Halloran herself. Rather it was filled with tumultuous ramblings about Lisa, the girl who had vanished so long ago.

"When I saw your picture you are so like her it made my heart stop and for a minute I could not get my breath," wrote Linda. "I have talked to Turner Gibson who says you are a smart, wonderful woman like what she would have been."

She doesn't want me, Jaye thought. *She wants Lisa to come back from the dead. She wants me to mend the past for her. I can't.*

She could not bring herself to answer that letter, either, and Linda O'Halloran did not write again.

Turner wrote her, too, often. He said he was staying in touch with O'Halloran, and that she still hoped to hear from Jaye. The woman was trying to better her lot, he said. And he himself wanted to see Jaye again, he said.

She could not bring herself to reply once. She wrote a short note that thanked him again for helping Patrick, and in it she enclosed a check to pay for his flight to California.

He never cashed it.

But she kept his letters. Somehow she could not make herself throw them away; it seemed too cold-hearted, too ungrateful. But, paradoxically, neither could she bear to reread them. She kept them in a box in her closet, out of sight.

"Patrick wants to know if you've gotten in touch with *her* yet," said Nona. "That woman from Oklahoma who had you."

"No," Jaye said. She really didn't want to talk about it.

It was a bright Saturday afternoon in September, and she had driven to New Hampshire to see Nona over the Labor Day weekend. But Nona's house, crowded with its pictures and memorabilia, oppressed her.

"You should go see her and be done with it," Nona argued. "It's eating at you. I can tell."

"Maybe someday," Jaye hedged. "I don't feel ready yet."

"I'll admit she doesn't sound like any bargain," Nona said. "But you at least ought to get your health history. Look at what happened to Patrick. He worries about you. What if you have children someday and—"

"I don't plan on having children," Jaye said. "It's getting a little late for that."

"Nonsense," said Nona. "You should find a nice man, get married, raise a family." It was her familiar theme, but it had a new twist, one Jaye flinched to hear.

"Why don't you get together with that nice lawyer?" prodded Nona. "He's crazy about you. He'd give you a good life."

"I can make my own good life, thank you very much," said Jaye.

Turner had sent flowers to Patrick in the hospital in Belgium, bouquets to Nona and Jaye in their Brussels hotel room.

After she and Nona had returned to the States, he'd made it a point to phone Nona to see how Patrick was doing. He utterly charmed her, of course, and told her he'd love to hear from Jaye. Nona had been nagging ever since, as only Nona could.

Jaye refused to argue about it with her. How could she and Turner build a relationship on a week of crazy emotions and terrible violence? And, of course, lies. She'd had one man who'd lied to her, and she told herself she would be a fool to want another.

"I see by the Philadelphia papers he's involved in a new trial," Nona said.

"Since when do you read the Philadelphia papers?" Jaye asked suspiciously.

"I read them at the college library," Nona said with an air of righteousness. "He's defending this man accused of money laundering or junk bonds or some complicated thing."

Jaye said nothing.

"You think because he's a criminal lawyer, that makes him a criminal, too," Nona scolded. "Well, that's not true at all. We have to *have* criminal lawyers. It's a constitutional necessity, a cornerstone of democracy. Alan Dershowitz says so."

Jaye gave her a disbelieving look. "And since when are you reading Alan Dershowitz?"

"I checked out a book," she said airily. "I've been discussing it with Brother Maynard. *He* says it would be criminal not to have lawyers who defend criminals. Brother Maynard takes a great interest in the law. He's quite insightful about it."

Jaye sighed and turned to look out the window. The yard was bright with the first autumn colors of the sugar maples. Suddenly she wished she were up in the mountains, hiking, all alone, with nothing to do but put her tangled thoughts in order.

"I heard from Turner," Nona said, an edge in her voice.

Jaye said nothing. *Why can't everyone leave me alone?*

"That man is dead," Nona said. "That Mr. DelVechio person. He died of a stroke. Turner said he thought you should know."

DelVechio is dead. The words dropped into her mind like stones, heavy and numbing.

"And," said Nona, "they never found the son. Turner says he'll stop looking now. That it's probably for the best. That the money that DelVechio set aside for the son will go into a fund. To help the other Hunsinger children and birth parents. They're setting up a database."

Jaye kept staring at the red and gold leaves. She could think of nothing to say.

"Oh," Nona said, "and he said to tell you he found out about the little girl. The one you stayed with. What's her name? It's *odd*."

Jaye turned to Nona, her heart starting to beat unaccountably fast. "Bright? He knows what happened to her?"

"Yes," Nona said. "He talked to her. She's still in a foster home. She had the baby. A girl. She gave it away, but the adoption was legal and open. She said she didn't want her child to be in a fix like you and Patrick."

Jaye shook her head. "I didn't think she ever noticed or cared. An open adoption. That's good, I guess."

"Maybe," Nona said. "And if you ask me, the whole thing is a two-edged sword. I mean, this whole Hunsinger business. The man *became* evil, but he didn't start out evil. He *did* help people. He *did* give children to good homes. I never would have had Patrick and you without him. But to let out all those names—well, people have a right to their secrets if they want. And some people don't *want* to know. Look at you. And Mr. DelVechio's son. Turner's right. It's better he never knows."

Nona rattled on, arguing both sides at once, not really making a coherent statement. Jaye stared out again at the changing leaves, and she stopped hearing the words, she heard only Nona's voice, as familiar to her and as much a part of her as her own memory.

I love her, she thought. *I've always loved her, and she's loved me, but it's been so hard to show.*

She felt something deep within herself change, as if some part that she needed for her own completion had at long last fallen into place.

Nona's chatter dwindled to an end. "Well," she said, "if I'm going to make dinner, I have to get started. Brother Maynard and Brother Gerard have permission to come tonight, and I've made my famous rum cake. Come into the kitchen and keep me company."

Jaye turned from the window. "Mother," she said, "you're right."

Nona looked at her in shock. It had been years since Jaye had called her "Mother." And Jaye had seldom told her that she was right.

"I should go see Linda O'Halloran," Jaye said. "Maybe it *is* time."

Nona looked taken aback. "Oh. Yes. I mean as long as you aren't *expecting* too much."

Jaye felt a strange and heady sensation of freedom. "I think I haven't wanted to go alone—"

"Well, I'll certainly go with you," said Nona, nodding primly. "I mean, it will be no great joy for me, and I know she's not the same caliber of woman as Suzanne, but if you need me, of course—"

"No," Jaye said. "Maybe another time—if there is another time."

"Oh," Nona said, with an air of relief and realization. "You meant *Patrick*. Of course, Patrick would be the one to go. He knows exactly what you're feeling. And he'd do anything for you, you *know* that. I don't want him wearing himself out, I'll be firm about that, but—"

"No," Jaye said with a slow smile. "Not Patrick. I need somebody else. Would you mind if I made a call in private?"

"Private?" Nona said, bristling slightly. "I don't know why you need to keep secrets from me, but—" She went suddenly silent.

She gave Jaye a long, questioning look. "Of course," she said. "Take your time. I'll be peeling the carrots."

She went into the kitchen and shut the door behind her.

Jaye went to Nona's phone and hesitated for a moment, holding her breath. Then she picked up the receiver and dialed. She still remembered the number.

The phone rang, seven times, eight. Then he answered.

She took a deep breath. "I know you're in the middle of a trial," she began, then paused, searching for a way to put it.

The beats of silence lengthened between them. He said, "Jaye?"

"Yes."

"Do you need me for something?"

"Yes," she said. "Oh, yes, I do."

• • •

Together they walked up the sidewalk that led to Linda O'Halloran's apartment. Jaye's stomach fluttered with apprehension. Her heart beat so hard it seemed to rattle her ribs.

The two of them had spoken little during the drive to this place. Turner seemed to understand her apprehension. He had not pushed her to talk.

A child rode a tricycle back and forth in front of the ground-floor apartments. A mongrel dog ran loose. A man in an undershirt was patching a broken window.

Linda O'Halloran lived in apartment number one. There was a mat in front of the door. It did not say WELCOME or announce her name. It was blank and a bit worn, a bit soiled.

Her name was hand-printed on a card that was taped beside the bell.

Turner looked down at Jaye. She tried to keep her chin at a steady angle, her eyes dry.

"Okay?" he asked.

She straightened her back and wished her knees didn't feel so unsteady. She had trouble getting her breath, but she said, "Okay." Her own voice sounded strange in her ears.

"Want me to do it?" he asked.

She nodded.

I don't know what this door leads to, she thought. *When it opens, I don't know where it will go.*

He took her scarred hand in his. He rang the bell.

ABOUT THE AUTHOR

BETHANY CAMPBELL was born and raised in Nebraska. She has taught at colleges and universities in Nebraska, Illinois, and New Hampshire. She and her husband make their home in Arkansas with three cats and a dog passionate about rodents and their pursuit.